THE SHAAR PRESS

THE JUDAICA IMPRINT
FOR THOUGHTFUL PEOPLE

THE JUDGE

A NOVEL BY
LIBBY LAZEWNIK

Published by **SHAAR PRESS**
Distributed by MESORAH PUBLICATIONS, LTD.
4401 Second Avenue / Brooklyn, N.Y 11232 / (718) 921-9000

Distributed in Israel by SIFRIATI / A. GITLER
10 Hashomer Street / Bnei Brak 51361

Distributed in Europe by J. LEHMANN HEBREW BOOKSELLERS
20 Cambridge Terrace / Gateshead, Tyne and Wear / England NE8 1RP

Distributed in Australia and New Zealand by GOLD'S BOOK & GIFT SHOP
36 William Street / Balaclava 3183, Vic., Australia

Distributed in South Africa by KOLLEL BOOKSHOP
Shop 8A Norwood Hypermarket / Norwood 2196, Johannesburg, South Africa

ISBN: 1-57819-548-9 Hard Cover
ISBN: 1-57819-549-7 Paperback

Printed in the United States of America by Noble Book Press
Custom bound by Sefercraft, Inc. / 4401 Second Avenue / Brooklyn N.Y. 11232

PART ONE:
REVENGE

I t was night, and she was running.

It had rained earlier in the evening, and now a fine mist draped a shimmering curtain in the air. Dim shapes along either side of the street were ghostly suggestions of houses. The trees were vague outlines that appeared briefly through the fog as she sprinted past, and then they receded. It was a rather beautiful scene, if also an eerie one. The young woman, however, saw neither the beauty nor the mystery because of the film of tears that filled her eyes.

There, on the quiet Baltimore street at 1 o'clock in the morning, her heart was in the painful process of breaking in half.

The furious, glorious moment when she had flung her ring into the face of the man responsible for the heartbreak was past — but blessed numbness had not yet arrived to ease her pain. Sobs bubbled up from deep inside, to emerge in tiny gasping cries that kept time with the tap of her high heels as she ran down the block in search of her car.

Her shoes were frivolous rather than sturdy. They were meant for a leisurely evening spent in the company of the man she was going to marry, not a mad sprint through the darkness of a strange street in an unfamiliar town. Her ankles ached. Tiny droplets settled on her shoulders and sparkled like glitter in her hair. Blinking away the tears from her eyes, she narrowed them against the fog. Where was her car, to take her far away from the scene of her humiliation? Distance had no meaning in this opaque world. Had she parked it in front of this house? Or was it that one? She could not remember.

Dimly, she registered a sound: a second pair of running feet.

It was impossible to tell from which direction the sound came. In any case, there was no time to figure it out. Out of a driveway, into the pool of yellow light from a street lamp, hurtled a figure full tilt, and she just missed careening into it.

Her breath left her in a gasp. The fog parted momentarily to give her a glimpse of a young man's face beneath a baseball cap. The face could have been called handsome, had it not been so surly — and had it not been disfigured by a long white scar that ran from the corner of one eye nearly down to his mouth.

"S-sorry," she stammered, breathless. The man stared at her for one wild instant, as though doubting the reality of her presence at this hour, in these surroundings. Then, ferociously, he shouldered past her and was gone, swallowed in the fog.

Something on the ground caught her eye. Stooping quickly, she picked it up. It was a man's handkerchief, white once, but stained now with some black, sticky substance. Uncertainly she looked into the fog, as though expecting the handkerchief's owner to materialize and claim his property.

Sanity returned with a thud. She dropped the handkerchief and shivered slightly, suddenly aware of how quiet the street was, and how lonely. Behind those shutters, good people slept. Somewhere close by, her car waited. And inside, her heart was still crumbling.

She began running again. Within two seconds, all was forgotten but the urgent need to get away.

Get away, get away —

June — Five Years Later

"The last day of school," Sara Muller remarked to a fellow teacher on a sun-soaked day in June, "ought to be declared a national holiday."

Her colleague laughed. "No declarations necessary. Just take one look at the kids' faces. It's holiday time, all right — official or not."

"Forget the *kids'* faces," Sara retorted, an irrepressible grin breaking out over her own. "Have you looked at yourself in the mirror today?"

The two young women were preparing to leave the staff lounge for the last time. The other teacher picked up her briefcase and, with its long straps, slung it jauntily over her arm. With a sidelong glance at

Sara, she murmured, "Look who's talking!"

When Sara laughed, her cheeks turned as pink as the early roses in her parents' garden at home. She looked all at once far younger than her thirty-one years. As she stepped out of the lounge, a passing student glanced wonderingly at her, searching in vain for the severe expression that was usually stamped there.

"G-good-bye, Miss Muller," she ventured.

"Good-bye, and good luck!" Sara answered gaily. She would not be seeing that girl in these corridors again. For Sara Muller, this was not only the last day of the school year — it was also her final day in this school. She had given ten years to this place. She still could hardly believe that she was leaving.

The roots she had sunk in this building seemed to cut right down through the bland, tiled floors, into the molten heart of the earth itself. No one — least of all Sara — had dreamed she would do anything but leave them there until she hardened in place, like some sad species of petrified tree.

But she *had* pulled free. She was moving on at last.

At the front door, she paused. It seemed to her that the school was reluctant to let her go. Strangely, for all her earlier anticipation, Sara felt herself infected with some of that same reluctance. The building — or her fears — sucked her back, even as her mind urged her on.

This was a good thing she was doing, she reminded herself. She must open herself up to new challenges, broaden her horizons, dare a little.

And still, there was the crazy backwards pull — the urge to run back to her classroom, familiar as a mother's arms. The future was a risk, a gamble of the dice. A new school, a new city — and old demons that must, sooner or later, be faced. Did she have the courage?

"Are you coming?" her colleague asked, from the top step where she stood blinking in the sun.

Sara turned away slowly, and drew a deep breath.

"Yes," she said evenly. "I'm right behind you."

She walked through the door and let it swing shut behind her. Then she stepped lightly down the stairs, never looking back.

❧✻☙

"Say cheese," the photographer urged.

Judge Daniel Newman bared his teeth in what he was sure must be his thousandth smile of the evening. The muscles in his cheeks rebelled at the effort. The photographer's lights were very hot on this early summer's day, like a pair of artificial suns beating down on Daniel's head.

Behind the judge, just above shoulder level, volumes of the Talmud were lined up in a row on the oak bookshelf. The photographer had wanted the other bookcase as backdrop to the photo — the one with all the legal tomes — but Daniel had quietly insisted on having it done his way. As a judge, he could summon an aura of authority to wilt even the hardiest resistance. The photographer was not equal to the struggle. The row of Gemaras had stayed.

Daniel watched the man fiddle with his camera, wishing he would get on with the job. He was tired; it was hard to be patient. Presently, he heard a click, and stirred thankfully.

"Not yet, please," the photographer said, holding up a hand. "Just one more."

Behind him, a girl and a boy stood watching. The girl — Daniel's 14-year-old daughter — was dressed in her best, on the off-chance that the photographer sent by the prestigious law journal would decide he needed a picture of the judge's family, too. Her younger brother was watching just for the fun of it. At 12, Mordy was interested in anything that was out of the ordinary. It was not every day that a professional photographer came to visit.

Suddenly, the girl's eye fell on her father's tie. It was red and black, but his suit was gray. Were the two awfully mismatched? She thought it looked all right, but there was a gnawing uncertainty that made her angry with herself.

Ma would have known. Ma knew . . . everything. People would see the picture in the magazine and raise their eyebrows, knowing that she, Yael, was not able to care properly for her father. There was just so much she did not know yet. It would be a long time — years, maybe — before she would be able to truly take her mother's place in the home.

But even as she thought it, she knew it wasn't true. She would never take Ma's place. Ever.

"Smile, Dad," Mordy called encouragingly. "This is the last one!"

That did make Daniel smile. He looked over the photographer's shoulder at his children, and the smile grew indefinably softer. There was paternal pride there, and a fierce love — and a hint of sadness.

The camera clicked.

It was that picture, the last in the roll, that would appear a month later above the newest article Judge Newman had authored. Attorneys and law students, who normally skimmed over such things in their rush to get to the printed word, would find their eye arrested by the photograph. Here, they would know without really articulating the knowledge to themselves, was a man with humanity. A man who had known great joy — and great suffering. A man touched by the finger of blessing, and also of tragedy.

The photographer packed his gear, wished them a good evening, and left. Daniel stretched gratefully, then turned to his kids.

"Well, what's on the agenda for tonight, guys? Any homework?"

"Daddy," Yael said reproachfully, "don't you remember? Today was the last day of school!"

"I still have nearly a week to go," Mordy sighed. "And a last Gemara test tomorrow. I studied for it already."

"Great. I'd like to go over it with you."

"Now?"

"Why not? If you know it as well as you say, this shouldn't take long."

The man who ruled his courtroom with an iron fist was not a person his children often argued with. In short order, the boy was seated beside the father at the large desk in Daniel's study, and there was a gap in the row of Gemaras that had moments ago served as a photographic backdrop. Strains of piano music wafted their way from the living room. The curtains were drawn against the night, and the air-conditioning kept the temperature comfortable after the heat of the day.

Everything and everyone was in its place. The house seemed to purr with quiet contentment. It hadn't always done so. It had been a struggle to get to where they were today. These peaceful walls were soaked with tears, and with a longing for something that could never be recaptured. But in the past five years something — a good thing — had been achieved.

For the first time in a very long time, Daniel allowed himself to feel safe.

As he was to learn the following day, however, the feeling was premature.

"A box of plain white stationery," the man in the corduroy jacket snapped. "And some white envelopes. The small kind."

The items duly produced, the young clerk glanced timidly up at her customer. "Anything else, sir?"

"Black indelible marker."

He liked that word — indelible. There were some things that could never — should never — be erased. He wrote with a heavy hand, and the black marker would make the words more forceful still. They would never wash away. Just as the years had not washed clean his memory . . . or his thirst for vengeance.

"Indelible," he repeated, sending the girl scurrying among her supplies. He pulled a battered imitation-leather wallet from his pocket.

With the bag tucked under his arm, he made his way from there to a supermarket, where he found the next item on his list: a pair of plain latex gloves. Again, he paid in cash.

Good thing he had thought of the gloves. A couple of dollars for freedom from worry: a fine investment. Fingerprints were the last thing he wanted to sow in the next days.

Right now, he was interested in only one kind of harvest.

Fear.

1

When Daniel Newman turned 13, he read the Torah portion for the congregation in a sweet soprano, after which, in a rush of relief, he downed six pieces of potato kugel and three cups of soda at the *kiddush* his parents gave in his honor. The shul newsletter took due note of the occasion, adding in the boy's praise: "The eloquence of Daniel's speech more than matched the careful thought and research that had so obviously been invested in it. We predict a bright career. Our newest bar mitzvah is going places!"

True to its early promise, that career was swift and brilliant as a comet. Unlike a comet, though, it shifted direction once or twice.

At his parents' urging, Daniel learned in yeshivah during the day while devoting his evenings to the pursuit of a college degree. He veered briefly into dreams of an English professorship, followed by an enthusiastic but short-lived foray into political science. It was not until his final year that Daniel's ambition solidified. Gradually he became aware that he had always been fascinated by the legal process — or, more accurately, the pursuit of justice. At the age of 21, he applied to law school and settled firmly into the groove of his studies.

Summers saw him clerking at a series of high-profile legal offices strung across the heart of downtown Baltimore. He worked hard; he made connections. Upon graduation, he turned down no less than four impressive job offers in favor of one, much more modest, that appealed to him most of all. Daniel Newman became a criminal prosecutor.

Those who followed his career with interest — and there were many — saw him launch a one-man crusade to clear the city streets of its most violent dregs. Baltimore courtrooms rang with the reasoned and impassioned speeches of the assistant state's attorney who always wore a trademark black yarmulke atop his thick dark hair.

Daniel also had a personal life, which he kept very separate from his public one. Here, too, the milestones came thick and fast.

At the age of 23, he married Ella Stavinsky, formerly of Elizabeth, New Jersey.

At 24, he became the proud father of a dark-haired baby girl, the light and joy of his life. They named her Yael.

Two years later, Mordechai was born. From the first, Mordy was a clone of his father: intelligent, alert, and outgoing. Though both Daniel and his wife hoped earnestly for more children, they were disappointed. He began to spend a little more time over his prayers, to add an extra *shiur* to his schedule whenever possible, and to thank G-d ever more fervently and frequently for the daughter and the son that he had.

At 29, he and Ella bought their first home. It was what is known in realtors' vernacular as a "starter house"; that is, it was not very large and not very expensive. But for Ella and Daniel, moving day was a taste of ambrosia from Heaven's own buffet. The house was unpretentious — it squatted on a minuscule lot on an undistinguished street just north of Park Heights Avenue — but they knew they could be happy there.

They *were* happy. Daniel did his best to make sure of that. More than ever, he was determined to keep his private life apart from his public one. The more lurid aspects of his career must never be permitted to cross the sacred threshold of his home. Let the cold winds of crime blow their mightiest through office and courthouse; at home, all must be forever warm and safe.

In this determination he was successful — until the day he found that determination was not enough.

That was the day the bottom dropped out of his world. The day his heart broke, smashed into tiny fragments beneath the grimy boot of catastrophe.

On a storm-tossed morning just a few weeks after Yael's ninth birthday, as he was running out of his office on the way to court,

Daniel's telephone shrilled. He could have ignored it. Responsibly, he snatched it up instead — to learn that he had just become a widower.

He was 33 years old.

With ears that seemed to have turned to stone and a mind that had slowed to a dreamlike pace, he heard something about heavy rain and a slippery road and brakes that, unaccountably, had failed to do their job. The voice at the other end was very sorry, but would Mr. Newman mind coming down to identify the remains?

He did not remember hanging up, nor did he retain any memory of the drive down to the scene of the accident. It was only as he stood in the slashing rain viewing what was left of his car — he was not ready, yet, to face the ambulance — that his mind leapt to life again. What woke it was a stab of sudden pain, sharp and deep beyond experience.

It was a pain he would carry the rest of his life.

The next few months were a blur. When the clouds of grief and shock had cleared enough for him to take a look around himself, he saw that his life had changed, irrevocably, in more ways than he could count.

One of the ways it had changed was that he was no longer a promising young prosecuting attorney. Somewhere along the line, though he had been scarcely aware of it, he had been promoted.

Daniel Newman had become the youngest district court judge in Maryland.

"All rise."

At the bailiff's sonorous command, there was a shuffle of feet. The benches emptied. The door from the judge's chambers opened and Daniel emerged, looking solemn and preoccupied.

He looked solemn because his was an important job and one that he took seriously. But his preoccupation, at the moment, had very little to do with the American legal system. A thorny question had arisen in his *Daf Yomi* class earlier that morning, and Daniel was never one for leaving questions unanswered. During the drive to the courthouse he had struggled with it, and some inner sense told him that the clarity he sought was close — just out of reach of his questing mind. A little more effort might succeed in jarring the truth out of the morass of legalistic Talmudic detail in which it was presently housed. But effort requires time, and time was one luxury Daniel did not have this morning.

Evicting the question from his mind called for a Herculean effort, which Daniel made. He succeeded in banishing it to a waiting area in a back room of his consciousness. With stately stride and sibilant swish of his robe, Judge Daniel Newman ascended the bench.

As he took his seat, so did the others. Calmly, he surveyed his domain.

The courtroom, this morning, was sparsely attended. There were no headline-catching criminals awaiting their turn in the limelight today, and therefore no hordes of reporters in the press section, clicking pens and tapping notebook-computer keypads with a noise like a colony of hungry termites. Daniel glanced down at the day's docket. It was the usual mixed bag: a few cases of breaking and entering, two assault and batteries — with and without a deadly weapon — and a sprinkling of shoplifting charges.

"The United States versus William Ortell," the bailiff read in a dogged monotone. Daniel picked up the first file and slipped a pair of glasses onto his nose, the more closely to examine both the nature of the crime and the sullen young black man being charged with it. Like a diver, he felt the waters of the law close over his head. The man was instantly and totally submerged in his role as the judge.

It would be five hours before he came up for air.

The last case of the day was thrown out on a technicality, and then Daniel was back in his chambers. It was time for the daily transformation from courtroom to living room — from supreme authority to struggling single parent.

Quickly he divested himself of his robes and brushed his hair before the small oval mirror that some anonymous decorator had hung on the wall of the room. There was a respectful rap on the door.

"Yes?" In the mirror, he saw the door open and a shaggy head appear. It belonged to Paul Hencken, his clerk. He looked excited.

"I was wondering if you'd heard the news, sir."

"What news?" Daniel asked Paul's image in the mirror.

"The Simmonds case. You know, the one they call the Baby Bottle Baron. He —"

"Was murdered. In his partner's home — or rather, out in the garden, if memory serves me. The partner's been indicted and is awaiting trial. So, what's the news?"

"You've pulled the case, sir."

Daniel paused, hairbrush frozen halfway to his head. "Have I?"

"Yes, sir. It was originally Judge Lionel's, if you remember."

Daniel nodded thoughtfully. Irvin Lionel — feisty, white haired, and owner of a well-earned reputation for striking terror in the hearts of litigators — had recently suffered a massive coronary. His calendar was being divided among the other judges — and Daniel, from what Hencken said, had pulled the big one. The Simmonds murder trial.

Looking back later, from the vantage point of hindsight, he would be amazed at the thrill, the intensely pleasurable apprehension, that overtook him at the thought of presiding over that trial. He had no premonition that, in very short order, his own life was going to take on aspects of a trial, too. Only this time, Daniel Newman would not sit gowned and imposing on his lofty bench. He would not wield a gavel with which to impose his order or his will.

In the ordeal he was about to face in the weeks ahead, Daniel would stand — figuratively — in the dock like the most common of criminals, hands cuffed securely behind his back as, helpless and trembling, he awaited the verdict.

2

He quickly regained his composure. His hand started moving again, mechanically brushing the rest of his hair. Finally, he put the brush down, replaced the yarmulke, and turned to face his clerk.

"Well, this promises to be interesting, Paul. When does the case come up?"

"Downing — the defendant — is due to appear before you next week, sir. There's a lot of pressure for an early trial date. Simmonds had a lot of friends. Influential friends."

"Hm. . . Well, we'll have to see what we can do about that." Still moving mechanically, Daniel began collecting his papers and slipping them into his briefcase.

The Simmonds case. Despite himself, his heart began to beat a little harder, its tempo slow and suspense filled, like the start of an Indian rain dance. He would have to bone up on the details, but the outlines of the case were as well known to him as they were to the millions of others who had been following the story. The murder had created a commotion when it occurred, some eight months before.

Al Simmonds — the "Baby Bottle Baron" — had dazzled the consumer world with a series of glitzy products whose novelty, combined with good, well-funded advertising, had captured the market's imagination. He was best known for his last, widely advertised offering: a newly patented baby bottle. The innovative design, and the advertising, had paid off in spades. An instant success, the bottle had garnered huge profits for its producer and its backers.

But Simmonds was more than just a shrewd entrepreneur. He was a jet-setter, a social fixture up and down the Eastern seaboard, and endless fodder for the town gossips. He had been married three times and was hoping to have better luck the next time. Though he owned an apartment in Manhattan and a beach house on Cape Cod, for reasons best known to himself Simmonds had elected to maintain his primary residence in Baltimore, from where he frequently drove down to Washington to grace some highly visible party or political dinner. His had not been a particularly admirable life, but it was a busy, animated one. And a wealthy one.

On the night of May 21st, that life had ended with the thrust of a knife between two ribs.

The uproar at his murder had revolved around his business partner, Henry Downing. Downing had come out of nowhere to hook up with Simmonds just a year previously — throwing in his lot with the entrepreneur on the eve of the baby bottle's market debut.

A man of late middle age, Downing had risen from obscurity on the wings of the New York State Lottery. Buying the lucky ticket together with Elsa, his wife of forty years, had been a smart move; the same, apparently, could not be said about his decision to invest his winnings with Simmonds.

By all accounts, in the weeks before Simmonds' death there had been a falling-out between the two. Henry and Elsa had invited Simmonds to dinner in their home, ostensibly in an attempt to clear the air. Simmonds never left. At a few minutes past midnight, a shaken Elsa Downing had phoned the police to report his murder. Three days later, her husband was arrested for the crime.

Daniel roused himself. "'Well, thanks for the news, Paul. By the way, how's your mother?" Hencken's mother was nearly crippled with arthritis, and bedridden nine days out of ten.

"Pretty much the same, sir. I'll tell her you asked. She'll be pleased you thought of her."

"Give her my best." Daniel tried not to betray his impatience as Paul lingered, discussing various aspects of the Simmonds case. The younger man was eager as a puppy on the scent of a rabbit. Daniel could not blame Paul; just thinking about the case made his own pulse race. A murder trial, especially the murder of a well-known personality, was something even he could never approach with calm. It represented a supreme challenge, almost an adventure: the judicial equivalent of the racing man's Indy 500.

Well, there would be time enough to think about that in the morning. Right now, he was expected home.

His clerk caught his involuntary glance at the door. With a respectful, "See you tomorrow, sir," Hencken left. Moments later, Daniel followed, closing the door of his chambers behind him.

His footsteps echoed in the empty corridor. The sound seemed to reflect his own inner hollowness. He was hungry. Lunch, he recalled, had been an unsatisfying sandwich at his desk. He was looking forward to dinner. It would be broiled chicken tonight, prepared by his daughter, Yael.

In the years since his wife was so tragically torn from them, the family had been fed nourishing, if not overly imaginative, meals by their housekeeper, Mrs. Marks. That worthy widow had been referred to them by an aunt of Daniel's who had known her family for years. "She's a widow. Her husband passed away not long ago. There was no insurance," the aunt had told Daniel sadly. "And Mrs. Marks won't accept charity. You'll be doing both of you a favor if you hire her. By the way — she's an immaculate housekeeper."

That she was. Mrs. Marks was nearing 60 when Daniel brought her aboard, but the passage of the years only seemed to heighten an already indefatigable energy system. She appeared on the Newman doorstep each morning like a force of nature, to steer the family's domestic course with an unerring hand. Mrs. Marks was neat, sensible, tireless. How Daniel would have managed to run the house — not to mention the kids — without her was unimaginable to him.

Then Yael decided that it was time to take matters into her own hands.

While not prepared to assume all responsibility for their domestic life, she had informed Daniel that some of the cooking, at least, was well within her scope. He had looked with barely concealed pride at his daughter — passionately convinced, at 14, that there was nothing she could not do if she only tried hard enough — and agreed to let her try.

Her brother had, in typical 12-year-old fashion, made gagging noises and asked for the phone number of poison control.

"Computer privileges in this house," Daniel reminded him mildly, "are dependent upon gentlemanly behavior. Gagging at the thought of sitting down to your sister's cooking definitely doesn't qualify." Mordy, an ardent computer buff, hastily subsided.

Mrs. Marks had put up a fiercer resistance to having her kitchen invaded by alien hands. At last, grudgingly, she gave way to a compromise. Twice a week, on Mondays and Thursdays, Yael would try her hand in the kitchen.

And a surprisingly competent job she made of it, too. Mordy made no further references to poison control. In fact, his most frequent comment, when partaking of his sister's more successful efforts, was, "Seconds, please."

Smiling, Daniel walked into the parking lot under a threatening sky. For the last week in August, the weather was unusually chilly. Early withered leaves skittered past him on the wind, harbingers of the changing season. The sight of those dried, orangey-brown leaves sent a twinge of melancholy through him, poignant as a cry. For all its beauty, autumn, with its visible reminders of death and decay, was definitely not his favorite time of the year. He hurried to his car as if trying to outrun the flying leaves — or time itself.

He was about to open the driver's door when a glimpse of white on the windshield caught his eye.

There was an envelope there, tucked under one of the wipers.

Daniel stared at the white oblong shape for a long moment before walking around to the front of the car. A faint uneasiness stirred in him as he scanned the black block letters that spelled his name on the front of the envelope. JUDGE NEWMAN, read the legend. There was something harsh about the way the letters were formed on the paper: The over-heavy pressure made them look as though they had been skewered in place. Skewered right through the heart.

With a soft bark of laughter at his own silliness, Daniel reached for the envelope. He was ripping through the top with a thumbnail when the first fat gray drops began to fall. A storm was about to break. It had been just such a storm that had caught his beloved Ella that morning, five years earlier, stealing control of the car away from her and hurling it over the edge of the highway —

A flash of lightning blinded him for a second — so much like the lightning that had penetrated the window of his office on that July day, just seconds before he had received the fateful call. An anonymous police officer had placed that call, like an old-time messenger sent back from the battlefield with evil tidings from the front. With sober courtesy, he had broken the news: In the deadly skirmish between Ella and the storm, the storm had won —

So compelling were the memories that, at first, the words on the unfolded page hardly came as a surprise. They were a natural continuation of his thoughts. It was only an instant later, as Daniel reread them, that their full import hit him. When it did, it was with the force of a wind-driven tree trunk, slamming into his chest at the height of a hurricane.

His eyes bulged as they ran over the neatly printed words yet a third time. A trickle of perspiration started at the back of his neck. The rain fell faster and harder on his head and shoulders, unheeded.

YOUR WIFE'S DEATH WAS NO ACCIDENT, the message read.

(YOU'RE NEXT.)

3

  "**C**edar Hills is not so far away," Debbie Muller Stein said, more to console herself than her sister. "Just four hours, right?"

    "Less, if you don't hit any traffic," Sara Muller replied with dogged cheerfulness. "Its not far from Baltimore, and that's practically around the corner. I'll be back in Flatbush so often, you'll be sick of the sight of me." She reached for the pot and poured herself another cup of coffee she did not really want.

    "As if I ever could. But you'd better be here for the kids' birthdays. They'll be devastated if their Aunt Sara doesn't come to help them blow out the candles."

    "Throw the party on a Sunday, and you're on."

    Both sisters smiled over their coffee cups, pretending that their words were fooling themselves and each other. It was a flimsy pretense; either of Debbie's 4-year-old twins could have poked healthy holes in it with little effort. Both women knew that it was not the physical distance between New York and Cedar Hills that was at issue here. Miles of highway were almost irrelevant beside the psychological distance Sara's move would impose. There was no getting around the fact that Sara's life was about to undergo a transformation, with a capital T.

    "Why do you have to go so soon?" Debbie asked, with the plaintive note her older sister remembered well from many a childhood whine. "School doesn't start until after Labor Day. That's — what? — ten days away."

"I can't waltz in on the first day of school, you know that. I have to get there earlier, to set things up. My apartment. My classroom."

"You sound excited," Debbie said accusingly. "I think you're actually looking forward to leaving all of us behind and starting over somewhere new."

Sara said slowly, "I'm not looking forward to leaving you, you know that. But I have to admit, the starting-over part does sound kind of attractive — Stop sulking, Debbie. Right now you look about 6 years old."

"Thanks a lot. You always were good for my ego!"

"You're welcome. Really, now — cheer up. As you just pointed out, it's not so far away. And besides," Sara added, somewhat less convincingly, "it's only for a year."

Debbie nodded, but she didn't believe it for a second. The probationary first year was a mere formality for a teacher of her sister's experience. She knew as well as Sara that a crossroads had been reached.

Sara, subconsciously, had been working her way up to this for a long time now. For years — too many years — she had been running in place, nourished by routine, subsisting on hope. In accepting the new position, she had accepted, also, the stark reality of her own existence. It had been some time in coming, but Sara had recently faced facts with a ruthlessness that left no room for self-pity: At 31, she was a spinster. An old maid. On the shelf.

That being the case, she decided she had better do something constructive with her life. Or more constructive, at any rate, than what she had been doing up until now, which was teaching an endless stream of seventh graders, year after year. She had been teaching the same material for so long that it practically tumbled from her lips without thought or meaning. That was not fair to the girls she taught, and it was not fair to the school. It probably was not even fair to Sara.

It was time for a change.

The Cedar Hills offer came along just in time. It came at the point in the year when schools undertake to solidify their teaching staffs for the following year. Sara had been summoned as usual to the office, to renew her contract with the Brooklyn school where she had taught for ten years. A decade of routine had propelled her to the office on the appointed day, like an automaton or a dreamer. The secretary ushered her into the principal's inner sanctum with a bored nod. Even the principal's voice seemed, to Sara, to hold a bored note, or at least a hurried one, as though he begrudged the time he was forced to spend on this formality — time that might be put to better use elsewhere.

It was that note that finally pierced the dead skin of Sara's consciousness. For the first time, she pricked up her ears and listened, not only to the content of the rather mechanical speech with which the principal initiated the contract-renewal ceremony, but also to the promptings of her own heart. Listening closely, she heard a mysterious, far-off wail. It was the wild cry of a phantom, as it realizes with awful suddenness that it is completely invisible to the human eye.

Sara had become that phantom.

And so, instead of signing on the dotted line, she had stood up.

"I'm sorry," she said. "I need a little time to think things over."

For the first time, something approaching interest flickered in the principal's eye. "I'm afraid I don't understand. Time to think over — what, exactly?"

My life, Sara could have told him. *My history, and* — *if I can see past the smoke* — *my future, too.*

But all she said was, "I just want to sort things out for myself. I feel I've lost sight of my direction." And then, to avert the need to deal with his reaction, she had murmured hastily, "I'll be in touch just as soon as I possibly can. Thank you," and fled the office.

That night, Sara lay awake in her small attic bedroom in her parents' home, thinking long, somber thoughts. They were not pleasant thoughts, but they had to be faced.

She had been engaged once, but miracles did not happen twice. That had been five years ago. Her life was set in a certain pattern now, and that pattern, apparently, did not include husband and children or the joy and security of marriage. That much she could not change; after all, it was not as if she could purchase a husband through a classified ad. But there were other things that could be changed — and should be. She settled down to do some planning.

It was not until the small hours of that long night that self-discipline faltered. Constructive thinking drowned in a whimper of pain. For the first time since the night she broke her engagement, Sara fell asleep with tears on her cheeks and broken words of prayer on her lips.

The next morning, the letter from the new girls' school in Cedar Hills arrived in the mail. Sara, reading it, had felt a tremulous wonder steal into her soul.

Maybe she had been wrong. Maybe miracles *did* still happen.

A clatter in the family room brought the twins running. "Ma, Raizy knocked over my tower!" Estie cried.

Raizy was not slow in registering her own complaint. "Ma, Estie tried to make her tower bigger than mine!"

Like matching furies they stood on either side of their mother, small fists planted on hips, wearing identical frowns of indignation. Debbie sighed, rolling her eyes at Sara. "Here comes the judge," she murmured. "I hate this." Raising her voice, she said, "Raizy, what's the big deal about Estie's tower being a little taller than yours? Sometimes yours is bigger, sometimes hers is. I don't see why you had to knock hers down for that."

Raizy's eyes filled. "But we're building the *Twin* Towers! They *have* to be the same size. I was going to just take off a little of her tower at the top, but then the whole th-thing f-fell down —" She gulped perilously.

Sara quickly left her seat, coming around to crouch beside the little girl. "Sweetie," she said, "don't you know that the Twin Towers aren't exactly the same height? One of them is actually a little taller than the other."

"It i-is?"

Sara nodded. "So why don't you and Estie rebuild her tower together? And if you want, I'll come in soon and put together the Empire State Building — to keep the Twin Towers company."

"The Empire State Building? That's *tiny!*" Estie said scornfully.

"I know." Sara smiled. "That's why I'm giving you girls a head start. Go ahead, now, rebuild that tower real fast."

The twins scurried back to the family room, curls bouncing. Debbie took a thankful sip from her mug, then cradled it between her hands. "Good work, Sara. You're the world's best aunt."

Sara laughed. "You tell me that at least three times a month."

"Not often enough." Debbie sighed again. "At the risk of being boringly repetitive, we're really going to miss you."

"I'll miss you, too. All of you. A small town like Cedar Hills is going to be — different."

"It's not New York, I'll grant you that. But it can still be plenty dangerous for a woman on her own. Please, *please* take care of yourself over there, Sara. Don't go out alone late at night, lock your car whenever you drive anywhere, get a chain for your apartment door —"

"Relax. Mommy already went through all that with me."

"She's worried," Debbie said. "Daddy, too. And I'll admit it — so am I."

So was Sara — but not about crime. Where that was concerned, she would take all due precautions and then place her trust in Heaven. Her worries were about something else altogether.

She was 31 years old, unmarried, and about to leave the only home she had ever known to embark on a new career in a new town. She did not know a soul in Cedar Hills, a relatively new community that had sprouted up in recent years to accommodate Baltimore's overflow. Sara was acquainted with one or two families in nearby Baltimore itself, but they were scarcely the people she wanted to see: her former fiancé's family.

All her life, she had been surrounded by familiar faces and had walked familiar streets toward the expected goals. Now, for the first time, she was about to launch herself into the unknown. The faces around her would be strangers' faces. The streets would bear names she did not recognize. She would lose her way at first. She would gaze longingly at people walking together, old friends and neighbors, and she would be lonely. It was a prospect to daunt the staunchest heart, and Sara was under no illusions about the fragility of her own.

She was uncharacteristically subdued while playing with the twins. The Empire State Building was constructed in record time out of the odds and ends of blocks left over from her nieces' more ambitious efforts. A few primitive Duplo buildings were thrust here and there among the skyscrapers. She was just putting the finishing touches on the Manhattan skyline when a crack of angry thunder sent the twins running to the window. They huddled together with cries of delicious terror. Sara slipped away and made her good-byes to her sister.

For a moment, as she stood by the front door buttoning up her jacket against the sudden downpour, Sara wondered if she had done the right thing in accepting the job offer. It had not been an impulsive move. She had done it for three reasons.

The first was the need she had belatedly acknowledged, that day in the principal's office, to reassess the direction her life had taken — to broaden her professional horizons — to challenge herself. The fledgling Cedar Hills Bais Yaakov needed a teacher of her caliber and experience in a way that more established schools did not. Up till now she had been helping to maintain a structure; now she would be called upon to pour the concrete and lay the timbers and pound in the nails. Much as she had tried to hide it from her sister, the prospect definitely excited her.

The second was the very real respect she felt for the woman who ran the Cedar Hills school. She had admired Rebbetzin Goodman from afar when she attended a lecture series the educator had once given in New York. Ever since that time, she had followed, with genuine interest, first the rumors, and then the reality, of the Bais Yaakov the Rebbetzin had launched, 'way down in (so it seemed to Sara, the New Yorker) uncharted territory in Maryland. On the strength of that admiration and respect, and goaded by a desperate need to shake up her life, Sara had sent in her résumé.

She had fully expected it to be buried in some dark dungeon of a filebox, never again to see the light of day. But the facts gleaned from that resume had clearly impressed someone. The letter of response from Rebbetzin Goodman, inviting her down for an interview, had caught Sara by surprise. In accepting the invitation, Sara stepped onto the slippery slope that led — inevitable as gravity — to her decision to move.

The third reason was the most secret, but also the most cogent.

In the five years since that fateful July night that saw her fling herself out of her betrothed's car and out of his life, she had not set foot again in Baltimore or its environs. She told herself that it was distaste that kept her away; in the more honest places of her mind, she knew it was really cowardice. The city, in her fancy, was alive with grievous memories waiting to taunt her, and to dance on the grave of her hopes. Her demons, as she had come to think of them.

The time had come to rid herself of them.

I

t was more than just a question of revenge.

Revenge was something he could have any day of the week. There were any number of ways. A drive-by shooting. A convenient hit-and-run "accident." Or his old favorite: tampering with a guy's brakes, then enjoying a game of cat and mouse, the end a foregone conclusion. It was fun, toying with the mark as death stared him in the face —

Or *her*, as the case might be.

On that morning, five years ago, it had been disappointing to see the wife get into the car instead of the husband — the one the hit had been meant for. But only at first. He quickly saw the possibilities written in a new script.

He hung around the scene of the accident, watching the police cut the body out of the car; there was not much worry, in the heavy rain, about being noticed or remembered. There were others there, too, gawking at the flashing red lights reflected in the puddles, the paramedics in their yellow slickers, the ambulance that, it was all too obvious, would not be needed — So he had been on the spot when the husband showed up. Had seen the look on the state prosecutor's face when he identified his wife. The police had contacted him on the strength of the ID she carried, but it was the husband who made the identification a positive one.

He had been startled by the prosecutor's youth. When Sal had told him to get the guy who had put him behind bars, the one who had shortly after been appointed to the judge's bench, he had pictured someone pompous and old: silver haired, with deep lines on either side of his mouth, and bifocals. But Newman had looked absurdly young as he had gazed down at his wife's lifeless body. The look on his face — worse than death. Much worse. Anything that came after that would hardly be felt. As his brother, Sal, had always said, you can't kill a man twice.

That had been revenge.

This time, he was after more. It was justice he wanted now. Didn't the Bible talk about that? An eye for an eye — a tooth for a tooth.

A death for a death.

Man, he was angry. Raging mad! Sal had been more than just a big brother. He had been like a father, beating him up when he needed a lesson, but also teaching him everything he knew that was worth knowing. Just thinking about Sal made him see red! For his big brother to die like that in a mangy prison cell — and all because that prosecutor — judge, now — had pulled every trick in the book to land him there. If he did not do something about it soon, he would go crazy. Utterly and absolutely crazy —

No, not him. *He* was not going to go nuts over this. He would do something about it, if it was the last thing he ever did.

Justice.

This time, he would do it differently. This would be no sudden strike by an anonymous hand. Oh, the suddenness would be there, and anonymity was necessary for now. But this time, the judge would *know* he had been targeted. The mark would have plenty of time to stew in his own juice — time to get good and rattled before the hand of justice struck. He would prove that even judges can get scared.

This time, he would do it right. He conjured up again the look on the judge's face when he saw the car, and his wife's lifeless body. It was a look he would enjoy seeing again.

Putting it there, though, would take some careful planning. The judge had already died inside when his wife was killed. As Sal said, you can't kill a man twice.

But Sal was wrong. There *were* ways of killing a man, again and again, even before you physically blew him away.

This time, he would go after the kids.

5

The kids. Daniel's first thought, after refolding the note and slipping it back into its envelope, was: I've got to protect the kids.

He slid behind the wheel of his car and leaned his head back. The isolated drops had massed into a sheet of gray fury, smashing into the windshield and rattling the roof with a noise like machine-gun fire. Daniel felt his pulse pound in time with the rain. His heart was galloping. Breathe, he reminded himself. In and out. Out and in. Sit on your hands if they won't stop shaking. Breathe.

Your wife's death was no accident.

What was that supposed to mean?

Ella had taken the car — *his* car; hers was in the shop for a tune-up — to work that morning. Daniel had insisted on making the trip to court by subway. He really did not mind the commute, he had told her, and he had not been lying. Even today, the occasional journey by public transportation was, he felt, beneficial. It kept him in touch with his fellow citizens in a way that was impossible from the awesome height of the judge's bench. If there was one thing he missed from his days as a lawyer, it was rubbing shoulders with people — all kinds of people, all day, every day. At times, it had been too much of a good thing; now there was far too little of it. His job made him too remote.

He always found the anonymity of the subway refreshing. No one stood up when he walked in, and no one sprang up to offer him their seat. For a full hour, he was just another face in the crowd. That was good.

So he had told Ella, "Go ahead, take the car today. Really, I don't mind."

"Thanks, Danny. I'll pick you up from the station later," she had promised. A promise she would never keep.

Your wife's death was no accident.

The words would not leave him. Already, they were branded indelibly on his mind. Who had written that note, and what had he meant by it? Not an accident? What else could you call it when a car skidded on a highway in a heavy rainstorm? What else was losing driver control and veering onto the shoulder, slicing through the guardrail as if it were butter, and ending up headfirst in a wall of rock?

It *had* to be an accident — and yet, somebody had gone to the trouble of telling him that it was not.

Daniel forced his racing mind to address the next problem: the identity of that somebody. Certainly no benevolent motive had inspired the message: that much was clear from the note. The words constituted an unabashed threat.

Suddenly, he felt better. His heartbeat slowed and his hands stilled their trembling. A death threat was something he could deal with. Judges — though never Daniel himself, until now — had been known to receive them before. An irate convict might pen one, or an accused man's family, or even an unbalanced attorney. It had been the reference to Ella's death that threw him.

He started the car. Very possibly, that reference had been nothing more than the twisting of a knife, painful but meaningless. Whoever had taken it into his head to send the death scare had known about Ella's end and used it to create an effect. It was the second half of the note — the threat — that was the significant part. The final two words made it a police matter.

He would call Garrity tonight. A police detective and an old friend from his prosecutor days, Garrity would know what to do about the threat to Daniel's life. He would know whether, and how seriously, to take it.

That resolved, Daniel recovered the last of his composure. He was actually whistling as he drove home through the rain, though the words "whistling in the dark" kept invading his thoughts with uneasy persistence. With the iron discipline that had kept him afloat through good times and bad, he forced the ominous message from his mind.

When he walked through his front door and greeted his children, he was no longer the mighty Judge Newman. He was Daddy.

"Daddy!"

"Dad!"

"Mr. Newman."

Daniel closed the front door behind him and held up a hand. "No one comes a step closer until I wring myself out. I'm wetter than a mop. It's a deluge out there."

He took off his coat, shook it gently onto the mat, then stepped up to the staircase to drape it over the banister. Mrs. Marks scooped it deftly out of his grasp before the damp coat had touched the wood.

"I'll just hang that over the bathtub, where it won't drip onto the carpeting," she suggested primly.

"An excellent idea! Thank you, Mrs. Marks."

She nodded without speaking, then started up the stairs, a solid woman with a solid tread. Her flowered apron was neatly tied in back, and spotless. Daniel's son and daughter came over to stand beside him as the housekeeper ascended, coat held out in front of her at arm's length like a warrior's shield. They watched in silent tribute until she had disappeared around the bend in the landing.

Yael and Mordy turned eagerly. Adroitly sidestepping his sister, Mordy whipped out a sheaf of papers and waved it at their father.

"Today's messages, hot off the press. Nothing very interesting."

"Mordy!" Yael chided. "You know you're not supposed to read Daddy's mail."

"This is *e-mail*, Yael. How can I print it out for him without seeing what it's about? Besides, Daddy lets."

Yael questioned her father with her eyes, and received a nod in reply. "He can read anything that's not marked 'Personal' or 'Confidential.' "

"Well." Yael reserved her judgment. "Daddy, I have some bad news."

Daniel started sharply. "Bad news? What is it?"

"You look like you just saw a ghost," Mordy grinned. "Don't worry, Dad. Yael probably just chipped a fingernail or something. A real life crisis."

"Daddy!"

"That," Daniel informed his son, "was not gentlemanly at all."

"Aw, I was only kidding. Yael knows that."

"Nevertheless," Daniel said. "If there's one thing I keep trying to hammer into you — both of you — it's the need to treat each other respectfully."

"Okay. Sorry." Mordy's hair was dark and springy, like Daniel's, but the large brown eyes were Ella's. Daniel nodded silently, betraying nothing of the tiny pain that worked its way through his heart at the sight of those eyes, like a caterpillar gnawing its way to freedom. A rush of feeling — a cocktail mix of tenderness and sorrow — threatened to overwhelm him. Mordy, misreading the silence for disapproval, prudently left the pile of electronic messages on the hall table and disappeared in the direction of the study, where his beloved computer was in residence.

Impulsively, Daniel called after him. "Mordy!"

"Yes?"

"We have an appointment after dinner, you and I. To learn together."

"Okay. Here, or in shul?"

Daniel considered. "Mrs. Marks can stay until we come home from *Ma'ariv*, but I don't want to keep her any longer than that. We'll learn here." Though Yael would never admit it, Daniel knew his daughter was nervous about being home alone at night. The uncharacteristic fear had surfaced nearly five years before, when they had moved to this house — yet another legacy of her mother's untimely death.

"Okay." Mordy's head, which had reappeared during this brief interchange, vanished again. Daniel turned to his daughter.

"Now, what's all this about bad news?" he asked.

Yael brushed a strand of fine dark hair from her face. "I didn't mean to scare you, Daddy. It's just that Mrs. Goldenheimer's retiring."

"Mrs. Goldenheimer?" He fished around in his mind, and came up blank.

"My piano teacher," Yael reminded him patiently. "My new one. Or newest one, anyway. The one I've been taking lessons from for the past four months, ever since Mrs. Mirsky moved to Israel. And now" — she sounded discouraged — "I need another teacher. How am I supposed to make any progress when all my teachers keep dropping out of my life like this?"

Daniel stifled a smile. This was the kind of life crisis he could cope with. "Not to worry," he ordered. "I'm going to institute inquiries. You do the same thing among your piano-playing friends. We'll come up with someone, never fear."

"None of my friends take lessons anymore. These days, they'd rather listen to music than make it." Yael strolled slowly alongside her father to the kitchen, where her chicken dinner was waiting to be popped into the broiler. Daniel wondered whether there was a hint to be read in her last words.

That was something Ella would have known instinctively. From the subtlest nuance in Yael's voice just now, she would have decided how to interpret what the girl had said. Daniel had been trying for five years to learn that skill, and was coming to the dismal conclusion that it was unlearnable. Either you were born with it, or — especially if you were born male — you were not.

Lacking a woman's intuition, he was forced to fall back on direct cross-examination. "Are you saying you're tired of taking lessons, Yael? Would you rather stop?"

She paused in the act of sliding the broiler tray into the oven, and peered up at him over her shoulder with incredulous eyes. "Daddy! How can you even *ask* such a thing? Don't you know me at *all*?"

Biting his lip, Daniel said feebly, "Just kidding, honey." *Mordy and me, we're great kidders.*

"After I practically broke into *tears* just now because Mrs. Goldheimer's retiring — not that she's the best teacher I've ever had, but she was someone to *learn* from at least! — how can you ask if I want to stop taking lessons? I know it's a bother for you to keep finding me teachers, but is it my fault I keep losing them? Mordy can sneer all he wants about a 'life crisis,' but this is *important* to me!"

"It's important to me, too, Yael. And Mordy doesn't sneer. He likes your playing. We both do."

Yael blinked rapidly, then closed the oven door with a snap and stood up. She faced Daniel, head high, her tone contrite but cool. "I'm sorry, Daddy. I didn't mean to shout."

"I'll find you another teacher." The words rang hollow in his own ears. He felt as though he were offering a Band-Aid to the victim of a four-car collision. She nodded once, without speaking, then turned to the counter where her vegetables lay ready for the chopping board. With a sinking feeling that was becoming very familiar, Daniel watched her pick up knife and tomato and begin slicing vigorously, her silence more eloquent than any words.

He had always been close to Yael, and they generally interacted well together. But these past couple of years, since her bas mitzvah, had been increasingly difficult. He was trying to read his daughter like a foreign language, and not succeeding very well.

His mother's words came back to haunt him. She had spoken them just the other week, on the porch of her summer home in the Catskills during Daniel's last weekend there with the kids. He remembered the way she had looked, sitting very straight and tall in a white wicker chair. Yael had just lapsed into one of her inexplicable crying jags — he forgot just why — and run off to her room. Daniel's dismay and befuddlement had been apparent.

"She used to be such an even-tempered kid," he'd mused. "What's gotten into her?"

"Adolescence," his mother said shortly.

"Was I so prickly at that age, Mom? To be honest, I don't remember it that way."

She fixed him with her characteristic gaze, which was at once aristocratic and warm. "She's a girl."

"I'm aware of that. But —"

"And that girl needs a mother, Daniel. You know that as well as I do."

"I've been —"

"Trying to be both mother and father to the children. I know." Her eyes were kind, but her voice had a don't-argue-with-me edge. "The fact is, you can't be both. Heaven knows, you have your hands full just being *one* of them! What you need —" She stopped, suddenly smiling. "But you've heard all this before."

"A wife."

"Exactly."

"It's too soon," he said, as he had said a hundred times over the past five years. "Ella's death was such a trauma. The kids need time." *I need time.*

He might almost have spoken the words aloud. Gently, she patted his hand. "It's natural to be afraid," she said, very quietly. "But sooner or later, you're going to have to start living again."

"Afraid? Me? This is Judge Newman you're talking to, Ma'am. The big, bad judge ain't afraid of nobody. There are inmates up and down the grand old state of Maryland who can attest to that."

So he had said. And on some level, he had meant it.

But now, as the first strains of piano music came wafting at him — Yael's surefire refuge when solace was needed — he felt a twinge of doubt. He had done his best to keep things going after Ella's death. The first was to sell the house they had lived in together and purchase this one, in Cedar Hills. A new Bais Yaakov-style high school had just opened here, headed by a woman with a fine reputation as an educator. That would do for Yael, when the time came; until then, she would carpool to her old school in Baltimore. For Daniel, the commute to courthouse from Cedar Hills was not so long as to make a real difference, and there was a bus to take Mordy and other neighborhood youngsters directly to their Baltimore yeshiva. The children seemed as relieved as he to start over, someplace new. Yael had scarcely begun bemoaning the friends she had left behind when a new crop of them came along to console her. All in all, it had been a wise move, and a comforting one.

In these less painful surroundings he had begun, brick by careful brick, to construct a new life for the kids. They were only 7 and 9 then, and they needed him badly. What kept him sane during those first terrible months was the necessity to be there for them.

Hours of intense talk and even more intense listening, of holding a weeping child in his arms for hours, of speaking to teachers, helping the kids with school assignments, hiring household help, arbitrating childish squabbles, chasing away night terrors — he had done them all, and, he thought, done them well. He looked around now, at the homey kitchen with its good supper smells. He thought of Mordy, tapping away at the computer, and listened to Yael at the piano. He had made them a real home. A good home.

A line from a nursery rhyme played through his mind. *This is the house that Daniel built.*

Like a hawk's shadow swooping low over sunlit fields, the recollection of the anonymous note rushed in on him. He reached into his pocket and fingered it with loathing. He would call Garrity right after the meal. He had fashioned a life for his family, stable and secure, to hold back the world's terrors. The note was like the first, ominous rush of distant water. Allow just one tiny crack, and the whole dam could burst wide open.

Strains of music filled the house. In the den, the printer beeped and whirred. The broiler sizzled, sending up the aroma of home and love and security.

Your wife's death was no accident.

You're next.

6

Nervously, Sara looked up at the beige brick building with its raised black lettering. The school looked deserted as a tomb, and about as uninviting.

She turned to the cabdriver, gray, grizzled, and uncommunicative. "Someone is supposed to be meeting me here. Do you mind waiting while I check that I can get in? It'll only be a minute."

She tensed for the answer she more than half-expected: "*Wait?* Ya think I got all day, lady?"

It never came. Instead, the cabbie turned to smile at her — a polite, neighborly smile. "Sure. Take your time." He switched on the radio.

This, she reflected as she swung open the door, was definitely not New York.

She had been living in Cedar Hills only a few days, but had already been struck by the routine civility, so different from what she had been accustomed to in her native city. Here, people held doors open for you, offered helpful advice, said "Hi, there," even if they did not know you. It made being a stranger in town that much easier.

With both hands clutching her handbag, she ran her eyes over the building. It was attractive in an understated way, a definite presence on the block without overpowering it. She liked the shade of brick: a beige so pale it was nearly white. It reminded her of the stones of Jerusalem, where she had spent a part of the previous summer. For four glorious weeks she had been an American abroad, savoring the exotic sights and sounds and smells even as she basked in the sun of a reinvigorated spiritual excitement. Those weeks had been a respite from routine, a flight from the excessively familiar. In winging away to Israel, she convinced herself — almost — that she had bought freedom. She almost managed to escape her own unhappiness.

When, at the trip's end, the wheels of her departing jet lost their final contact with Israel's tarmac, Sara had wept bitter tears — not only for what she was leaving behind, but also for what she was rushing back to embrace once more.

But she had not embraced it, or at least not for long. A chance for change had come, and Sara had found the courage to seize it. Here she stood, facing the building that, in a few days' time, would come to embody and solder that change. Forcing her steps into a confident rhythm she did not feel, she approached the front door and placed her finger on the intercom button.

An indistinct "Yes, who is it?" reached her through the box. She moved closer to call, "It's Sara. Sara Muller! I'm supposed to be meeting — ?"

"Yes, yes. Come in, Sara!" Filtered through the intercom, the voice was calmly welcoming. A harsh buzz followed almost immediately. Sara said frantically, "Wait, please, I have to pay the —" The buzz continued to rend the air with a noise like angry bees. She waited until it had ended, and then pressed the intercom button again.

"Yes?"

"It's still me. Sara."

"Didn't the buzzer go off?" The voice was puzzled, but not, Sara was thankful to note, impatient.

"Yes, I heard it. But I can't come in yet." Sara explained, shouting into the intercom in her effort to make herself understood. She ran back to the cab, thrust some bills into the driver's hand, offered a quick smile to atone for her haste, then literally ran back to the school building. For the third time, she placed her finger on the button and pressed.

This time, the buzzer sounded without any preface. Sara grasped the handle and twisted. The door opened; she stepped inside. A blast of air-conditioned comfort swept over her, making her aware for the first time just how hot it was outside. She smoothed her hair, already frizzing with the humidity, and caught her breath.

Here I am.

Getting here had been a long journey, both literally and figuratively.

What awaited her in this building? She had pulled up roots in the old place. Would she throw down new ones here, or would this school offer only a transient welcome? What lay along the path she had — bravely or foolhardily — chosen to walk last spring?

Right now, the only path she wanted was the one that would lead to the principal's office. As she peered this way and that, she caught a faint strain of music, far off, like a fragrance too delicate to be captured. The music halted, then stopped. Sara moved forward in the hush.

Second door on the right, Rebbetzin Goodman had said. The music started up again, but Sara had no time for it now. Nervousness assailed her, making her heart race and her stomach leap. In coping with these internal gymnastics she walked right past the door she wanted.

Belatedly, she turned back, quickening her step. She found the door marked "Office," started inside, and just missed — by a neat, if startled, sidestep — a head-on collision with a woman in the act of hurtling out that very door.

The woman had been throwing a final remark over her shoulder to some invisible listener. At Sara's involuntary exclamation, she whipped around, staring.

"Who — ?"

"Sara Muller," Sara said quickly. "Excuse me."

If she had been surprised at the suddenness of the stranger's appearance, she was doubly astonished at the reaction to her name. "*You?*" she squeaked. "You're Miss Muller? Teaching *Chumash* and *Navi* to the ninth grade this year?"

"Yes. Also science to the tenth and eleventh grades in the afternoons. And you are —?"

"Henya Davidson." Mrs. Davidson's eyes narrowed. "What a coincidence! I was just talking with Rebbetzin Goodman about you." The words were friendly; the tone was not.

"About me?"

"That's right." Mrs. Davidson fixed a pair of very dark, very hard eyes on her. "You taught a niece of mine last year, in Flatbush. Rina Pollack's her name."

"Ah, Rina," Sara said as she forced a smile. Rina Pollack had been the laziest, most unruly student she had ever had the dubious pleasure of trying to teach. Single-handedly, the girl had turned what would otherwise have been a rather nice class into a theater of horrors. "Yes, I remember her well."

"Well, let me tell you, *she* remembers *you*, too! That's exactly what I was talking to the Rebbetzin about just now. I've got a daughter starting the ninth grade here this year, and let me tell you, Rina has made her, and my husband — not to mention *me* — very nervous!"

Sara was at a loss. "I'm afraid I don't —"

"Thank you for dropping by, Mrs. Davidson," a voice interrupted firmly from behind. Rebbetzin Goodman had Mrs. Davidson by the elbow and was propelling her gently, in an unwavering line, toward the front door.

"Well, I'll be in touch," Mrs. Davidson said, wrinkling her nose as if she smelled something bad. "I hope —"

"Everything's going to be fine." Still walking beside her visitor, the principal smiled. "My best to Sima. Tell her I'm asking her to bring just one thing to school next week: a positive attitude. All right?"

"Of course, Rebbetzin." Mrs. Davidson allowed herself to be guided along the hall to the exit. Only when the glass doors were plainly in view did Rebbetzin Goodman relinquish her grip on the other's elbow. Mrs. Davidson turned to offer one last word, but, "Good-bye, Mrs. Davidson," the principal said, still in the same gentle tone. The words wore an unmistakable air of finality.

She watched the glass door open and shut, then turned back to where Sara stood frozen in the center of the corridor. There was something pathetic and yet courageous about the young woman with the uncertain expression and the big, no-nonsense handbag.

With a very different smile, Rebbetzin Goodman said, "Sara Muller. Welcome."

Moving very slowly, as though through an unknown medium, Sara stepped forward to meet her.

7

"hat was that about?" Sara asked.

She had intended to dance around the subject indi-
rectly, but meeting the principal's eyes across the desk
made her change her mind. There was something
about Rebbetzin Goodman that elicited the straightforward approach.
Frankness called to frankness.

The principal took a little time to frame her answer. "A nervous
mother," she said finally, "as she herself told you."

"But what did my former student — her niece — say to make her so
nervous? Did she make me out to be some sort of monster?"

She smiled as she said it, then saw with a sinking feeling that the
principal was not smiling back. She waited tensely for some reassuring sign that all this was trivial, bordering on meaningless, not to be
fretted over for an instant. Instead, the Rebbetzin murmured, "I take it
that this niece was not one of your better students?"

"That's correct. Not to mince words, Rina was my worst headache
last year."

"Apparently, you were also hers. Or so she told her aunt, uncle, and
cousin — the Davidsons. She made you out to be inflexible and overly
harsh. 'A tyrant,' to quote her exact words."

Rebbetzin Goodman was watching Sara closely as she spoke. At the
word "tyrant" Sara flinched. Then she lifted her head a little higher.

"I see. May I ask where this is leading, Rebbetzin Goodman? Are
you trying to tell me that you regret hiring me?" Was she being fired
before she even began? Her head began to pound.

The principal leaned back in her chair. "You're very quick to feel slighted, Sara."

Silence.

"Have I given you any reason to believe I regret my decision?"

"But Mrs. Davidson —"

"— is not running this school. I am. Suppose you tell me, Sara, what might have given Rina the impression she has of you?"

Every mortified nerve fiber was screaming at Sara to get up, pull the tattered shreds of her dignity around her, and leave. Leave the school, leave Cedar Hills, run back to the safe cocoon of home. Why was she called upon to defend herself against these unfair charges even before her first day on the job? Was she a naughty child, to be seated before the principal's desk and asked to give an accounting of herself?

She looked up from her lap, leaving her fists lying clenched there. Her eyes met the principal's. All at once, her outrage, her humiliation, fell away. She was not a naughty child — but she *was* an unknown entity. Rebbetzin Goodman was well within her rights in asking these questions, and she was doing it in a courteous and respectful manner. It was up to Sara to respond in a similar fashion. She was not an errant schoolgirl, outraged at some classroom injustice. *Behave like an adult!*

She filled her lungs and tried.

"As I've said, Rina was a difficult student. Apart from caring very little about her schoolwork, she consistently disrupted my class and led others to do the same. At times, these disruptions took the form of actual chutzpah. Disrespectful behavior is something I've never tolerated, and I was determined to try and correct it in Rina.

"I tried imposing various consequences, from sending her to the principal's office, to assigning essays on proper classroom behavior, to sending notes home to her parents. Nothing did more than make a dent in the situation — and even that, only temporarily.

"Finally, after a particularly bad stretch toward the end of the year, I decided that more serious action was called for. I took away Rina's right to join the class on our end-of-year trip. It was an overnight trip, and the girls had naturally been looking forward to it. Rina was furious."

The Rebbetzin nodded. "I imagine she must have been. What happened?"

"Her parents called, trying to convince me to change my mind.

When that didn't happen, they appealed to the principal. He backed me up as a matter of policy, though privately he told me he wished things hadn't reached that point. Her parents were raising quite a ruckus. But I wouldn't back down. Rina deserved, in my opinion, to be asked to leave the school. Missing a class trip was mild punishment in return for her behavior all year."

"I see." Rebbetzin Goodman tapped a pen against the desktop. "And the rest of the class? Did they also see you as a — tyrant?"

Sara flushed. "I don't think so. Oh, one or two of Rina's closest friends were a little hostile, but I got along well with the other girls. In fact, when word got out that I was leaving the school, the class got together to throw me a farewell party. I don't think they were lying when they told me they'd enjoyed having me as their teacher."

For a few moments, Rebbetzin Goodman was silent, studying Sara's face as though trying to read there the secrets of her soul. Abruptly, she put down her pen. "I believe you. We'll forget about the Davidsons, shall we? Now, on to more pleasant topics. We've got a ninth-grade curriculum to discuss . . . "

Some forty minutes later, Sara left the office, head swimming with the details of their talk. In such a new school, the curriculum was far more fluid than she was accustomed to. Instead of being presented with her year's work as though it had been etched in stone from time immemorial, she was actually invited to offer an opinion about what she would be teaching! If her excitement had been intense before, it soared now into an intellectual stratosphere. Her mind whirled with ideas, possibilities.

She walked quickly, heels tapping down the empty corridor. There were one or two supplementary materials the principal had recommended for teaching high-school *Chumash*, and Sara wanted to catapult herself into the nearest Jewish bookstore as quickly as humanly possible. The dismay she had felt at the start of the meeting — the Davidson encounter, and the Rebbetzin's interrogation — seemed to have happened days ago. She was brimming with energy, fired up with a fierce new enthusiasm for her profession.

"Fire" was an apt word. For too long, she had been raking over the cold ashes of her commitment to teaching — feeding her seventh graders stale, if nourishing, dishes at lukewarm temperatures. For years, her dream had been to teach high school. Somehow, she had mentally linked the fulfillment of that dream to another longed-for "promotion": marriage. It had been a revelation to her — a rather sheepish one — to realize that the two did not have to go together. If there was nothing she could do to bring the one to fruition, there was a definite move she could make toward the other. Given her years of experience, it had not proved too difficult to land this job teaching the ninth grade. All she had really needed was the willingness to try.

She had taught science in a desultory way through the years — though never on a high-school level — and was not sorry to take it up again now. Living on her own would be a much more expensive matter than staying under her parents' roof, and the extra money would come in handy. Besides, she was grateful for anything that would serve to fill her days. By teaching full time, then spending her evenings preparing the next day's classes, she hoped to keep both loneliness and boredom at bay. She knew from bitter experience just how long an evening can be when you are waiting for Mr. Right — or at least the local matchmaker — to call.

She stepped along the corridor with a quick, sure stride, already beginning to feel at home. Her footsteps echoed on the tiles now, but next week the place would be filled with students and teachers and noise. From every open door would stream the beautiful cacophony of learning. And she would be a part of it.

Right now, there was another sound streaming into Sara's consciousness. She halted, listening. It was the piano player again, the one she had heard on her arrival. The melody was Mozart's, the execution sophisticated, if not yet perfected. Without being aware of making the decision, Sara abruptly changed course. The bookstore could wait a few minutes longer.

The music seemed to be coming from the far end of the hall.

Along that side lay the lunchroom-cum-auditorium. The corridor ended in a few steps down, with the auditorium on the other side of a pair of heavy double doors. Sara had just reached the top of the steps when the music stopped. A moment later, the doors were pushed open from the inside, and a girl stepped out.

She had fine dark hair, eyes that were a bright hazel and — just now — absorbed inwardly. There was a radiance about her that told Sara, without question, that this was the piano player. The sight of an unexpected figure on the steps stopped the girl in her tracks. With the width of the stairs between them, they regarded one another, Sara gazing down and the girl craning her neck slightly upward, the better to see.

"Sorry if I startled you," Sara said softly. "You play beautifully."

"Um, it was nothing —" Collecting herself, the girl offered a sheepish smile. "I mean, thank you."

"That's a difficult piece."

"I don't have it right yet. I'm in between piano teachers at the moment." She sounded frustrated.

"Keep working. You'll get it."

"Do — do you play?"

"A little." Sara smiled. "Well, have a nice day." She descended the rest of the steps and, with a pleasant nod, walked past the girl into the auditorium. The doors swung shut behind her.

The room yawned ahead of her like a chasm. Sara saw nothing of the long rows of tables and benches, nothing of the raised stage at the opposite end, or the giant, colorful posters that decorated the walls on either side. Her eyes flew straight to the piano at the foot of the stage.

In a moment, she was seated on the bench, fingers poised over the ivory keys with a sense of exquisite anticipation. She was far from being in a position to afford a piano for the tiny apartment she was renting, but she sorely missed the one she had left behind in her parents' home. Finding this fine instrument here at school was a stroke of luck. At the end of her day's work, when the building emptied enough to afford her some measure of privacy, she would be able to come here to find the best kind of relaxation she knew.

She closed her eyes, hearing in her head the symphony she had chosen, letting her fingers come down on the keys. Music was born.

On the other side of the double doors, Yael Newman listened.

8

"**M**ark. Thanks for coming."

Mark Garrity nodded his shaggy head in greeting, then ducked to pass through the doorway into the Newman house. The doorway was not particularly low, but a series of bumped foreheads in his teens — coming in the wake of a truly breathtaking growth spurt — had left Garrity perpetually cautious. He followed Daniel into the living room, walking close on his host's heels, like an elongated shadow. They sat down at right angles to each other, Daniel in the recliner and Garrity on the sofa, one long arm slung across the back.

Without asking, Daniel popped open and handed his guest a can of diet cola — Garrity's lifeblood. The police detective nodded his thanks, then guzzled half the can before setting it down. He wiped his mouth, crossed one lanky knee over the other, and said, "You asked me down here to discuss something. A worrisome matter, you called it."

When Daniel did not answer, he formed his fingers into a gun, pointed it at Daniel, and said, "Shoot."

"Worrisome," Daniel acknowledged, "but not necessarily a police matter. At least, not yet. That's why I asked you to come here to the house instead of meeting me at the station house. I appreciate it, Mark."

The policeman waved a hand. "It's all the same to me. But I do go on shift in half an hour, so suppose you get down to it, pal."

Mark Garrity was almost the caricature of a detective: dark, lean, taciturn, ever given to actions over words. During Daniel's years as a prosecuting attorney, Garrity had been his most useful contact on the police force. He was energetic, utterly reliable, with a single-minded passion for his job that left little room for a personal life. Like Daniel, he was unmarried. But, unlike Daniel, there was no tragedy in Mark Garrity's past. He was a bachelor simply because he had not made the time to find a wife.

As Daniel hesitated, Garrity said again, "Get down to it, Dan. Worrisome, you said." His lips twitched. Daniel's penchant for what Garrity called "book words" had been the subject of much teasing between them in the past. With Daniel's ascendancy to the judge's bench, his former colleague had turned a shade more respectful. But just a shade.

Daniel hesitated, automatically listening to his surroundings — as though his ears were a gauge of his children's safety. The house was quiet. Yael was at a friend's house, commiserating or partying or whatever it was that kids did on the eve of the new school year. She had promised to be home by 9 o'clock and to get a good night's sleep before the big day tomorrow. Mordy was in the study, using the computer and oblivious to the rest of the world. If there was any time to talk privately, it was now.

"Okay." Daniel leaned forward, hands clasped. "Mark, I received a note yesterday. Anonymous."

The detective was instantly alert. "What kind of note?"

"An unpleasant one. Threatening."

"A death threat?"

"I guess you could call it that. It — mentioned Ella." Daniel was surprised at how naturally the words emerged. Until not so long ago, he would stumble and all but choke whenever he had occasion to pronounce his wife's name.

Garrity held out a hand. "Let's see it." True to his word, he was wasting no time.

Reluctantly, Daniel pulled the note from his pocket and passed it to the detective. The moment it left his possession, he felt a ridiculous urge to pull it back, to wad it up and hurl it as far as it would go — as if that action could remove the threat, could undo what was done. He also wanted very badly to wash his hands; they felt soiled from contact with the venom-filled message.

Garrity read through the note carefully, turned the page over, then turned it back and read it again. When he looked up, his dark eyes were thoughtful. Tapping the paper with one finger, he demanded, "When did this arrive, and where, and how?"

"A few days ago . . . Thursday, I think. Yes, it *was* Thursday. I found it on the windshield of my car when I left work at the end of the day."

"Where was the car parked?"

"My usual spot in the courthouse parking lot."

"Was there an envelope?"

Daniel nodded. "I threw it away. Sorry."

"You should have known better than that. There might be fingerprints."

"Mark, as I told you over the phone, this visit is strictly unofficial. I didn't call you down here to open an investigation."

"No? What, then?"

"Just advice. How seriously would you take this, and what steps — if any — would you take if you were me?"

Garrity needed no time to formulate his answer. "The first step I'd take," he stated, "would be to call me in — officially. The second would be to request police protection — for you and the kids — until the perpetrator is caught. And the third would be to help track down the piece of scum who wrote this."

"That last bit is fine. But leave out the first and the second."

"Why? Don't you value your life?"

"Of course I do!" Daniel flared. "But I'm not about to turn my life — not to mention my kids' lives — upside down because of one stupid little note. As a prosecuting attorney, and now as judge, I'm used to being on the receiving end of a lot of hate. That doesn't bother me."

Garrity shot back, "Hate has a way of hurting sometimes. Hurting bad. We can protect you, Dan."

"I won't have my home turned into a garrison."

"We're talking death threats, man!"

"*One* threat. Only one. And very possibly nothing more than a sick prank." Daniel shook his head. "I want my kids to lead normal lives."

"Things will be a lot more 'normal' with their father still living."

The two men glared at each other.

Ten seconds ticked past. Daniel drew a deep breath. "No police," he said evenly. He inflected the words with judicial hauteur, but Garrity was not impressed.

"How about if you get another note? Do we open an investigation then? These guys don't usually stop with one, you know."

"Sometimes they do."

Garrity snorted. Daniel thought for awhile, then proposed a compromise: "Tell you what. If another note comes, I promise to call you. We can decide together then."

Garrity nodded slowly, in resignation rather than agreement. "Fair enough. Now, what do you think of this business about your wife?"

Behind Daniel, in the kitchen, the refrigerator began to hum. The ceiling fan above his head whirred peacefully. Why couldn't life work like an electrical appliance — just plug it in, then sit back and enjoy? He smiled inwardly at the notion (it was a wry smile) because it painted a portrait of an existence that bore no resemblance whatsoever to life as he, or humanity as a whole, knew it. Wishful thinking had never been a weakness of his. Why start now?

Shaking his head, he addressed the detective's question. "I've been trying to think, and I keep coming up blank. You know the story, Mark. Ella took my car that morning because hers was at the shop. It was a stormy day, with high winds, the roads were slippery, and she lost control. How could it have been anything *but* an accident?"

Mark Garrity could think of several possibilities — especially in light of the sinister note — but he said nothing. "Any enemies, Dan?"

"Only a thousand or two. Come on, Mark, you know what happens in our line of work. Every criminal I've ever helped prosecute, or anyone I as judge helped put behind bars, is a potential enemy."

"Didn't you become a judge *after* the accident?"

"Oh, that's right. We can eliminate anyone I've spooked in these past five years, anyway. That cuts it down."

"How," Garrity mused aloud, staring down at the note, "would this guy have information about the way your wife died? Was the accident written up in the papers?"

"A straightforward skid-in-the-rain? No."

"Then what does he know about it that we don't?"

"Nothing, probably." Testily, Daniel rose and began pacing the living room. "Ella's death is a matter of public record. It's no secret."

"Maybe not. But I'd say there's a strong chance that the reference to your wife dates the perpetrator to the general time frame of the accident. It happened — when, exactly?"

"October of '93. Five years ago next month."

It had been a week after Sukkos. The box of decorations had sat where he had left them, in a corner of the living room when he dismantled the sukkah days before. Ella had reminded him several times — the last time, on the final evening of her life — to carry the box down to the basement when he had the chance. Sometime after the accident, but before he started sitting *shivah*, some kindly soul had whisked the decorations out of sight. He had found them the following year, in the wrong part of the basement, slightly the worse for wear because of some minor flooding —

"It was a very rainy October," Daniel said sadly.

Garrity kept his mind on the business at hand. "If there's another note," he said, "even one more, I'm going to want to start pulling records from five-six years ago. Maybe we'll come across someone who has a habit of making threats — or worse."

"Aren't you jumping to conclusions, Mark? As we just said, any number of people might have written that note. You're assuming, a) that the writer is a criminal I once prosecuted, b) that I dealt with him more than five years ago, and c) that he'll send another note. That's a lot of assumptions."

"All of them sound," Garrity argued, "and all based on experience and the law of probability. Or do I mean the law of averages? "

"Murphy's law is what you want. Not that I believe it'll hold true in this case."

"Believe what you want, my friend. Just remember to call when the next threat comes in." Garrity stood. "It's been nice seeing you again, Dan. Regards to the kids. And — take care of yourself, will you?" He extended a hand.

Daniel shook it, saying, "Wipe that look off your face. I probably shouldn't even have mentioned this thing to you at all. Just a stupid prank."

"It was you," Garrity reminded him, "who called it worrisome."

"I'll downgrade that to 'annoying,' if it makes you feel better."

"I'll feel better when I see you safe." From his superior height, Garrity looked him in the eye. "You asked me another question before, one I haven't answered yet."

"Oh? Remind me. "

"You asked how seriously I'd take this threat."

"Oh, that."

"Yeah, that."

Daniel waited.

"I'd take it seriously, Dan. Very seriously. You get me?"

"I get you," Daniel sighed. He walked his guest to the door. As Garrity ducked Daniel added, "If there are any more notes, you'll be the first to know. I promise."

"I'll hold you to that." Garrity walked away to the unmarked squad car parked at the curb.

Daniel watched him get in and drive away. Then, slowly, he closed and locked the front door, wishing that, by that simple action, he could lock evil out. He glanced at his watch. Nearly time for Yael to return home. Her friend's older sister, newly empowered with a driver's license, had offered to drive her.

Daniel frowned. Just how good a driver was this big sister? Yael was only a few short blocks away. A brisk walk certainly would not do him any harm, not with the excess poundage he had begun to pick up since sitting on the bench. He would walk over now and get her himself. The older sister would just have to find someone else to practice her new driving skills on.

Before he left, he went to check on Mordy. He found his son staring blankly at the computer monitor, hands unmoving on the keyboard.

"Mordy?"

The boy jumped. "Hi, Daddy. What's up?" He sounded casual enough, but there was a glassy look in his eye.

"Anything the matter?"

"Matter? Not at all. I'm fine. Just — thinking."

"A useful occupation. "Daniel smiled. "I'm going over to pick up Yael. Will you be ready to learn when I get back? "

"Sure. I'm all through here, anyway."

"Finished your summer homework?"

"Just a few math problems left."

Mordy regarded his math assignments the way other kids might view shooting basketball hoops — as a pleasant way to unwind. On the other hand, he got the cold shakes when faced with the prospect of writing an original composition. Danny tousled his son's hair fondly.

"You get those out of the way while I'm gone, then. Any English homework?"

"No, thank goodness," Mordy said fervently.

Daniel laughed, and turned to go. His back was to the boy, so he did not see the glassy look return, nor did he see the way Mordy stared after him as he walked away. Just as he had not heard the silent tread of his son's sneakers as he had sat talking with Garrity earlier.

Mordy had not meant to eavesdrop. In fact, he had had no idea that anyone was in the house with his father. He had gone into the kitchen for a drink, then stood transfixed by the words he caught from the living room.

You asked me how seriously I'd take this threat . . .

I'd take it seriously, Dan. Very seriously . . .

What threat?

Daniel slipped on his jacket for the short walk. When his father was gone, Mordy ran upstairs to fetch his homework assignment. He sat at the front window, mechanically solving a series of — for him — ludicrously simple math problems, until he saw the shadowy figures of his father and sister coming down the street toward him. Quickly he turned away, facing the room with his notebook on his lap, so that they would not catch him looking out for them.

It was not until they came through the front door that Mordy realized how tightly his jaw had been clenched the whole time his father was gone. His teeth ached!

With a vague, "Hi, "Yael disappeared upstairs to her room. She had already packed and repacked her schoolbag for tomorrow, but felt compelled to look through her things again, if only to assure herself that she was as ready as she would ever be for the big day. As an incoming sophomore, she felt worldly wise and experienced in the high-school world she had inhabited for one whole year. Still, the first day of school was the first day of school.

Downstairs, Mordy closed his notebook.

"Ready?" Daniel asked, shedding his jacket. He tugged at the drawstring behind the couch that closed the living room curtains.

"Sure, Daddy! "They made their way to the study. The blinds were still raised in this room, letting in the silver of the streetlight until Daniel flipped a switch and the room was flooded with electric light. Instead of sitting opposite Daniel, as he usually did, Mordy pulled his chair close to his father's on the same side of the big desk, so that their shoulders almost touched as they bent over their Gemaras.

They made a pretty picture for anyone who might happen to glance through the undrawn shades of the broad window which, like that of the living room, fronted the street. And someone — though they had no inkling of it — *was*, at that precise moment, availing himself of the sight. Father and son were nicely framed in a pair of binoculars trained on them from a discreet vantage point across the street.

The binoculars were not lowered until much later, when the lights had been doused and the house lay shrouded in uneasy sleep.

9

"Tell me, Sara, why are you here?"

Sara looked out the window, framing a few late roses and a section of dull brick from the house next door. She looked down at the couch she was sitting on, at the cushion propped up against one brown curve, at the beige shag rug at her feet. She looked at the bookcase on the opposite wall, with the interesting titles she had only had time to notice briefly as she walked in.

Only then, reluctantly, did she raise her eyes to meet those of the woman seated across from her in the burgundy swivel chair.

She was a few years older than Sara, though she did not look it. In contrast to Sara's casual skirt and sweater, Miriam Schumacher wore a crisp, up-to-date navy suit, with a cream blouse and navy pumps. She was poised and professional, self-confidence radiating from her in almost palpable waves. Her eyes were the kind of blue usually associated with electricity. They questioned, they searched, they probed. They made Sara very uncomfortable.

"To get help," she answered at last, dropping her eyes once more. It was a difficult admission.

"We all need help of one kind or another," Mrs. Schumacher said calmly. "What kind are you looking for?" When Sara did not answer at once, she added a touch more firmly, "Sara, as in any endeavor, the first and possibly the most useful step is defining our goals."

"I — I suppose you're right."

"Then help me understand. You've come to me seeking — something. Obviously, there is a specific issue or issues you'd like my assistance in working out. What are those issues?"

Sara sat helpless, wondering where to begin. Miriam watched her for a moment, then said, "Let me put it another way. How would you like to see yourself when our time together is over?"

"Wearing a wedding ring!"

The words burst out of Sara before she could stop them. Amazed at herself, she laughed aloud. Miriam Schumacher laughed, too. Suddenly, the ice was broken.

"We're getting somewhere," the therapist said encouragingly. "You're here to deal with the issues that you feel are preventing you from being married?"

"That's it in a nutshell," Sara admitted. "Oh, I've got all sorts of things I need to improve in myself — like anyone, a lifetime's worth of work. But this is one area where I seem to be — stuck."

"Tell me about it." Miriam sat back in an attitude of listening.

"It's so stupid! Whenever I meet anyone who seems even remotely suitable for marriage — I run in the opposite direction!"

"And yet, you say you *are* interested in marriage."

"Very much so."

"And therefore — "

"Therefore — I'm running away in spite of what I really want. In spite of my own best interests."

"You run because — ?"

"Simple. I'm scared."

Sara paused thoughtfully. Already, under the therapist's calm gaze, she was forcing herself to become more analytical than she generally allowed herself to be on this sensitive topic. She was like a patient newly released from the dentist's chair, probing with her tongue the sore spot where a tooth had been. Only, in her case, it was not a tooth that had been brutally wrenched from her five years ago, but her heart.

"And bitter," she added now, not without an effort. "Furious and bitter."

"At — ?"

"At men in general, I guess."

"Because of one man in particular?"

Sara was startled. "How did you know that?" Did Mrs. Schumacher investigate her prospective clients' backgrounds before agreeing to meet them?

Miriam laughed. "That's usually the way it goes. We tend to generalize from the particular. I bang my head on an oak tree; therefore, all oak trees are bad. True?"

Sheepishly, Sara smiled. "When you put it like that, I feel silly."

"Never mind that. I want to hear about the big, bad tree that left you with such a nasty bump."

"Oh, the story is straightforward enough. I know exactly why I'm so stuck — so bitter about men, and so scared of commitment. I've got that part all figured out. What I don't know is how to change it."

"Tell me anyway."

Sara was quiet a moment, collecting her thoughts. "About five years ago, I was engaged to be married." She marveled that she could say those words now with only a faint ghost of the ache they had once brought. "I was 26, which is late by the standards of our community. By that time, I'd been dating for nearly seven years. Naturally, I was thrilled to have found the right one at last. My family was thrilled. My friends were thrilled —"

"Your engagement spread light and joy on every side," Mrs. Schumacher grinned. "I get the picture. Go on."

"This is the hard part." Sara drew a breath. "Apparently, the light and joy were — one sided."

The therapist nodded encouragingly.

"I guess I should have waited to get to know him better, but the logistics of our dating were complicated. You see, my *chasan* and I were not from the same city. I grew up in Flatbush; he lived in Baltimore. We could only meet on weekends, and often only on Sundays."

"So, the feelings were one sided. Why did he propose?"

Sara shrugged. "What his reasons were for getting engaged to a girl he didn't really want to marry are not important. At least," Sara amended, with a sideways look at the therapist, "I don't think they are. The point is that he was — unenthusiastic — from the very beginning. Oh, he sent me all the usual cards and flowers, but when we'd meet — still only on the weekends, since we lived hours apart and each of us had crazy-busy schedules — he could hardly bring himself to discuss the wedding, or our future plans."

"How did that make you feel?"

With a grimace, Sara admitted, "I was hurt, naturally. Bewildered. I felt — unloved. Unlovable."

"I see." In Miriam Schumacher's face, Sara read understanding — and compassion. This last was similar, but different in quality, from the pity she had glimpsed in the faces of friends, family, and casual acquaintances when news of her broken engagement emerged. Sara found she did not mind this look nearly as much.

"Well, things reached the point where I couldn't hide my head in the sand anymore. I couldn't pretend we were in this thing together. I was racing ahead at top speed, while he hadn't even left the starting post —"

"Who broke the engagement?"

"I did. And thank G-d for that! That made it a little easier to bear — afterwards."

"Tell me how it happened."

Sara found she was breathing hard, as though running a race. She willed her pulse to slow down.

"It was very late one Sunday night. We had been out somewhere and were sitting in the car in front of his house, talking, before saying good-night. I had spent Shabbos in Baltimore with his family. My own car was parked further up the block . . . "

It was not raining anymore, but there was a foggy dampness in the air that had the same effect as rain in blocking out the rest of the world. A shimmering curtain of mist hid the street from Sara's sight. Inside the car, Moish had the heater going full blast, but Sara's fingers and toes still felt chilled.

She glanced over at her *chasan's* profile. It was slightly averted as he gazed out at the street. His house, in front of which they were parked, was dark except for a light that had been left burning in the front hall. In a little while Sara would go inside, while Moish would drive on to his uncle's house, where, for propriety's sake, he had been staying while Sara was a guest in his parents' home. In a little while. It was late, but they were an engaged couple with so much to talk about.

Only — they were not talking.

Sara hated these silences, which even at her most optimistic she could not pretend were companionable. Even though they were engaged, it was always this way now. As long as they were out doing something, Moish was chatty, informative, and fun to be with. But then, on the drive home, a mask would descend over his face. All of Sara's conversational gambits would fall into a black hole that gave back either silence or monosyllabic answers.

Gradually, her despair mounted. What had she said or done to offend him? Before they became engaged, she would wonder whether his occasional silence meant he regretted having taken the relationship this far, and if he was trying to formulate the sentences with which to break it off. Now that they were engaged, Sara was, frankly, at a loss. She did not know what to make of the silences. Proposing marriage meant that you wanted to be with the person forever. For two such people, conversation should surely flow with joy and abandon! What was the problem here?

And why did she have the gnawing feeling — a feeling that she kept telling herself, with ever decreasing conviction, was absurd — that her presence was unwanted?

"Tired?" she tried.

"What? Oh — no. Not very." He roused himself. "But *you've* got to make an early start back from Baltimore tomorrow morning." He shook his head. "Four hours of driving, then a full day's work. I don't know how you do it."

"It should take closer to three and a half hours, that early in the day. And it was worth it, to spend the weekend here with you."

No response.

Sara drew a breath. "Moish, we've been engaged for more than three weeks already, and we still haven't set a date or picked a hall."

"So do it. What's the problem?"

"I — I want this to be a joint effort. We're in this together, remember?"

"Look, whichever hall you pick will be fine. That is not the kind of thing I'm into, that's all."

"And our marriage?" Sara flared, suddenly sick and tired of playing cat and mouse with the man to whom she had agreed to entrust her life and her happiness. "Are you 'into' that?"

He finally turned his head at that. "What do you mean?"

"You heard me. From the day we got engaged — no, even before that — I've had the feeling that you wish you were somewhere else.

Tell me the truth, Moish. *Do you?*"

He hesitated. It was as if he had been waiting for this moment, for permission to speak the truth at last. In that instant of hesitation, she *knew*. And still, a faint flicker of hope refused to die. Fighting back a rising sense of dread, she urged, "Tell me what's wrong."

He told her. Sara listened, a cold hand clutching her heart, as he confessed that there was a girl he had been seeing seriously just before he met Sara. She had broken up with him after two whirlwind months, leaving him heartsick.

She said, when we broke up, that she wasn't interested in marrying me. I thought I couldn't have her, so —"

"So you caught me on the rebound? Or do I have it the wrong way around?" Sara was amazed that she could speak. The words had to fight their way past a football-sized constriction in her throat.

"Sort of." For the first time all evening, Moish looked her full in the face, pleased and grateful to find her so calm at the news. What had he expected, tears and tantrums? Fainting? Hysteria?

And how long had he been planning to continue this deception? "If I hadn't brought this up tonight —" Sara began shakily.

"I was planning to tell you, sooner or later. I — I didn't have the courage, I guess." He spread his hands and talked faster, more urgently, seeking expiation. "I didn't mean to hurt you, Sara. I really thought I'd managed to put her out of my mind."

"Well, one person's bad fortune can turn out to be another person's good luck." Sara tugged the diamond off her finger.

She could not finish, not without the humiliation of letting him see her cry. She hurled the diamond in the general direction of his face, then groped for the door. His voice sounded behind her as she fumbled blindly for the handle, the words coming jumbled and as if from a great distance. Through her grief, her fury, and her shame, she felt a distinct sense of relief that she need not ever hear that voice again.

Then she was out on the street, slamming the car door and cutting off his voice forever.

Her own car was parked halfway down the block from where she stood. She would drive back home tonight, back to her parents and her own life. Let Moish's mother pack her things in the overnight bag she had left in the guest room; let Moish get them to her somehow, through the mail or some accommodating traveler. She did not care about any of that. She would not set foot in Moish's house again. Home was where she needed to be now, at this very moment. And home was hours away.

The thought of her mother and father, asleep in the house they had shared for thirty years, filled Sara with longing and an exquisite pain. They would not be sleeping as soundly after this, she predicted drearily. Let them cherish these last hours of contentment. She would slip in quietly with her key, to spend what was left of the night in her room. The bad news could wait for morning ... "That's it," she finished, unaware of the tears that glistened on her cheeks. "Three months later, Moish married his dream girl." She made a bitter face. "And five *years* later, here I am."

In silence, Miriam Schumacher handed her a box of tissues. She watched impassively as Sara wiped her eyes and blew her nose. Then she remarked, "You made that last comment as though expressing two polar opposites. *He's* happily married — (presumably, anyway) — while *you* are seated on a therapist's couch, wishing you were. His life — and yours. Joy — and misery. Success — and failure." She waited a beat, then asked, "Am I right?"

"Do you have to ask?" Sara sniffed into the tissue a final time, then resolutely crumpled it in her fist.

"No," the therapist said quietly. "That's something that *you* have to ask yourself." She glanced at the clock on the wall above Sara's head. "We'll discuss the answers next time."

Sara was astonished. Had it been fifty minutes already? Along with her surprise came a pleasing sense of — peace, she had to call it. She supposed that was natural, after unburdening herself to a sympathetic listener. Whether or not the therapeutic process would accomplish anything more than that remained to be seen. In her desperation to make this move to Cedar Hills a fresh start in every way, Sara had made the appointment of her own free will. Still, she was reserving judgment about the outcome.

As she said good-bye to Mrs. Schumacher though, she was conscious of an emotion she had not expected to feel: anticipation. She was looking forward — eagerly — to being here again.

"Till next week, then," Mrs. Schumacher said at the door.

"Next week," Sara agreed, feeling unaccountably shy now that the professional part of their session was over. The therapist seemed to expect this, for she smiled comfortably at Sara as she held the door open. "Good-bye for now. And good luck on the first day of school."

"Thanks," Sara smiled wryly. "I think I'm going to need it."

10

On second thought, just killing them was not good enough.

It was too easy. No big deal to knock off an unarmed man and a couple of unsuspecting kids. Besides, he wanted — needed — to make them suffer the way he had suffered over Sal. That was only fair.

But there was more to it than that. There was also the practical side. Justice was one thing — but a guy had to eat, too. Late one sultry night in early September, he lay on his lumpy mattress, swatting mosquitoes and listening to a tinny radio playing on the other side of the flimsy wall and some frazzled mother screaming a hoarse, monotonous tirade about lowering the volume. As he lay there, he suddenly had the inspiration that would make all the difference. A way to get out of this rat hole, to move into a decent apartment, buy himself some good threads and shoes that would not fall apart in a month.

The judge had money, and plenty of it. Before being helped to his eternal rest, he would have to be induced to part with some cash. A lot of cash.

That, too, was justice.

Because of the judge, Sal had spent the last years of his life in some dingy jail cell, deprived of an earning capacity (albeit a criminal one) that had once dressed him in designer suits and seated him proudly behind the wheel of a Mercedes. Sal's little brother deserved a piece of the good life, too. It was time for the judge to pay up.

And the brilliant thing was, neither goal contradicted the other. Justice would be just as well served after he had helped himself to a generous handful from the judge's wallet. The money-making angle could lead right into the more permanent solution.

As a prelude to death, kidnapping for ransom was as good as anything else.

The bedsprings creaked as he struggled to his feet. He went to the rickety table that served him as dining area and desk together. Shoving aside an empty mug, an ashtray overflowing with cigarette butts and cold gray ash, and the remains of the salami he had had for supper, he found what he was looking for.

It was a picture. A pretty family picture, clipped from the back pages of a small New England newspaper, snapped the summer the Newmans had vacationed there. He needed it to help him identify his victims — and to feed the fuel of his blood lust. Whenever he found his courage ebbing even the tiniest bit, he would pick up the picture and stare at the figures in it, the way a hunter might give a bloodhound a sniff of his prey to start the juices flowing.

A pretty picture. Father, mother, daughter, son. Only there were just three of them left now. After watching the paramedics go through their futile motions at the accident site, he had gone home, taken a thick, black, indelible marker, and slashed a large "X" across Ella Newman's face.

He still had the marker. One down, three to go.

But he would squeeze whatever he could out of this before the others went.

A few minutes ago he had been red eyed, exhausted; now he found sleep the furthest thing from his mind. He had some planning to do. He picked up the picture again and focused on the children.

The daughter — or the son? Which one first?

11

Judge Lionel's house came as a surprise to Daniel. The low-slung, ranch-style brick house was not what he would have expected. Something with a lot more personality would have seemed fitting for the feisty old judge — something definitive, imposing, with sturdy white columns, perhaps, to go with the famous mane of hair.

The ranch — situated, aptly, in Baltimore's pretty Ranchleigh section — was modest by any standard, though a closer look revealed the care and money that had been lavished on things like windows, doors, and garden. Its most impressive feature was the front entrance: Of heavy, shiny oak, it was a portal through which one must earn his passage. Daniel felt privileged as he stood on the stone doorstep, waiting for his ring to be answered.

He had admired the owner of this house from his own first day on the bench. Young and untried, he had been fascinated and — he was not ashamed to admit it — awed by Judge Lionel. The older man's legendary sagacity and iron-fist authority stood in towering contrast to Daniel's own inexperience. Despite the tales of eccentricity that circulated in the courthouse halls (Lionel had once, on a stormy Monday morning, forbidden anyone wearing wet galoshes to enter his courtroom, saying the smell of damp rubber was more than he could stomach), he was regarded with special reverence by his colleagues and his contemporaries. Judge Lionel's working days might be over, but he had left behind a distinguished and well-founded legacy.

"Yes?" A housekeeper, gray hair pulled back primly from her face, opened the door. She wore a starched white apron over her dark-brown dress.

"My name is Daniel Newman. I have an appointment to see the judge."

She eyed him narrowly. "An appointment? You called?"

"Yes, earlier today. He said 5 o'clock would be a good time."

Grudgingly, she moved aside to let him precede her into the house. "He's just woken from his nap. I'll see if he's ready for you."

"Thank you."

"He mustn't be overtired, you know. Doctor's orders."

"I won't stay long," Daniel promised.

The housekeeper uttered a skeptical sound, but she led him into the living room and pointed to the sofa. "Wait here, please. I'll see if he's up." She put a finger to her lips, as though suspecting him of planning to raise the roof the moment her back was turned. Smiling, he nodded his obedience. The woman walked down a long hall and stopped at a door at the far end. She went inside, closing the door after her.

Daniel whiled away the time admiring the decor: a desert motif. Beige carpets, ridged sand-colored wallpaper, tan sectional sofa with plump, light-brown cushions. The art on the walls was muted rather than eye catching, mostly blues and pale greens: a horizon for the desert. Daniel had always enjoyed this kind of look, and in fact had done up the living room of his own home in much the same colors — in contrast to their former living room, which Ella had decorated in dark woods and rose and cream. Interior decorating was only one of the million and one areas he had left to his wife — and which he had had to face the overwhelming task of mastering once she was gone. Cooking had been another, and gardening a third. But none of it even touched the most bewildering hurdle of all: figuring out how to be father and mother to the two small, grieving people entrusted to his care.

As always when he was away from them, Daniel felt a surge of protective love for his children rise up in him, so strong that he unconsciously doubled up his fists as though ready to take on anyone who threatened them. It was this aggressive stance that greeted Judge Lionel when he wheeled himself slowly into the room.

"Daniel."

He whirled around, relaxing his fists. "Judge Lionel! It's good to see you, sir." Swiftly he crossed the room and bent to shake the old man's hand.

"Stupid doctors insist on incarcerating me in this thing," Lionel grumbled, casting a look of intense dislike at the wheelchair. "I'll be on my feet soon, though."

Daniel smiled. "I don't doubt it."

"Sit down, sit down. I'll have Mrs. Sauder get you a drink. A cocktail? Wine?"

"No, thanks, I don't drink. But don't let me stop you, sir."

The elder man sighed. "I'm not supposed to drink either. Something else, then? Juice, or soda?"

Daniel shook his head.

"Well, sit, anyway. I can't bear craning my neck to look up at people."

Daniel chose a corner of the sectional sofa and watched Lionel roll his wheelchair across to face him. The piercing blue of the legendary eyes — "meltdown eyes," certain courthouse figures had called them, with a shudder — was slightly faded now. There were more lines in the old judge's face than there had been the last time Daniel saw him up close, and they were etched deeper. Though the shoulders were as square and the thick white hair as magnificent as ever, a new sense of frailty made Lionel look somehow diminished. The man's working days were clearly over.

The notion saddened Daniel. Lionel's absence would be felt. The wheels of the law would grind on without him, but the old courthouse would never be the same.

His host permitted the scrutiny for a few seconds, then said testily, "Yes, I'm old and I'm sick, and I don't want to talk about it. I presume you came here because there's something you want to discuss. What is it?"

Daniel collected himself. "There is, sir. The Simmonds murder trial."

"Ah, so you've pulled that one?"

"Yes, sir. I wish," Daniel said simply, "it could have been you. Justice would have been more nobly served."

"Well, well, never mind that." Lionel dismissed the comment with a wave of his hands, but seemed pleased nonetheless. He wheeled himself closer to the sofa and positioned his chair at right angles to

Daniel's knees. "It's an interesting case. To be perfectly frank — though I won't have you quoting me on this — I have much more sympathy for the defendant in this case than for the victim. I never had the dubious pleasure of meeting Al Simmonds personally, but by all accounts he was quite a nasty one. Not that you could tell at a glance, though."

Daniel leaned forward, interested. "What do you mean?"

"On the outside, he was all suave businessman. Social animal, jet-setter, man-about-town — But I have my ear to the ground, Daniel. There are a good many stories circulating — stories that don't show Simmonds in a very good light."

"Anything criminal?"

Lionel shook his head. "Apparently, he was too careful for that. Always kept to this side of the law — just. But an unsavory character all the same. His private life won't bear very strict scrutiny, either."

"You mentioned some sympathy for the defendant. Tell me about him, please, sir."

"Henry Downing?" The old judge permitted himself a smile. "Or should I say, Henry and Elsa Downing."

Startled, Daniel asked, "I understood that she — the wife — was not a defendant in the case."

"No — Not officially. But I presided over the arraignment, and I tell you she might as well have been standing right there by her husband's side. I've never seen a more devoted couple. There was almost something — well, *spooky* is the word I'd choose, if I may be forgiven such an unjudicial expression — about the connection between them. It was as though an invisible line ran from Downing, at the defendant's table, to his wife in the back of the room. She never said a word, but I swear I could hear echoes of her voice whenever he spoke."

"Do you think they were in this together?"

"In what — the murder?" Lionel glanced at him sharply. "Aren't you presuming guilt here? Not exactly an impartial stance, *Judge*." He laid sardonic emphasis on the word.

Slowly, Daniel said, "I didn't mean that the way it sounded. I have no idea whether or not they conspired to commit a crime together. But there does seem to be some type of — complicity, I suppose you'd call it — between the two of them with regard to Al Simmonds. At least, that's the impression I've picked up from following the case to the extent that I have. And it's the primary reason I've come to sound you out, sir."

As Judge Lionel pondered this, his hawklike eyes fixed on some spot out the window. On this early September day, 5 o'clock was still bright as noon, though a golden cast to the light hinted at the waning to come. Daniel watched his host. The old judge's head nodded once, then he said quietly, "Good instincts. You have the instincts a judge needs — But then, I already knew that about you."

He swung his wheelchair around to face Daniel. "There's more to this case than meets the eye, Daniel. That's what these old bones are saying, and they haven't often lied to me."

Daniel leaned forward and said urgently, "Tell me, sir."

12

"Henry Downing pleaded not guilty," Judge Lionel said slowly, "but the way he said it, it might as well have been 'guilty.' He seems to be an honorable man — his reputation is spotless — but there's an air of defeat about him that makes one wonder."

Daniel leaned forward and asked softly, "Do *you* think he's guilty, sir?"

"No way of knowing. We know there was a dispute between him and Simmonds, centering around their partnership in Simmonds' last enterprise — the baby bottle. A dispute over money. Did financial pressures — or his wife — lead Downing to commit a crime that's left him feeling horrified?"

"You say Henry Downing has a good reputation. What about the wife?"

"Elsa Downing has stayed very much in the background. A private person, I'd say. I thumbed through the newspaper accounts of their big win in the lottery. It was Henry who fielded the questions and submitted to the inevitable curiosity by the press. Elsa stood smiling at his side, always there, but not saying much." Lionel shook his head. "But one doesn't get the impression of weakness. No, if you ask me, Elsa Downing is no doormat. Fairly intelligent, too, I'd guess, though neither of them has had much education."

"And there are no other viable suspects in the case?"

"At the moment, none." Judge Lionel looked regretful. "The murder was committed on the Downing's private property — in their back garden. A locked gate would effectively keep out intruders. Wired for security, too. Don't forget, this was the Downings' new dream house. Before the lottery, they'd lived very modestly indeed, I believe."

Daniel said thoughtfully, "Winning that money must have made all the difference to the Downings. They were in their 50's, with grown children, and nothing to look forward to at retirement except a careful subsistence on their pensions. Then the lottery — and joining up with Al Simmonds in the hope of maximizing their earnings." He recited the facts as though hoping that, in the recital, a pattern would emerge. "And then the dispute over the profits. Henry Downing claimed that Simmonds was systematically siphoning them into his own pocket. The bulk of Henry and Elsa's good fortune appeared in real danger of vanishing — and all because of Simmonds.

"The invitation to dinner was, or so they say," Lionel inserted, "an attempt to try and settle the matter once and for all. But something went wrong."

Dryly, Daniel said, "Very wrong, apparently." Off came the judge's hat; on went the prosecuting attorney's. The years rolled back. "They met to discuss the Downings' allegations. Simmonds must have heard them out — tried to justify himself, perhaps. What happened next?"

The wheelchair made a half-circle, leaving Judge Lionel with his back to Daniel.

"Next," the judge said heavily, "came murder."

The Beltway around Baltimore lay directly in the path of the low sun, causing the "road glare" that was notoriously responsible for headaches, irritability, and accidents. Traffic, mercifully, had so far managed to avoid rush-hour gridlock, but movement was slow. Putting on a pair of sunglasses that he kept in the glove compartment for just such occasions, Daniel eased into a middle lane and gave himself over to thought.

But his mind, normally so disciplined, would not settle down. Maybe it was the late-summer sunshine slanting against his windshield that distracted him, or the fresh breeze that made him roll down his window instead of punching the a/c button the instant he entered the car. The kids were back at school — his little girl in the tenth grade this year (where had the time flown?)! And Mordy was starting the seventh. His thoughts touched on them, lingered briefly, lovingly, but did not stay. For some reason, he kept returning to the picture that Judge Lionel had painted. The portrait of Elsa and Henry Downing.

A devoted couple . . . .

An invisible line from Henry, at the defendant's table, to Elsa at the back of the room . . .

He might have been describing a pair of exotic aliens. Daniel and the older judge had sat together, two lonely widowers, noting — as outsiders — the devotion that could exist among the happily married. And remembering —

But there was a difference. Judge Lionel was 70 and he, Daniel, decades younger. Thirty-two years younger, to be precise. He was only 38 — surely not too old to start over. Gentle proddings by his mother, by a concerned neighbor, by an interested aunt, came to mind. They were all urging the same thing: that he go out and find himself a new wife. A replacement mom for Yael and Mordy. Another Ella —

In the privacy of his car, he shook his head. No one could ever be that. But until very recently, he had been unable to even imagine wanting to build a life with anyone else. It was either Ella, or do-it-yourself. And he *had* done it himself: got his emotions in check, made a home for the kids, filled the twin functions of father and mother. None of it had sat naturally on his shoulders. Every morning brought its fresh struggle, as he tried to contort himself into the necessary shapes. Most of the time, he succeeded. The kids were flourishing. He had done his job, and done it well.

But do-it-yourself had one major drawback. It was very, very lonely.

This was not something he felt comfortable discussing even with those closest to him. He kept his feelings hidden away from his mother, his father, and his best friend, Yehuda Arlen, who now was in Israel for a sabbatical year. Chaim, his brother, might have been a confidant, except that Daniel suspected him of harboring some unconfided problems of his own. Daniel had several times made a mental note to pursue this, but Chaim was reticent and Daniel had more than enough on his own plate to distract him from his resolve. So he had left Chaim to his problems and continued to struggle silently with his own.

But keeping his feelings to himself did nothing to blunt their cutting edge.

Loneliness was his constant companion. It had settled in early — dropping in, as though for a brief visit, shortly after Ella's death — and it rapidly pushed its way in for the long haul. It peeked out at Daniel from his morning coffee, winked over the rim of the toaster, waved wickedly from between the pages of his Gemara. He had tried to fill his life, his heart, with his children; but somewhere along the way, he had been forced to admit that it was not enough. Hashem had given all living creatures a partner. Hard as he had tried to convince himself otherwise, Daniel was fast coming to admit that he needed one, too.

But the game was too painful — and it felt so ludicrous! Oh, he had tried once or twice in the past couple of years. Got himself decked out in his best suit and taken some woman to dinner at whatever restaurant was all the rage at the moment.

The first time, he spent 90 percent of the evening talking about his kids. The woman had none of her own, and it was impossible to ignore the glazed look of sheer boredom in her eyes as the meal progressed.

The second time — this had been a different woman — his beeper had gone off in the middle of dessert. *Please, Daddy, call home,* the plaintive message had read. *Nightmares. Yael.*

As soon as politeness allowed — if not a tiny bit sooner — he had rushed home to comfort his daughter. His date sent word, through the matchmaker, that she had been insulted. Clearly, his priorities did not allow for the normal course of courtship. And, just as obviously, neither of the women he had dated was a candidate for the kind of wife he needed: a wife who would be willing and able to lovingly fill the additional role of caring stepmother to his children.

His kids depended on him. He was determined to be there for them, in the face of every social nicety — and despite Loneliness's hideous leer, coming at him in his bathroom mirror, in the rear-view mirror in the car, through every window and door. He would be a father first.

And yet — and yet —

A most devoted couple . . .

Maybe he would pick up a phone one of these days, call one or two people. Somewhere, there must be a woman who would be willing to take on him *and* his children. Someone to fill the empty spaces — to be the partner he so sorely missed.

Maybe, someday.

Traffic picked up again. Daniel drove at higher speeds, letting the wind rush through the car, sweeping across his face and brushing away the sadness. The kids were waiting.

He had just walked through his front door when the phone started ringing.

"I'll get it!" he called out to whomever might be interested. The house felt empty. Then he remembered: it was Mrs. Marks' half-day off. Scooping up the mail from the doormat, he went to the phone.

"Chaim!" Daniel exclaimed with pleasure when he heard the familiar voice at the other end.

It had been some time since his younger brother had phoned him. In fact, it seemed to him that they had been drifting apart lately. If one of them did not snag the other soon — the way one floating log might hook another in mid current — they might let the stream of their affairs carry them ever farther away, until they were beyond each other's reach.

It looked like Chaim had been the one to reach out first. Daniel was pleased, and made no attempt to hide the fact.

"It's good to hear your voice!" he said warmly, as he scanned the top envelope in his hand and moved it to the bottom of the stack. The second letter was marked *Airmail*. With pleasure, Daniel saw that it was from his friend Yehuda Arlen. He looked forward to hearing what Yehuda had to say about life in the Holy Land. Flipping through the pile — which were mostly bills — he forced his attention back to his brother. "It's been a long time, Chaim. What's new?"

"Nothing much, Daniel. You're right — it's been too long. How's everything? The kids?" He sounded nervous.

"Fine, they're fine, *baruch Hashem*. They started school today. Do you believe my Yael is in the tenth grade already? Yes, and Mordy's in the seventh. Time really does fly, doesn't it? It seems like only yesterday —" His voice trailed off.

"Daniel? Are you there?"

Daniel stared at the envelope facing him. After an endless moment, he found his voice. "Yes," he croaked.

"You were saying —?"

"Time. Time moves — fast —" It was all he could do to keep the phone from slipping through his nerveless fingers. His eyes were riveted to the letter at the top of the pile. He would have recognized that writing anywhere. Big, block letters in black, indelible marker. Letters that looked skewered in place.

"FOR JUDGE NEWMAN" the words read. "PRIVATE AND CONFIDENTIAL."

"Daniel?" His brother was growing alarmed — and irritated. "What's going on?"

With a mighty effort, Daniel forced himself to speak calmly. "Nothing. What were you saying?" His mind raced like the hands of an overwound clock. Any minute now, Yael and Mordy would be traipsing in. He had to have himself under control — and the letter out of sight — by then. He drew a deep breath and went directly to the point.

"What can I do for you, Chaim?"

If his brother was taken aback by the suddenly businesslike tone, he did not show it.

"Actually," Chaim said, sounding nervous again, "Since you ask, I need a little favor, Daniel. See, here's the story . . ."

13

I f Chaim Newman was not exactly a successful man, neither was he a failure. That consoled him, in some measure, for the indifferent respect he encountered in his dealings with his fellow men, and for the discouragement he sometimes glimpsed in his wife's eyes.

Not that Gila ever threw his mediocrity in his face. If truth be told, she desired nothing more for herself or her children than a sort of middle-of-the-road prosperity. If the family was not rich, it was also not poor. Socially, they had staked a modest claim beyond which Gila had little ambition. Chaim faithfully attended his shul and his *shiurim*, making him a visible — if not an especially dynamic — member of their community. Though his job as administrator for a small yeshivah would never lead to dazzling leadership possibilities, it was steady.

The discouragement came not so much from the circumstances of their existence as from the knowledge that those circumstances would probably never change.

Given the type of man Chaim was, his horizons were limited. At 35, he knew himself well enough to accept that he would never be a towering Torah giant, never strike out on a course that would win him great wealth or celebrity — never, in short, be more than the plodding and rather unimaginative administrator he was. If his wife felt dismayed by her husband's inability to let his reach exceed his grasp, Chaim felt doubly so.

They hid it well. Optimism, not discouragement, was the tone in their home. Every year, at the start of the new school term, Chaim and

Gila would solemnly enact the ritual they had initiated early in their married life. She would announce the amount of money they had managed to save in the year's Home Improvement account, and whip out their ever-growing list of projects. Planning their modest renovations had become, for the two of them, a way of aspiring together. Stymied though they might be on more ambitious fronts, they could watch with satisfaction the slow — the very slow — transformation of their home into something approaching an ideal.

In recent years, however, some stress had crept in to replace the satisfaction. What had started out as the purr of luxury had changed, with the coming of the children one after the other, to a howl of necessity.

"Tova needs a room of her own," Gila told him this Tuesday night immediately after Labor Day. "A girl of nearly 13 sharing a room with two sisters under the age of 5? It's just impossible."

"Impossible — why?"

"They have very different bedtimes, for one thing. Tova has to tiptoe around her own room once the little girls are asleep — and can't even turn on the light to read. She's been straining her eyes with a flashlight under the covers. Besides which, she has zero privacy, not a good thing for a girl this age." With the finality of a legal summation, Gila repeated, "She needs a room of her own."

"So go to the supermarket," Chaim suggested mildly, but with the nervous twitch that always accompanied his feelings of inadequacy, "and buy a room."

"Very funny. Chaim, this is serious."

He sighed. "I know it is. But — *seriously* — how can we create a room out of nothing? Or were you thinking about finding another house altogether?" The thought filled him with a vague sense of trepidation. Change of any kind held the possibility of mistaken decisions, of botched executions — of failure.

Gila rose from her seat at the kitchen table, where all their financial discussions took place amid a litter of papers, calculators, and clipped dreams, and began to pace restlessly around her husband. Chaim watched her apprehensively, for the first time seeing the kitchen through his wife's eyes. The old porcelain sink that should, according to Gila, have been two sinks of shining stainless steel. The linoleum, painstakingly saved for and selected just five years before, worn and unfashionable now. The wooden table which bore the scars of many childish skirmishes, and the chairs, stained with the patina of the years.

Gila paused again beside her own chair, resting her hands on its back. Chaim tore his eyes away from the linoleum's soothing pattern and brought them back to his wife. Uneasily, he wondering what her restlessness portended, and where it would lead.

"No, not a new house," she said. "This is a good block, with good neighbors, and the house — old as it is — has its pluses. All we need is a relatively minor renovation, Chaim. Listen to this: We switch the girls' room with the boys' room, because the boys' bedroom has that back porch nobody ever uses. We enclose the porch, borrow a little bit from the bedroom — and Tova has a room of her own!"

Chaim looked dubious. There were many holes in the scenario his wife had just painted; he was not sure where to begin pointing them out. "A pretty small room, wouldn't you say?" he remarked at last.

"Tova won't mind," Gila said eagerly. She slid back into her seat, leaning forward on her elbows in a stance that shouted of her determination to persuade him. "She would happily sleep in a closet, if only we could spare one. Of course, to get to her room she'd have to walk through the little girls' room, but that won't be a problem. Chaim, it's a great plan. No expensive extensions, no major plumbing or electrical work — just a simple enclosure and a little creative shifting of furniture. And," she finished triumphantly, "Dini and Shiffy will be only two to a room then, with more space for everyone."

"You're forgetting heat. We'd have to put in heating on the porch. There's a light out there, but no electrical outlets." Not to mention a roof.

"I said no *major* plumbing or electrical work."

"And the money for this is supposed to come from where, exactly?" He hated to ask, but it was necessary.

"I know we don't have enough in the account. It's been a hard year to save, what with Mendy's braces and starting Shiffy in school." *And no raises at your job,* she almost added. That she refrained from doing so was not so much from a sense of tact as from the knowledge that it would be useless. For years she had been urging him to assert himself, to demand the pay hike he deserved for his long and loyal service. But Chaim, it seemed, was completely nonassertive.

"What, then?"

Gila fixed her husband with a bright and steely eye. "You have to talk to Daniel."

Letting out the breath he had not been aware he was holding, Chaim felt a familiar wave of futility wash over him, unpleasant as used bathwater. They had had this discussion before.

"Daniel has his own problems," he said slowly. "He is not required to shoulder ours."

"But not *money* problems! Money has never been a worry of his, the way it is with us. For one thing, he earns a lot more, and for another, he has only two children, while we have seven. Your parents have already helped us in so many ways, that we can't go to them again. It's Daniel's turn now."

"Why does it have to be anyone's turn? Why do we have to ask for handouts?" Chaim sounded uncharacteristically bitter.

"We're not asking for charity, Chaim! Just a small loan to help us make the house more livable. Daniel likes Tova; he'd be happy to help her get a room of her own. Remember when she was born? He was so proud of becoming an uncle, he went out and had a custom-made blanket crocheted for her that said 'World's Best Niece.' You don't do that for someone you don't care about."

"I don't question my brother's love for Tova, or any of the others," Chaim said. "That's not the point here. Nor am I arguing with you about the fact that he could probably afford to lend us the money we need. It's — something else."

Gila was not about to let him get away with that. Challengingly, she crossed her arms and asked, "What is it? Tell me." Her tone implied that nothing he might say could be proof against the validity of her position.

How could he explain the horror of appealing to his older brother — his *successful* older brother — for the things he himself was unable to provide for his family? This was no question of simple sibling rivalry. From the day he was born, Chaim had been well aware that, where their abilities and potentialities were concerned, Daniel was an astronaut skimming the stars while he, Chaim, was doomed to crawl the surface of the earth. He did not expect admiration from his brother, or even the respect one accords one's equals. Self-respect was a skill Chaim had yet to fully master, and he could hardly demand from others what he begrudged himself. But to go to Daniel, hat in hand, seemed an outrage to even Chaim's modest image of himself as father, husband, provider.

"Well?" Gila was waiting.

Suddenly, like air from a pricked balloon, the fight went out of him. This battle, apparently, was one he could never win. Tova's happiness, and Gila's contentment, depended on it. Over the years, in like situations, he had managed to avoid soliciting his brother's help by putting off, cutting corners, doing without. This would be the first time he actually asked for a loan. Maybe it would not be so bad.

"All right," he said.

Gila blinked. "What?"

"All right, I said. I'll ask him."

Her eyes blazed with joy. "Chaim, you're the best!"

"Right," he said heavily, and went up to their bedroom to make the call.

" . . . We still need to get some estimates and all that, but I have a pretty good idea of what it should cost to get the job done right," Chaim said into the phone, trying to pretend that this was not a personal call asking his brother for money, but one of the countless financial appeals he routinely made in the course of his work for the yeshivah. He swallowed, then added the hard part: "We don't have enough right now, Gila and I. That's why I'm calling you, Daniel. I hate to do it, but we both feel this thing is really necessary."

"Oh, I'm sure it is." Daniel sounded as though his mind was on another planet.

"So — should I go ahead and get the estimates?"

"Hm — Estimates? For what?"

Chaim frowned. Daniel was being either deliberately obtuse, or rude beyond belief. Chaim chose to believe the former, though why Daniel would play the fool was beyond him. "I just told you, Daniel. For the room. Tova's room."

"I thought you said something about a porch."

"Daniel, are you listening? I told you, the porch is going to *be* the room, as soon as we make the renovation."

There was a rustling of paper. Was Daniel actually sitting there and *reading* as they spoke? Then a strange sound emerged — involuntarily, it seemed — from Daniel's throat. It sounded almost like a moan.

"Daniel, are you okay?"

"What?"

"You're acting very strange. What's going on?"

"Going on —? Nothing. Nothing. Chaim, listen, it's been nice chatting, but I've got to run. The kids'll be home any minute. Talk to you later in the week, okay?"

"But — what about the estimates?" Chaim asked, bewildered. His face burned as though he'd been slapped.

"What? Oh, get them, by all means. Great idea. Estimates are always good. Let me know how it turns out. 'Bye, now."

The line went dead.

Chaim held the receiver for a full minute, unable to believe his brother had hung up on him. He had not actually gotten around to asking for the loan, not in so many words, but he thought he had been pretty clear about where his story was leading. It was very unlike Daniel to brush him off the way he had. Was that the judge's way of saying, "Not interested?"

He stood up, picked some imaginary lint from the knee of his pants, and addressed himself reluctantly to a more pressing question. How was he going to tell Gila?

His own hurt and humiliation he would deal with later, after his own fashion.

YOU WERE THE ONE SUPPOSED TO BE IN THE CAR THAT DAY.

EVER HEARD OF AN ACCIDENT-PRONE FAMILY?

COOPERATE . . . OR ELSE.

STAND BY FOR DETAILS.

14

He did not know what to do with his rage.

The intense feeling of fury itself was not unexpected; how else does a father react when his children are threatened?

What astonished him was its strength. The rage literally lifted Daniel off his feet. He stalked to the window, whirled wildly and started back the way he had come, only to start the savage trek all over again. It was a wrenching effort of will not to crumple the note and hurl it out the window, back into the black regions from which it had come. Somewhere in the saner depths of his mind, words like *police*, *fingerprints*, and *investigations* tried to make themselves heard. But his blood was beating a vicious tattoo in time to his ragged heartbeat — mad music that drowned out sanity's voice.

Parallel with the sofa, he abruptly paused. Lifting both hands, he brought them down with all his force on the broad arm. The impact hurt his palms, but the pain sent out a tiny measure of returning calm. He had nothing against the furniture, of course: It was the evil stranger he wanted to smash, the stranger who had invaded his life without invitation, bearing the twin weapons of malice and intimidation.

After a while, still shaking, Daniel went into the kitchen to pour himself some cold Coke from the supply he always kept there for the kids. Mrs. Marks had left behind a spotless kitchen. A chicken stew bubbled softly in the Crock-Pot, though at the moment Daniel doubted he would ever have an appetite again. He picked up the soda bottle and squinted at the label. *Caffeine-free*. Just as well; he had no need for further stimulants. His rage had sufficiently stirred his blood.

He was primed and ready for battle.

But just who was it that he was supposed to fight?

There was a blank space where the answer should have been. The question, and the blankness, triggered in Daniel a sudden quenching weariness. All the pumped-up energy leaked away, leaving in its place a tired, impotent anger. Helplessness was a novel sensation for the judge. He did not like it at all. It was not meant to be this way! At the slam of Judge Newman's gavel, a crowded courtroom fell respectfully silent. At a word from His Honor, criminals trembled, glimpsing the bleak outline of their futures.

But though his heart slammed like a piston gone berserk, the fear and the fury hurled themselves into empty space, vainly seeking an object. Because of two anonymous letters, the future held terrors he had never anticipated. And now — because of those same letters and their veiled reference to his wife's death — the past was equally uncertain. What had really happened on the day Ella died?

Your wife's death was no accident.

You were the one supposed to be in the car . . .

As he sipped his Coke, an inconsequential phrase rose up in his mind: "All dressed up and nowhere to go." Daniel was all set to engage the enemy — to the death, if need be — only he did not know whom he must fight. His enemy had chosen the coward's way, hiding his identity behind paper threats. Vague allusions to Ella were his sword, and unspecified threats about children its sharpened edge. This was not the way a man fought — not an honorable man, anyway. But then, the judge had no doubt in the world that he was dealing with someone as unscrupulous as they came.

The possibility that it was all a cruel hoax remained with him, but it was quickly shrinking — a small, shriveled question mark that had no power against his terror. He could no longer cling to that hope and still protect his children. He must react as if the threats were as real as could be.

Slowly, he put down his cup. He had promised to call Garrity if another anonymous letter arrived. And he *would* call — as soon as he would see his children arrive home safely. Daniel rose from the kitchen table, leaving his glass where it was. He forgot that Mrs. Marks was not there tonight to benevolently clean up after him. He forgot his Tuesday-night chore of chopping the tomatoes and cucumbers she had left for him in the vegetable crisper. Every nerve was riveted to the front door, willing it to open and admit his darlings into the safe haven of his presence. He would not relax until they appeared.

The really frightening thing — a thought he would successfully push away all evening, but knew he would be forced to face in the quiet of his room that night — was the reality that even his protective presence might not be enough to keep them safe. It had not been enough to save Ella.

Something tightened in his stomach. Clenching his fists, he walked mechanically to the couch and sat down. When, some ten minutes later, Yael waltzed in, and half an hour after that Mordy, he rose and hugged each one in turn, holding them as though he could not bear to let them go.

It was Wednesday.

Someone was following him. Daniel was positive of that fact.

It had begun the moment he had pulled into the courthouse parking lot: the prickling sensation at the back of his neck. Daniel was a man who lived by logic rather than intuition, but that did not mean that intuition was dead in him. On the contrary, the cases — both as prosecuting attorney and judge — that had most often won him the label'' brilliant'' had been ones in which he had relied not so much on his mental powers as on some undefinable sixth sense.

That sense was working overtime now. Someone was following him, and had been at it all morning.

Again and again, Daniel had tried to catch a glimpse of his stalker. A heavy downpour forced him to rush from the parking lot into the building with his head down, so that he lost his chance to look around him. The courthouse halls teemed with people, any of whom might be the one he sought. There were moments when he thought the follower had gone, but always it came back — that prickling warning. Was it *him*? The letter writer?

His courtroom was very full that day. Determined to clear his docket as quickly as possible to accommodate the upcoming Sim-monds trial, Daniel had permitted the court clerks to give him an extra-long and extra-tight schedule today. There would be no more than a quick bite of lunch at his desk, preceded and followed by hour after hour of pleas for Daniel to hear and adjudicate. He peered into the crowded benches, wondering if any of the men seated there might be *his* man.

No face in particular caught his eye. It might be anyone — or no one. He might be imagining the whole thing. But he didn't think so.

When he phoned Garrity the night before, the latter had been out, his message machine informing callers that he would be away until Thursday — tomorrow. In any case, Daniel was not sure how he felt about soliciting the police for active guard duty. It would disrupt the kids' lives, something he wanted desperately to avoid. Even more, it would frighten them. If police were needed, that meant that their Daddy was helpless to keep them safe. And a helpless Daddy was not what these motherless children needed in their lives. No, they did not need that at all.

Right now, with Garrity out of the picture, it was all up to Daniel. His prayers that morning had been recited with extra intensity: essentially, one long plea for his children's safety. As he slipped into his seat for the first hearing, motioning the court to be seated, he quickly ran through his mind the measures he had taken for his children's protection that day. In the morning, he had personally seen Yael and Mordy into their respective car pools. Mrs. Marks would be there when Yael came home that afternoon, and Daniel himself expected to be on hand to greet Mordy when he returned. They would have dinner together, and then a quiet evening at home. He would betray nothing of the anxiety that gnawed away at him from the moment he opened his eyes until the moment he closed them again — and tormented his dreams even then.

Until this mess was cleared up, he would find some excuse not to let Yael leave the house to study with friends at night. She would not like it, he knew — would protest that he was being unfair. About that possibility Daniel was philosophical. It is the lot of parents everywhere, even the kindest and most balanced, to find themselves periodically accused by their children of gross unfairness. As a man who had made it his life's work to be utterly and unequivocally just, the accusation sat uncomfortably on Daniel's shoulders. But, though Yael's resentment might trouble him, he could not let it deter him.

"Better safe than sorry" must be his credo, until the letter writer was behind bars.

Mordy would be less of a problem. His son was something of a homebody, chained to his computer and his hobbies and routines. Much as Daniel had bemoaned that fact on all the sunny afternoons Mordy declined invitations to play outdoors, he was fervently grateful for it now.

❦

His workday ended unusually late, at 6 o'clock. A hurried call to Mrs. Marks — made by his clerk, Paul Hencken, just before the last rush of hearings — had elicited the information that both kids were home and cheerfully avoiding their homework.

"I told her you'd be home soon, sir," Paul said, a respectful grin creeping across his broad face. "She promised to save dinner for you. She said to hurry, though, or it would dry up and taste like leather."

Daniel smiled. "I'll do my best. Let's get these last couple of hearings out of the way so we can all enjoy some dinner tonight."

"It's been a long day," Paul ventured.

"You can say that again," Daniel agreed. "Or rather, don't. Let's get back inside and wind things up instead."

Paul chuckled, and opened the door to let the judge precede him from the chamber.

Pleasant, comfortable chatter. Normal. Safe.

But the sense of normalcy — and certainly of safety — fled as Daniel stepped out into the parking lot after the final hearing. The sky retained considerable light on this early-autumn evening. The lot held only a sprinkling of cars. Before he had crossed halfway to his own, the prickling at his neck started up again, with a vengeance. There was a faint sound: less than a footstep, but more than silence. Daniel strode briskly forward, willing himself not to turn.

At the door of his car, he spun suddenly around. He saw a figure in the next row crouch low, quickly swing a car door open and slip inside. Without stopping to think, Daniel ran over. "Stop!"

The other man had been on the verge of switching on his motor. The hand that held the key at the ignition stiffened, hesitated, then fell. The stranger looked up into the judge's face.

Daniel stared, falling back a step in his confusion.

"What — ?"

The other driver was young, in his middle 20's by the looks of it, with a shock of auburn hair under a black yarmulke. The hazel eyes were intelligent, the nose patrician, the chin firm. Taken all together, it was an attractive, Jewish face.

Right now, it looked scared.

15

"You were following me," Daniel said, when he had recovered from his shock.

Whatever he had expected, it was not this. Some thug from the sleazy underworld would be more the ticket — or perhaps the kind of slick, well-dressed crook he had so often encountered in the course of his work, smugly prosperous from drug or other illicit earnings. In his neat jacket and tie, this fellow looked like any one of the dozens of lawyers that roamed the courthouse on any given day. If this guy had criminal leanings, he was hiding them well.

The young man swallowed, a finger tugging at the collar of his shirt. He opened his mouth as if to answer, thought the better of it, and closed it again. Finally, he threw open the car door and stepped out. He was much thinner than Daniel, but at least three inches taller. He stood awkwardly, with the hangdog air of a boy sent to the principal's office for some schoolroom misdemeanor.

"I didn't want you to know," he said, a rueful smile briefly lifting a corner of his mouth. "I sort of hoped I was invisible."

"You nearly were. But not completely. And not soundless, either."

"No, I guess not — But I meant no harm, honest. I just —"

"Yes?" Daniel crossed his arms, waiting.

With a sigh, the other said, "You must hear this all the time. It's embarrassing to have to admit it, but I've been admiring your work — well, to be perfectly honest, *worshiping* would be more accurate — from afar for some time now. I'm a third-year law student, and you're — my role model." He seemed unburdened after he spoke the words.

Daniel did not know whether to laugh aloud with relief or to cry out in exasperation. "You scared me half out of my wits, do you realize that?"

"I'm sorry, sir," the young man said, sincerity stamped on every feature. "I really am. I heard that you've drawn the Simmonds trial, and I — I've been following you around all day, trying to work up the courage to talk to you."

"Next time," Daniel said, finally smiling, "please do us both a favor, and be more direct."

"I will," the other said, beaming back in the enormity of his relief.

"What's your name?"

"Jacob E. Meisler. My friends call me Jake."

"What's wrong with 'Yanky'?" Daniel asked, eyes twinkling.

Jake looked uncomfortable as he answered, "Maybe one day. I grew up in a very American home, you see. Even Jacob was a concession — a big one. But that was my mother's father's name, and he had passed away just weeks before I was born. My father couldn't refuse her that."

"Yet you've obviously moved far to the right of your parents."

Surprised, Jake nodded, then asked, "How did you guess?"

"The yarmulke."

"Oh, that. I didn't always wear one this size, or this color. It's a long story, sir —" He looked uncertain.

"And a very wet day." For the first time, Daniel became conscious of the fine drizzle drifting down onto both their heads. Pulling up his coat collar, he said, "I'd like to hear the story, but there's no need to get soaked to the skin while we do it." He thought a moment. "Since you've spent all day waiting to talk to me —"

"Longer than that, sir," Jake said earnestly. "Much longer. I've been reading up on your most famous cases for months now. More recently, the Simmonds case has got me intrigued. I'd already decided to try and sit in on that one, as my classes allow. Then I found out that you're going to have the bench! It seemed like a sign."

"A sign?"

"That I should finally muster the courage to talk to you."

"But not, apparently, today." Daniel threw a pointed look at Jake's car.

With a shamefaced grin, Jake admitted, "I lost my nerve at the last minute."

Daniel smiled. "As I was saying, I think this conversation had best proceed elsewhere. Would you like to follow me home? You could join us for dinner if you'd like. " He had taken an instant liking to this young man. The forthright, enthusiastic personality might almost have belonged to an earlier version of Daniel himself, before life — and death — had worked their subtle changes. At 38, he was far less sure of things than he had once been, and certainly far more moderate in his hopes.

Jake's hair and yarmulke were beaded with drops of rain, beneath which his green eyes glowed like a pair of lanterns in a storm. He seized eagerly upon the invitation. "Could I really? If you could spare the time, sir, I'd *love* to come — and to talk a little afterwards, if that's possible? I don't mind about the food, if there's not enough, I mean. I'm not that hungry."

Daniel laughed. "Our housekeeper rarely prepares less than a mountain of a meal, though there are only three of us to eat it. Come on, the rain's getting stronger. Let's go."

He turned back toward his own car, registering the sounds of Jake Meisler behind him, leaping into his own vehicle and starting up the engine with a roar. Daniel barreled down the Beltway, then drove at a much more sedate rate through the familiar, rain-washed streets toward his own house.

Whenever he looked, Jake's car was always in place in the center of his rear-view mirror.

He was slightly later arriving home than he had planned, but Mrs. Marks had managed to keep dinner edible. She welcomed their unexpected visitor with calm aplomb. Mordy and Yael greeted the newcomer shyly at first, but quickly warmed to him. Jake, Daniel saw, had an easy way with children. For all his ingenuousness, there was a keen intelligence there that piqued Daniel's interest. Intelligence and ambition — a potent combination, if one could only remember to leaven it with humility and good sense. He was pious, too, *bentching* with indrawn concentration. Daniel suspected that, with proper guidance and the seasoning of the years, Jake Meisler could become a real asset one day — and not only in his chosen field of the law.

The meal over, Daniel dispatched the kids to their rooms to attack their homework, while he closeted himself in the study with his guest. Over cups of cranberry tea, Jake shared a little of his life history.

"I suppose you could call the home I grew up in 'Orthodox,'" he said pensively, cradling his cup in both hands. "But, as a kid, I felt as if I were floating in an ocean filled with waves. At specific points in the year — the High Holy Days, Pesach — the wave called 'religion' lifted us a little higher than the rest. But just as often, the other waves — education, career, keeping-up-with-the-Joneses — were the important ones. And they pulled us down.

"As I grew older, I began to move gradually to the right. I had a terrific rebbi in the tenth grade, more authentically attached to the yeshivah way of life than the other teachers in my school. He influenced me, almost without my realizing it. I transferred to a real yeshivah in the twelfth grade, and spent a couple of years learning in Israel after that, before my parents dragged me home to go to college. I was reluctant to leave yeshivah —" Here, he grinned. "Well, that's an understatement; they had to practically carry me home kicking and screaming. But before leaving home I'd promised to get an 'education,' and I had to honor that promise . . . Still, I managed to put in a good few hours a day in yeshivah while completing my degree, though it never felt like enough."

"And now you're in law school?"

"Yes," Jake said. "I also manage to learn *daf yomi* early every morning and have a *chavrusah* almost every night."

"When do you study?"

"A better question," Jake answered with a swift grin, "might be, when do I sleep?"

Daniel returned the grin. "And the law? How do you like it?"

"I like it." Jake's face altered, grew more serious, even a little shy. "I think that practicing the law is one of the ways that a Jew can bring light into the world. Everyone makes fun of lawyers. They're depicted as grasping and unscrupulous. But so were the Jews depicted that way, for years." He leaned forward earnestly. "Law and justice are the highest concepts that a human society can aspire to. There can be, and has been, much abuse — I'm the first one to concede that. But the ideal is a sound one, and so are many of the people who aspire to it." Passion infused the young man's voice as he ended with quiet intensity, "It is possible to do so much *good* as a lawyer, sir. I really believe that!"

Daniel said gently, "You don't have to convince *me* of that."

With a blush and a bark of sheepish laughter, Jake sat back in his chair. "Of course not. I nearly forgot who I was talking to. Did — did you choose the profession for the same reason?"

Daniel sipped his tea as he pondered the question. "You know, I don't recall doing much thinking at all when I was young. I had a decent mind and the drive to accomplish. The law fascinated me the way an intriguing puzzle might. A nudge here, a tug there, and I was pointed in this direction. I hardly recall even making the decision." He smiled, self-deprecatingly. "Sounds strange, I know. But that's the truth."

"Don't worry, sir," Jake offered kindly, as if in consolation. "I don't think all that much, either."

After a startled pause, both men burst into laughter. When he could speak, a pink-cheeked Jake exclaimed, "I really didn't mean that the way it sounded!"

"I know it. So tell me, Jake," Daniel said. "Why did you want to talk to me? Was it just the urge to get acquainted with Judge Newman, or did you have something more specific in mind?"

Jake drew a long breath. "Here it is, sir. I would give my right arm — in a manner of speaking, of course — to be able to clerk for you. This year, or if that's not possible, then starting this summer."

Daniel frowned. "You'll be finished with law school by summer, won't you? Won't you be hooked into a real job by then?"

"If you'll have me, I'd postpone the search for a job in a law firm. I think I could learn so much from working with you, sir."

Taking small sips of his cooling tea to avoid the need for speech, Daniel mulled over this proposition. At last, he shook his head.

"There are two problems, Jake. One has to do with me, the other with you."

Jake's face, lit with eagerness a moment before, fell sharply. Daniel held up a hand as though to prevent an emotional landslide. "Hear me out, please."

"Of course, sir." The rain lashed the study windows with a sound like rasping zippers. Watching his guest, Daniel said softly, "You're going to have to learn to mask your feelings a little better, Jake, if you want to become a successful lawyer."

Jake's eyes opened wider. He flushed, then offered a reluctant grin. "Advice noted, sir. Actually, I've been told that before."

"By someone who has your welfare at heart, I'm sure."

The grin widened. "My mother."

"Good!" Daniel's manner became brisk. "Now, here are the problems. First, I already have a clerk. He's a fine young man named Paul Hencken, and there's nothing in the world wrong with him except for the fact that he's not Jewish — and I certainly can't fire him for that. In any case, I wouldn't want to. Paul has been clerking for me for the past year, and he's done a fine job."

"I see." For all his effort to conceal it, disappointment rendered Jake's voice thick.

"Of course, there's always the chance that he might decide to change jobs by summer, which would leave the slot open for you."

"I graduate in May, sir. That's just eight months from now."

Daniel nodded. "Which brings me to the second problem."

Jake looked up.

"Frankly, I think you're overqualified. During law school, you might have already clerked for a judge."

"Actually," Jake confessed, "I did. Judge Lionel."

"Lionel?" Daniel looked astonished. Then, laughing, he said, "Want to hear something funny? He's *my* role model!"

"Then you know how I feel, sir," Jake said, setting down his teacup and clasping his hands together. "I'd rather clerk for you than pile up billing hours for clients in some big, impersonal law firm."

"And I'd be honored to have you, Jake. But your career will suffer, you must know that. The others in your class will snatch up all the best positions out there. When you're finally ready to start job-hunting, you'll be at a disadvantage."

Jake said simply, "It would be worth it."

Daniel crossed his ankle over his knee and tapped the heel of his shoe with a thoughtful forefinger. "Tell you what, Jake. If it means that much to you, why don't you act as a sort of informal clerk this year? If you can handle it alongside your school workload, that is."

"I can handle it!" Jake sat up, eyes sparkling. "I arranged this year's schedule so that two days a week can be set aside for clerking. The eternal optimist!"

"I don't know exactly how we'll work it," Daniel said slowly, "but I'd like to have you aboard. Paul is often forced to take personal days off because of an invalid mother at home, so your help would be useful. Especially with the next big case I'll be trying —"

"The Simmonds murder trial!"

"Exactly. Have you read up on it?"

"Yes, sir. *Thank you*, sir! You won't regret this, believe me. And —" Jake hesitated.

"Yes?"

"If your other clerk — Paul — does leave in the summer, would you consider me as your full-time clerk then? Despite your reservations about my career?"

"If Paul leaves," Daniel said slowly, "I'll consider it. But remember, my boy — a lot can happen in eight months."

"I know it," Jake said, obviously not convinced at all. Eight months from now, he was sure, he would be exactly who he was tonight, with no greater ambition, for the moment, than to clerk for the judge he so admired. Like all young people, he believed in changes of circumstance far more than in changes of heart. The way he felt now was the way he would always feel.

Daniel was not so sure. But he had said his piece, and would say no more for the moment. Besides, who was he to claim he had cornered the market on wisdom? He had many years on this boy, but that did not mean there was not a lot that he himself had yet to learn — as his mother and various other members of his inner circle made no bones about reminding him, often.

He smiled warmly at his new assistant as they settled down to discuss the upcoming trial.

16

There was no question about it: Sara was on trial.

Her roll book sat open on the desk before her, its long row of student names snaking down the leftmost edge of the page. Usually, on the first day of school, those names seemed mysterious — in an exciting way — like a box poised to spring open or a promise waiting to be kept. Sara would try to match up the names to the faces as quickly as she could, making a private game of it, challenging herself and her memory. She knew how good it felt to have someone remember your name after hearing it only once.

But this morning, the names seemed as devoid of warmth as the girls to whom they belonged.

They stared back at her from their seats: twenty-six stony faces. Fifty-two watchful eyes. No, she had been mistaken. There was no trial here. The trial had already come and gone. Though this was only the first day of school, judgment had already been rendered.

It's not fair! she wanted to shout. She felt like stamping her foot, the way her little nieces did when they were angry. *They didn't even give me a chance, Ma. It's just not fair!*

But she was the teacher here, and no matter what these girls might expect from her, even they would be taken aback at a full-blown tantrum. And so, keeping foot-stomping and impassioned cries strictly within the bounds of wistful imagination, Sara continued to recite the roll in a calm, amazingly steady voice.

Her poise was tested afresh when she came to the name "Sima Davidson." If there was a center to the amorphous hostility in the classroom, it resided in this girl with the hard brown eyes and the wavy dark hair resting carelessly on her shoulders.

"Here!" Sima's tone rang like that of a warrior meeting its enemy on the field. *I won't give in without a fight*, her voice promised. How could Sara let her know that she had neither the desire nor the intention of engaging her in battle? It was Sima's cousin, Rina Pollack back in Brooklyn, who had poisoned the girl's mind against the new teacher. Sara could have forgiven her that; what she found harder to forgive was the way Sima had spread the poison throughout the class.

Here and there, she spied a few faces that looked as thought they might be won over. Eyes that held at least a tinge of openness; postures that said "wait and see." But they were a woeful minority.

"By the way, everyone calls me Simi," the girl continued.

"I'll be happy to do the same," Sara said, mustering a smile.

Simi smiled back, a tiny, meaningless twitch of the lips, then looked away to meet a friend's eyes. The friend winked. Someone in the back row snickered.

Quickly, Sara ran through the rest of the roll. That chore behind her, she came around the desk to perch at the front, the way she did every year on the first day of school. It was time for the welcoming speech she had so successfully delivered to each new crop of students, year after year. This was one thing she had decided to bring with her from Brooklyn. Part introductory, part inspirational, in the past her opening words had held her classes mesmerized.

The fact was, Sara spoke well. Words had a way of coming alive when she uttered them. She did not consider her personality an especially colorful one — particularly since her broken engagement, which had sapped a large portion of the self-confidence that makes for charisma. But for all the loss of self-esteem, she had never lost her articulateness, or her ability to inspire others with what she said.

Until now.

There is nothing like a hostile audience to murder the gift of gab. The words stuck in Sara's throat. Several times, she lost the thread of her speech and had to grope embarrassingly, under the gaze of those twenty-six pairs of eyes, until she found it again. She could almost hear the wheels turning in Simi Davidson's mind. *Rina told me she was an interesting teacher, at least. You call this interesting? She can hardly string two words together!*

It was no use. Sara brought her talk to a premature close and walked around the desk to pick up her *Chumash*. She would try to recoup her losses through the absorbing lesson she had sat up long into the night to prepare.

In the course of the lesson, a few of the girls — but only a few — seemed to thaw to a small degree. Under Sara's gentle but unrelentingly firm pressure, first one and then another unbent enough to volunteer a question on the subject matter. Her gimlet eye brooked no whispering or other misbehavior, but she need not have worried. For now, the girls — following Simi Davidson's lead — seemed content to wait and size her up. What tomorrow would bring, Sara could not know. Today, she had done her job.

But her shoulders, as she dismissed the class, remained erect only by the sheerest willpower. A leaden feeling had crept into her heart, and her spirit sagged like a sack of rocks slung over her back. She went on to teach two more classes before lunch, the second of them, *Navi*, to this same ninth-grade class. Later, as she unwrapped her sandwich, she was forced into a silent confession: She was discouraged.

Sara had planned to eat her lunch in the teachers' lounge and start becoming acquainted with her colleagues. Now, she had lost any desire for socializing. In silence she chewed her tuna on rye — which had seemed appetizing enough when she put it together that morning, but now tasted like nothing at all — and reflected on the turn her life had taken. In the cold light of the unfriendly classroom, it seemed a decided turn for the worse.

A month ago, she had been living in her parents' stately Flatbush home. She now inhabited a tiny, two-bedroom walk-up on an undistinguished street in Cedar Hills.

Where she had scores of acquaintances back home — though only two or three really close friends — here she was a stranger in a strange land. Her family, a support system she had hardly acknowledged as long as it was anchored in place, was hours away. They might as well have been living on a distant planet for all the good they were to her now. A disembodied voice on the phone is no substitute for loving dinner-table companions or a sympathetic, sisterly face over a coffee cup. She was missing her parents and Debbie more than she had ever expected.

Mechanically, Sara peeled her orange. She was bent over the wastepaper basket beneath her desk, disposing of the peel, when the door of her classroom opened. Quickly, she looked up.

"Oh, hi! I was hoping to find you!" A teacher stood there, smiling in a way that struck Sara, in her vulnerable state, as unbearably self-assured. She had masses of light brown hair, held together with a pair of matching clips on either side of her head. The smile faltered slightly as Sara slowly straightened up and adjusted the position of the wastepaper basket. The other teacher had no way of knowing how wildly Sara's heart was beating, or that Sara felt caught off guard, exposed, vaguely ridiculous. She could not know that Sara felt herself, today, to be a failure at her chosen profession.

The teacher gazed at Sara, uncertain of her welcome. "I'm Faygie Mandelbaum. And you're — Sara Muller?"

"That's right." Sara inclined her head formally.

"When I didn't see you in the teachers' lounge at lunch, I thought you might be — well, a little overwhelmed. This being your first day and all." Faygie waited hopefully.

"Not really. I just wanted to be alone. To — go over my first impressions of my classes. To 'get my head together,' as the girls would say."

Faygie laughed. "That's definitely the way they'd put it."

Sara smiled, too, but offered nothing more. After a moment, Faygie ventured, "So you'd rather be alone at the moment?"

Sara hesitated, then nodded. "At the moment. But thanks for asking."

Faygie nodded back and withdrew, closing the door very softly behind her. Sara stared at that door for a full minute, as though willing the young woman to reappear. When she did not, Sara felt unaccountably sad, as though the other had rejected her overture and not the other way around.

I'll be friendlier tomorrow, she promised herself, looking down with distaste at the orange, cold and moist, in her hand. She knew, though, that her coolness toward Faygie Mandelbaum today would only make her isolation that much harder to bear tomorrow.

Whichever way she looked at it, life seemed a pretty uphill piece of work.

It was hard not to feel sorry for herself. Back home, despite any problems with her personal life, she had been an undeniably success-ful established teacher — a fixture in the school, it was true, but a respected fixture — with legions of students and their parents counted among the ranks of her fans. Here, she was a newcomer who had yet to prove herself. And, to cap her sorrows, the class she would mostly have to do it with seemed to despise her already.

She pictured her sister's face when she called later to hear all about Sara's first day on the job. Though she would be unable to see it across the miles of phone wire, she knew that Debbie's expression would hold a mixture of pity and I-told-you-so.

"You should never have moved away," Debbie would imply without even saying the words. "You had it good here. You had me, you had Ma and Ta and all your friends — and a job you knew you could do. Take a look at your life now!"

Easy, Sara told herself. It's only the first day. Some of her natural optimism flooded back as she gazed out the window at the brilliant blue of the Maryland sky. The tops of some trees just brushed her view, and they were a glorious green, still untouched by autumn's russet. Exactly one day — no, half of one day — had elapsed since she embarked on this new phase of her life and career. Wasn't she being just a tad premature with the forecasts of doom?

Her spirit inched higher. She would not tell Debbie. She would not tell anyone. Most likely, things would look better tomorrow. In the meantime, there was only one place to confide her troubles. She finished her sandwich, decided to skip the cookies she brought along for dessert, and quickly *bentched.* Then she took out the *Tehillim* she always kept tucked into her purse, and spent the rest of her lunch hour talking earnestly to the only One Who really understood.

17

Yael Newman always felt funny when the final bell rang during the first few days of a new school year.

Later in the year, she and her friends would be so closely knit that they would find it hard to tear themselves away from one another at day's end. Together they would linger in the high-school halls, attending practice sessions of the various clubs to which they belonged, discussing the day's events, laughing at well-worn witticisms as though they were fresh and original. But club tryouts still lay in the future, and the distance imposed by summer vacation had not yet completely worn off. On this, the second day of school, no one seemed disposed to linger. The girls bade each other slightly self-conscious good-byes and started briskly for car pools and home.

Yael expected to do the same. At the last minute, however, she changed her mind.

"Coming?" Her friend Tzippy was impatient to go.

"Not right now. Go ahead without me."

"What about car pool?"

"If my father comes before I'm there, please tell him I'll be right out."

Tzippy looked at her quizzically. "What are you hanging around here for? There's nothing doing in school today."

Yael shrugged. Tzippy waited, but nothing further was offered. It was Tzippy's turn to shrug then. That was Yael: moody and unpredictable. Of course, there was her artistic temperament to blame — a temperament she richly earned with her wonderful talent on the piano. And losing her mother when she was only 9 was enough to make anyone's moods erratic. Sometimes Tzippy could not understand how Yael could ever *not* feel miserable! She swung her bag over her shoulder, said, "Oh, well, see you later," and left at a rapid clip.

After a moment, Yael made her way to the door of the empty classroom. The halls were nearly empty, too. She stood in the doorway, trying to decide how the sight of that deserted corridor made her feel. On the one hand, it was lonely — like being a survivor of a shipwreck, with nothing but ocean and sky as far as the eye could see. White-capped waves, though, would have been kinder to the eye than these institutionally painted walls and banks of look-alike lockers.

On the other hand, Yael kind of liked being on her own in a place that normally teemed with life. It gave her a sense of power. The rest of her life, in contrast, was a study in helplessness. She had been helpless to hold onto her mother, just as she was helpless to make her father smile again the way he used to. The only place the helplessness dropped away was on the piano bench. There, her roaming fingers were little monarchs who knew how to dominate their black-and-white kingdom. There, Yael spoke with another voice — a voice that made people pause in what they were doing, and listen. Sometimes Yael got a lump in her throat from her own music. If she had an ambition in the world, it was to make others feel the same way.

Which brought her to her reason for staying late at school today. She returned to her seat, grabbed her schoolbag, and hurried out of the room and down the hall. She had only a few minutes. Yesterday, as she had been about to leave the building, she thought she detected the faintest strains of music in the air, floating like an almost-imagined undercurrent to the noisy chatter of students set free for the day. Her friends had not noticed, or had not remarked on it, but the memory had not left Yael since. As she came closer to the auditorium, she broke into a run.

There it was again. Someone *was* playing the piano. She tiptoed down the four steps to the auditorium doors, hesitated, then rapped lightly.

There was no response, probably because a crescendo in the melody made it impossible for the musician to hear anything but the music filling her ears. Yael was about to knock again when she reconsidered and, with an impatient grimace, she pushed the doors open instead.

The piano was positioned at a right angle to the stage, parallel to, but slightly in front of, the doors. That placed the player with her profile to the audience and her back to the doors. Walking as silently as she could, Yael came to within a few feet of the piano before Sara Muller became aware that she was there.

Sara's fingers froze in midchord. Her soul, radiantly uplifted by the music she had been making, crashed to earth with heart-stopping suddenness, the way it does at the tail end of an early morning dream when the alarm shrills. With a painful jerk, she twisted around on the bench. Seeing a student staring at her, she felt the flush of annoyance mount to her cheeks. Couldn't she have even a few minutes of precious privacy, here at the piano? It was not as if there were club rehearsals going on. All too soon, she knew, these private sessions would have to come to an abrupt halt as girls danced, sang, or acted after school on the stage to her left. That knowledge made her cherish these moments all the more.

Go away, she felt like telling the intruder. Instead, she smiled mechanically and said, "Hi. Is there anything I can do for you?"

"Just keep playing," Yael blurted. "I mean, *please* keep on playing. It's beautiful."

A veil seemed to drop from Sara's eyes. Looking more closely, she recognized the girl she had met on the auditorium steps on the afternoon of her meeting with Rebbetzin Goodman the previous week, before school began. Only that time, it had been Yael at the piano, and Sara offering the compliments.

There was something in the girl's eyes that Sara had been longing to see from the moment she stepped into her classroom the day before. She had not found it there — but here, in Yael's eyes, she saw nothing but the sincerest admiration. It was all she needed to relax her completely. Her annoyance was magically transformed into pleasure.

"I remember you," she said warmly. "We met here one day, about a week or so ago."

"That's right! And I — I heard you playing here yesterday. That *was* you, wasn't it?"

Sara nodded.

"I was hoping you'd be here," Yael said simply.

Sara felt an unfamiliar sensation in the region of her heart. It took a few seconds for her to identify the emotion as simple happiness.

Someone in this city of strangers had been hoping to meet her again. After the two days she had just endured in a classful of hostile strangers, she felt inordinately pleased.

"Do you play duets?" she asked.

Yael's eyes sparkled. "Yes!" She threw down her schoolbag and came over to the bench. She hesitated. "May I?"

"Of course!" Sara moved over. "Let's make music."

And that is just what they did. No one was there to hear, or to appreciate it, but that did not matter. Yael knew she should be outside, joining her car pool. Her father would be waiting. But she could not stop. Daddy would understand. For ten exalted minutes Sara and Yael were outside themselves, soaring on the currents of the harmonies they wove. By the time they finished their piece, it was as if they had known each other forever. There was no need for words or explanations. They shared something precious; it was as simple as that.

They stopped at the last note, turning simultaneously to look at each other. "I don't even know your name," Sara laughed.

Yael grinned. "It's Yael Newman. And I know who you are. You're Miss Muller, the ninth-grade teacher, right?"

"That's correct. Well, Yael Newman, it's a pleasure to meet you — again. You're a very good piano player, but I'm sure you know that."

Much as she instinctively liked her, Yael was glad that Miss Muller was not her teacher this year. It would have been hard to balance what they had here, at the piano, with the give and take that went on between teacher and student in the classroom every day.

Though she did not know it, Sara Muller was feeling the same way. And she was also — to her astonishment — coming to recognize that she had just made her first friend in Cedar Hills.

"Miss Muller," Yael said, cracking her knuckles once, nervously, before resolutely placing them in her lap, "do you have a minute?"

"I do. What is it?"

"Can I talk to you about something? It's kind of important. But only if you're not in a major rush."

Sara thought of her lonely little apartment, and the leftover meatloaf waiting for her in the fridge.

"Go ahead, Yael," she said. "I'm listening."

18

The first day of a new trial was like the first day of school. And, like schoolchildren, the various parties were of two minds about the roles they were called upon to play.

They were eager, because something new was beginning, something dramatic and charged with possibility. The ambitious looked forward to finding fresh toeholds in their relentless upward climb. The merely curious looked forward to a spectacle that would fill the tedious hours.

But the eagerness was tinged with a genuine reluctance, as the players remembered that this was the business of real life — and death. Like school halls as the year's first bell rings out, the courthouse corridors were charged with excitement mingled with apprehension.

Defense attorneys, prosecutors, witnesses, the media, and spectators converged on the courtroom in a state of anticipation, pitched to a point as sharp as the pencils in the hands of the newspaper artists seated in the press benches. In his chambers adjacent to the courtroom, Judge Newman listened to the murmur of the crowd which, his clerk, Paul, had informed him, already filled every seat. For Paul, this was high drama — something to savor with an almost schoolboy relish. He was clearly enjoying every minute.

Not so Daniel. This was a sober moment. As judge, he held the life of the defendant in his hands. Though a jury of twelve would be the ones to decide Henry Downing's guilt or innocence, Daniel knew that he held undeniable power to influence that decision. The power would lie in the way he ruled on various motions brought before him by the defense and prosecution teams, and by the manner in which he instructed the jury at the trial's conclusion. The regulation black gown, the elevated seat, the long-handled gavel — all these were calculated to inspire awe in the jury who were, after all, only a dozen ordinary citizens with the ordinary citizen's respect for such symbols. The twelve men and women in the jury box tended to follow the judge's lead, subtle though it might be.

It would not be Judge Newman who decided this case — but Judge Newman would be a mighty force in it. The Simmonds murder trial was a responsibility as heavy as any he had ever carried.

He sat at his desk, reviewing for a final time what he knew of the case. Some of it he had gleaned from transcripts of the proceedings to date, as recorded by the court stenographer, Mary Connelly. Mrs. Connelly was a grandmotherly woman with a shrewd eye and a seamed, give-nothing-away face. Once she had overcome her shyness at being summoned to the judge's chambers, she had proved voluble.

"The facts are there, Your Honor, but there was more that I didn't put down. Things that had nothing to do with the indictment, but a lot to do with the person being indicted."

"What do you mean?"

"A lot of what went on at the indictment was nonverbal. I mean things like Henry Downing — the defendant — looking into the spectator benches for his wife, and her shaking her head, and he waggling his eyebrows. It was kind of like a silent conversation between the two of them. It continued all the time that I could see."

"A devoted couple?"

"It looks that way, sir." She paused to wipe a sentimental smile from her doughy features. "Which is not to say, of course, that he's innocent."

"Of course not. The jury will determine that." Daniel hated himself for his own pomposity; the stenographer seemed to find it perfectly fitting. She nodded approvingly, but there was a lingering thoughtfulness in her eyes.

"The evidence looks black for Downing," she mused, "but I still can't help hoping that something will come to light to acquit him. Losing her husband to a life term in prison will shatter his wife — shatter her. She's such a pleasant-looking woman, too. Not pretty, exactly, but her face has character." Mrs. Connelly laughed self-consciously at herself. "I find myself rooting for her. For them."

"The best we can hope for," Daniel reminded her gently, "is for the truth to triumph. Whatever that truth might be."

Mary sighed. "I know —" Pulling herself abruptly together, she said, "Will that be all, sir?"

"Yes. And thank you. You've been very helpful."

Daniel Newman picked up the volume of *Tehillim* that he kept on his desk, recited several chapters as was his custom before every trial, and replaced the volume. Then he gathered his papers and turned to take a last look in the mirror. His judicial robes were clean and pressed and looked ready for action. He hoped the man wearing them was just as prepared.

It was time. In approximately five minutes, the Simmonds murder trial was slated to begin, with Judge Newman on the bench. By the time he stepped down from it at the trial's end, Henry Downing would be either a free man or a prisoner for life. Downing's wife, the devoted Elsa, would be delirious with happiness — or plunged into a living death. Al Simmonds was dead and gone; he could no longer be touched by human hand or the inexorable workings of the law. But a living man waited to be judged in the next room, and a living woman was sitting there, too, hoping for a miracle.

The responsibility weighed on his shoulders like a physical burden. As always at such times, Daniel tried to lighten the burden by throwing it onto greater Shoulders than his own; by fervent prayer this morning at the early *Shacharis minyan*, and the extra recitation of *Tehillim* just now in his chambers.

Paul, his clerk, knew better than to disturb him in the minutes just before a trial began. He had once opened the door at such a moment, only to find Daniel so absorbed in his devotions as to be oblivious to the clerk's presence. Paul had never forgotten the look on the judge's face as, gowned in his judicial robes, he swayed in silent prayer. The picture was etched permanently in his memory: the image of human authority, utterly bowed to the Authority above.

Daniel walked slowly to the door and opened it. Paul was waiting. The clerk had been leaning against the wall with a vacant expression, but at the sight of the judge he sprang to attention. Daniel walked into the courtroom.

From the front of the room the bailiff threw out his chest and bellowed, "All rise!" With a shuffle of feet and a rustle of clothing, every person in the courtroom stood. Judge Newman climbed the steps to the bench, sat down, and picked up his gavel. He noticed Jake Meisler, notepad and pen in hand, perched eager as a spaniel in the front row.

"The United States vs. Henry Downing," the bailiff intoned. "The charge: murder in the first degree."

From the spectator benches came the sound of a muffled gasp. Daniel would have laid bets that the sound had come from Elsa Downing.

In light of Mary Connelly's observations, he wanted to study both the defendant and his wife — but this was not the moment. There would be plenty of time for that once the trial was under way. Right now, there were prospective jurors waiting to be interviewed and a trial to be put into motion. The public prosecutor and the defense attorney stood on either side of the room, like dueling opponents — which was exactly what they were. The first skirmish would take place in the arena of jury selection. The precise composition of those twelve men and women would be a major factor — if not the deciding one — in Henry Downing's fate.

Daniel took a deep breath, let his gaze rake the crowded room, and lifted his gavel. It came down with a sonorous *bang.*

"Good morning, ladies and gentlemen," the judge said. "I think we all agree that the biggest favor we can do the defendant, the prosecution and defense teams, the jury — and, of course, the quest for true justice — is to make this a speedy trial."

He permitted himself a flicker of a glance at the defendant. He saw steady, blue-gray eyes over a rather bulbous nose, and thick salt-and-pepper hair cut short. From the collar of Downing's white shirt peeked a workingman's thick, muscled neck. The suit was navy and new looking.

Daniel focused his commanding gaze on the two attorneys.

"Let's begin."

Six long hours later, five men and seven women sat in two rows facing the judge. They were no longer plumbers, shopkeepers, housewives. They formed a new entity now. They were the jury.

Neither the prosecution nor the defense was completely happy with the mixture. The former had tried to disqualify the less prosperous jury candidates, individuals who might logically be disposed to root for the underdog — in this case, Henry Downing: everyman turned lottery winner. "Poor Henry," as they would see it, had miraculously stumbled onto a pot of gold at the end of his hard-earned rainbow only to see good luck turn to bad when — with a naivete that served to highlight his basic human decency — he took up with the rich and ruthless Al Simmonds.

The defense, of course, had strained every sinew to keep those same jurors very much in the running — while doing its level best to throw out the more prosperous, entrepreneurial types who might look to Simmonds as a role model.

In these aims, both sides had been only moderately successful. The final panel satisfied no one — but then, that was usually the way it was. With a combination of science and instinct, the attorneys had concocted a volatile human mix. A jury had been created in the test tube of the courtroom, and it would mature, Frankensteinlike, into its own vision.

Judge Newman glanced at his watch, then at the faces of the jury, the attorneys, the reporters, and the thinned-out ranks of spectators. They looked as tired as he felt. Though it was only 4 in the afternoon, his back ached, his arms felt heavy, and his neck was stiff. Most of the distress, he knew, was mental rather than physical. And only a portion of it was linked to the burden of presiding over a murder trial.

An accident-prone family — He would be meeting Mark Garrity again tonight. But he had a couple of stops to make first.

"This court is adjourned until 10 o'clock tomorrow morning," he announced. "At that time, we will hear opening arguments."

It was only then that he permitted himself to gaze fully at the face of the defendant. But Henry Downing was already twisting in his seat, trying to catch his wife's eye to offer a fleeting smile before the two beefy guards clamped their hands on his arms and led him back to his cell.

❧

"Daddy!" Yael smiled brightly as she slipped into the passenger seat beside her father. The station wagon overflowed with other tenth-graders, including the faithful Tzippy.

Daniel did not smile back. Instead of starting the engine, his fingers tapped impatiently on the driver's wheel. With a sideways glance at his daughter, he said grimly, "Notice that we're the last car in this place? Not one of the last. Not the next-to-last. The very last."

"I'm sorry, Daddy. But I'll explain everything. You see —"

"Save the explanations for later, please. Right now, I want an apology from you — to me, and to the girls you've kept waiting."

Criminals in the courtroom had heard this particular tone in Judge Newman's voice. Yael never had. She stared at her father with wide eyes, in which an involuntary tear had begun to form. She knew nothing of Daniel's rising panic as he waited for his daughter. He watched the stream of girls that first gushed, and then trickled, through the doors of the high-school building. Tall girls, short girls, blond and brunette and redheaded girls — but no Yael. A thousand scenarios played themselves out on the screen of his mind, each one more horrifying than the last. Another sixty seconds would have seen him bursting into the building in frantic search of his daughter. If not for the fact that Tzippy had warned him that Yael would be late, he would have done so already.

"I'm sorry," Yael whispered. She dashed the back of her hand across her eyes, and then — for the benefit of the back-seat watchers — lifted her head. "It won't happen again."

Seeing her safe, the hard knot of anxiety in Daniel's chest melted. He wanted to erase the frown between her brows, to bring back the happy-hearted girl who had skipped down the school stairs just a few minutes before. Breathing deeply to dissipate the tension, he said, "Well, tell me then. Why so late, Yael?"

She sniffed, and brightened. "Oh, Daddy, I met the most wonderful person! She's a teacher in the school — the ninth grade — and she's new in town. She used to live in New York, and she plays the piano *scrumptiously*! We played a duet together, and then I asked her — would you believe I actually found the nerve to do it? — if she would give me piano lessons! And she said she's not really a piano teacher, in fact, she's never given an actual lesson in her life, but I begged and begged, and she said she'll think about it. Daddy, isn't that fantastic?"

Yael's eyes were shining like twin headlamps.

"Yes, of course. That's fine, Yael. But this wasn't exactly the right time to make new friends, was it? I was — worried. Everyone else came out of school ages ago."

Something in her father's voice penetrated the elephant's hide of Yael's euphoria. She turned to face him, surprised, and wary without quite knowing why.

"I told you, we were playing the piano. I lost track of the time. I *said* I was sorry —"

"Well, please don't keep me waiting next time. I wouldn't be surprised if I earned myself a few more gray hairs in this past half-hour. And Heaven knows I've got enough to spare already." Jerkily, he switched on the motor. The car purred to life. He negotiated the long, narrow driveway that led down to the road.

Suddenly, Daniel realized how strained and odd he must appear to Yael and the other girls. In his own ears, his voice echoed harshly — desperately. As the car began to move forward, he concentrated on relaxing the muscles in his jaw.

In a small voice, Yael said, "Daddy?"

She spoke softly, for his ears only. Behind them, the other girls cheerfully chatted among themselves, exchanging lively impressions of their new teachers, the new school year.

"I've been late before. Why are you so nervous about it all of a sudden?"

Sure, she had been late before. But never on the heels of two death threats. He felt his heart stutter, then begin to hammer painfully. He had to remind himself to breathe. The car surged forward with the unconscious pressure of his foot on the gas pedal.

He slowed down, merging with care into a five-way intersection, as he tried to think of some way to answer his daughter's question.

19

He wanted to apologize. He longed to hold her in his arms and soothe her, the way he had done so often when she was little. Instead, in a voice that fear made more curt than was strictly necessary, he asked, "Has it occurred to you that I might occasionally have some more pressing business than hanging around the school parking-lot? At 14, I know, time seems an endless commodity. But for me, it is not endless — it's very precious."

"Oh!" Yael nodded, enlightened. "Are you in a rush? Where are you going?"

"I'm not going anywhere. I do have work to do at home, though. We started a new trial today." As a rule, Daniel did not share details of his work with his children. This afternoon, however, in a bid to distract Yael — to prevent her antennae from pinging wildly at what she was picking up from him — he deviated deliberately from his usual practice. "The Simmonds murder trial. Heard of it?"

Yael shook her head, but another girl, in the seat just behind him, called excitedly, "That's the businessman who was knifed to death by the guy who won the lottery, isn't it, Mr. Newman?"

So much for innocent until proven guilty. With a half-smile for his questioner in the rear-view mirror, Daniel said, "Actually, that's for the jury to decide."

"It was a kitchen knife, wasn't it?" another girl asked.

Tzippy shuddered, "Ugh. Spare me the gory details."

Yael said, "How's the trial going, Daddy?" She seemed to be just as relieved as her father to discuss something other than her lateness.

"This was the first day. All we did was pick the jury — a long and tedious process, let me tell you."

Tzippy leaned forward curiously. "Why? I thought people just got a letter telling them they have jury duty."

"They do. But many more than just a dozen people show up on the morning of a trial like this one. We get hundreds. And, out of those hundreds, the attorneys for the defense and the prosecution each try to pick a jury that they think will be most sympathetic to their case . . . " In a few well-chosen words, Judge Newman explained how the system worked. The homily brought the car to its first drop-off point. One girl climbed out.

Daniel watched her until she was safely in her house. As he pulled out again, Tzippy leaned forward to tap Yael on the shoulder.

"Yael, did you say you were playing a duet with the ninth-grade teacher?"

"Yes. Miss Muller's her name. She's so nice!"

"That's not what *I* heard. Simi Davidson says her cousin had Miss Muller in New York last year. She says she was a dragon!"

"Well, I don't know anything about anyone's cousin," Yael retorted hotly. "All I know is that Miss Muller plays like a dream — and she *is* nice."

"Calm down, Yael. All I said was that I heard —"

"Girls," Daniel interposed mildly, "don't you think we're drifting into forbidden territory here? I refer to things like *lashon hara*, gossip, and slander. All that nasty stuff."

"But, Daddy —"

"Besides," Daniel went on, inexorably, "speaking as a judge, Tzippy, I strongly advise against making premature judgments. Despite whatever impression some third party might have had of this teacher, don't you think you should wait to see for yourself?"

"The way I did," Yael put in piously.

"After what I heard from Simi, I'm scared to get near her," Tzippy muttered.

Daniel felt a stirring of sympathy for this unknown teacher. "And here we are," he announced, swooping into a spot in front of a still flourishing, end-of-summer garden. "Your rhododendrons are looking good, Tzippy. My best to your parents."

"Thanks. Well, bye, Yael." Tzippy gathered her backpack and

slipped awkwardly through the door.

"Bye." Yael still sounded a little sullen at the slur cast on her new friend, the piano-perfect Miss Muller.

In short order, Daniel drove the last two girls home. Conversation was sporadic. Yael contributed hardly a word apart from "See you tomorrow" when each left. The drive to their own home was completed in total silence. Daniel would have liked to believe that it was a companionable silence, but something in his daughter's profile told him otherwise.

After pulling the car into the driveway, he busied himself with small things: unbuckling his seat belt, turning off the headlights that he always kept switched on, night or day, since his wife's accident, opening and locking the car door. "We're having lasagna for supper, Mrs. Marks tells me. Maybe we can have some of that vanilla fudge ice cream for dessert. I saw a box in the freezer the other day."

It had been years since Yael had allowed food to play a very important role in her life. Mordy might have been sidetracked by such a tempting offer, but not she. Yael maintained a determined silence as they walked up the path to their front door. As her father groped in his pocket for his house keys, she wheeled around to face him.

"Daddy, wait a second, please."

"What is it?"

"Something's going on. Please tell me."

She wanted to sound mature and adult, but the face that met Daniel's tore at his heart. It was so unconsciously fragile, so vulnerable in its unprotected youth. He would do anything to spare this girl as much as the bruising of a thumb, the stubbing of a toe. And Mordy, his good-humored, computer-addicted, funny, brainy only son — what wouldn't Daniel do to keep *him* out of harm's way?

With a stab of pain, he thought of the shadowy stranger penning notes to him and slipping them, unseen, where he would be sure to find them. *Stand by for details.* Well, Daniel had no intention of standing by. He was going to protect his children, if it was the last thing he ever did.

They had taken his Ella from him. With G-d's help, they would take no more.

Yael did not get her answer that night. After hardly tasting Mrs.

Marks' good lasagna, she went up to her room in not a very happy frame of mind. She could not put her finger on what was bothering her — and that bothered her most of all.

There was very little homework tonight. Restlessly, she thought about going downstairs for a snack, then discarded the idea as unnecessarily fattening. She wanted to play the piano, but knew her father would remind her before the first chord was struck that it was nearly her bedtime. At last, with a sigh, she succumbed to hunger pangs and, going to the kitchen, plucked an apple from the basket on the table that Mrs. Marks always kept filled. After that, pajamas on, teeth brushed, and schoolbag readied for the morning, she climbed into bed to read herself to sleep.

A chapter or two in her new library book kept her awake for another half-hour of her day. It was not as absorbing as it had been billed; by 10:15, Yael was yawning.

It was nearly 10:30 when she turned out her light. Scarcely had she closed her eyes when the front doorbell sounded. She heard her father open it, then the low murmur of exchanged greetings. Her eyes flew open. Who could be visiting at such an hour? Curious, she climbed back out of bed, threw on a robe, and went to the door.

She had to open it only a crack to learn what she wanted to know. It was Detective Garrity. She saw him duck in order to enter the living room, and heard the quiet, indistinguishable flow of words as he crossed the living room. Daniel led his guest into the study, closing the door firmly behind him.

Knowing that she would hear nothing more, Yael returned to her bed. She was really drowsy now, eyes and ears already attuned to the dream-life waiting to claim her. That was why she did not hear the door to Mordy's bedroom open, or the soft padding of his feet as he tiptoed down the hall to the bathroom.

Mordy closed the bathroom door very quietly, and turned the lock. Then he went over to sit on the floor by the radiator grille in the corner. To his great delight, he had long ago discovered that the grille carried sounds up from the room below. By positioning yourself just so, you could hear, with remarkable clarity, every word that was spoken there.

The room directly underneath the bathroom was his father's study.

20

"There's been another threat," Garrity said. It was a statement, not a question.

Daniel nodded. In silence, he produced the envelope, handling it by the corners with the tips of his fingers. Just as silently, the policeman took it from him. With tweezers that he whipped from his pocket, he gingerly opened the envelope flap. By the same method he extracted the single handwritten page. He scanned it quickly.

"Accident-prone?"

"That's what it says. And notice that it doesn't say an 'accident-prone person.' It says 'family.' " Daniel was angry at himself for the lump in his throat that made the words emerge hoarsely. He cleared his throat and tried again. "But there is one hopeful part."

Garrity studied the message. "The part about cooperating?"

"Yes. The other message just threatened. This one seems to imply that — violence — might be averted through cooperation."

"Hopeful!" Garrity snorted. Then, with a quick glance at Daniel, he said, "Sorry, Dan. You're worried, so it's only natural for you to, ah —"

"Grasp at straws. I know. But the word 'cooperate' tells me that there's at least something I can do to keep this guy at bay. And something is better than nothing."

"A whole lot better." Garrity nodded. Himself wedded to action, he knew all too well the frustration of being powerless to act. Those times when circumstance or judge's whim kept him from laying his hands on someone whom he *knew,* with every shouting nerve-ending, to be a lawbreaker — But all the gut instinct in the world counted for nothing in the eyes of the law. It was evidence that was needed, and legal evidence at that.

Grudgingly, he supposed that was a good thing — the kind of caution that keeps democracy alive. In a society where the police may storm and search private premises without a warrant, what guarantee was there that other freedoms — including, eventually, his own — would not be next to disappear?

Garrity took a plastic evidence bag from his pocket and carefully dropped the envelope inside. "I'll have this checked for fingerprints. It's not likely we'll find any useful ones, though — not after it's been through the postal service." He looked up. "Dan, this would be a good time to check the other note — the first one. You said you found it on your windshield, didn't you? That eliminates the postal system. A long shot, but you never know."

Daniel opened a drawer, pulled out the first letter with open distaste, and passed it across the desk to Garrity. As he watched that note disappear into the depths of the detective's jacket pocket along with the more recent one, he wished the threats they carried could be made to vanish just as easily. He closed his eyes, inhaling the comforting aroma of the *sefarim* and legal tomes that lined his study walls. Of all the rooms in his house, he loved this one most. In the small hours, even without a light, he could lay a hand on virtually any volume he sought in this room.

A scene flashed into his mind: himself as a young boy, no more than 10 or 11, propped up on a daybed in a study very much like this one, a pile of books at his elbow. It was Shabbos afternoon, that leisurely hour when souls and stomachs are pleasantly full and time has been banished to the outer reaches. His parents were napping upstairs, his sister and brother were out with their friends, and young Daniel was enjoying the delicious prospect of a whole afternoon in which to read to his heart's content. As he drowned in a sweet sea of words, the rest of the world receded. Words wrapped around him then like a comforter. But where was that sense of infinite security now — that illusion of a protected existence? All children believe they lead a charmed life. For Daniel, books had only deepened the enchantment.

He could use a little of that magic now, to bind his enemies and render them powerless — He opened his eyes, and sighed. There was no magic — but he did have Mark Garrity, waiting.

"So what's the next step?" he asked.

"I'm glad you asked that. Police protection is indicated. And, of course, you'll have to have —"

Daniel held up a hand and broke in, "Please, Mark — not so fast. Much as I appreciate the offer, I still don't want my home turned into a garrison. I don't want to frighten the kids. I can look after them myself."

"Can you?" Garrity pressed his lips together and gave an impatient shake of the head. "Dan, we're not playing cops and robbers here. There's a dangerous man out there who's gunning for you. He's probably done this kind of thing before. Are you —"

Again, Daniel interrupted. "Aren't you jumping to conclusions? Several of them?" He held up an index finger. "First, that the threat is a genuine one. I know what the notes said, but after all, they're just words. This might be nothing more than some disgruntled ex-con's way of trying to shake me up. If sweet revenge is what he's after, he can get it easily by turning my life into one long look over my shoulder — and without doing a thing to incriminate himself."

A second finger joined the first. "Second, you're assuming that the person who wrote these notes is dangerous. Not necessarily, Mark. Again, all we have are words. Those can just as easily be a weak man's weapon. We've seen no evidence at all of violence."

"Yet," Garrity reminded him grimly.

Daniel inclined his head. "Granted."

"Except for your wife's accident."

"We have no proof that that was anything *but* an accident — or that the writer of these notes had anything to do with it."

"He implies that he did. We can't ignore that," Garrity said quietly. "And he also says that you're next. Or rather," he corrected himself, "he talks about an 'accident-prone family.' That could mean the kids."

This last point had the desired effect. A tremor of fear ran through Daniel. He sat silently, choosing his course. As he considered, he rested his elbows on his desk, fingers steepled in proper lawyerly fashion. It was the gesture of a judicious man, though at the moment Daniel felt decidedly un-judgely. It was his fate to render opinions for others — to pass down words of wisdom for the edification of his fellows. Just once, he wished there was someone — apart from the police — who would tell *him* what to do.

Suddenly, the image of his mother came to mind.

He smiled inwardly, then gave the idea an unequivocal mental veto. Mom was the most level-headed woman he knew, but even the bravest mother can shrivel in the face of a threat to her fledglings. Confiding in her might halve his own worries, but it would treble hers. That was something he would not do to her.

Briefly — very briefly — he considered talking the matter over with his father. But Dad's health was not all it should be these days. And, apart from that, Daniel would not submit him to the strain of keeping secrets from his own wife.

Chaim? Instantly, Daniel dismissed that possibility. His younger brother was the weakling of the family, the one who needed to be shored up and encouraged at every turn. Not much hope of guidance from that source.

There was a pang as he thought of his best friend, on sabbatical in Israel. Yehuda Arlen was the person he would most naturally have turned to in this crisis. There were few people whose intelligence and good old common sense he respected as much as Yehuda's. Ever since their yeshivah days, they had been firmly — though never brutally — honest about their own and each other's faults. Together they had navigated many new rivers, pausing often to pull one another from the shoals. They were friends, in the best sense of the word.

But there was a limit to the demands one can impose even on such a friendship. Yehuda's last letter, which arrived on the same day as the most recent threat, had waxed effusive over his new life in Israel. Yehuda's wife, too, was thrilled to be back after so many years. The kids were enjoying the change, making new friends. Daniel would not intrude on his friend's serenity. He would answer the letter soon, omitting any mention of spine-chilling threats, or the fears that kept him awake into the wee hours, night after night.

The one he really longed to confide in was much farther away even than Yehuda. He thought he had grown accustomed to Ella's absence, but he found himself missing her more keenly now than at any time since her death. He needed a wife's sympathetic ear, a wife's intuition, a wife's discretion. Many people cared about him, he knew — cared deeply. But only a wife had one's interests so deeply at heart that they were interchangeable with her own.

Garrity watched the swiftly changing reflections of thought on Daniel's face. He was a man blessed with a greater than usual supply of patience, something he found very useful in his line of work. Lose your capacity for waiting, he believed, and frustration would claim you faster than a blindfolded stroll across the highway. He watched Daniel now, and waited.

At last, the judge turned to face his visitor. He lowered his steepled fingers and rested them lightly on the desktop. "Mark, here's what I think. A two-pronged approach is indicated. On the one hand, we pursue this thing as though we know it's genuine. I'll get my clerk to dig up the court files on everyone I sent to jail as prosecuting attorney in the period leading up to Ella's — to the accident. Particular emphasis, of course, on the more violent criminal offenders. You have my permission to go through those files with me, and to tackle the case in best police fashion — up to a point."

"That point being — ?"

"Overt police protection. I'm sorry, I can't do that to the kids. Not yet. Not unless this thing proves itself more than a lot of hot air."

"My gut tells me it's more than that now, Dan," Garrity said quietly.

Daniel sighed. "I know. My own gut is not very happy — But until and unless we're sure, I have to try and let Yael and Mordy lead normal lives."

"They'd be more alert if they knew what was happening."

"They'd also be panic stricken — especially Yael." He shook his head. "No. I can do the worrying for all of us, Mark."

"So what exactly do we wait for?" Garrity burst out in frustration. "An actual attack of some kind?"

Daniel hesitated, weighing the conflicting voices inside his head. Meeting the detective's eyes, he said in a low voice, "Mark, listen. Yael was 9 when Ella — went. She'd been comfortable in the dark for years by then, but suddenly she wouldn't go to sleep without a light on — both in her room and in the hall outside. She also asked me to position her bed so that, with both of our bedroom doors open, she could see me even if she woke up in the middle of the night.

"Mordy's reaction wasn't so obvious. He just became very quiet, and very, very studious. It was as if he were trying to chase away the bad thing that had happened by being a super-good boy. He never played outside, rarely invited a friend over."

Garrity waited. When Daniel showed no signs of continuing, he prompted, "And now?"

"It's better now. Yael and Mordy are leading happy, normal lives today, Mark. This is what I've been working for, these past five years. *I don't want to destroy that for them.* I don't want to see the haunted look return to Yael's face, or see Mordy shrink back into himself the way he once did. *I don't want them to know that I tried to keep them safe — and failed.*" His eyes pleaded with Garrity to understand.

Whether he actually understood or not, Garrity knew when he was beaten. He had achieved at least a portion of his goal in coming here: the green light on police involvement in the case. While he had his reservations — serious ones — about leaving the family unprotected, he was willing to let that go for the moment. If the threatener made further contact, as Garrity suspected he soon would, Daniel would surely be made to see that even the most committed father was just not enough. No one could be in three places at once. And the best intentions in the world were no match for a ruthless, evil spirit and a well-aimed pistol.

The detective kept his thoughts to himself. To Daniel he said, rising, "Well, that's it, then. I'll get the ball rolling down at the station." He patted his pocket. "Starting with this."

"Low profile, right?" Daniel asked. "I don't want to see this on the front page of tomorrow's newspaper."

Garrity gave him a weak smile. "Not tomorrow's, maybe. But how long do you think you can keep something like this under wraps? Especially once we start investigating?"

"As long as possible" Daniel said determinedly. "For the kids' sake."

"For the kids," Garrity echoed. With a quick, two-fingered salute, he turned and left the study, Daniel following behind to see him to the door.

Upstairs, Mordy began to shiver uncontrollably. Though crouched just inches from the radiator, he felt chilled to the bone. It was a long time before he could force himself to move, or to make the endless journey back to his bedroom. And it was even longer — though he curled the quilt tightly around him like the snuggest of cocoons — before the shivering subsided.

September was wearing its most unbecoming face as Judge Newman prepared to leave home for the courthouse, where the cast of characters was moving into place for opening speeches by counsels for the prosecution and the defense. Daniel found himself wishing that the sky was less leaden, the wind less biting, and that the withered leaves still danced at the ends of their branches, lush and green. On a day like this, it was easy to believe the worst of anybody.

He packed his briefcase, thinking of the day lying ahead. It had been a long time since he had taken such a personal interest in a case. It had been a long time since he had taken a personal interest in anything. Something had awakened in him, even as the year had begun to settle down for its long sleep. Fear for his children's safety had uncapped the bottomless well of his love for them, and that love, in turn, had allowed other, more insidious, longings to set in. He thought of Henry Downing seated at the defense table and of his wife, anxious-looking in the row behind.

A year ago, they had been an unassuming couple, eking out a placid, uneventful existence on his salary as a postal worker. In one of life's bewildering changes, he was now a multimillionaire staring into the hollow eyes of the justice system. The wheel turned and turned, making for a ride that was dizzying at the best of times and incomprehensible all the time.

At a footfall on the carpeted stairs, Daniel turned.

Mordy looked pale, and there were circles under his eyes that testified to a sleepless night. Normally, he woke at 6:30 and joined the school *minyan* for *Shacharis*, optional for sixth-graders in his school. This morning, pleading exhaustion, he had drowsily requested permission to *daven* at home and be dropped off in time for class. With a quick call to the bus driver to inform him of the change in plans, Daniel had allowed his son to sleep an hour longer.

Judging by the way Mordy looked now, it did not seem to have done him much good.

"Hi, Mordy. Ready to go?"

"I guess so." The boy sounded listless.

"Have you *davened*? Had breakfast?"

"I finished *davening* —"

"What about breakfast?" the father asked patiently. "You know how I feel about your leaving for school with nothing inside to keep you going till lunch."

Mordy shrugged. "I tried to eat, but I felt too nauseous."

Daniel peered at his son. "Nauseous? How long have you been feeling this way?"

Since eavesdropping on you and Detective Garrity. "Since last night, I guess."

"Why didn't you say anything then?"

The reply was another shrug.

"Do you want to stay home from school today?" Mordy, he knew, was not the boy to take advantage of such an offer; he enjoyed the challenge and the structure of school life and actually regretted the rare occasions when he was too sick to attend. Somewhat to Daniel's surprise, after a brief hesitation his son nodded. "I guess it would be best. Mrs. Marks will be here today, right?"

The father's surprise deepened. "Of course. At least, she hasn't phoned to say she's not coming. What's the matter, Mordy? You don't usually mind staying home alone."

"I *don't* mind," Mordy said quickly. "It's just —" He trailed off.

"Just what?"

"Nothing."

Something tickled the edges of Daniel's mind, where a parent's worry-nerve centers live. While alarm bells were not actually ringing, Daniel was aware of a certain restlessness — the far-off chime of muted anxiety — in that area. He asked again, "What is it, Mordy?

Is anything wrong?''

"What should be wrong?''

Gently, Daniel said, "That's what I asked *you*, son.''

Mordy moved closer. Impulsively, he asked, "Can't — can't you stay home today, Daddy? You could take a day off. We could learn together.''

Daniel's eyebrows shot nearly to his hairline. He laid the back of his hand on Mordy's forehead. "You don't *feel* feverish.''

"Seriously, Dad. It would be fun.''

"It would indeed.'' Daniel shrugged into his raincoat; the forecast had predicted considerable activity from those leaden clouds. "Unfortunately, there are things I must do today — namely, earn a living for all of us. It's the Simmonds murder trial.''

As he had hoped, these last words served as a perfect distraction. "The baby-bottle baron? I read all about him! They say his partner did him in.''

"*May* have done him in. Defendants are innocent until proven guilty, remember?''

"But everyone thinks he did it. Who else could have? It happened in his own back yard!''

"That,'' Daniel said, picking up his briefcase, "is what's known in the business as circumstantial evidence. We must keep an open mind.''

"Maybe it was the wife,'' Mordy speculated, accompanying his father to the door.

"And maybe it was the milkman. I'll let you know when the jury decides. Oh, Mordy, can you give Mrs. Marks a message for me? I may be bringing a guest home to dinner.''

Instantly suspicious, Mordy asked, "Who?'' Was it Detective Garrity, and did that mean more trouble?

His odd reaction was lost on Daniel, who was slapping his pockets for his car keys. "Jacob E. Meisler. You remember Jake?''

"Sure! I liked him.''

"Me, too,'' Daniel said ungrammatically, fishing out his keys at last. "He's a bit of a character — but a smart one. Works hard, and I suspect he doesn't eat too much when he's hitting the books. If I can induce him to take an hour or two out of his hectic schedule to sit down to a home-cooked meal, you'll be seeing him this evening. You'll tell Mrs. Marks?''

"Sure, Daddy. Uh, when is she coming?"

Daniel consulted his watch, then looked up the street to where an ancient, pale-blue sedan was making its sedate way toward them. "That'll be her right now. I can't wait, though — I'm running late. Feel good, Mordy!" Stooping, he planted a quick kiss on his son's forehead, then hurried for the car parked in the driveway.

Mrs. Marks pulled up at the curb just in time to catch the judge's parting smile and wave. Mordy was waiting in the open doorway, but his eyes were not on the housekeeper. They were fixed with longing and a despair born of fear on his father's car, moving away from him down the street like a vanishing dream of security.

Martin Bedeker, state prosecutor, was tall and very thin, and that lent him an air of aristocracy. His face completed the impression. The nose was Roman, the thin lips fine for pursing with disapproval, the eyes small and filled with arrogance.

It was his hands that gave him away: Stubby fingered and graceless, they were the bane of his existence. If he could, he would have hidden those hands in his pockets like a schoolboy. It was his wife's pleasure to joke that Martin ought to have been a waiter in an upscale restaurant or hotel, where white gloves are *de rigueur*.

Gloves or no gloves, the prosecutor made a powerful impression on the twelve men and women of the jury. His appearance — or perhaps the magnificent Roman nose — seemed to fascinate them. Erect and unsmiling, Bedeker faced the twelve as though he were about to be knighted.

"Good people of the jury," he began. "You have here before you a case that is, at the same time, both ludicrously simple and infinitely complex."

Out of sheer habit, he paused. An attention-getting introductory sentence was part of his personal courthouse style. Making sure to catch each juror's eye in turn, he went on.

"The complexity does not lie in the crime's execution: There is nothing more straightforward than the stab of a knife. It derives, rather, from the tangled motivation behind that crime — the shadowy workings of the human mind. What leads one man to lift up his hand against another? What level of evil, of contempt for human life, permits one individual to rob another of his most precious possession — his very life?

"We cannot answer this question for all murderers. But in this case, we have an answer that seems all too obvious.

"At its core, as in many violent crimes, there was greed."

Here, again, the prosecutor paused — this time for breath, and to gauge the effect of his opening remarks on the jury. They seemed spellbound. Nodding slightly, satisfied, he continued.

"Let us pause for a moment to review the facts.

"Two men formed a partnership for the sake of producing an innovative type of baby bottle. Think of it, ladies and gentlemen: a baby's bottle, the very image of innocence. But what followed the formation of that partnership was the opposite of innocent.

"One of the partners — the victim, Alexander Simmonds — was an entrepreneur with many successful business ventures behind him. He'd personally designed the new product and, excited about putting it onto the market as swiftly as possible but finding himself temporarily strapped for ready cash with which to do so, sought a silent partner to back him. He turned to a man who had recently come into big money. In good faith and the desire to continue serving the public he had already served so long and so well, Al Simmonds turned to the multimillion-dollar winner of the Maryland State Lottery. He turned to Henry Downing."

The touch of ice that crept into the prosecutor's voice at the mention of the accused's name was nothing short of masterly. One jury member — a middle-aged woman with a mop of gray hair and motherly eyes — actually shivered. The judge observed the proceedings narrowly, while appearing hardly to be watching at all. At the defense table, Downing sat rigid as a statue. Bedeker leaned both hands on the rail of the jury box and looked earnestly into the faces of the jurors.

"But the venture which had started out in such innocence and good faith was doomed to end in tragedy. It was doomed by one man's greed. We will prove in this courtroom that it was Henry Downing's insatiable lust for money that led to the harsh words he exchanged with his partner before witnesses. It was avarice that sat at the root of the accusations he made to Mr. Simmonds, of foul financial dealings — accusations, I may add, unsubstantiated in any court of law.

"It was blind greed, afterwards, that led him to do an apparent about-face, to extend the so-called olive branch and invite Mr. Simmonds to dinner at his home. And it was his idolization of the almighty dollar that caused Henry Downing to pick up a sharpened kitchen knife and in his garden stab Al Simmonds repeatedly in the chest that same night.

"If Al Simmonds died, he, Henry Downing, would be sole beneficiary of the sales of that baby bottle — sales projected to soar into the millions. He would accumulate those millions on top of the ones he had already won. The lottery jackpot was his by sheerest chance. But once he had sampled the sweet taste of affluence, Henry Downing was prepared to leave nothing else to chance. We are going to show that he planned his partner's murder meticulously, down to the last detail."

Bedeker wheeled around to point dramatically at the defense table. "The defense is going to try to convince you that he did not do it at all. They will try to play on your sympathy, to remind you that Downing was, until recently, a relatively poor man. They will urge you to consider him a victim rather than a killer. You, of course, will reject that as the nonsense it is. Victims do not plunge knives into other people's hearts.

"After hearing the evidence we have to offer, ladies and gentlemen of the jury, you may begin speculating: Was it a crime of passion — a sudden, almost uncontrollable fury that led Henry Downing to lift his hand against his partner and dinner guest?

"We will show otherwise. We will demonstrate that the crime was not impulsive, but cold-bloodedly planned. In accepting an invitation to his partner's home that night, Al Simmonds unwittingly accepted an invitation to dine with death."

The hush in the courtroom was total. In the benches, artists were silently sketching the scene for their newspapers. Bedeker allowed the silence, and the tension, to stretch for one more delicious moment before intoning, "No one should be allowed to get away with a crime like this one! As the jury in this case, it is your responsibility to see to it that Henry Downing does not get away with it. It is your duty to see that justice is done." He inclined his head. "I thank you."

Bedeker turned away and, in a few swift strides, returned to his seat.

At a nod from the judge, the defense counsel rose just as swiftly, if less gracefully. Buttoning his jacket as he went, he strolled in the direction of the jury box.

Neil Palladin was the opposite of Martin Bedeker in a variety of ways, only some of them obvious. For one thing, he was short where Bedeker was tall, stocky where the prosecutor was lean, and amiable where the other was aloof. Where Bedeker was pressed and immaculate, the defense counsel was gently rumpled. The more subtle differences that had led one to choose a prosecutor's life and the other to serve as defender were hidden in the recesses of the human personality. The jury studied Palladin curiously as he marched with short, deliberate steps up to their box. Slapping both hands down on the railing, he began to speak without preamble.

"As my esteemed colleague has just reminded you, justice must be served. I agree with him there — wholeheartedly. I also agree with his assessment of the psychology of this case. It is greed that stands at the bottom of this case. But that greed was not that of the man sitting in the defendant's chair today. It was another man's 'lust for money' that led directly to Al Simmonds' downfall. And that man's name is — Al Simmonds."

From the spectator and press benches came a stir at these words — of interest and, here and there, of protest. The judge frowned at the benches, hand poised on his gavel. The stir subsided.

Palladin appeared supremely oblivious. "Simmonds and the defendant," he declared, "formed a partnership. The very word implies equality, probity, fair dealing. Instead, Henry Downing found himself foundering in a quagmire of double-talk and dubious figures. As the months went by, and his share of the profits with them, he naturally raised a protest. He had invested a considerable sum in the venture, with commitments — written commitments — that were simply not being met. He knew that sales of the product were booming, yet according to Al Simmonds, there were no profits available to be shared. When, in desperation, Downing demanded his investment back, Simmonds just laughed. Harsh words passed between the two partners, words that, as the prosecutor has reminded you, were overheard by witnesses. Henry Downing was looking into the face of great financial loss — a specter more frightening for him, so recently risen from near-poverty, than for most of us. The security he'd hoped for in his old age appeared to be evaporating. Worse, he nursed the humiliating knowledge that he was being systematically, and ruthlessly, made a fool of. Such a fear, and such knowledge, might conceivably drive a man to violence.

"Some men, maybe. But not Henry Downing. We will bring character witnesses to testify to the basic decency, the gentleness and consideration — the essential *goodness* — of his nature. Henry Downing, however provoked, could not harm the proverbial fly. *And he did not harm his business partner, Al Simmonds.* That somebody chose to do so in Downing's own back yard is indisputable; the fact that Downing himself is not constitutionally capable of committing either cold- or hot-blooded murder is equally indisputable.

"But you, of course, must come to see that for yourselves. I trust that you *will* see clearly — and act accordingly."

Slowly — in contrast to Bedeker's swift exit — Neil Palladin turned away from the jury box. For a moment he stood with his back to it, head bowed as though feeling the weight of his responsibility. The defendant's eyes, Daniel noted, never left his attorney. And the defendant's wife's eyes, he noted as well, never left her husband.

Elsa Downing wore a plain, though well-tailored, charcoal suit a few shades darker than the pale gray of her hair. She was wan and haggard, with blotches of red high on each cheekbone that had nothing to do with cosmetics. The eyes above those cheekbones were brown, large, and filled with a determined calm — a calm overshadowed by fear.

As Palladin walked slowly toward his seat at the defense table, Daniel shifted his gaze to the prosecuting attorney. "Mr. Bedeker, are you ready to call your first witness?"

Bedeker rose. "I am, Your Honor."

The preliminaries were over. The quest for the truth with regard to Al Simmonds' murder was about to begin.

I f not for Faygie Mandelbaum, Sara would never have survived her first week at school. They would have had to carry her out — figuratively speaking, of course — feet first. A bona fide, grade A, classroom casualty.

"Nonsense," Faygie said crisply, when Sara confided this thought over tuna sandwiches and oatmeal cookies in the teachers' lounge. "I *know* you're more of a fighter than that, Sara. Don't give up so quickly."

"Quickly? It's been a whole week!" Sara grimaced. "It feels like a year."

"Okay, so you've had a rocky start. It's bound to get better soon."

"That's what I like about you: your endless — if unjustified — optimism. Tell me something, Fagyie. Have you set foot in my classroom lately? Well, don't try it without a fur parka on. Each morning, when I walk in, the temperature drops down to around the freezing point. And that's even before I open my mouth."

"They're testing you, Sara. Hang in there. They'll see what a good teacher you are."

"Who says I'm a good teacher?" Sara was wallowing in a swamp of oddly satisfying self-pity; she knew it, but felt no inclination, at the moment, to haul herself out. "I used to think I was a decent one. Now, I don't know anymore."

"Who says?" Faygie echoed. "Mrs. Goodman, for one." She sliced delicately into a late peach.

"Mrs. Goodman." Sara wondered, as she had been wondering for days, what sort of stories were filtering through to the principal about Sara's classroom reception. Cowardly, she had been avoiding the administrative offices. When she had papers to xerox, she went into the Rite-Aid drugstore nearest her apartment and made her copies there. Imagining disapproval in every face, she had erected barriers against all the other teachers, maintaining a cool, keep-your-distance air that won her a sort of semi-isolation on the faculty. The only one who had been allowed to come close was Faygie — and that had been achieved by nothing short of bulldozer tactics.

Every day for the past week, Faygie had dropped by Sara's room at lunchtime. And, every day, she had found Sara drooping over her lonely sandwich, or marking papers, or — on more than one occasion — studiously reciting her *Tehillim.*

"I'm fine. Really," Sara said each time. "I'm just not in the mood to socialize. Maybe tomorrow."

Each time, Faygie simply nodded, withdrew with a cheerful word, and patiently continued to wait her out.

The siege had not lasted long. To someone as friendless as Sara was at the moment, any nonthreatening presence seemed positively inviting. And Faygie was more than just nonthreatening: She was openly, and unabashedly, eager to be friends.

"Come on, Sara, have a heart. All the other teachers are either old hands — teaching for decades — or babies fresh out of seminary. Help! I need you!" These words, spoken with refreshing frankness on the fifth day of the school year, did more than anything else to draw Sara out of her self-imposed exile. She looked at Faygie, standing in an exaggeratedly pleading stance in the doorway, and smiled despite herself.

"Who can resist being needed?" she murmured.

"Exactly. So *don't* resist! Come eat lunch with me. Here, if you want, or in the lounge. The lounge is much more comfortable."

So Sara had gathered up her brown paper bag and her thermos and followed Faygie out the door and down the hall. With a nod or a few vague words she greeted teachers she knew only by name, and others she knew not at all. To her relief, there was no sign of Mrs. Goodman.

"She eats in her office," Faygie told Sara, when she had finally asked. "Sometimes alone, other times with a parent or some bigwig supporter. It's not the Rebbetzin's style to mingle with the faculty in a casual way. We get to see her at our bimonthly staff meetings — and boy, do we receive her undivided attention then!"

"What goes on at those meetings?"

"Everything. We talk about curriculum changes, school policy, problems with individual students — you name it. Mrs. Goodman sets the agenda, but anyone can bring up an issue he or she thinks is important."

Sara made a face. "Would having your whole class hate you be considered important?"

Faygie laughed. "Are those girls giving you a hard time?"

"You could put it that way."

"Don't worry about it," Faygie advised. "It'll pass."

That was easy for her to say, Sara reflected sourly at the end of that first lunch together. Lively, intelligent, and outspoken, Faygie was a favorite with the students. *She* did not have to face a sea of hostile faces every morning, or practically put on a circus act just to get the girls to pay attention. Sara was aware of a seedling of envy, which she quashed forcefully and at once. This had nothing to do with Faygie Mandelbaum, or any other teacher. Sara was not foolish enough to measure herself against them. It was her own self she was measuring against, and finding herself lacking something. She knew she had been a good teacher once — even a superlative teacher. What had happened?

But even that, she knew, was not the real question. There was nothing really wrong with her teaching skills. The sad fact was that girls had been prepared to dislike her before she ever set foot in her classroom. Nothing short of twisting herself into a pretzel was going to make them change their minds.

She tried to mask the forlorn feeling that swamped her as she pushed open the door for the start of her afternoon classes. Once again, an almost palpable wave of rejection rose to meet her. Over the last days, some tiny measure of the hostility had become tempered with a sporadic and very tentative openness by a few of the girls. She clung to the one or two faces that were neutral or slightly better, wishing she were anywhere but in this classroom, and hating herself for feeling that way.

Teaching, her beloved profession, seemed now an intricate form of self-torture. And she had done nothing — not a thing! — to deserve this treatment! There is nothing easier than disliking someone, if you are determined to dislike: Her students, led by Simi Davidson, were living proof of that. Liking is harder won. In her moments of deepest discouragement, Sara felt that she might as well try to scale Mount Everest than attempt to win these girls over.

It was Faygie who was helping her to survive. Though she had known her fellow teacher only a week, Sara never thought of her without warmth, and never saw her without succumbing to an irresistible urge to smile. And, as a sort of bonus, she had discovered that they had something in common: Like Sara, Faygie was a single woman anxious to get married. Though her new friend, at 25, was a full six years younger than Sara, that mutual longing had formed an instant bond.

The river of their lives was carrying each of them, swiftly and surely — but not necessarily where they wished to go. The two women, still virtual strangers, were clinging to the same log and fighting the same buffeting current.

At the moment, that meant more than all the shared history or common tastes in the world.

A car pulled up in front of the Newman home. A moment later the passenger door opened to emit Yael, who shot out as though spewed by a cannon. Slinging her backpack over one uniformed shoulder, she waved good-bye to her friends, called "thank you" to the car-pool mother, and flew up the path to her house.

"Daddy!" The word was out of her mouth even as she burst through the front door. "Oh, hi, Mrs. Marks. Is my father home yet?"

The housekeeper, newly emerged from the kitchen, wiped her hands on her apron and calmly answered, "I'm expecting him any minute, Yael. Your father's started a new trial and said he would probably run a little late."

"Oh, that's right! Well, please let me know the second he comes in. There's something I need to ask him." Flushed with her sprint and some secret excitement, she bumped the backpack up the stairs to her room and closed the door.

Mrs. Marks followed her progress fondly. She had been a surrogate mother, in a manner of speaking, to Yael for the past five years. Many changes had taken place during those years — there is a world of difference between a 9-year-old girl and one who is 14 — but the essential Yael had remained the same.

So had her most fundamental needs. In Mrs. Marks' unwavering opinion, Yael required more, in terms of a role model, than a middle-aged housekeeper who went home at night. She needed a mother — and with all due respect, it was high time Mr. Newman realized it, too.

There was a noise behind her, and then Mordy was saying, "Mrs. Marks, was that my father?"

"No, dear. Yael just came home. Your father should be here soon." She peered at him. "How are you feeling?"

"Much better, thanks." He paused, eyes raking the street through the picture window behind the living room couch. No sign of the Newman sedan yet. Mrs. Marks watched him trot back to the study, and the computer. Such a bright boy, but he needed to get out with friends more. Why, in her day boys played in the street until the sun went down. There was none of this sitting indoors staring at a computer screen until your eyes went bad. But then, her day, as she well knew, was long past. With a tiny sigh, she turned and made for the kitchen, feeling every minute of her age.

Her spirits lifted as the aroma of her cooking greeted her. It was chicken cutlets tonight, prepared Mr. Newman's favorite way. There was more than enough for the family and for Mr. Newman's guest, too, if he decided to come — even after Mordy's predinner sampling. She inhaled appreciatively, then set about starting the rice pilaf that would accompany the dish.

From his vantage point across the street, the watcher could not smell the cutlets frying on the stove — but he could, by angling his binoculars, follow Mrs. Marks' progress across most of the kitchen. He lost her near the kitchen door, but that did not matter.

Neither did the kitchen matter. The important place was the living room, and he was able to look directly into that room from where he crouched, without anyone being the wiser. Until the judge drew the curtains later this evening — and the watcher had learned, to his satisfaction, that he often waited until quite late to do so — the stalker was in a position to witness everything that went on in the hub of the house.

The knowledge filled him with a sense of gloating power, more electrifying than any stimulant. Things were moving! Sal would have been proud. He would get that judge, and he would get the judge's kids, and he would get the judge's money. He would have his revenge.

He had been clever to find this hideaway. It was situated in the basement of the house almost directly across the street from the Newmans. The house featured three floors of flaking siding, a sagging front porch, and a lawn that ought to have been fighting off crabgrass but had long ago given up the struggle. It was the "For Sale" sign, planted in the center of that lawn, that had attracted his attention.

The place had been on the market for months now, and several days of patient watching had brought to light the fact — sad for the owners anxious to sell, but just the opposite for *him* — that very few people were eager to view it, much less make it their own. In the week since he began his surveillance, only once had a house agent come by with a prospective buyer. The tour had not lasted long, and the buyer had not returned.

It was an estate sale, a home that had once belonged to a vibrant, growing family but had passed into neglect and decay with the parents' aging. With their deaths within months of each other, the children — a son and a daughter living, respectively, in Boston and San Francisco — had placed the house on the market. Neither one was pressed for money. Both could afford to wait for the right buyer to come along, at the right price. Meanwhile — to the watcher's satisfaction — the house sat empty, and looked like it would remain so for some time to come. For all intents and purposes the place was his own: a perfect base of operations.

He had had no problem jimmying the back-door lock to gain entry. A quick trip to the supermarket had garnered several bags of groceries to see him through the next few days. His eyes went to the cardboard cartons he had stacked beneath the window that served as his spy-hole on the Newmans. They were laden with canned goods, bags of chips and pretzels, soda and beer. Within seconds he could whisk the cartons out of sight into the boiler room should a real-estate agent wander in: He had done a test-run as an experiment. For variety, he had already found some half-decent takeout places within a few blocks of the house, though he would have to travel a little farther afield if he wanted anything stronger than beer to drink. He was not yet certain how long it was going to take for this thing to play itself out — but one thing he did know: He would not go hungry while he waited.

Across the street, Mrs. Marks gently flipped the cutlets while Mordy tapped away at his computer and Yael, upstairs, listened to her favorite tape and waited for her father to come home.

Outside, the watcher waited and watched.

23

Daniel was used to being greeted effusively by his children as he walked through his door, but he was unprepared for the bombardment — he could call it nothing less — that met him this evening. Mordy's eruption from the study was perfectly timed to coincide with Yael's clattering descent from her room. The twin missiles converged on Daniel.

"Daddy! You're home!" The relief in Mordy's voice was unmistakable, and caused Daniel to raise his eyebrows. Mordy hastily modulated his tone to one of elaborate casualness. "You got a couple of e-mails. Nothing important."

"Then they can wait," Daniel said. "How are you feeling, Mordy?"

It took the boy all of ten seconds to remember why he stayed home that day. He had not lied — his stomach *had* been upset upon waking, and he had been sorely in need of additional sleep after his troubled night — but the morning seemed years ago. A full day in Mrs. Marks' soothing presence had done much to restore his faith in life, and an unexpected but satisfying nap had finished the job. While it would be too much to say that Mordy was feeling cheerful, the terror of the previous night had slowly abated. He was no longer feeling scared to death — just scared.

"I'm okay, Daddy. I took a nap today, and that helped. Mrs. Marks made me chamomile tea and that helped too."

Daniel remembered the morning's distant alarm bells. "If there's anything troubling you, Mordy — at school, maybe — ?" He let the question hang.

Drawing a deep breath, Mordy prepared to do his best to assure his father that his little world was perfectly rosy — a performance bound to tax his acting talent to no small degree. Daddy might see through the act, and then what? An admission that he had eavesdropped on his father's talk with the detective would be decidedly uncomfortable. It would probably cause Daddy to make doubly certain to keep such consultations very private in the future, leaving Mordy completely in the dark about the threat hanging over their heads. He could imagine nothing more horrible than not knowing.

Fortunately for Mordy's peace of mind and limited histrionic abilities, Yael chose this moment to break in urgently. "Daddy, you have to call Miss Muller right away! I mean," she amended with a blush, catching sight of his quizzical glance, "could you *please* call her when you get a chance — as soon as possible?"

"Who," Daniel asked, divesting himself of briefcase and coat, "is Miss Muller?"

"A teacher in my school. I told you about her — the one who plays the piano. She's out of this world! Remember, I asked her if she'd give me lessons, and she said she'd think it over. Well, she's thought it over — and she's agreed!" Yael was radiant.

The kitchen door swung open, and Mrs. Marks emerged in her flowered apron. Daniel nodded pleasantly. "Hello, Mrs. Marks. I understand that you've been sustaining my son with cups of tea. I hope he didn't give you too much trouble today."

"No trouble at all, Mr. Newman." She glanced past his shoulder to the still-open front door. "Mordy did mention something about a guest for dinner?"

"Jake should be along any minute. He was following me here in his car but was less lucky than I was at catching the green lights. I hope it's all right with you."

"It's fine. We're having cutlets and pilaf."

"My favorites!" Daniel smiled. "Thank you, Mrs. Marks."

Smiling back, pink cheeked, she bobbed her head and returned to the kitchen. Yael, who had been jiggling impatiently at her father's side during this interchange, tugged at his sleeve. "Will you call her, Daddy? I've missed a couple of weeks of lessons already. I'm so thrilled that she said yes! I'd like to start as soon as possible."

He turned to his daughter and asked, "Will you be meeting this —
Miss Miller, is it? — at her house?"

"Muller. Her name's Miss Muller. And no, she just moved to
Baltimore and doesn't have a piano. That's why she's been playing the
one in our auditorium after school hours. That's how I met her." She
held out a scrap of paper, obviously torn from her notebook. "Here's
her number, Daddy."

He pocketed it, promising to call right after dinner. The slam of a car
door made him hurry out to welcome his guest. Jake Meisler ambled
in, lanky, rumpled, and wearing his engaging grin. He greeted Yael
and Mordy, who responded with shy hellos, then stepped into the
kitchen to see Mrs. Marks — from whom Jake won an instant stamp of
approval by asking what he could do to help.

"Nothing, nothing," she said, making shooing motions with her
hands. "You know what they say about too many cooks —"

"Who, me — cook? Not me, Mrs. Marks. I'm no chef — but I do
know how to set a table. And I promise not to break anything."

Laughing, Mrs. Marks said, "Thanks, but Yael will take care of
that."

"I'll remind her," Daniel said, and went to do so. He found his
daughter playing the piano. It was a dreamy piece, each note lingering
sweetly like crystal drops of dew.

"That's pretty," Daniel said, when the song was over.

Yael glanced up, startled. "Oh, hi, Daddy. I was working on this
piece with my next-to-last teacher. I would probably have played it at
the next recital, but she moved away —"

"You really love your music, don't you?" As Daniel spoke the
words he felt slightly surprised, and ashamed of his surprise. He had
known of Yael's passion for the piano, of course — but had he really
understood how deeply it ran? After Ella's death he had plunged into
his responsibilities, new and old, finding in them a panacea for his
grief. Perhaps music played the same role for Yael.

The things we do to distract ourselves from the cold, hard facts of
our lives, he thought with a twinge of uncharacteristic depression.
Determinedly, he shook off the feeling. "Sorry to break up your
practice session, but it's that time again," he said with forced cheer.
"The table awaits your delicate touch."

"Can't Mordy — ?" Yael broke off the half-hearted plea in

midsentence. "I know, I know, it's my job. Okay." She hopped off the stool, closed the piano lid with a pat that was almost a caress, and wandered off to the kitchen in search of plates and silverware.

"She's pretty good."

Daniel turned, to find Jake standing in the doorway. "I think so too," he acknowledged. He patted his pocket. "Have to remember to call this new piano teacher later. Remind me, will you, Jake?"

"Will do."

Daniel led Jake into the living room, where his guest proceeded to enrapture Mordy with a series of fairly proficient magic tricks. Mrs. Marks appeared soon and announced that dinner was ready. In short order, the family was seated around the dining room table, chatting with the gangly law student as though they had known him all their lives. Jake had clearly made a hit with them all.

Yael cleared the table afterwards, throwing significant glances at her father and the telephone. With a mock sigh, Daniel rose from his seat. "Excuse me, Jake. I have an important call to make."

Yael paused, a stack of dirty plates in her arms, to beam at her father.

When the phone rang, at exactly 7:30, Sara jumped six inches.

Living alone was proving surprisingly pleasant — a balm for the soul — but the flip side was a vague nervousness that made her start at every unexpected noise.

She had been standing with her hand poised on the receiver, about to make a call, when the jangle erupted under her fingers. It took four rings for her to recapture her breath.

"H-hello?"

"Hello. May I speak to Miss Muller?"

"Speaking."

"I'm sorry, did I take you away from something? You sound out of breath."

Sara laughed, a trifle shakily. "No, really. The phone startled me, that's all."

"Oh? Then I apologize again." The man at the other end laughed, too. "I seem to be starting off this conversation with one apology after another — My name is Daniel Newman. I'm Yael's father. I understand that she's badgered you into agreeing to give her piano lessons."

"Oh! I'm glad you called, Mr. Newman." Yael had mentioned that her father was a judge. An image flashed instantly across the screen of Sara's mind: someone very tall — at least seven feet in her imagination — and very stately, with gleaming steel-gray hair, black judicial robes, glasses, and a frown. The frown did not go with the voice she was hearing, though — Firmly, she brought herself back to the matter at hand.

"Yael *has* been after me to give her lessons — but there was no badgering involved, honest. She's a sweet girl; it'll be a pleasure to teach her." Sara broke off.

"What is it? Is there a problem?"

"Well, I feel obligated to tell you that I've never actually done this before — not professionally. I'm a schoolteacher by trade, Mr. Newman, not a piano teacher. But Yael is certainly past the stage where she needs the strict format of beginning lessons. She knows the drills on her own by now, and can concentrate on perfecting her technique. I do think I can help her there."

"She says you play beautifully. 'Out of this world,' I believe, was her exact expression."

Sara blushed, glad he could not see through the phone. "Thank you," she said simply. "I love the piano."

"And so does Yael. Why don't we start right away — if you're available, that is — and see how it goes. If either one of us feels that Yael is not getting what she ought to be getting at this stage, we can always terminate the agreement."

"That sounds very businesslike."

"Well, isn't that the best way to conduct business?"

Sara's manner became equally brisk. "Of course it is. Shall we discuss my fee?"

That discussion lasted only a minute or two, with agreement being reached almost at once. Then came the question of logistics.

"I'm afraid I don't have a piano, Mr. Newman. I'm new in town, and —"

"I know, Yael told me. No problem; you can give lessons here at our house. Our housekeeper is usually here when Yael gets home from school, if that's a good time for you. In any case, I have a learning *seder* after work on Tuesdays so I get home later than usual. If you can make it every Tuesday, you and Yael will have the house to yourselves until I come home."

Sara considered. "I could drive Yael home on Tuesdays and give her the lesson immediately. I'd be out of your way by — oh, 5:30 or so."

"Is that all right for you? Good! It's all settled then. Yael will be thrilled. She reminded me at least a hundred times tonight to call you."

"Only a hundred?"

Daniel chuckled. "I'm exaggerating, of course. But she did seem anxious for us to settle the arrangements. Was she afraid you'd change your mind?"

"Well — I *was* reluctant, at first. Being new both in town and in the school, I've got plenty of adjusting and preparing to do. Yael was pretty persistent, though. And the more I got to know her, the more I liked her — and the idea of giving lessons."

"So that's what changed your mind?"

Sara hesitated. Looking around at the bare apartment, with its lone shelf of family pictures to remind her that she did belong to someone, somewhere, she threw caution to the winds and went for the truth.

"Actually," she said, "outside of work, there's not much else going on in my life right now."

Four minutes later, they hung up. And a minute after that, Sara was on the phone again, this time with her sister in New York. The sound of Debbie's familiar voice, droning on about the twins and the baby and a recent luncheon she had attended, helped fill some of the holes that loneliness had drilled into Sara's apartment, and her life — for the moment, anyway.

24

Hilda Newman often bemoaned the fact that time and the informality of the American culture had done away with the custom of afternoon tea. When the occasion permitted, she loved the ritual of cutting the tiny sandwiches, slicing the cake and, most of all, pouring tea in a fine, steady stream from her beautiful silver teapot. Hilda made sure to create numerous such occasions. This latest one was a meeting of the shul's sisterhood Executive Committee. Hilda Newman was serving as committee chairwoman this year. The current meeting was the first of the season.

She had trimmed the crusts off dainty cucumber-mayonnaise sandwiches and set them out on lace doilies. The cake was always something delicate: angel food, or air-light coconut sponge; this time both were present on the shining silver tray. Her friends smiled behind their hands at the way Hilda presided over her tea table like some old-fashioned character out of a Victorian novel — but the smiles were indulgent, and liberally laced with respect. There was nothing weak about the sisterhood chairwoman, as she proceeded to prove in the first moments of the meeting.

"While our membership is not exactly decreasing, it's also not growing the way it ought to be. I don't like standing still," she announced vigorously. "We've got to double our efforts this year — triple them! The more dynamic we are on behalf of the shul, and the more funds we manage to raise for it, the more appeal we'll have for those women who've been content to send their husbands to shul and leave their involvement at that."

She gazed around the table, her hazel eyes direct. In her genteel way she could be demanding, especially when there was a principle at stake. It was no coincidence that the son she had raised had grown up to become first a firebrand prosecution lawyer and then a judge. "Any suggestions? Ruth?"

The conversation became general, as the women bandied ideas for expanded sisterhood activities. Esther Mintz, acting secretary, wrote down every suggestion in her laborious script, making sure to include the other members' reactions to each one. The minutes ended with a quick summary of the chairwoman's closing words, before the meeting was formally adjourned and the ladies turned their attention to the fine tea Hilda had prepared.

"Action requires leadership," Hilda Newman concluded forcefully. "As your leader this year, I intend to do more than my share to generate funds and increase membership. I view this in the light of a personal quest. Except for the months of January and February which, as you know, my husband and I spend in Florida each year, I pledge myself to work harder than anyone to achieve our goals."

These words were received with a smattering of applause. No one — least of all Hilda herself — had any reason to guess that before too long, she would have to unsay them.

"Hilda?" Jonathan Newman turned his head toward the study door. "Is that you?"

His wife stepped lightly into the book-lined room. There was a smell of new leather here, from the matching easy chair and loveseat she had installed when Jon retired from his job last month. The walls were richly paneled, the thick carpet a comfort to aging soles. A small fireplace was there to dispense welcome warmth as the days grew shorter.

Hilda never walked into this study without a sense of satisfaction. Retirement was the next stage in a long and rewarding life together; as with every other stage, she was determined to approach it with vigor and efficiency. She smiled at her husband as she sank into the loveseat opposite his armchair. "Yes, we're all finished. It looks like a busy year coming up for the sisterhood."

"That's nice." There was an odd, strained note in Jon's voice. Even in the midst of her pleasant musings on the horde of activities lying in wait for her, Hilda's ear caught it.

"What's the matter, dear? Are you feeling all right?"

Looking more closely, she noticed the pallor in his cheeks, under the receding but still thick silver hair. He had removed his reading glasses when she had walked in, and the hollows beneath his eyes were dark and pronounced.

When he did not answer at once, she got up and went to him. Crouching to look into his face, she insisted, "Tell me, Jon. Is it the pain again?"

He nodded. "I took the nitroglycerin just before you came in. I'll be all right in a minute."

Hilda hesitated, then straightened and said decisively, "I'm calling the doctor. You don't look good to me."

"Hilda, I'm fine. This has happened before, and it'll happen again. The pills are all I need."

"We'll see what the doctor says about that."

Jon Newman was an old and valued patient. Apart from recommending a host of his acquaintances as patients, he had donated a generous sum toward the building of a new wing at the hospital where Dr. Blaustein practiced. At Hilda's request, the doctor had his receptionist clear a space on his calendar that very afternoon.

Turning a deaf ear to her husband's grumbling, Hilda coaxed him into the passenger seat of their Lincoln and pulled carefully out of the driveway.

An hour later, Dr. Blaustein smiled reassuringly at his patient and told him he could put on his shirt. "I'll just step outside while you get dressed, Jon. Be back in a minute."

"What is it, doctor?" Hilda asked, almost before the door to the consulting room had swung shut behind them. He motioned her into his private office, just a step away, and waited while she sank into a chair in front of his massive desk. The hands she clasped in her lap were long fingered and beginning to show faint brown age-spots. Right now, they were trembling. "How is he?"

The doctor rounded the desk and took his own seat. Once again, the reassuring smile appeared on his face. "He's not substantially worse,

Mrs. Newman. Then again, he's no better. I don't like his color, or the fact that his blood pressure is slightly more elevated than the last time I checked."

Hilda leaned forward, clasping her hands tighter to still the trembling. "Is there anything you'd suggest? Some new treatment?"

"As a matter of fact, there is."

"Not — not surgery again."

"No, not this time. Your husband's not a good candidate for further open-heart surgery, Mrs. Newman. But with proper diet and care, he could live many more years."

"I feed him exactly what you told me! Jon can complain till he's blue in the face, but no steaks or eggs or whipped cream. What else can I do?"

The doctor tilted his chair back so that he was viewing Mrs. Newman along the bridge of his nose — an arrogant angle which his accompanying smile rendered completely inoffensive. "Tell me, Mrs. Newman. How has Jonathan taken to retirement?"

"Oh, he's been keeping himself really busy. He walks miles every day, works in the garden mornings and afternoons, sits over his Gemara at least a few hours a day, putters in his garage work-room —"

"The part about the Gemara is fine," Dr. Blaustein said, sitting abruptly upright, "and so is some mild form of exercise. But I've suspected — and you've just confirmed — that Jon's overdoing things. Given the state of his heart, he needs a routine that is quieter, and certainly less arduous. Can you see that he gets it, Mrs. Newman?"

She frowned doubtfully. "I can try. But I'm not always home, and he does love to get under the sink to tighten a nut, or work at his workbench. You know Jon."

He nodded. "Yes, I do. And that's why I'm going to suggest that the only way to slow him down would be to remove him from temptation."

"Remove —?"

"Get him away from his toolbox and his garden for a while. Mrs. Newman, the two of you go down to Florida in the winters, don't you?"

"Yes, we do. But that's in January — nearly four months away."

The doctor spoke slowly, and with enough gravity to lend his words a chilling emphasis. "*Go now*, Mrs. Newman. Get Jon away, someplace as quiet and as boring as possible. No late nights, nothing more strenuous than a gentle stroll along the boardwalk. Someplace where you can keep an eye on him, away from all the distractions that keep you both so busy outside the home."

"I take good care of my husband," Hilda protested, sitting up straight, face flushed. "Are you implying —"

"Please, I am implying nothing. I only want to impress upon you the importance of what I'm saying. Take him to Florida soon, this month. Jon needs peace and quiet. His *heart* needs it."

"He'll hate it. He'll be bored to tears."

"Better that," Dr. Blaustein said, fixing her with a level gaze, "than the alternative." Hilda blanched.

"Is — is it that serious?"

He sighed. "It could be. Your husband's heart is not strong, Mrs. Newman. Tenderly coaxed along, it could tick on for years. But we've got to be careful. Very careful."

With a sleepwalker's dazed look, Hilda stood up and took a step toward the door, murmuring, "He'll be wondering where I am so long."

The doctor rounded the desk again and came to stand beside her. "Will you take my advice?"

She looked at him in surprise. "Of course I will! Did you have any doubt of that? You're the doctor — and he's my husband!"

"In that case," the younger man smiled, "I have no worries for Jon. He's in good hands."

"The best," Hilda said firmly. "You can bet on that." Wide awake now, and brimming with resolution, she started for the door, and her husband.

A quarter of an hour later, they were pulling into the driveway of their handsome brick home. The garden was in its fading stages, summer's vibrant palette beginning to pale to muted browns. Rich green stems had turned to brittle stalks. There was little that needed to be done here now. In due course the garden would take its long winter sleep, and in the early spring, please G-d, she and Jon would be back to oversee its awakening.

She walked up to the front door behind her husband and watched him grope for his key. More than ever before, she would be the protector. Jon would not be pleased, but he would be given no choice in the matter. This was a battle for his life.

Coming home in the car, she had already outlined the doctor's plan — and her intention of following it to the letter.

"Florida — now?" Jon had protested. "But it'll be hot as blazes down there in September. Let's at least wait for the fall to set in."

"We can't wait," Hilda had said stolidly. A patina of calm overlay a huge abyss of panic — an abyss she refused to recognize. "At the risk of sounding heartless, dear, if you're hot, you can stay inside in the air conditioning. Please don't take this badly, Jon. You're only making the inevitable more difficult. The doctor says it's absolutely necessary."

Every further protest was met with the same courteous but implacable resistance. Eventually Jonathan subsided, staring gloomily out of the window as his wife navigated the car along the broad, shaded Baltimore streets, toward home.

"Why don't you lie down and take a little nap?" Hilda asked as they went inside. "I've got some calls to make."

Grumbling, he went off to do as she had suggested — more tired than he cared to admit. Hilda kicked off her high-heeled pumps and made for the telephone.

Her first call was to the sisterhood, to resign her chairmanship. With a pang, she recalled her impassioned words earlier that afternoon. *"I view this in the light of a personal quest."*

The sisterhood and its goals seemed almost trivial now, and incredibly remote. As of today, she had a different quest. Even if she vaguely regretted the need to sharply curtail the scope of her own interesting and varied activities, the feeling was so overshadowed by her fear for her husband's health, and her love for and sense of obligation toward him, as to become nearly irrelevant.

Her second call was to her travel agent, to book their seats on a flight to Miami later in the month. There would be another call, perhaps in the morning, to the employment agency she used down there for cleaning help. She would have to contact the newspapers and periodicals to which they subscribed, as well as arrange for someone to take in the mail and water her plants.

But all that would come later. Right now, she picked up the phone to make her third and last call for the moment — to her older son, Daniel.

At any other time, her finely attuned maternal ear would have caught the unusual nuance in Daniel's voice as he picked up her call. But right now all her senses, and all her anxiety, were directed toward her husband. She was like a radio set on a single frequency, unable for the moment to receive any other signal.

Ignorance played its part, too. Hilda had no way of knowing that the phone had already rung three times that evening in Daniel's house, and that each time his "Hello?" had been met with a silence that grew progressively more ominous. He had been at the point of slamming down the receiver yet again, when he heard his mother's "Danny, it's me," at the other end.

He made an effort to steady his breathing. "Oh, hi, Mom. How are you?"

"Thank G-d, I'm fine. Your father's not doing so well, though." Before Daniel could break in with the inevitable questions, she hurried on. "Danny, listen. We're going down to Florida early this year — this month, in fact. I'd like to leave right after Rosh Hashanah and stay until after Purim. Doctor's orders."

"Rosh Hashanah?" Daniel echoed, stupefied.

"And I just had a marvelous idea. I want you and the kids to join us in Miami for Sukkos!"

What Hilda expected to hear was a prompt, and pleased, "Of course!" She would not have been surprised at an elaboration on the theme, as Daniel reflected aloud on his children's pleasure at the prospect.

What she did not expect was the loaded silence that met her invitation — or the hesitation in her son's voice as he said, "Mom, that sounds nice. But this may not be the best time for us to go away — I'll have to think it over and get back to you."

"Think it over? What's there to think about?" Astonishment edged quickly into dismay — and anger. Didn't Daniel know that she needed him, now more than ever?

But Daniel was not saying what he did or did not know. At the moment, he preferred to keep his thoughts to himself.

25

At first glance, Sukkos in Miami seemed the answer to his prayers. It represented escape — escape from the nightmare threats and unanswered questions that were keeping Daniel's nerves dancing at razor's edge almost continually.

Last night's silent caller had shaken Daniel more than he cared to admit. While he could not be positive that the caller and the letter writer were one and the same, it would be stretching coincidence too far to deny that the possibility existed. His intuition, for that matter, was screaming "probability." And Garrity, when Daniel had phoned him to report this latest unsettling development, emphatically agreed.

"Can we meet tomorrow afternoon?" the detective asked. "I'd like to start going through those records right away. You never know when some name might jump out at one of us."

"Tomorrow it is," Daniel had answered quickly, grateful for the prospect of some action, other than the worry gnawing at his innards.

"And I'm ordering a car to be stationed outside your house, Dan."

Automatic resistance flared up, and then died on Daniel's lips. Hesitantly, he asked, "Can you use an unmarked one?"

"Sure. That's what I had in mind. No need to advertise our presence in the neighborhood." Garrity paused. "On the other hand, maybe we *should* make our presence known. That would serve as the best deterrent to anyone with evil intentions."

Daniel thought about that. "Let's start with the unmarked car," he said finally, "but only after the next written message comes."

"What makes you so sure that another one will come before a bullet does?" a disgusted Garrity demanded. "Dan, gimme a break!"

"We had a deal."

"All right, all right. No unmarked car until we hear from our friend again. It won't be long, Dan."

Daniel sighed. "I hope you're wrong about that."

"But you're afraid I'm not. Right?"

"Terrified," Daniel confessed.

Abruptly, Garrity asked, "So what time do we meet?"

Sharing his fears with the detective calmed Daniel to the point where he was able, for the first time in a while, to fall asleep within minutes of hitting the pillow. He carried the elusive newfound calm along with him to the courthouse that morning — where it rapidly evaporated in response to the prosecutor's line of questioning in the Simmonds trial.

The prosecution's opening witness was the police officer who had been first on the scene of Al Simmonds' murder. A man of broad shoulders and a ruddy complexion, the officer clearly savored his moment in the spotlight. As he testified with gruesome pleasure to what he had seen in the Downings' garden — putting special emphasis on the quantity of blood found on the body and surrounding area — Daniel found himself clenching his fists out of sight behind his podium.

This enthusiastic witness was followed by the state medical examiner, who described the death wounds in gruesome — and, in Daniel's opinion, quite unnecessary — detail. The grisly images mingled in the judge's mind with his memory of Ella, huddled shapelessly behind the wheel of her crumpled car, blood spread in a grotesque new-age design all around her. This, in turn, gave way to a nightmare vision of his children, Heaven forbid, held at gunpoint by some vindictive madman. His forehead was damp, his nerves stretched taut as a piano wire. His agitation grew so extreme that he had to struggle violently against the urge to call a short recess. Such weakness ran contrary to every habit and precept he owned. Mustering all his reserve, he asked his clerk for a glass of water instead.

All day long — like a photograph of white beaches and palm trees glimpsed in a travel brochure and filed away in some anticipatory mental compartment — Miami lay at the back of his mind. The image offered a blessed, if temporary, reprieve from the strain of his existence — a strain his children knew nothing about, but whose effect they would certainly begin to feel, sooner rather than later, if they had not begun to feel it already.

And "strained" was the very word he would have used to describe the look on Elsa Downing's face as she followed the progress of her husband's trial with the rapt intensity of some medieval lady watching her champion battle for life and honor on the jousting field. Her fingers twisted together constantly, eyes darting from attorney to witness to judge and back again in never-ending motion.

By contrast, the defendant himself was calm, almost listless. He heard various witnesses speak about events that had taken place in the garden of his home, without seeming to really listen. Daniel recognized this apathy; he had seen it often in trials of hardened criminals. But he knew enough to understand that the air of uncaring might just as easily be the child of despair.

This trial had gripped Daniel's imagination as nothing else had done in a long while. *Had* Downing, in a passion of rage, picked up a knife on that night, months ago, and repeatedly stabbed his partner with it? There had been no weapon on Simmonds' person, effectively ruling out a plea of self-defense. Nor was there evidence that the two had engaged in any sort of physical scuffle before the actual murder. Simmonds had trusted his assailant, up until the second the knife had plunged into his heart.

Who was he, the man behind the knife? Was there another player in this game, waiting to step up and be identified? And if so, what was his relationship to Simmonds, and what motive had goaded him — or her — to dispense so violently with him?

Was Henry Downing a ruthless killer or an innocent victim? And what, if anything, did his wife know about the events of that tragic night? She had begun the evening by playing hostess — tossing a salad, and basting a roast perhaps, as she waited for the guest to arrive — and ended it by phoning the police to report a murder. What had occurred in between?

Difficult questions, though he hoped the trial would answer most of them to his satisfaction. For the amount of time that he sat on the judge's bench, the questions distracted him from the equally difficult ones that plagued his own life.

Questions. Were the death threats legitimate? Had they been written by someone he knew — someone, perhaps, whom he had sent to prison in the past?

What were the threatener's intentions? What had he meant by saying that Ella's death had been no accident? How far should he allow the police into his and his children's lives? And what should he do about his mother's invitation to Miami for Sukkos?

He thought, initially, at least he had the answer to this last question. At first glance, it seemed like the answer to his prayers.

But only at first.

It was at the end of his day's work, as he waited in his chambers for Garrity to appear, that emotion receded, and logic, with a painful whirring of rusty gears, reasserted itself.

Sukkos in Miami would be fine — but only if the stalker had been apprehended by that time. Otherwise, the move would be a foolish one. It made no sense to suspend activities for nine days while he basked in the Florida sun. Coming home, he would only have to face the threat again, with that much time lost that might have been spent tracking down the shadowy figure. What Daniel needed to do now was to concentrate on pinning an identity on the writer of the anonymous letters. He needed to resolve the matter, quickly and definitively, so that he could sleep at night. So that Mordy and Yael would not just *seem* safe, in far-off Florida, but would actually *be* safe.

Another horrifying possibility struck him. If he and his kids could board a plane to Miami, so could a stranger intent on doing them harm. Away from their home turf, they would be that much more vulnerable. Or he might be waiting for them, armed and ready, the moment they returned — waiting to catch them off balance.

Running away for a week or more prior to the stalker being caught would only prolong the suspense — and the danger. The decision made itself: His response at this time must be fight, not flight.

His mother would not be happy about it.

His mouth twisted wryly. Not happy? She would be furious! Especially now, with his father's health more precarious than ever, she would expect a rallying around of the troops. Chaim, the younger son, was no substitute: His large family would never fit into the compact Florida condominium. Besides, since Ella's death Daniel's parents had

made a point of spending holidays with him and the children. Refusing his mother's invitation would make him seem ungrateful and
even lacking in proper respect. And Daniel could make no attempt to
ease that impression by explaining just how matters stood with him.
Now, more than ever, Mom and Dad needed to be protected.

A rap at the door heralded Garrity's arrival. Daniel rose to greet
him, glad for the interruption to an unpleasant train of thought. Most
of the courthouse staff had left for the day, and the detective's steps
echoed sharply beneath the splendid, high ceilings.

"Hi, Mark, have a seat. I'd offer you a Coke, but I see you've come
equipped." Garrity had walked in with a can uptilted to his mouth.

Lowering the can, Garrity grinned. "Sorry about the lack of
manners — but it's a scorcher out there. Hasn't anyone been informed
that summer's over?"

"It's this crazy Baltimore weather," Daniel said, pulling a heap of
files into the center of his desk. "Chill you to the bone one day and
simmer you in a gravy of humidity the next. But it's nice and cool in
here, Mark. Let's get cracking."

"Sure." Garrity grabbed a stack of files. "By the way, that last letter
was useless. As I expected, all we got was a jumble of overlapping
fingerprints, belonging apparently to the postal workers who handled
the thing."

"And the first?"

"Again, as expected. Clean as a whistle." He hefted a few folders,
squinting at the date on the top one. "These five years old?"

"Yes. I went back to about twelve months before Ella's accident."

Thoughtfully, Garrity said, "Don't forget, we're looking for someone you sent up the river. However vengeful he was feeling, he'd have
had to wait till he got out."

Daniel glanced up sharply. "So we're looking for short sentences?
Say, under a year?"

"Maybe —"

"A short sentence means we're talking petty crime. First-time
offenders, mitigating circumstances, low prospect of recidivism.
Mark, that doesn't sound like the type of guy who would push a
woman off the highway in a rainstorm."

Daniel was vaguely astonished to hear himself speak in so detached
a fashion of his life's greatest tragedy. As much as he had refused to

believe the well-wishers who had tried so earnestly to convince him, time really did work a change all on its own. The simple passage of the years had blunted the pain he had thought he would carry around forever like a bullet lodged permanently in the heart. The pain was still there, but muted, like a memory.

Garrity lifted the can to his mouth in search of the last elusive drops. "Easy now," he said, as a well-aimed toss hurled the can into a wastepaper basket. "We're jumping to a whole series of conclusions here. In fact, the whole premise of letters-as-revenge is a leap. But we've got to start somewhere, and this seems to me to be the most logical place." He tapped the stack of folders in front of him on the table. "Here's another thing. Your wife's accident — assuming the letters are right, and it *was* no accident — could have been perpetrated by someone else. A buddy of the crook you put away, or a relative."

"That's a possibility," Daniel admitted. "He could have had someone act for him almost immediately after sentencing. That way, the length of the sentence wouldn't matter. In fact, a longer sentence would give us more of a motive."

"A quick worker — and one with a long memory. He's held this grudge for at least five years."

Daniel chewed his lip in frustration. "So where do we start? I served as prosecuting attorney for nine years. That's a lot of trials, and a lot of jail sentences. Do we go all the way back to my first day on the job?"

"It may come to that. But I always like to start with the simplest route first, the most obvious. Revenge comes from anger, and anger can stay fire-hot only so long. I say we stick to the original plan and look for someone you put away not long before Ella's death. A year sounds about right."

"Okay." Daniel drew a long breath, then divided the stack of folders in half and drew his portion toward him. "Let's stop to compare notes in twenty minutes or so."

A silence descended as judge and detective pored over the files. To Garrity, they were only an anonymous list of names and crimes. For Daniel, each case he reviewed brought back a flood of memories: Hours of burning the midnight oil in advance of a trial, searching for the one clue, the single piece of evidence, that would convince the jury he had nailed their man. Performing on the courtroom stage, drawing on every persuasive trick he could think of to make sure that yet another criminal spent the next weeks or months or years away from the society he had abused. Living and breathing each trial until he succeeded in sending another crook off to prison — or conceded defeat.

"I've got a couple of names," Garrity said, when the twenty minutes were up. "I skipped what I'd call the small-time wimps — the Peeping Toms, the shoplifters, the petty thieves. If we're barking up the right tree, it makes more sense to look for harder crime and longer prison sentences."

"A big 'if'," Daniel pointed out dryly. "But I've been barking up the same one. Let's see who you've got."

Garrity handed Daniel two files. Daniel skimmed them, nodded once, then added the two names to the three he had jotted down on a notepad by his elbow. He sat still, staring down at the list.

1. Mario Esplanada - Armed robbery. Fifteen years.
2. Carl Sandhurst - Grand-scale embezzlement. Fourteen years.
3. Gerry Towson - Felony involuntary manslaughter. Twenty years.
4. Salvatore Mercutio - Armed robbery, attempted murder, and inflicting grievous injury. Twenty-five years to life.
5. Alexander Freehy - Theft and attempted arson. Eleven years.

26

The pervasive smell of plaster hung over the Chaim Newman household in a persistent cloud. A white pall had settled everywhere — on the surfaces of the furniture, on the floors, draped over the family's shoulders like a second skin. It tickled throats and even turned the children's hair prematurely gray.

The Newmans were renovating.

Tova, the 12-year-old on whose behalf these discomforts were being borne, was beside herself with excitement. "A room of my own! Ma, Ta, you're the greatest!"

Chaim did not feel like the greatest. He felt like a man in debt. The *gemach* (interest-free loan) he had managed to wrangle would cover, he hoped, the cost of converting the unused porch into a bedroom for Tova. As for the finishing touches that were needed to turn four walls into a room, Chaim supposed they would have to dip into their savings for those — their nearly nonexistent savings. The family was just managing to meet its monthly expenses on what he made in his administrator's job, plus Gila's much more modest earnings; she worked out of their home as a billing clerk. Squeezing the budget to allow for putting away even a minuscule amount for a rainy day was like extracting water from the proverbial rock. And they were still paying off Mendy's braces.

Financial anxiety gnawed at Chaim incessantly, even as he tried, ostrichlike, to escape into an illusory sense of well-being. He kidded Tova about her imminent rise in life, expressing the hope that she would deign now and then to poke her head out of her new room to say hello to the family. For Gila's benefit, he maintained a determinedly cheerful facade even in private. But the anxiety remained — not a single adversary, but a thousand burrowing worms making themselves at home in his innards. They made good companions to the mole of shame — over his lackluster earning power — that had already dug its snug domicile deep inside the man.

Apart from Tova, no one else in the family was particularly cheerful at this juncture. The boys, whose bedroom adjoined the porch presently undergoing surgery, were shifted willy-nilly into the living room, where people were constantly tripping over them or their belongings. Tova's little sisters, upset by all the chaos, burst frequently into tears that grated on everyone's nerves. The workers were loud and obtrusive, tramping often into Gila's kitchen for cold drinks or hot ones, or to use the telephone. She shared brittle laughter with her friends over this, and waited with mounting impatience for the work to be done.

The thumping went on, and the sawing and drilling, and the drone of strangers' voices in the sanctum of their home. And all of it resting on a foundation of borrowed money.

Chaim was brooding over this point one evening as he played the dutiful husband and father. The workers had lingered late, leaving Gila running behind with her supper preparations and the children hungry and cranky as a result. Somehow, as his mind added up figures in an ever-narrowing budget, Chaim marshaled the kids through the last difficult hour before the meal. Finally, at Gila's signal, they sat down to eat. A rose-colored sunset stained the windows and lay a fairylike patina over the clutter in the adjoining living room. Chaim was trying — without any great measure of success — to enjoy the sunset and banish his omnipresent anxiety, when the phone rang.

"Let the machine get it," Gila suggested, ladling soup into bowls with robotlike efficiency. But Mendy had already sprung out of his chair — the kid must, Chaim had often reflected, have jack-in-the-box blood in him — to snatch up the receiver.

"It's Bubby! Who wants to talk to Bubby?"

"You take it, Chaim," Gila said, her ladling arm never breaking its rhythm.

"Hi, Mom." Chaim cleared his throat and began again. "How are you? And Dad?"

His eyebrows flew into his hairline as Hilda Newman filled him in on the abrupt change in their plans. "Is Dad feeling all right? I mean, is this an emergency, or what?" he asked anxiously.

As usual, his worrying seemed only to annoy his mother. "Dad's fine," she said testily. "He just needs to slow down, and that's why we're making the move to Miami this month." Her tone sharpened. "I invited Danny and the kids to come down for Sukkos —"

"And — ?" he prompted.

"And he just turned me down! I've never heard a poorer excuse, either. He said the kids would miss their friends over the holiday. I know he's always trying to give Yael and Mordy all the security they lost when Ella died — but this is ridiculous!" She drew a shaky breath. "I can't believe this is my Daniel. He really hurt my feelings."

Against his will, a thrill rippled through Chaim. It was unusual for his mother to confide in him this way — and she never voiced any complaints about Danny, her golden boy. Chaim knew his mother thought of him as spineless, unambitious, and careless about the respect and the salary that she believed ought to go along with his responsibilities at the yeshivah. It was only Danny's tumble from favor that had catapulted him temporarily into the vacancy of her favor. The instant that mother and son reconciled their petty difference, Chaim would be relegated to the shadows again. This he knew all too well.

But the moment was too precious to renounce. He would savor the feeling for as long as it lasted.

"That's too bad, Mom," he said cautiously. "I'm sure Danny knows what he's doing — doesn't he always? But I can understand why your feelings would be hurt."

"With Daddy not well and both of us worried, wouldn't you think he could put his own affairs aside for once? It's not as if I drag him down to Florida every year. Usually we spend Sukkos together at *his* house."

"I know, I know." Chaim was soothing. "Look, there's no use being upset over something you can't change. Let's think of ways to brighten up the time until you and Dad leave." He hesitated. "How about a Sunday visit? Gila and I can pile all the kids into the station wagon and stage an invasion. Sound good?"

"Sounds good," Hilda admitted, grudgingly allowing herself to be diverted. "If the weather holds out, we can barbecue out on the patio."

"The kids'll love that. And it'll give all of us a chance to get away from this awful dust and clutter."

"What's that?" Hilda asked, instantly alert. "What dust?"

"Didn't we tell you?" Chaim was genuinely surprised. "I thought for sure Gila must have said something. We're doing some renovating, Mom. Tova's finally going to get a room of her own. We're making it out of the little porch off the boys' room, the one that's never used."

"Gila did mention something, but I didn't know you'd already begun work . . . "

Hilda had a hundred questions, and a thousand pieces of sage advice. The conversation proceeded very satisfactorily from that point, with Hilda apparently having pushed Danny's defection to one side to concentrate on her younger son's affairs. It ended with her decision to drive to Baltimore the next day to see how the work was progressing.

"I would have liked for us to spend a Shabbos together before Dad and I leave for Miami." She sounded genuinely regretful.

"Can't you find the time to come?"

"Rosh Hashanah's just a week away, and we're leaving right after that. But tell Tova that Zaydie and I plan to give her something nice to dress up her room when it's finished," she promised.

"Thanks, Mom. She'll be delighted."

"Or, better yet, let's surprise her!" Hilda amended gaily.

"You got it, Mom. It'll be our secret."

"Our secret. "

They hung up seconds later on the most cordial of terms. Despite himself, Chaim could not help feeling as smug as a small boy whose parents have favored him specially. Danny was in the doghouse, while Chaim and his mother shared a happy little secret. He was smiling as he returned to the table.

"How's everything with Mom and Dad?" Gila asked, looking up from her plate.

In a few words, Chaim updated her on the state of his father's health, his parents' travel plans, and the invitation that Daniel had inexplicably declined. Skipping over his mother's wrath, he informed the family of the projected Sunday visit to the grandparents.

"A barbecue — yay!" Nachum whooped.

"Will Uncle Danny and the cousins come up from Cedar Hills?" Tova asked eagerly.

Chaim frowned. "I'm not sure if they're invited. A crowd might be too much for Zaydie just now."

"What's three more people?" Tova persisted. "They *have* to come! I'm going to call Yael later to make sure they know about it."

Something in Chaim's manner alerted his wife. "Your father is right," Gila said firmly, turning to fix a piercing eye on her eldest daughter. "Don't make any calls, Tova. It's up to Bubby and Zaydie to decide whom they want to invite."

Wide eyed, scenting something she did not understand but instinctively wary of finding out what it was, Tova persisted, "But of *course* they'll want Uncle Danny. Why shouldn't they?"

Gila and Chaim exchanged a quick look. Tova waited expectantly for an answer to her question. But — "Finish your soup, it's getting cold," was all her mother would say.

In nearby Cedar Hills, the same sunset was spreading its rosy net. On Daniel Newman's block, a stealthy figure took advantage of the gathering gloom to slip through a side door into the twilight shadows. As far as he had been able to discern from his basement lookout, the block was empty at the moment. Everyone was inside, enjoying their dinners and a few moments of well-earned repose after the day's labors.

The watcher was going out for his own dinner. Somewhat in the nature of an appetizer, he wolfed down a couple of stale chocolate bars before setting out. Sugar always settled his stomach when he was nervous — and the combination of boredom, indecision, and the need to be invisible just to get himself a hot meal was proving lethal to his calm.

Hands in his pockets, he slouched up the street toward the bus. Nobody passed him; nobody noticed him. In his workman's overalls, he was truly as good as invisible.

27

He was not quite sure what he was waiting for.

This letter-writing business was all right as it was, he thought as he boarded the bus (he had considered bringing his battered old jeep into the neighborhood but had rejected the idea as too risky). The pacing of it was what had him stymied. On the one hand, he did not want to rush things. Instinctively, he sensed that it was good to let the judge go several days without any sign of him. Good to let the suspense build, to let the not-knowing become intolerable . . . On the other hand, too much waiting made him feel like climbing out of his skin.

His job was to find the right pace and the right methods. There was no doubt that this campaign of psychological terror was deeply satisfying. The problem was how to structure that campaign for maximum effectiveness.

There would be, he had decided from the start, six in all: a letter for each year of Sal's imprisonment. A layer of brick in the wall of terror surrounding the judge for each year the watcher's brother had rotted in his cell. Then the kidnapping, and the extortion of cash: recompense for all the money Sal, in jail, had never got a chance to lay his hands on.

And then — the crown of his plan. Death — to counter the death of his beloved older brother.

Justice.

The other night's silent phone calls had been a spur-of-the moment thing, something to pass the time and stretch the judge's nerves a little thinner. He had derived an almost physical pleasure from dialing the Newmans' number from a phone booth several blocks away. He had heard the judge's voice tighten in rising panic with each successive call. That had been good. That was the way he wanted it. He hoped that knotted nerves — if not actual terror — had kept the judge tossing in bed all night. The watcher had slept exceptionally well.

But it was time for something more concrete. Tomorrow, he would pull out the stationery and the latex gloves for another round of letter-writing. This one would be number three.

The thought should have been laced with anticipation. It was not. Repetition was dull. The campaign itself was exciting, but the weapons at his disposal needed varying. Just how to vary them was the question that had been vexing him as he peered through his binoculars into the Newman windows, night after night.

His answer came unexpectedly, and from the most unexpected of sources.

The watcher was not an especially dutiful son, but his mother made life miserable for him if he did not stop in at the old house at least once every few weeks. There, for an hour or two, he would fill up on pasta and Mama's recriminations. The latter had increased in length and become laced, now that Sal was gone, with a grievous self-pity. With the hope of the family gone, it was up to the younger brother to make a success of his life. Mama was not optimistic about his chances.

"I'm gonna be a rich man soon, Mama," he boasted as he dug into a plate of steaming ravioli. "I'll buy you a fur coat just like Aunt Gina's, you wait and see."

"I'm waiting," Mama said sourly, placing a green salad and some oil-and-vinegar dressing on the table, though she knew he never touched vegetables. She was a small woman with graying hair worn pulled back from a pinched, sad face. Her apron sagged at the hips. "All my life I've been waiting. Sal, at least, remembered to call. He ended up in jail, the sainted boy, but he was still the best son a mother could have. I carry him here "— mournfully, she thumped her chest — "every day. Every night, I pray for him. Even in heaven, I know he's looking out for his old momma. But you —" she turned resentful, tired eyes on her second son, "you don't call, *and* you don't make anything of yourself. Your poor Papa would turn over in his grave!" The tears began flowing, as, cynically, he had known they would.

He made a valiant effort. "Mama, I may not call a lot, but I do come to visit, right? Look, I'm here now! I'm eating your ravioli. It's great ravioli!" To prove his point he forked up another mouthful.

"Yeah, you come to eat. For food, you'll come. But for your poor old Mama, all alone in the world, do you come? Do you care? "

Her voice had risen dramatically. Next she would remind him about the time he had called the nun a bad name and been expelled from Catholic school. She attributed all his subsequent failures to that pivotal episode. He strove hastily to avert this.

"Mama, are you listening to me? I'm gonna be rich. It won't be long now. You'll have furs, a diamond ring like Aunt Gina, high-heeled shoes like Aunt Marie. You'll have everything you want!"

"Can I wear high heels, with my poor feet worn out from standing in the store all day? High heels!"

"Ma, I promise —"

"All I get from you is promises. Empty promises! Your brother Sal, at least he used to call —"At the mention of her dead son's name, tears began to spurt again from her tired eyes, to dribble in hopeless little rivulets down her cheeks.

It was always the same.

He bolted his ravioli and escaped as quickly as he could, thankful to step away from the walls that breathed recrimination, to pass through the door that screamed his guilt. It was good to breathe the impersonal early-evening air — the nonjudgmental air. There was a soft breeze tonight, mild as summer. The stars hung low, almost brushing the tops of the slow-swaying trees. The thought of his dank basement hideout seemed hideous at the moment. On impulse, he decided to visit Vinny Fouza, an old school friend.

Vinny lived down the block. They had hung around together as youths and fallen into various scrapes together, repeatedly skirting the edges of the law. Surprisingly, Vinny had straightened himself out this past year, started going to college. His passion was computers.

As he opened the door, Vinny blinked at him in the uncertain light of dusk. "Hey, Joey, is that you? Howya doing, man? Come in. "

He led the way into a shabby but painfully neat living room. The carpet had once been emerald and was now the color of the sea — an indeterminate grayish-green. A suite of matching floral couches faced each other over a glass coffee table. Joe slumped onto one of the couches and helped himself to a handful of peanuts from a ceramic dish. Vinny remained standing, hands in his pockets. From the kitchen, vague splashings and the squawking of a radio spoke of Vinny's mother at the sink.

"Busy?" Joe asked.

"Nah. Just fooling around on the computer. You know, e-mail, Internet, all that stuff."

Joe did not want to look foolish. Straightening the cuffs of his leather jacket, he asked with elaborate casualness, "E-mail?"

"Yeah. You know, sending stuff over the computer. It's like mailing a letter, only faster. So fast that we call the regular kind 'snail mail.' Get it?" Vinny chortled.

A light ignited in Joe's brain. Popping peanuts into his mouth to hide the excited trembling of his hands, he drawled, "Wanna show me how it works?"

Vinny needed no further prompting. "Sure, come on." Abandoning the frightfully correct living room, they climbed a narrow staircase to Vinny's bedroom. The bed was unmade, with clothes strewn over the end of it and spilling off onto the ancient rug on the floor. With the tip of his sneakered foot, Joe shoved aside a pile of what looked like freshly washed laundry next to the doorway. Vinny seemed unaware of anything but the gleaming computer sitting proudly in its place on a scarred wooden desk against one wall.

He sat down in front of the machine, calling over his shoulder, "Hey, Joey, pull up a seat." Vinny flipped a switch and the monitor came to life.

Joe stared into the blue depths of the screen, mesmerized. Finally tearing his eyes away, he dragged a spindly chair across the room and lined it up beside his friend's. Under Vinny's questing fingers, icons flashed and metamorphosed.

"What e-mail does, "Vinny said conversationally as he deployed his mouse, "is cut through what we call cyberspace. That's just another word for thin air. All you have to do is put in the address you want, type the message in here "— he indicated a large white box — "and off it goes," he snapped his fingers, "just like that. Pretty cool, eh?"

"Pretty cool," Joe said absently. His mind was spinning furiously, turning over possibilities. "Vinny, if I wanted, could I send an e-mail from your computer?"

"What? Oh, sure, sure. No problem." Vinny was intent on the changing windows on the screen. "Do you know the person's address? That's an e-mail address, not the number on the front of the house."

"No. I don't know it." Joe was first nonplused, then angry. "Is there any way you could help me find it out?"

"There are ways. But are you sure this guy *has* e-mail? Not everyone does yet, you know."

"I'm not sure. I'm not sure of nothin'! But let's find out — right now." There was an edge to Joe's voice that made Vinny glance at him, curious. Then he shrugged and returned to his screen." I'm game." He mobilized and switched search engines until he found the one he wanted. In suspenseful silence, Joe watched his friend work the keyboard, mysterious as an artifact in some exotic and incomprehensible tribal ritual. Computers were a locked room to him and always had been. Probably always would be. But there are ways of jimmying the lock on even the stoutest of doors — and Vinny was the tool he was going to use to do it.

"Okay," Vinny said at last, fingers poised. "Name?"

Joe hesitated. "This stays between you and me, Vinny."

"Sure, no problem." Vinny paused, half-turned in his chair to peer at him. "What's the matter — you in trouble, Joey?"

"Nah. Not me." *But someone else is going to be, real soon.* "And one more thing."

"Yeah?" Vinny was growing impatient.

"I need to type the message myself. It's private."

"Okay, okay. Let's get started already. What's the name?"

"Newman," Joe said slowly, relishing every syllable. "Judge Daniel Newman."

Mordy Newman slipped off his backpack, thrust it into the front closet, and made a beeline for his father's study. He was thirsty, but stopping in the kitchen for a drink would only slow him down.

Mrs. Marks would be there, and there would have to be small talk and the predictable "How was school?" to get through before he could make his escape. Daniel believed in letting the kids relax before dinner and tackle their homework afterwards. Playing around on the computer was the best way Mordy knew of relaxing.

With practiced fingers, he activated the machine and sped through the preliminaries. There was a new game he was interested in trying out, and a letter he was in the middle of writing to his grandmother — his mother's mother — in Israel. But the first thing he would do, the first thing he always did when he got home, was check his father's mail.

Or, more accurately, his father's e-mail.

28

"She's met someone," Sara said mournfully.

Mrs. Schumacher swiveled gently in her chair and asked, "Who did?"

"Faygie Mandelbaum. You know, the teacher at my school. The one I've become friendly with."

"I see. She met a man?"

"Last night. It seems the *shidduch* was arranged some time ago, but he only just came in from Israel. All day today, she hasn't been able to stop talking about him. And when she wasn't talking, she was dreaming! I tried about half a dozen times to have a reasonable conversation with her, then, I finally gave it up as hopeless."

"You sound upset, Sara."

"I am upset."

"What's making you feel that way, exactly?"

Sara flushed, and hesitated. The therapist coaxed her with a faint smile, "Where can you be honest if not in here?"

Where else, indeed? Sara looked around at the office, so trim and compact — so secret. Or, more accurately, so respectful of secrets. She had been spilling a great many of her own lately, savoring the incredible relief of having someone to listen, weigh, and assess them with her. Beginning with the secret shame of her broken engagement.

The secrets had led, inevitably, to dealing with difficult questions. Did the prospect of marrying her, so disagreeable to her former *chasan,* strike other men in the same way? How — short of crawling inside another's mind — could she ever possibly know the answer? And was fear spurring her to put an abrupt end to every relationship — so that she would not have to learn what the answer was?

From there, they had moved on to Sara's childhood. She secretly envied her sister, Debbie, who was outgoing, cheerful, and always surrounded by a flock of friends. Sara, on the other hand, struggled with her own serious nature and almost stern solitude. It had not been until high school that Sara had come into her own, forming several lasting friendships that gave her endless delight to this day. But those friends were long since married, mothers now with growing broods of their own, and little time available for Sara anymore. Here in Cedar Hills, Sara's solitude had returned in full force. Except for Faygie.

"I couldn't bear it if she went and got married before I've even had a chance to know her," she said softly. After the first difficult sessions, the habit of expressing emotional honesty came easily. "We've just barely become acquainted, but being so new here I've become attached to her company very quickly. We have lunch together, talk about teaching, laugh about being single, compare *shidduch* stories, and our hopes for the future — Then suddenly, overnight, she's in a different category." Bleakly, she repeated the dismal litany. "She's met someone."

"How many times has she seen this fellow?"

Sara's smile was wry. "All right — it's only been once! But she walked into school so starry eyed this morning that she might as well have been announcing her engagement." She buried her face in her hands, her voice emerging muffled and plaintive. "I hate myself for being so jealous! Why can't I just be happy for her? *Why is it so hard for me?*"

"It's awfully premature to be jealous," Mrs. Schumacher said calmly. "Faygie is not engaged yet. She has not even formed a serious relationship. She has had *one*" — she held up an index finger for emphasis — "date. However," she continued, stopping Sara who was on the verge of responding, "let's assume that your crystal ball is functioning at peak form. Suppose Faygie does walk in one day soon to announce her engagement. What then?"

Sara was silent.

" 'If Faygie got engaged soon,' " the therapist prompted gently, "I'd feel . . . ' What?"

"Angry," Sara whispered. "I'm older than she is. I've already suffered a broken engagement — and a broken heart. It just wouldn't be fair!"

"Ah!" With a meditative flick of the fingers, Mrs. Schumacher removed a speck of dust from one immaculate navy sleeve. "Unfairness. That does seem to be a theme in your life, doesn't it, Sara? It wasn't fair that Debbie had all the charm and all the friends. It wasn't fair that your beloved father had to work such long hours that you had little chance to talk to him about the things that were important to you. It wasn't fair that your *chasan* had another girl on his mind while courting you."

Sara was silent, looking down at her interlaced fingers in a cloud of shame.

"Come now, Sara. You're not the first person in the world to feel that the deck is stacked against her. What you need is a shift in perspective. But before we can get to that, I think a little more digging would be in order. The most easily conquerable enemy is the one we best understand. Are you with me?"

Without looking up, Sara mumbled, "I guess so."

The therapist spoke briskly. "Then let's get started. We have work to do."

Mordy swept his mouse across the pad with the ease of long familiarity. A few clicks brought the e-mail screen up on the computer monitor. *"Four new messages"* read the legend at the bottom of the screen. Mordy brought the mouse into play one more time, and was looking at his father's "inbox."

Idly, he ran his eye down the list. One message had come from his father's good friend Yehuda Arlen, in Israel. A second was a technical message from the e-mail server. The third name was unfamiliar to the boy, but in the space reserved for jotting down the subject of the message, the sender had written, "Changes in Court Calendar, October." Just another bureaucratic memo. His father received dozens of them monthly.

It was the fourth message that intrigued him. Mordy had a good memory, and to his knowledge his father had never received a communication from a Vincent Fouza before. The "subject" line said only, *"Number Three."*

Mordy hesitated. His father's rule was crystal clear: Mordy might, if interested, read any message that was not marked "personal" or "confidential." This "Number Three" said neither. It was probably no big deal — but the boy's curiosity was piqued.

He clicked on the message.

As he read and then reread the words on the screen, Mordy's fingers gripped the arms of his chair, the knuckles turning white.

HEY THERE, JUDGE! YOUR DAYS ARE NUMBERED. YOUR KIDS TOO. AND SO IS THIS LETTER: NUMBER THREE, RIGHT? HA, HA.

STAND BY FOR INSTRUCTIONS . . . UNLESS YOU WANT NUMBER FOUR TO BE YOUR LAST.

"It's a joke," Mordy mumbled, unaware that he was speaking aloud. "Some stupid, perverted mind is playing a trick on Daddy." But he remembered all too well the subject of his father's conference with the police detective. *"There's been another threat . . . "*

A thrill of fear swept through the boy. It made his heart pound and his palms grow suddenly slick on the computer controls. Mixed in with the fear was a childish excitement. Who was it that kept hounding his father, first by letter (if he had understood Daddy's conversation with Garrity correctly), and now via e-mail? Was it some lunatic who belonged in a padded cell — or a vicious criminal with genuine evil on his mind? Mordy was determined to try and find out. He had had enough of watching fearfully on the sidelines while wicked strangers threatened his father — threatened them all. Here was a chance to act in his own right, to stand up and protect his father and Yael.

Mordy never stopped to think what a ludicrous picture of valiant knighthood he must make, with his feeble armor hanging loosely and sword and shield sagging pathetically in his thin arms. The fleeting possibility of trying to have the message traced did cross his mind, but he dismissed it at once. Things like tracing e-mails were adult work, and Mordy wanted with all the strength of his young heart to tackle this threatening stranger himself.

"I'll answer this Vincent character," he decided, eyeing the screen warily, as though the sender of the message might leap out at him from its depths. "I'll try to find out what his game is — why he's after

Daddy. Maybe I can scare him enough to make him back off." The tone of the letter had been unsophisticated. Surely the writer was not counted among the world's superintelligent criminals. It should not be too hard to find the key to dispelling the danger he represented. And how relieved his father would be then!

Even if he was unsuccessful at this goal, Mordy reasoned, he would at the very least have bought his father, and the police, some extra time.

He was dimly — and uneasily — aware of misgivings. His father, he knew, would not want him to get tangled up with bad guys. But then, he was not going anywhere near any bad guys. He was not even setting foot out of this house! That was the beauty of cyberspace communication. What could be safer than tapping out a swift message on his computer keyboard, here in his own house?

Nothing, that's what. Nothing could be safer.

Then why was he sweating as though he had just run a marathon? Why did it take such an effort of will to muster the nerve for what he was about to do?

He shook off his trepidation. He would do it — now.

Carefully, he pressed the "Reply" button. The message from Vincent Fouza reappeared in a new box, in a tighter format, leaving lots of blank space for Mordy to type in his return message:

WHOEVER YOU ARE, YOUR THREATS AREN'T SCARING US AT ALL. THE POLICE ARE ON YOUR TAIL ALREADY. BETTER GIVE UP BEFORE IT'S TOO LATE!!

He read the message aloud, softly, to register its impact on its unknown target. He was satisfied. In the mythical scene in which he might be required to explain his actions to his father, Mordy would say, in essence: Turnabout is fair play. The guy had threatened them; Mordy was simply sending the threats right back! Boomerang —

The rationale pleased him. He pictured his e-mail curved into a hefty weapon, hurling through the vacuum of cyberspace to whack that bad guy on the side of the head. Bam!

And the reason he had not printed out the message at once and shown it to his father?

"I didn't want you to worry," would be the obvious answer. Mordy felt strong, protective. He liked the feeling. It was not often that a boy gets to do for his father what fathers do for their children every day of their lives.

Mordy hesitated, then pressed the "Send" button. A series of beeps and whistles led to a brief whirring, and then the confirmation: "1 message sent."

He quickly printed out the remaining three messages, then sent the one from Fouza into an electronic "folder" he created for the purpose. Daddy never touched his e-mail, and knew next to nothing about folders and outboxes. Mordy's secret was safe.

Whistling, he disconnected from the server and wandered away to find out what was for dinner.

29

"Fur our next witness," Bedeker intoned from the prosecutor's table, "I call on Ms. Julia Friend."

A young woman rose from her seat and made her way self-consciously along the aisle, between the packed spectator benches, to the witness box. Though it was obvious that she had dressed with care — the inexpensive suit was fresh from the cleaner's, the collar of a white cotton blouse lying pristine against the pea-green jacket — she had erred in her choice of footwear. The over-high heels caught on the step leading up to the box, causing her to stumble awkwardly before judge, jury, and spectators. A brick-red flush mottled her cheeks as she took her seat and was sworn in.

It was in Bedeker's interest to help her regain her poise. He decided, strolling up to face the witness, that this was best achieved by simply ignoring the mishap. In a gravely courteous voice, he said, "Ms. Friend, I appreciate your taking the time to come down here to be of assistance to us."

"You're most welcome," she fluted, in an attempt to match his manner. "My pleasure." A titter rippled across the room, bringing the crimson flooding back into Julia Friend's cheeks. Bedeker dropped the urbanity and became briskly businesslike.

"You were personal secretary to Mr. Simmonds, were you not?"

"Yes, sir," she answered, glancing nervously at the jury and then away.

"How old are you now?" Before she could answer, he added apologetically, "Just for the record, Ms. Friend. I would never do this to you otherwise." The spectators chuckled, with sympathy this time, and the young woman on the witness stand visibly relaxed. With a smile, she said, "I'm 26."

"And Mr. Simmonds hired you — when?"

"I got this job with the firm right out of secretarial school. I worked in the secretarial pool for three years, then got promoted to Mr. Simmonds' office when his own secretary got married and went off to live in another state."

"Were you and your employer on cordial terms?"

"Sure we were. He treated me fine. I got a big bonus at New Year's."

Martin Bedeker strolled several feet to the right, then abruptly reversed direction. The jury followed him with their eyes, exactly as he wished them to do. It was his pet theory that certain impressionable jury members could fall into something resembling a hypnotic trance in response to a skillful counselor's voice, gestures, and movement. Certainly some were more suggestive than others. For these, the greater the show of confidence on his part, the more easily swayed they would be. He concluded the brief performance with a full turn, in slow motion — bringing him to face first the jury, then the spectator benches, the judge, and finally the witness — before uttering another word. From the defendant's table, Neil Palladin looked on cynically, as though debating whether to applaud. Daniel, looking down on them, felt inclined to share Palladin's sympathies.

"Ms. Friend," Bedeker said, "were you acquainted with the defendant?"

The young woman's eyes flickered toward Downing. "I spoke to him on the phone, setting up meetings between him and my boss."

"Where did these meetings take place?"

"Sometimes they went out to lunch. Other times, Mr. — uh, the defendant came to the office."

"How did he treat you on those occasions?"

"Oh, fine. No problem there."

Bedeker pounced. "But there *was* a problem between him and Mr. Simmonds?"

"Objection!" Neil Palladin called. "Counsel is leading the witness."

"Sustained," Daniel ruled. "Counsel will let the witness speak for herself."

Bedeker nodded, unruffled. "Ms. Friend" — his tone became

confidential, as though they were children sharing secrets on the playground — "In your opinion, and based on your personal observations, how did relations stand between your employer, Mr. Simmonds, and the defendant?"

The witness took a moment to formulate her reply. "They got along fine in the beginning. Then, when the new baby bottle took off, Mr. Downing started complaining that my boss — that Mr. Simmonds — wasn't cutting him in on his share of the profits."

"Which one of them told you about this complaint?"

She blushed. "Neither one. They happened to be talking in Mr. Simmonds' office one day, and the door wasn't completely closed. Mr. Downing got mad at him and raised his voice. I overheard."

Strolling to the jury box and back, Mr. Bedeker asked over his shoulder, "You sit at your desk in an outer office, is that correct?"

She nodded. "Yes."

"How far away is that desk from the door to your employer's inner office?"

"About um, about six feet, I guess."

"Six feet. And from six feet away, through a partially closed door, you clearly heard Mr. Downing shout at Mr. Simmonds?"

Neil Palladin struggled to his feet. "Objection. Witness did not use the word 'shout.' "

"She said he raised his voice, Your Honor," Bedeker said quickly. "Same thing."

Daniel peered down into the witness box. "Let's go straight to the source. Ms. Friend, did Mr. Downing merely raise his voice, or did he shout at your boss?"

Julia Friend threw the judge a scared glance, then turned to meet the more reassuring eyes of the prosecuting attorney. In a small voice, she answered, "It's not like he bellowed or anything like that. But he was *loud*. And — " she hesitated.

"And what?" Bedeker prompted.

"And he thumped on the desk, too."

"How do you know that?" the prosecutor asked swiftly. "You weren't in the room with them."

"I heard him." The witness spoke with confidence now. "I didn't have to be in the room to hear what he said, or the way he banged his hand down on my boss's desk, *hard*. I didn't have to be there to know that Mr. Downing was — " She stopped.

"That he was what, Ms. Friend?"

"Good and mad."

"Mad?" Bedeker repeated, with a significant glance at the jury.

"Yes. Mr. Downing was seeing red that day, that's for sure."

Martin Bedeker smiled at the secretary, then inclined his aristocratic head courteously. "Thank you, Ms. Friend. That will be all."

ം<ട്ട്ര്യ

Sara was seething, but she could not allow her fury to surface. Outwardly, her face was set and unnaturally pale as she faced Rebbetzin Goodman across the expanse of the principal's desk.

"*Which* girls asked to be transferred out of my class?" she asked quietly. "Am I allowed to know their names?" Simi Davidson was, beyond a doubt, one of them. The other two? Simi's cronies and cohorts, of course — any one of four or five classmates who trailed after her like so many mindless sheep.

"I don't think that would be a good idea," the principal answered. "I challenge any teacher to be completely objective toward a student who has asked to leave her class. The average teacher will either freeze that student out, or else do the opposite — bend over backwards to win her over."

"With all due respect," Sara said stiffly, "I don't think I'd do either."

The principal smiled, and let the comment pass. "I'm not going to divulge their names, Sara, because the names are not important. None of the three girls had any specific complaints to lodge against you, nothing that had occurred specifically between you and them. Their complaints were more general in nature."

"The attitude of the class, in *general*, has been hostile," Sara admitted. She forced the defensive note from her voice, eyes pleading with Rebbetzin Goodman to understand, to take her side. "Frankly, I'm not very surprised about this delegation that came to see you. Maybe we'd all be better off if they were moved to the other ninth-grade class."

The weather had turned cold again. Gazing out the window, Sara saw the branches of trees shedding their burden even as she watched. Crimson, yellow, and orange-brown, the leaves flew on the wind like souls in torment. Others lay in great heaps at the curb, raked together by some industrious homeowner. Inside, the radiator hissed.

"Tell me, Sara," Rebbetzin Goodman said suddenly. "Why did you take this job?"

"E-excuse me?" Sara was startled, and wary. The question reminded her of the one her therapist had asked on Sara's first visit there. Everyone, it seemed, was interested in hearing her account for her motives.

"You left a secure position in a good New York school to come here. You left your family and your home town and your friends. Why?"

"I suppose — because I wanted a challenge."

"A challenge? How do you define that?"

Sara did not know where this was leading, but she warmed to the topic, which was one she had spent a considerable time thinking about when making her decision to take the job. "I really believe that people don't grow until they're faced with something they've never had to deal with before. When things are going smoothly, we just coast along, using the skills and talents we were born with, ones that come naturally to us. We rest on our laurels. But when things get rocky and difficult — well, that's when we have to invent new skills, innovate new ways of doing things, create new solutions to brand-new problems." Her natural pleasure in speechmaking had taken over, helping her to find the language and form the cadences that made music of her words. "That's when the best in us comes out. That's when we *daven* harder and discover new wells of creativity we didn't even know we had! *That's* what a challenge does to us."

All at once, Sara came down to earth with a thud. Imagine, getting onto her soapbox in front of the principal! Coloring faintly, she said, "I'm sorry for going on so long — but you did ask."

"I did, indeed," the Rebbetzin answered, smiling. "And I think you've answered your own question, Sara. I will not transfer the girls to the other class. You're all going to have to learn to deal with each other this year."

"But —"

Though her the smile widened, the principal's manner became, at the same time, unmistakably dismissive. "Sara. Consider yourself challenged!"

Sara walked out of the office in a turmoil she did her best to hide from the openly curious secretaries. She was stuck with the job of teaching a group of girls who had taken a silent struggle and escalated it into open warfare. The principal had been made aware of their antipathy — if she had not known about it before — and would monitor Sara's progress even more closely from this point on. If she had been on probation as a newcomer before, Sara now felt as though her very career as a teacher was on trial.

Until today, she had been confronted with a class full of girls who seemed to loathe her. Now she was faced with a worse problem.

She was beginning to loathe them back.

Perhaps it was her depression over her meeting with the principal and her uphill struggle with her class that made Sara dream of the repairman that night.

She had scarcely thought of him in years, and then only in the context of the more harrowing points of the night, long ago, when she had — literally — run into him. But she dreamed of him tonight, dreamed of the startled dark eyes and the long, livid scar that ran down one cheek to his mouth. Even in the pale lamplight, with her vision diluted by the mist, the surrounding darkness, and the tears that stood in her eyes, she had seen his face clearly.

She had managed to leave her ex-*chasan's* car with her dignity intact, but the moment she had her back to Moish her eyes had inexorably filled. Shoulders shaking, she willed her legs to carry her down the block. Soon she was running. She must not think. More important — she must not feel. Let the impersonal highway carry her far from the scene of her shame. Her car — her car — Where was it?

There was a sound of running feet that were not her own. As she passed underneath a streetlight, a figure suddenly darted out of a driveway. Sara gasped and ground to a halt, only narrowly avoiding a collision. She could see the long white line of a scar that ran from the top of one cheek down to his mouth. Above the scar was a glimpse of dark eyes and coarse black hair under a Yankees cap. He wore workman's denim overalls.

Yellow lamplight poured down on them as the man sidestepped Sara with a muffled oath. More startled than afraid, she stammered, "S-sorry. I —"

He didn't wait for her to finish. The meeting was bizarre enough, taking place in the dead of night, with the thin lamplight highlighting Sara's swollen eyes and sodden hair, frizzed and glittering under its hood of mist. As the man ran away into the fog, Sara wondered vaguely about the overalls. Maybe he was some sort of repairman. But, at 2 o'clock in the morning?

The question did not really take root in her mind, which was too full of other, weightier matters at the moment. But as Sara turned away, she saw something crumpled and white lying at her feet. Instinctively, she stooped to pick it up.

It was a man's handkerchief, and it was covered with some black, sticky stuff. A vague smell of oil wafted up at her. She peered up the street through the mist, as though expecting the repairman to show up at any second, demanding his handkerchief back.

Then, harsh as a hammer blow, the absurdity struck her. It was the middle of the night. The stranger would not be back for his handkerchief. Sara threw it down, then fled for her car, wondering whether Moish had witnessed the encounter.

It was only when she was seated safely in her own car that she dared peer over her shoulder at her former *chasan's* house. Though not more than two or three minutes could have passed since she had left him, the hall light had already been extinguished. In its place, an upstairs light glowed behind a curtain on the second floor. Nurturing the seeds of a bitterness that would grow and grow with the years, Sara wondered how soon after her flight Moish had made his frenzied, relieved scramble for home.

All that had been the reality. The dream was a little different.

In the dream, the repairman darted out from a driveway, as he had that night — but there the parallel to real life ended. He began turning weird, unbalanced cartwheels down the street, the pinpoints of mist swirling and playing around him as though performing gymnastics of their own. Just before the fog swallowed the figure, a hand shot up, waving a stick on which a white handkerchief fluttered. Sara woke with the word "*Surrender*" lodged in her mind.

The bedside clock announced in red: 3:50 a.m. Surrender what? she wondered, with drowsy, middle-of-the-night curiosity. Or, surrender *to* what? Generally, she enjoyed analyzing her dreams, but this one baffled her. Surrender her hopes? Her grief? Her memories?

She was too sleepy to take it any further. As she settled herself comfortably for what remained of the night, Sara suddenly remembered a detail that she had forgotten these five years. It had been just another small annoyance to cap the monumental anguish she had endured that night.

After the endless drive back from Baltimore, as she was preparing for bed by the light of her desk lamp before dawn the next morning, Sara had noticed a stain on the cuff of her sleeve. It was dark, and sticky, and it smelled of oil. Some of the stuff from the handkerchief she had picked up had apparently found its way onto her good beige jacket.

It was a small thing, unimportant in itself — but so was the proverbial straw that broke some poor camel's back. Now, five years later, as she lay in the dark courting a fickle sleep, Sara remembered the look of that oily stain. She remembered, too, the way she had stared at it for an interminable minute, and then collapsed on her bed, to let a blackness such as she had never known wash over her till morning.

She banished the memory now, and tried to sleep. The apartment was very quiet, but the quiet did not seem to her a contented one. The peaceful slumber she craved continued to elude her. Eventually, she did doze off again, just as the sky was turning from charcoal to pearl.

Less than two hours later, Sara awoke exhausted and red eyed, to face whatever the coming day would bring.

30

Wiping floury hands on her apron, Mrs. Marks opened the door. Her welcoming smile perched first on Yael, then flitted over to her companion.

"This is Miss Muller," Yael explained, pulling off her jacket and dumping her backpack in the front hall in one eager motion.

"In the closet," the housekeeper murmured automatically. "Pleased to meet you, Miss Muller. Yael's been pining away lately with no piano teacher."

Sara smiled. Mrs. Marks reminded her of several of her mother's friends, back in New York: hardheaded, motherly, and ultimately as solid as goodness itself. "I don't feel right calling myself that until I've given my first lesson. I hope this works out —"

"It will!" Yael called from the piano bench, where she was already firmly ensconced. The schoolbag had found its way into the hall closet with some help from her sturdy foot. "Can we start now?"

"A drink first, Miss Muller?" Mrs. Marks asked, with a quick frown at Yael for her lack of manners. There was an etiquette to be followed when a visitor stepped through the Newman portals, especially for the first time. "There's fresh coffee, if you like, or some soda or juice."

Yael took the unspoken reprimand well, but could not stop herself from squirming on the bench like a child much younger than her years. Her fingers trilled a quick ripple of impatience on the keys.

Sara's eyes twinkled. "Yael, I'll be there just as soon as I can get my coat off," she promised. To Mrs. Marks, she said, "I'd love a glass of plain ice water. Thank you!"

The housekeeper took Sara's coat and hung it in the front closet. Benevolently, she followed the piano teacher with her eyes as Sara took her place beside Yael on the bench. The girl handed her some piano books, pointing out various pieces she had mastered. With deep concentration, Sara studied them to assess her pupil's progress, then indicated to Yael the piece she wanted her to play. Yael steadied herself, raised her hands above the keyboard with the fingertips just brushing the ivories, then closed her eyes and plunged her hands down.

A series of chords, light as water, ascended from the instrument like a rising river. They overflowed the banks, pouring over Yael, over Sara, and, finally, over Mrs. Marks as well. Then, without warning, the melody changed from sweet to strident; the stream turned into a roaring tidal wave. The magic of this particular piece lay in these alterations in volume, which caught its listeners off guard and held them mesmerized. Under Yael's skillful fingers, the piano murmured and shouted. A tender whisper became a bellow — a crash of sound that rent the air with startling ferocity. Then, just as quickly, the music turned soft again, as winning as a child lisping an apology.

Mrs. Marks listened with appreciation, Sara with an intensity that furrowed her brow and darkened her gray eyes. When the girl was finished, Sara waited until the final note had died in the air before saying quietly, "Very nicely done, Yael. Now, here's what I want you to try in the third passage . . . "

Mrs. Marks turned away and started for the kitchen to fetch a glass of water. Miss Muller, she reflected with gentle amusement, could properly call herself a piano teacher now. Experienced or not, she was certainly teaching, and Yael was drinking in her instruction with a voracious thirst. This passion for music had been born after Mrs. Newman's death, and the housekeeper was acutely aware of a mother's absence at times like these, when Yael's yearning soul was revealed so clearly in her piano playing.

A section of melody — one of the resounding parts — burst from the instrument in a sudden torrent, startling Mrs. Marks into nearly dropping the glass of water she was carrying in for Sara. Despite her concentration on the music, Sara caught the involuntary jerk and jumped to her feet, hand outstretched, as Mrs. Marks made a clumsy recovery.

"Here," she gasped, handing over the glass with a hand to her heart.

"Thank you," Sara said softly, accepting it. "I'm sorry, Mrs. Marks. This is a loud piece."

"In certain places," Mrs. Marks agreed. "But other places are very quiet, I notice."

"True." Sara smiled, then glanced quickly down at Yael, who was still pounding at the keyboard, oblivious. "She's very good."

"I know. That's why she needs you."

It was just possible, Sara thought wryly as she resumed her seat by the girl, that *she* needed Yael just as much. But this was not a thought she was prepared to share just now.

"That last part again," she told Yael, when the fingers finally stilled.

Yael launched enthusiastically into the melody once more. As she played, she pictured the notes escaping the room, drifting down the street and across the sky to find their way to far, unimagined corners of the globe. Music, she fancifully believed, did not die, but only relocated.

Sometimes — most times — Yael played to obliterate the world. Today, with Miss Muller beside her, she wanted to embrace it, to lavish all of mankind with the pleasure she could bring with her music.

She played on until the allotted time came to its unwelcome end.

And hour later, Sara's tiny Ford was just vanishing around the corner when Daniel pulled up into his driveway. His mind was not on music. In fact, he had all but forgotten that his daughter was having her first lesson this afternoon. The judge's thoughts were focused entirely on the trial.

He had managed to push these thoughts away during the past hour, while he and Pinny Klein, his learning partner, argued their way through a page of Gemara. Klein's enormous appetite for debate was the primary reason Daniel enjoyed learning with him. His style served to sharpen Daniel's own appetite and made the sessions highly pleasurable for both. Their learning *seder* had been going on for nearly five years, since shortly after the Newmans had moved here to Cedar Hills — and Daniel hoped they would continue learning together.

But with the closing of the Gemara today, the trial had come rushing back to him. All the way home, Daniel had reviewed the testimony he had heard today from the judge's bench, and seen again with his inner eye the changing expressions on Elsa Downing's face as she listened to the nails being pounded into the coffin of her husband's good name.

Jim Brooks, a colleague of Al Simmonds, had taken the witness stand that afternoon, after a morning spent largely hearing and dismissing motions by counsel for the defense. He had been strident in his condemnation of Henry Downing.

"A nothing, comes up from nowhere — and my pal Al (here, Brooks paused to acknowledge the titter that swept the courtroom) was nice enough to give him a hand up into the big time. And what does Downing do? Takes every chance he gets to bad-mouth his partner."

"Did you, personally, hear the defendant, er, 'bad-mouth' Mr. Simmonds?" Bedeker asked, hands on the rail of the witness box and his tall, lean form inclined at a 45-degree angle. Behind him, the jury listened in rapt silence.

"Yes, I did. We had lunch on the very day he was killed, Al and me." Brooks, a stocky man with small, crescent eyes over hamster cheeks, appeared to consider the advisability of wiping a tear from the corner of one of those eyes, then to think the better of it. "He told me then."

"What was Mr. Simmonds' manner at that lunch?"

"He was happy — confident — filled with life! Not a clue in the world that, by that time the next day, he'd be lying in the morgue — with his partner's knife stuck in him!"

A sharp ripple of sound swept the courtroom, cut abruptly short by the judge's gavel. Brooks looked triumphant. Martin Bedeker turned slowly to exchange a significant look with the jury. Then, circling to face the witness again, he asked, "Mr. Brooks, did Mr. Simmonds say anything specific about the defendant during that last lunch?"

"I'll say he did! He said that Downing was harassing him!"

"Harassing him? What do you mean?"

"Downing wouldn't stop phoning. Even when his secretary assured him that Al was out of the office, Downing persisted in making a ruckus, saying how he had to talk to him. Finally, he just barged into the office one day, shouting a lot of nonsense about how Al had stiffed him."

"Cheated him, you mean?" Bedeker was at his most pedantically precise.

"Yes, that's exactly what I do mean. Cheated him! As if Al needed to take money from Downing, or anyone. He was rich as Midas, and all by his own doing." Brooks' pink face turned suddenly pious. "A great loss," he said, shaking his head dolefully. "A great loss. "

A moment later, Neil Palladin, defense counsel, stepped up to the witness box for his cross-examination.

"Mr. Brooks, what was the reason for the lunch date you've just described to us?"

Brooks looked startled, then apprehensive. "What do you mean?"

"Why did you and Al Simmonds meet for lunch?" Palladin rephrased patiently.

"We — we were friends! Friends have lunch from time to time, don't they?"

"Certainly they do. But I have the impression — correct me if I'm wrong — that this particular occasion was more in the nature of a business lunch. Am I right?"

"Al and I did conduct a little business from time to time," Brooks conceded cautiously.

Palladin wheeled away from the box. Speaking with an unconcerned air, half-turned away from the witness, he said, "That 'business' took the form of a loan, didn't it? Several loans, in fact." When Brooks did not answer immediately, the defense attorney added softly, "We can subpoena your financial records, you know, Mr. Brooks."

"Okay, so I did borrow some money from Al. We were friends. He liked to help me out now and then."

"A good friend," Palladin said dryly, facing the witness again. "But one who liked to get paid back what he was owed. He asked you to lunch in order to press you for repayment of the latest loans, Mr. Brooks, didn't he? *Didn't he?*"

"He — he might have mentioned something about the loan. I don't really remember." Brooks was visibly perspiring.

Bedeker was on his feet. "Objection! Irrelevant."

Daniel hesitated, then said, "Let's see where this goes. Please demonstrate relevance soon, Mr. Palladin."

Neil Palladin nodded, eyes riveted to the witness.

"You don't remember. Perhaps we might recall Julia Friend, Mr.

Simmonds' secretary, to the stand. She might remember the reason Mr. Simmonds asked her to set up a lunch date with you.''

''All right.'' Brooks sucked in some air, then exhaled noisily. ''I did owe Al a little money.''

''Did he ask you when you were prepared to repay it?''

''Yes.''

''And you said — ?''

''I needed a little more time.''

''And Simmonds' reaction to that?''

''He — he wasn't too happy —''

''Objection!'' Bedeker was on his feet, looking furious that the foregoing exchange had been permitted to go on as long as it had. ''Your Honor, I see no relevance between Mr. Brooks' financial obligations to Mr. Simmonds and the case at hand.''

''It provides another motive for murder,'' Palladin shot back. ''Another suspect.'' He glanced appealingly up at the judge.

Daniel fixed an eye on Bedeker. ''Prosecution may question the witness again after cross-examination. I'll overrule this one.'' He shifted his gaze. ''Go on, Mr. Palladin.''

''Where were you on the night in question, Mr. Brooks — the night after your lunch with Mr. Simmonds? I am referring,'' Palladin added, for total clarity's sake, ''to the night your *pal Al* was murdered.''

''Where was I? I was visiting my mother, that's where. She lives alone. A widow.''

''Where?''

''In Olny.''

''And you visited her at what time?''

''I went there for dinner. I stayed oh, two, three hours.''

''And afterwards?''

''I went home.''

''Are you married, Mr. Brooks?''

''No. At least, not at the moment. I have two ex-wives, though — that's enough for me right now.'' This raised a subdued chuckle from the spectator benches.

''Did anyone see you after you went home?''

Brooks shook his head. ''I don't recall meeting up with anyone.''

''What did you do for the rest of the evening?''

''Watched some TV. Had a beer or two. Fell asleep.'' Brooks smiled disarmingly. "Nothing very exciting."

"So no one can substantiate your whereabouts after you claim to have left your mother's house?"

"I guess not."

Palladin peered at him. "You *did* have dinner at your mother's that night, Mr. Brooks? Not on some other night?"

Brooks bristled. "You can call her up. My mom'll vouch for me any day!"

"I'm sure she will," the defense counsel murmured dryly. With a dismissive shrug he said, "I'm finished with this witness."

It was a sound technique, Daniel thought as he parked his car and doused the lights, to sow seeds of doubt in the jury's minds. Even before he had begun to construct his own case, Palladin had used the prosecution's to establish possible alternate motives for Al Simmonds' murder. He had not built up a particularly strong case against Brooks, but then, he did not have to. A seed of doubt — reasonable doubt — was all that was needed.

For the first time, as Palladin had hammered at Brooks, Daniel had seen the faint sparkle of hope on Elsa Downing's lined face. Beneath the neat gray hair her eyes had opened wide with something more than the usual muffled despair. Standing up to leave with his escort of guards, Henry Downing had, as always, turned to smile across the room at his wife. It was a reassuring smile, filled with the offer of courage, as though it was she, and not he, who was on trial for her life. Tremulously, she had smiled back.

It was the memory of that shared smile that stayed with Daniel as he strode into the house. Would there ever be anyone again who would smile at him that way?

He had scarcely greeted his children when the phone shrilled.

Mrs. Marks poked her head through the kitchen doorway, wearing a harried expression. "It's for you, Mr. Newman," she announced in what, for her, came across as a testy voice. Daniel's weekly learning session with Mr. Klein made Wednesday-night supper a late affair, which in turn put Mrs. Marks on edge.

"Thanks, Mrs. Marks." Daniel picked up the living-room extension, signaling an apology to the kids waiting for his attention. Into the receiver, he said, "Yes?"

"Mr. Newman? This is Sheila Erlanger. You know, your mother's old friend, from Boro Park. I'm calling because I have a *shidduch* for you. A wonderful woman! Recently widowed — very sad story. Do you want to hear more?"

The memory of the Downings' smile, of the dawning hope in Elsa's faded eyes, and the stoic devotion in Henry's, was powerful. For the first time since his own Ella had gone, Daniel found that he actually was interested in hearing more. He wanted to say "Yes. I'm listening."

But there was another memory competing for supremacy, and this one proved the more compelling. It was the memory of two anonymous letters, two definite threats, and a series of eerily silent phone calls. How could he in good conscience give himself over to a relationship with any woman while the specter of danger to his children hovered over his head like a freshly sharpened sword?

The children came first.

After the stalker was apprehended, then he would be free to explore the possibilities he had been denying himself. But only afterwards.

"That is so kind of you, Mrs. Erlanger. I can't tell you how much I appreciate it. But this is not a good time. I'm all tied up right now. Can I call you when I'm free?"

"Who is she? Someone interesting?"

"I'll call you," Daniel said softly. "Thanks again."

"Who was that?" Yael asked curiously, when her father had hung up.

"A friend of Bubby's. Nothing important." He smiled down at his daughter, then extended the smile to Mordy, hovering behind. "So what's new, guys?"

The words hurled at him then: Yael's rapturous description of her first piano lesson with Miss Muller, and Mordy's tale of a splendid showing on a Gemara test. Daniel let the words wash over him, letting them form a warm sea in which he loved — needed — to swim.

An essential part of what made him Daniel Newman had been slumbering all these years. As healing proceeded slowly in the subterranean chambers of his shattered self, he had engaged, unconsciously, in a waiting game.

Now — overnight, it seemed — the waiting had become conscious. And he knew what it was he was waiting for. Somewhere, there was another life partner for him. Sometime would come the peace of mind that made possible all the other things that made life worth living.

But — not yet.

He hugged his children and let them lead him, chattering, to the dinner table where Mrs. Marks stood guard over an ambitious new casserole. As they sat down, curls of smoke rose up from the dish, like tendrils of an almost-forgotten dream.

31

Scrutinizing his father's face as Daniel set the receiver into its cradle, Mordy had seen with relief that the call had been an innocent one. There was no residue of anger or anxiety in his father's manner as he headed for the dinner table. If he did seem slightly preoccupied, it was not, Mordy instinctively knew, with some new danger. In a frame of mind when every unexpected noise seemed to carry on its back a burden of fear, an ordinary phone call served as a reprieve.

Threats and violence seemed very far away as the three sat down to Mrs. Marks' good dinner. Mordy gave himself permission to relax.

The relaxation lasted through the meal and halfway through his homework. Then, out of nowhere, the anxiety struck again. Whenever he thought of the e-mails — the one he had read and the answer he had sent back — a trembling overtook Mordy, rendering him weak as a newborn baby. The worst part was keeping the whole horrible thing to himself. He longed to share his private drama, but could think of no one to whom it would be safe to confide.

Yael would be terrified, and go screaming for their father. Mrs. Marks would give him one horrified look and phone for the police. As for his father — well, Daddy, he admitted to himself with painful honesty, would be furious with him for taking matters into his own hands. All the justifications he had so eagerly woven before pressing the "SEND" button had, with the passage of the days, dissipated like smoke from the casserole they had just consumed for dinner. And with them, his courage had cooled. He felt vulnerable, exposed — while at the same time, paradoxically, hidden away from every friendly eye.

A friend to confide in. That was all he needed.

But Mordy would not share this thing with a friend. His yeshivah comrades were part of another world, one that knew no terror or evil. He could not mix the two.

He made a valiant effort to tear his mind from the churning of its dreary thoughts. Math homework helped, but only for the space of time it took to figure out the solutions and jot them down. The sense of quiet triumph that came with doing something well, quickly evaporated, and he was back to being afraid.

Finally, he gave up and went downstairs. His father was sitting at the dining room table, his Gemara opened in front of him, at his elbow a pile of other *sefarim* — some obviously having been recently used and others standing by for research — and on his face an expression of rapt absorption. Though he had stayed late at yeshivah for *mishmar* tonight, Mordy would not have minded learning a little more with his father when Daniel was finished. He lingered in the dining room, watching his father, feeling at loose ends.

It had been a warm day, and through the partially opened window a fragrant breeze drifted in, soft as summertime. Mordy was a product of his age: wired up and plugged in and savvy to all the modern technology that kept him confined, as a rule, inside his four walls. Tonight, inexplicably, the outdoors called. The soft, invisible wind, the autumn leaves meandering on its currents, the blazing new color trumpeting on every branch — and above them all, the stretch of velvet sky, impenetrable and mysterious and all protecting. He hesitated, on the brink of an impulse he could neither express nor understand. It was an impulse, had he but known it, to escape what was too difficult for his young shoulders to bear.

He started for the front door.

"Where are you going?" Daniel asked sharply, looking up from his Gemara.

Mordy turned, a hand on the doorknob. "Out. It's such a nice night, I thought I'd take a walk or something."

"Not a good idea, Mordy. I'd rather you stayed at home."

Surprised, Mordy blurted, "Why?"

What to answer? To tell his son that he feared a stalker who had already threatened them all at least twice was out of the question.

Nonplused, Daniel fell back on plain old authority. "Because I said so. Isn't there something you can find to do in the house?"

Mordy shrugged, and directed his footsteps instead to the study. The urge had passed as quickly as it had come. He knew exactly why it was not such a good idea for him to wander out alone. And, in any case, the computer was just as good a way to empty his mind of its worries.

He played a restless game of electronic solitaire, then checked his personal e-mail. To his surprised pleasure, there was a note there for him. The laconic letter was from his cousin Ari, out in Los Angeles.

His cousin was exactly his own age. They had been born within a week of each other, and though they met only rarely, there was a bond of friendship that transcended mere formal cousinhood. When Mordy's mother had been living, the two families had made sure to get together at least every other year, summers or Pesach. Those visits had petered out with Ella's death, but Ari and Mordy had found electronic mail a fine substitute for the discomfort of making conversation over the phone, or the chore of physical letter-writing. If it did not exactly advance or deepen their friendship, quick notes on the computer screen every few weeks did manage to keep what they had alive and well.

There was one thing about his cousin that loomed very large in Mordy's mind as he scanned the electronic letter. Ari could keep a secret.

As he had expected, the message said nothing much. A few words about school, another few about a recent basketball game, regards to all, good-bye. Mordy pressed the "REPLY" button and poised his tingling fingers over the keyboard, preparing like Yael to make a kind of music of his own. He wrote:

DEAR ARI, THANKS FOR YOUR LETTER. SCHOOL IS GOING WELL FOR ME, TOO, B"H. BUT LISTEN TO THIS! MY FATHER'S BEEN GETTING POISON-PEN LETTERS FROM SOMEONE. REAL DEATH THREATS!! HE'S TALKED WITH THE POLICE BUT THEY'RE NOT OFFICIALLY INVOLVED YET. AND GUESS WHAT? THE BAD GUY WROTE MY DAD AN E-MAIL, AND I ANSWERED HIM, TELLING HIM EXACTLY WHERE TO GO!! AM WAITING TO SEE IF HE WRITES BACK.

THIS IS A DEAD SECRET!!! I'M COUNTING ON YOU NOT TO SAY A WORD TO ANYONE ABOUT THIS, ARI. I'LL KEEP YOU POSTED ON FUTURE DEVELOPMENTS.
'BYE, MORDY.

Feeling much better, Mordy switched off his e-mail and wandered off to see if his father was ready to learn with him. He had never known that a secret could weigh so much. On the surface, it seemed lighter than a feather, something easily lodged inside a brain or a heart with no noticeable bulge. But now that he had shared his with someone, he felt at least two tons lighter. Amazing!

Daniel looked up from his Gemara, glazed eyes gradually focusing. "Hi, Mordy. Ready to learn?"

"That's just what I was about to ask *you*, Daddy."

Smiling, Daniel said, "I guess we're on the same wavelength, then. Pull up a seat, son."

"Son? What son?" The Italian woman was bitter — or more accurately, more bitter than usual. Vinny could imagine her at the phone, thin as a scarecrow, and almost as bedraggled in her faded housedress. "I never hear from Joey unless he needs something. Some food for his belly, some cash for his wallet, which is always empty. Sal, at least, sent me money once in a while —"

"I'm sorry about that, Mrs. M. But I need to talk to Joey. Could you let him know I'm looking for him? Next time you hear from him, I mean."

"I can tell him." Grudgingly, she added, "He usually shows up for Sunday supper."

Vinny hesitated. "Maybe you could give him a message for me?"

"What is it?"

"Tell him he got an answer to his e-mail."

"His what?"

Hastily, Vinny backed down. Old Italy and the mysteries of cyberspace were two things that, like oil and vinegar, just did not blend. "Never mind," he said. "Just tell him to stop by, or to call me, okay?"

"All right, Vincent."

"I appreciate it, Mrs. M. Good-bye, now. Nice talkin' to you."

"Good-bye, Vincent. You're a good boy." The heavy sigh that accompanied her final words spoke volumes about the contrast she was inevitably painting, and would always paint, between him — between almost anyone — and her hapless Joey.

Suppressing a sigh of his own, Vinny hung up.

Through his powerful binoculars, the watcher saw father and son beautifully framed between the open window curtains. He could have reached out a hand, almost, and touched them. He pretended to have them in his gunsight, encased in the fatal circle that he, personally, had drawn around them. Pointing his index finger straight at that circle, with his thumb up, he mouthed a soft, "*Bang!*"

Quietly, under cover of the darkness and protected by the stillness of the deserted basement in the empty house, he put down the binoculars and laughed and laughed.

32

The elderly professor of law had a fondness for the alliteration in the name "Mister Meisler." Accordingly, he tended to call on Jake rather more often than was the norm in the course of a lecture. On this Friday morning, unfortunately, he caught Jake in the throes of a vivid daydream.

"Mister Meisler, what is your opinion of this precedent?" the professor asked. When no answer was forthcoming, he cleared his throat loudly and rumbled, "*Mister Meisler*. Are you with us?"

Jake jumped, blinked, and hastily produced an engaging smile. Under normal circumstances, it was a smile that could disarm a fire-eating dragon. These, however, were not normal circumstances.

He met the professor's stony eyes across the length of the lecture hall. "I'm sorry, sir," he ventured. "I'm afraid I didn't hear the question —"

"Or much else, apparently," the professor said dryly. The class chuckled, which encouraged the lecturer to expand on his theme. "If your attentiveness in class is any indication of your ambitions in the law, I fear that your career in our illustrious field, young man, will be wholly unremarkable."

This quick retort produced more laughter. Good-naturedly, Jake grinned, too. If this was what it took to reduce the professor's umbrage, so be it. Besides, he was a good-enough student to survive the occasional slap on the wrist, and both he and the teacher knew it.

The question was duly repeated, and an answer offered and

accepted. Satisfied, the professor droned on. Jake relapsed into his daydream.

It was a dream of a small, comfortable home, and a nice, comfortable wife, and a wonderful, meaningful existence. But each time he pictured that existence, it bore no resemblance at all to the future he was at that moment preparing for in that lecture hall. In his third year of law school — which itself capped an educational voyage that had lasted, all told, nearly nineteen years — Jake Meisler found himself in the unenviable position of doubting his direction.

In his daydreams, he was dressed in a modest suit and hat, returning from a day at the *kollel* in time to greet his wife and then play with his children before tucking them into their beds. These imaginings were always especially compelling on Fridays, when the Shabbos of his dream future came up hard against the rather lonesome one of his present life. The battles he fought in these visions were not courtroom battles, but a matching of wits with fellow travelers along the high road of Torah.

He had been learning Gemara more and more intensively with each passing year, even as his legal studies had also intensified. Somewhat to his surprise — and to his great satisfaction — he had found that he had a real aptitude for the Talmud. With this realization had come a subtle shift in his perspective. Jake's ambitions in the illustrious field of the law, as his professor had so shrewdly remarked, were shrinking every day — even as other, more spiritual ambitions grew proportionately larger.

Jake did not yet know it, but a crisis of monumental proportions was looming in his young life. It would be a crisis of direction. He stood at a crossroads, and would soon be forced to choose: this way, or that?

But the crisis still lay a little way off, in his future. For the moment, Jake could relish his peace.

At the front of the lecture hall, a white-haired man droned about law and precedent while, near the back, a young man with auburn hair and a large black yarmulke dreamed on.

The high point of Jake's day came when classes were over and he could escape to the courthouse — and Judge Newman. He slipped into the courtroom in time to hear the tail end of testimony being provided by Lester Turkin, the late Alexander Simmonds' personal accountant.

As far as he could make out, the bulk of Turkin's testimony had dealt with financial transactions between the defendant, Henry Downing, and the late Mr. Simmonds. According to the accountant — a balding man of below-medium height, above-medium girth, and a singularly unpleasant smile — Simmonds had violated none of his written agreements with Downing.

"What about verbal agreements?" Neil Palladin asked quickly, on cross-examination.

The smile was actually more of a smirk. "*You're* the lawyer," he said in a tone that came very close to a sneer. "But it seems to me — correct me if I'm wrong — that a legal contract, a *binding* contract, is one that's in writing."

Palladin neither confirmed nor corrected this statement. Instead, he leaped to a different tack. Walking over to the defense table, he picked up a sheaf of papers and said, as he pretended to shuffle through them, "The partnership contract drawn up between the two men stipulates that profits from the patented baby bottle would be distributed on a fifty-fifty basis — with Downing providing most of the capital and Simmonds taking charge of the actual design, production, and marketing of the product."

The accountant nodded. "That's correct."

"Did this division of profits ever take place?"

"It hadn't take place by the time — by the time Mr. Simmonds was killed."

"When was it due to happen?"

For the first time, the accountant looked uncomfortable. "Actually, the date had already passed —"

"What?" Palladin paused for dramatic effect, just as though his entire line of questioning had not been leading up to eliciting precisely this piece of information. "Passed? Then why, according to both Downing's and Simmonds' financial records, did he not receive his share?"

"It seems there was a clause in the contract," the accountant said slowly, "stipulating for delays or postponements due to an act of G-d."

The defense attorney held his tongue for a full fifteen seconds, allowing the jury to fully absorb these words. Then, with a show of respectful curiosity, Palladin inquired, "And which such act, Mr. Turkin, did G-d see fit to rain down on Mr. Simmonds?"

The accountant's discomfort grew acute, and was readily apparent to every observer in the hushed room. He raised one pudgy finger as though to run it along his shirt collar, then thought the better of it.

"Well, the advertising executive in charge of the whole baby-bottle campaign was in a road accident. He was hospitalized, with an uncertain prognosis. This seriously handicapped Mr. Simmonds' marketing plans."

"There are other advertising companies, I believe?" Palladin asked sardonically.

"Of course there are. And other executives at the company he was already using. But, technically, the man's accident and hospitalization could be termed an act of G-d. As such, it gave my client — Mr. Simmonds — the latitude to postpone the profit sharing."

"Technically. I see." Palladin glanced at the jury with raised eyebrows, then back at the witness. "How long a postponement are we talking about, Mr. Turkin?"

"Until someone could be brought in to replace the injured man and the campaign was solidly back on its feet."

"In whose opinion?"

The accountant looked startled. "Pardon?"

"The campaign must be solidly on its feet — in whose opinion?"

"Why — Mr. Simmonds' after all, he was managing director of the operation."

"I see." Palladin tapped the fingers of one hand thoughtfully against the palm of the other. " Now let me see if I understand the situation, Mr. Turkin. Alexander Simmonds got to decide which events constituted 'acts of G-d,' and how long such acts lasted. And meanwhile, my client, Mr. Downing, who had put up the lion's share of the capital to fund the entire enterprise, had to wait around with empty pockets — and had no say in the matter at all."

The accountant shrugged.

"We'll need an answer in words, please, Mr. Turkin," Judge Newman prodded mildly from his perch.

The accountant glanced at the judge, then back at Palladin.

"That would be correct," he conceded coldly.

Daniel watched as the portly, balding accountant stepped carefully off the witness stand. He was the type to do everything carefully. The judge considered the foregoing testimony. Palladin's cross-examination had brought to light the fact that Simmonds was not beyond an unscrupulous interpretation of the law, if it suited his needs — and, apart from his lawyer, the man's accountant would be the most likely person to help him carry out that interpretation.

But the defense's line of questioning had also produced a side effect that the defense counsel would surely have done anything to avoid: It had strengthened Henry Downing's motive for murder.

Daniel wound up the day's proceedings almost mechanically, aware of not only a strong personal bias in favor of the defendant, but a growing dislike of the victim in the case as well. What he had seen of the people with whom Al Simmonds had surrounded himself did not impress Daniel at all. They seemed, all of them, to be fueled by motives of powerful self-interest, a motive that they apparently shared with Simmonds himself. Daniel would have to watch his step, do his utmost to remain impartial in his rulings. This was not simply a case of an instinctive partiality for the defendant, of championing the under-dog. Henry Downing, from everything Daniel had come to know of him, was not the killing type.

For the first fifty-six years of his life, Henry Downing had been a law-abiding and hardworking citizen. His first move, upon winning the lottery jackpot, had been to make a series of hefty donations to his favorite charities. He and his wife had moved into a home that was reasonably luxurious, but by no means overly opulent. Their new lifestyle had been comfortable, but not overly indulgent. Downing might have — legitimately — demanded his fair share of the profits. He might have shouted and rampaged and even threatened in his effort to see justice done. But when you came right down to it, would a man like that take another man's life in order to get his way?

Nothing that Daniel had read or seen convinced him that this was so.

And yet, murderers came in the most unlikely packages.

He was ruminating in fruitless circles as he stepped into his chambers and pulled off his judicial gown. He felt tired, which was not unusual at the end of a workweek. But behind the tiredness was a tentative ray of light. It had been days since the silent phone calls, well over a week since the last threatening letter. Dare he hope that the nightmare was over?

He could not be sure. In a war of nerves — and this assuredly was one — a waiting game could only play to the aggressor's advantage. He shrugged, and turned his thoughts doggedly away from that particular worry. As almost always on a Friday, he had dismissed his court early. He would set his sights on Shabbos instead.

Paul Hencken, his clerk, was already in the chambers, tidying up.

"How's your mother, Paul?" Daniel asked.

"Not very good, sir. The doctor is saying that a warmer climate would do her good. Florida, maybe." Hencken seemed anxious to change the subject. "What do you think of the way the trial is going so far, sir?"

"That's hard to say. Lacking solid evidence, the prosecution is obviously trying to build up a strong circumstantial case against the defendant. It's still too early to say how successful they've been."

"Will the defense bring character witnesses for Downing, do you think?"

"I'm sure they will." Daniel smiled. "The best character witness would be his own wife. Have you noticed how closely she watches the proceedings, and her husband's reactions to them? Their devotion to one another is so palpable, you can almost touch it."

Paul looked blank. "Sorry, sir. I can't say I've noticed."

"You haven't? Well, never mind. It's —"

He was interrupted by a deferential tapping at the door. Paul hurried to open it. Jake Meisler stood there, smiling eagerly.

"Hi, there, sir! Just finished my last class of the week, and thought I'd drop in to see how the trial is going."

Daniel was aware of a surge of warmth at the sight of the young man. He offered a hand for him to shake, along with a welcoming smile. "Hi, Jake. You and Paul have already met, I believe?"

The two young men eyed each other warily. Both nodded.

"The trial," Daniel said, answering Jake's question, "is coming along. Nothing very dramatic so far, but then most cases plod along in just this way. The fireworks are reserved for the crime novels."

"No!" Jake registered mock-horror. "Are you telling me that you find real-life courtroom drama to be rather less than dramatic?"

"Not all the time. I'll admit, a flamboyant witness or an unexpected twist can shake things up a bit. But, on the whole, day-to-day life in the courtroom is about as colorful as a trip to the supermarket."

"You don't really mean that, sir." Paul was reproachful.

Daniel did mean it, but his clerk was young and still filled to the brim with youthful notions. He winked at Jake, who grinned back. Having Jake in his chambers was like throwing open the windows for the fresh air of the outside world. He was about to offer the law student a chair, when the phone rang.

Both Paul and Jake started towards it, then fell back in confusion. Daniel stepped in and picked up the receiver. "Judge Newman speaking."

"Dan? Mark Garrity here."

"Hello, Mark. What's up?" Instantly, Daniel shifted gears.

"Got a minute?"

"I do. What do you have for me?"

"An update on our list of suspects."

33

"Do you? Good! Hold on a minute, will you, Mark? I've got to finish up in here."

Daniel placed his hand over the mouthpiece and said to both his young companions, "Sorry, guys, but I'm going to need a little privacy now."

"Shall I wait outside?" Paul asked quickly. Jake looked as though that question had been on the tip of his own tongue.

"There's no point — I'll be leaving for home right after this call. Thanks for everything, Paul; see you Monday. Jake, sorry to cut your visit short. Have a good Shabbos."

"Good-bye, sir," Paul said.

"Good Shabbos," said Jake.

Daniel would have liked to add a few words to Jake, newly arrived and so precipitately sent on his way. But a show of extra warmth to Jake would only hurt his clerk's sensitive feelings. He would call Jake later, from home, he decided, and wish him a more personal "Good Shabbos" then.

He saw them out, closed the door firmly, and only then removed his hand from the mouthpiece. "I'm back. Thanks for your patience, Mark."

"Don't mention it. Dan, I've had my men check out the five men on our list."

"Check out — how?"

"They talked to Esplanada and Towson in their respective jail cells, and tracked Freehy down at home; he's on probation. All three, of course, swear they know nothing about any anonymous letters and wouldn't dream of hurting a hair on your head.''

"They're bound to say that either way.''

"Naturally. So we're going to monitor the jailbirds' visitors, put a tail on Freehy, and see what we can come up with. Meanwhile, you might want to keep looking through your files in case we've missed anyone.''

"Will do," Daniel promised. "Mark?''

"Yes?''

"What about the other two? There were five names on that list, if I remember correctly.''

"You remember correctly. Carl Sandhurst, the embezzler, has seen the light. He got religion — and is a model prisoner. The warden gives him the highest marks for good conduct, says the guy's been showing some real remorse. It could be an act, but I don't think he's your man.''

"And the other one? The fellow I put away for armed robbery and attempted murder. A good-looking fellow, I recall, but nasty. What was his name?''

"Mercutio," Garrity said. "Sal Mercutio. We can cross him off our list, Dan. He's dead.''

"Dead? Since when?''

"Since about a month ago. Got knifed in prison and died in a maximum-security hospital room.''

Daniel exhaled, and sat down in the large leather chair behind his desk. "Well, there's one less person to worry about.''

"That's right. Let's concentrate our efforts on the living.'' A pause. "Sure you won't change your mind about having that police car outside your house, Dan?''

"I'm sure. There have been no more threats for some days now. Also, our holidays are coming up, and I want to preserve an air of normalcy for the kids.''

"And afterwards?''

"Afterwards — we'll see.''

Elsewhere, on that Friday afternoon, Joey Mercutio, brother of the deceased Salvatore, was sitting at a computer monitor carefully reading, and then rereading, the e-mail message that had come for him five days before and that he was seeing for the first time today.

"Thinks he's going to scare me off, does he?" Joey muttered.

"What's that?" Vinny asked. "What'd you say?"

"Nothing."

"Joey, what's going on? You in some kind of trouble?"

Joe Mercutio whirled on his friend, eyes bulging in sudden rage. "Stop asking me that! You, my mother — everyone's always asking me if I'm in trouble! I'll be in trouble if I wanna be in trouble, okay? Now lay off!"

The scar that ran from cheek to mouth gleamed whitely, as it always did when he was angry. It lent Joey a particularly malevolent air.

Vinny stepped back, hands up. "Okay, okay, stay cool. I didn't mean anything."

"If you don't mean anything, don't *say* anything!" Abruptly, Joey faced the machine again. "I want to send an answer. How do I do it?"

As he waited for Vinny to join him at the machine, Joey read the message one more time.

WHOEVER YOU ARE, YOUR THREATS AREN'T SCARING US AT ALL. THE POLICE ARE ON YOUR TAIL ALREADY. BETTER GIVE UP BEFORE IT'S TOO LATE!!

With Vinny's help, he found the REPLY button. Vinny stayed well back as his friend laboriously tapped out his answer.

The click of the SEND button sent the message winging its way toward the Newman house, where Mordy, blissfully oblivious, was preparing for Shabbos.

Mordy spent Shabbos quietly, feeling secure in his father's presence. Daniel seemed more like his old self, less jumpy and less preoccupied. The boy's jangled nerves stopped shrieking, settling instead into a low, dimly agitated hum, like a washing machine churning quietly in the background.

It was not until Saturday night that he checked his father's e-mail again. The name "Vincent Fouza" jumped out at him, punching him in the eye with a force that was almost physical. The low hum of worry escalated at once into a silent, high-pitched whine of panic. Mordy stared, electrified, at the newest communication from the anonymous menace to his family's peace of mind.

I THINK MY THREATS ARE SCARING YOU PLENTY. NOW THINK IT OVER — ARE YOU GOING TO PLAY . . . OR PAY?

The message was overbearing, hateful, terrifying. This time, Mordy did not stop to think. In a white fury, he dashed back an answer and sent it off at once.

Unlike his first reply, this one reached its destination almost immediately.

Joey Mercutio had arranged to phone his friend nightly until an answer came through. To his delight, the wait was short — only one day. It was late, with Saturday fading quietly into Sunday, when Vinny snatched up the ringing extension in his room.

"Joey? That you?"

"Yeah, it's me. Any word?"

"Yeah. You got a reply."

"What — already?" Wildly impatient, Joey was tempted to ask his friend to read it to him. Then prudence prevailed. "I'll be right over."

"*Now?* It's midnight, man. Come tomorrow."

"No way. I'm coming right over, *now.*" The phone slammed down.

Glumly, Vinny sat down to wait. Twenty minutes later, he had the front door open even before Joey knocked. "Sssh! You'll wake my old man — and then I'll never hear the end of it!"

Joey brushed past him, taking the stairs two at a time. He hardly waited until Vinny had walked into the room behind him and carefully shut the door before demanding, "Where is it?"

"Right here." Vinny hesitated. "But before I call the e-mail up for you, I got something to say."

"So say it."

"I think we should stop this, whatever it is, right now." Vinny was beginning to feel used. More, his antennae — fine tuned from years of associating with neighborhood hoodlums busy perpetrating varying degrees of evil — told him that whatever Joey was up to, it was no good. What had started as a lark, a way to show off his new computer knowledge to an old pal, was escalating into something Vinny was not sure he liked.

But Joey was beyond caring what Vinny did or did not like. "Oh, you do?" he countered. "You think I should stop, huh?" Negligently, he flicked open a small knife and waved it in a casual fashion a foot from the other's nose. "From now on, we do what *I* say," he informed his friend softly. "Get it?"

Vinny's eyes flickered from Joey's face, to the knife, and back again to Joey.

"Okay," he said. There was less fear in his voice than resignation.

Fifteen seconds later, Mordy's latest message was stamped boldly across the computer screen.

WE'LL PLAY . . . BUT NOT ACCORDING TO YOUR RULES. WAIT TILL MY FATHER GETS HIS HANDS ON YOU. THEN YOU'LL WISH YOU NEVER STARTED UP WITH US!

Joey stared. "Father?" he said aloud. "*Father?*"

"What? What is it?" Vinny asked, from behind.

"Nothing. Keep your nose out of this. *Father*," Joe Mercutio mused aloud, his dark eyes beginning to glitter with a mad new excitement. "I *thought* that last message sounded a little off — Too childish for a judge. But it wasn't 'off' — it was just a *kid* who was writing! It was the kid all along!"

This was beginning to get very, very interesting. Without trying, he'd got the kid writing letters to him! With a little bit of cleverness — and Joey had no doubts about his own — he'd get him just where he wanted him.

"*Whoo-eeee!*" he whooped suddenly, at full volume. Vinny yelped, darting frightened glances at the door. But his father, apparently, was a sounder sleeper than he thought. Joey jumped up from his chair and two-stepped his way to the door. "It's the kid!" he chanted as he danced — a little more quietly this time, but no less maniacally. "I've got me the kid!"

"What kid?" Vinny asked.

Joey did not hear. "We're going places!" he said gleefully. "Me and the kid — It won't take long now."

It was no use asking what he was talking about. Vinny slumped back on his bed, yawning. "Is that it?" he asked. "Wanna answer the e-mail now?"

"Not right this minute," Joe said, snapping his fingers repeatedly as if to burn off excess energy. "I've got to think things over first. I've gotta make me a plan." He gave a final, jubilant snap. "But first right now — tonight — I'm gonna go out and celebrate!" He headed for the door.

"Have fun," Vinny called after him, not at all sorry to see him go.

Joe Mercutio ran down the steps and out into the night, intent on finding a bottle of some good, strong stuff to help him savor the sweetness of his triumph, and to render it even sweeter.

It was almost 1 a.m.

Across town, people were streaming out of their own homes: mostly men and boys, with a sprinkling of women. All were headed for their local shuls. It was the last *motzaei Shabbos* before Rosh Hashanah, and they were on their way to *Selichos.*

Daniel and Mordy Newman got into their car. A few blocks away, Sara Muller got into hers. She was picking up Faygie and they would be going to shul together. Jake Meisler hitched a ride with a friend. Chaim Newman climbed into his battered old station wagon, and let out his breath with relief when the engine started.

All of them wore somber expressions, suitable to the moment. Most, in their various shuls, were out of hearing range of the police sirens that split the night some half-hour into their prayers — and those who did hear paid them not the slightest attention. They were otherwise, and more vitally, occupied.

They were busy begging forgiveness for their sins, and supplicating Heaven for a good year, a sweet year — a year when all their hearts' desires would be granted, and true justice rendered.

PART TWO:
JUSTICE

34

Sirens tore through the night. Whirling lights, red and blue, gouged out pieces of the darkness and hurled them carelessly away. People stirred on their pillows, wondering, through their dreams, where the fire was this time.

The sirens and the lights, however, belonged not to the fire brigade, but to the police. They were hastening, with all speed, toward a rendezvous with Joey Mercutio. Hearing the blare of their approach, Joey decided that the prudent move would be to let the night swallow him. He abandoned his treasure and ran.

Joey had left Vinny Fouza's house with the intention of purchasing a bottle of whiskey with which to celebrate his good fortune. Celebration certainly seemed to be in order. Establishing communication with one of the Newman kids had made his job that much easier. A hazy plan was forming in his mind, but he was too heady with excitement to think it through just then. He wanted a couple of stiff drinks first. He deserved that much, after days and nights living cramped and cold in the unheated empty house across the street from the Newmans.

Night after night, he had trained his binoculars on the Newman home, watching the family move about in warmth and comfort. Now that his dedication was about to pay off, he would treat himself to a little warmth, too — in his own style.

He started out intending to buy the whiskey, but the illogic of euphoria soon made him change his mind. Why shell out good money for liquor? He was *owed* that much. Society owed him — for what it had done to his brother Sal, and for what it was doing to him, Joey. They had never had a lucky break, either of them. Sal had tried, via armed robbery, to better his station in life, and where had that landed him? First in a jail cell, then dead in a prison hospital. As for Joey himself, he had fared even worse at civilization's hands. His teachers at school had never understood him, his friends did not take him seriously, even his own mother thought he was good for nothing! But he would show them. He would show them all.

Yes, society owed him. So when Joey walked into the liquor store, instead of pulling out his wallet he drew his switchblade. During the brief scuffle that ensued, the shopkeeper, long prepared for just such an emergency, managed to press a button on the floor with his foot. The sirens sounded soon after that, faint at first, then growing ominously louder.

Joey hesitated, his hands in the till. Then, grabbing only a fistful of the cash that lay there in such enticing splendor, he fled.

The shopkeeper, shaking and slightly scratched but otherwise unharmed, gave the police a fairly accurate description of the lawbreaker, laying particular emphasis on the long scar that disfigured the criminal's cheek and gave him a look more frightening than any knife. A citywide alert went out. Joey, cowering in his dank basement, knew he was a hunted man.

For the next few weeks, until the heat died down, it would be risky for him to appear on the open streets. Stopping at his rented room only to pick up some clothes and other essentials, he moved back, on a more permanent basis, into the empty house-for-sale where he had been keeping his vigil with the judge. It made a good hideout. He could last here indefinitely, if need be.

His only worry was the e-mail situation. How was he supposed to stay in touch with the Newman kid without a computer? Getting over to Vinny's house with the police on the lookout for him would be tricky.

And he had not even managed to get the bottle of liquor he had gone for.

Well, he didn't much feel like celebrating anymore. Impatiently, he set his bags down and turned to the more important business at hand. There was some serious thinking to be done. He had to decide how to turn his connection to the Newman kid to his best advantage. It was a connection unplanned and unhoped for, his first lucky break in a long time. With the force of habit, he picked up his binoculars and trained them on the house across the street. To his astonishment, the Newman car was not in its usual spot in the driveway. Where would the judge have gone at this time of the night? And had he taken the kids with him — or were they sleeping, virtually unprotected, with no one but that elderly housekeeper or a babysitter to stand guard?

His heart raced with the possibilities. To help him think, he lit a cigarette and puffed it standing at the window, the red tip glowing in the dark as he ran the binoculars across the length of the house.

The clock struck 2. Down the block came a car, so quiet as to hardly make a ripple in the deep silence of the sleeping street. Daniel Newman turned into his driveway and parked the car. The house was dark, except for a light on the front porch. Yael was sleeping over at a friend's house.

Yawning, Mordy climbed out even before his father had killed the engine. Mordy was not thinking about threatening strangers or e-mail messages at the moment; the only thought occupying his mind just then, with a magnetic pull that lured him irresistibly up the short walk to the front door, was his bed.

Daniel followed a moment later. As he pulled the door shut behind them, he glanced back over his shoulder. No, the pinpoint of light was not there. He must have imagined it. How *could* there be a light in that house across the street? It had, after all, been sitting empty for so many months, forlorn and unwanted, behind its weatherbeaten FOR SALE sign.

Closing and then locking the door, Daniel promptly forgot what he had thought he had seen. He, too, was more than ready for his bed.

A few blocks away, Sara rolled her car to a halt in front of the small, well-kept apartment complex where Faygie, her new friend and school colleague, made her home.

"This is nice," she said, peering up at the building and taking in the pretty landscaping. Security lights illuminated beds of winter pansies, yellow and royal purple, laid out in a neat grid in front. The grass looked newly clipped, and was bare of the leaves that littered the neighboring lawns. "Better than the place I'm living in."

"So move," Faygie suggested, patting back a yawn. She gathered her pocketbook and siddur and looked around for her jacket, which she had slung over the back of her seat.

"And break my lease? That would cost me, big time."

"Well then, move when the lease is up. We'd be neighbors — what fun!"

Sara twisted in her seat to face her friend in the light of a streetlamp that hung almost directly above their heads. "Do you really think you'll still be here eleven months from now?" Her tone was teasing; the look in her eyes was not. But Faygie could not see the eyes very well in the dimness.

"We-e-ell," coyly, Faygie dragged out the syllable. "That's not a question I'm prepared to answer right now." She chuckled. "But you do have a point, Sara. At our stage in life, it's dangerous to make long-term plans. You know what they say: 'Man plans, and G-d laughs!' "

"You'll be laughing, too — right down the aisle." Sara paused. Her friend smiled, but did not answer.

"So how's it going, Faygie?" Sara coaxed.

"Like a whirlwind," her friend admitted. "Five dates in less than two weeks! And all of them lasting hours and hours. I've been yawning so hard in class that my students asked me today what was wrong. 'It's all those late nights, preparing classes,' I kidded them. 'I ought to get some sleep and let you girls teach yourselves!'"

"Do you think they suspect?"

"Girls that age *always* suspect. But let's not be premature about this. All it is, so far, is a few dates."

"*Five* dates."

"All right, five dates —"

"Long ones, you said."

"So they were long. We both like to talk! But we've still barely scratched the surface. There's so much we still don't know about each other, Yoni and I. And there would have to be some big adjustments —"

"Adjustments?" Sara prompted, when her friend showed no sign of continuing.

"Yoni wants to live in Israel," Faygie said unhappily. "He grew up there, and he says it's a better place to raise children than America. But I've got my whole family here, and my parents aren't getting any younger, plus both my brother and my sister keep producing adorable nieces and nephews that I'd never get to watch grow up if I live so far away." The unhappiness in her voice intensified as the litany of her potential losses grew.

Sara struggled valiantly to suppress a stab of selfish pleasure at Faygie's dilemma: the pleasure of if-Faygie-stays-single-then-I-won't-be-alone, which was really no pleasure at all. She recalled Mrs. Schumacher's words, at their last therapy session. "I don't need to remind you, Sara, that you don't really wish your friend ill, G-d forbid. What you're feeling is simple envy — the kind you've struggled with before. If you had your own heart's desire, you'd be thrilled for Faygie, wouldn't you?"

The question had been a rhetorical one, requiring no answer. Sara genuinely, even fervently, wished to see her new friend blessed with the full measure of a woman's happiness. It was the contrast that depressed her: the prospect of Faygie's joyfully wedded future, side by side with her own bleak and continuing solitude.

Solemnly, because it was true, and because she needed to hear herself say the words aloud, Sara said, "I know you'll make the right decision, Faygie. I wish you every happiness in the world. You deserve it!"

Impulsively, Faygie gave her a quick hug. "Don't we both?" she murmured.

Laughing softly, Sara watched her friend leave the car and walk up to the front door of her building. Faygie turned to wave, silhouetted for a moment in the lighted frame of the doorway, before disappearing inside. Sara waited until a light went on in a second-story window before she started up the car.

The lateness of the hour, and the *Selichos* service, had made her tired, but not nearly as much as her inner struggles had done. Through her exhaustion, she felt a stab of genuine self-pride. She remembered that other late night, long ago, when she had driven this same car, alone, all but blinded by tears, lost in a physical fog and another of her own making. On that night, she had seen the bare patch on her finger where a diamond had so recently sparkled, felt it taunt her all through the long drive home from Baltimore, where she had left behind the wreckage of her dreams.

She had been robbed of her self-respect then, an angry and frightened and insecure girl. She felt stronger now, ready at last to tackle the demons that had kept her tied in place. Her *davening* tonight had been especially fervent. Heaven knew she had her faults, but she was making a concerted effort to change them. She was working on her attitude, too. Some of the apples in her barrel might be wormy, but she would pick through them and make the tastiest applesauce in her power.

The image brought the smile back to her face. Resolutely, she tore her mind from the past and addressed instead the immediate future.

The New Year was quickly approaching. Rosh Hashanah was slated to begin on Wednesday night. On that morning, she would be driving up to Brooklyn to spend the holiday with her family. The thought of seeing her parents and Debbie — not to mention her nieces — made Sara's spirit soar. Her career at the new school might be off to a rocky start, but there were things to look forward to. Over the holiday, she would use the detachment lent by distance to form her resolutions for the rest of the school year. In some way, she was going to make that class accept her. And if they never did, somehow she was going to survive that, too.

But even before her trip to New York, there was another event she was anticipating. On Tuesday night this week, because of the holiday, there would be a second piano lesson with Yael Newman. Somewhat to her surprise, Sara found herself looking forward to that meeting almost as much as the longed-for reunion with her family.

As she pulled into the parking lot of her own small apartment complex, she conjured the image of herself and Yael, side by side at the piano bench. The strains of their imaginary duet accompanied her, in friendly fashion, all the way up the stairs to what she now called home.

35

For no reason at all, that Sunday was a magical day.

None of the Newmans had planned it that way. With too little sleep because of their late-night session in shul, Daniel and Mordy might have expected to be groggy and grumpy in the morning. Instead, they woke to the sweetness of an Indian-summer day, with moods to match. Mrs. Marks did not come on Sundays, and without her there to preside over it, the day had a relaxed air, like tightly tied laces undone to let the toes wiggle.

On Sundays, Mordy did not travel to his Baltimore yeshivah with his usual car pool. Daniel always took him along to *daven* at a local shul and then drove his son to school himself. It was their time together — the only time, often, that the two of them got to spend alone, out of the house, with no agenda but the winding road and the short school day waiting at the end of it.

This morning, Daniel chose to walk to shul instead of making the short trip by car. Though Mordy complained mildly, he secretly enjoyed walking beside his father along the wide, tree-lined side-walks, with the yellow and scarlet leaves swinging above his head, and growing piles of dried brown ones to kick aside as he went. The sky was an especially clear shade of blue that morning. Through the thinning foliage, the sun shone brightly down on their heads.

Daniel was in a contented frame of mind — the combined result of last night's *Selichos* and the fact that each day that passed without any sign of his anonymous stalker was another link in the chain of hope that this unwelcome chapter in their lives was finally over. The mood filtered down to Mordy. They were quiet as they walked, exchanging only the occasional, desultory remark between house and shul. Despite his late night, Mordy felt clear eyed and rested. If his father was at peace, then he, Mordy, could give himself permission to follow suit.

There had been, to his knowledge, no further meetings with Detective Garrity. His father seemed less jumpy lately, less preoccupied with the worries that beset him. As for Mordy's e-mail correspondence, that was beginning to feel almost like a game — a sort of verbal chess match or test of nerves. Mordy was determined to make the other guy blink first.

He was only 12 and, for all his computer savvy, still very young in his experience of evil. Tragedy had struck at him five years before, but it had not done away with his innate belief that life was good. As he tripped along beside his father, the sun shone on his springy dark hair and filled his round brown eyes with light. With such a father walking beside him and such a sun shining above, nothing bad could touch him.

While Daniel and Mordy were still away at shul, a car dropped Yael and her friend Tzippy at the house. Yael had spent the night at Tzippy's and now, with Tzippy's parents headed out of town, Tzippy would be spending her day at the Newmans'. Energized by her friend's presence, Yael had a tantalizing-smelling breakfast on the stove by the time her father and brother stepped through the door. Eggs, sunny-side up, sizzled in their pan, and fresh bread lay ready by the toaster. Daniel and Mordy sniffed appreciatively as they entered the kitchen, and it was Mordy who said, before his father had the chance to, "Thanks, Yael! It's great to come home to a breakfast like this."

"Ditto," Daniel said, smiling at his daughter. He shed his jacket and hat, adding, "Hi, Tzippy. How are you?"

"Fine, *baruch Hashem,* Mr. Newman," Tzippy answered shyly. The mere fact that Yael's father was a judge always had the effect of rendering her tongue tied. Fair haired and hazel eyed, the faintest blush showed clearly on her cheeks. Much to Tzippy's chagrin, it was apparent there now.

"What do you think about Yael's abilities as a cook? Not bad, eh?"

Tzippy nodded admiringly. "I can't even boil an egg yet. My mom says I'll be able to cook one day, but I don't know —"

"Well, you know what they say," Daniel remarked, taking his place at the sink to wash his hands. "Necessity is the mother of invention."

The memory of the tragic necessity that had thrust Yael into service as cook in lieu of her mother was like a dark wing whose tip brushed briefly through the sunny kitchen. Then the shadow was gone, and it was just Sunday morning again. There were good smells in the air, and stomachs rumbled in anticipation. Yael bustled about the kitchen, putting the finishing touches on breakfast.

Daniel sat and watched her, swelling inwardly with what could only be described as *nachas*. Had there ever been a word in any language, he wondered, that precisely paralleled the full meaning of that one? He thought not. Joy, satisfaction, triumph at a job well done — none of those words came close to doing justice to the richness of "*nachas*." Yael was not full grown yet, not by any means, but Daniel had raised her for over fourteen years — the last five of them all on his own — and he was pleased with the results so far. More than pleased. *Nachas.*

Over eggs and toast, he asked, "Would you girls like to ride into Baltimore with us this morning?"

Yael and Tzippy exchanged a considering glance. They had no special plans, and the prospect of a jaunt into the larger city was tempting. To cap the matter, Daniel said, "I thought we'd stop off at Seven Mile Market after dropping Mordy, and pick up some ice cream."

"You won't eat it till I get home, will you?" Mordy asked quickly.

"Not a drop," his father promised, rumpling his hair. Mordy flushed with pleasure, and Yael said, "Sure, we might as well go along. To pick out the right kind of ice cream."

"That's why I invited you," Daniel assured her solemnly. "These crucial decisions should never be made without consulting a woman's intuition." His eyes twinkled.

Now it was Yael's turn to smile. But the smile soon faded at the sound of her brother's snort. "*Woman?*"

"Well, I *am* one — almost. I have the intuition, anyway," Yael retorted hotly. Then, recalling her dignity, she turned to her father and asked, "More coffee, Daddy?"

"I'd love some." He allowed her to save face by pouring him coffee he did not really want, and took a sip at once. He smiled. "Delicious.

Just the way I like it."

Mordy's eye caught sight of the clock. "Yikes! I'm going to be *really* late if we don't get started. Rebbe's pretty lenient about kids coming in after the bell on Sundays, but —"

Daniel took the hint. His son was a stickler for being on time. In short order, all four of them had *bentched* and cleared the table, leaving the dishes in the sink for later. They piled into the car, boisterous and happy under the warming sun — and blissfully unaware that their every move was being watched through a pair of high-powered binoculars, trained on them from a basement window across the street.

Mordy was duly deposited at his yeshivah, the ice cream was selected with deliberation, and the drive home was safely effected. The girls wandered off to Yael's room, while Daniel went to his study to catch up on some learning. An unusual peace — unusual since he had received the first threatening note — seemed to wrap itself around the house like a feather-light comforter. Seated in his leather desk chair, Daniel closed his eyes for a moment to let the sensation wash over him.

It was true what they said: You never really appreciated what you had until you lost it. Before the threats had started coming, he had taken for granted a Sunday like this, when the hours could slip by, carelessly cherished, like silent ducks across a pond. A Sunday when freedom from the workday schedule could be savored, when nerves were not jangled and insides were mercifully free of knots. He prayed that this serenity would prove permanent — that the anonymous stalker, whoever he was, had satisfied his sick mind with thoroughly terrifying Daniel and would let it rest at that. He amused himself with a brief fantasy, in which that unknown man tossed his indelible marker into the trash can before catching a Greyhound bus to — anywhere. Cedar Hills would breathe easier when that bus pulled out of the station.

For the return trip from school, Mordy rejoined his car pool. As soon as he was home, Daniel, Mordy, and the two girls sat down to a lunch of freshly delivered pizza, hot from the box. Dessert was the ice cream they had picked out that morning. When they were done, Mordy, leaning back in his chair, said lazily, "So what do you want to do today?"

"Something outdoorsy," Yael said at once. "It's too nice a day to sit around inside."

"I'd have to agree with that," Daniel said. Tzippy nodded and murmured, almost inaudibly, "Me too."

Mordy looked interested. "The park? With our balls and mitts, Daddy?"

"And what about the girls?"

"Oh, that's all right," Yael said with a gracious wave. "Tzippy and I can sit under a tree and watch the two of you get all hot and bothered. We'll take along books in case we get bored."

"I'll get the drinks and fruit," Mordy said, hopping off his seat. He was well versed in the drill. Before long, water bottles, washed fruit, and a bag of pretzels had found their way into the tote bag slung over Mordy's shoulder. A baseball cap and catcher's mitt completed his outfit. The girls came downstairs with their books, and they all piled again into the family car for the short drive to nearby Sunrise Park.

The sun poised at the apex of its vast blue climb, then began its graceful descent to the west. In the park, children and their parents lolled about on the grass, relishing the feeling of summer in autumn. Jackets were shed and hats discarded. Mordy's ball flew in high, soaring arcs toward his father, who tossed it back with an energy that brought back a whiff of his younger days. Under a nearby tree, Yael and Tzippy divided their time between watching the progress of the catch, dipping into their books, and idly chatting. It was a golden day. To Daniel, it felt endless — a day under a spell of enchantment, in which time held no sway and the hours had lost their meaning.

But even enchanted days are subject to the setting sun, and with dusk a chill sprang up. Daniel collected his children, who in turn collected their paraphernalia, and they all made their way back to the car.

Supper was an impromptu barbecue on the Newman deck: steaks and hot dogs and — at Yael's insistence — fresh salad. One by one, the stars came out to light their little party. Yael sighed, and said, "Wasn't this a perfect day?"

Tzippy, her shyness mitigated by the darkness, murmured, "Just scrumptious!"

Mordy considered a blistering comment on girls and their mode of expression, then thought the better of it. "A good day," he agreed, eyeing the last hot dog in a speculative way. "You can have it," Daniel said. Mordy grinned sheepishly and reached for the mustard and a bun.

Yes, Daniel thought, a good day. The star-studded sky seemed to enclose them like a protective dome. The love between parents and children was here on this patio tonight, and friendship, and good, plentiful food, and the Torah values to inspire and elevate them all. It was a moment that was completely *now*, with the past like a softly shaded background and tomorrow still only a glimpse of light in the wings.

This barbecue tonight had been a good idea, too. He recalled the last time he and his kids had barbecued: Labor Day weekend at his parents' home. Hard to believe that only a short few weeks had elapsed since then. The memory, in turn, brought his mother to mind. She had been unusually brief on the phone when he called her on Friday to wish her a good Shabbos. She was probably miffed about the way he had declined her invitation to Miami for Sukkos. Under the influence of the stressless Sunday and a good steak, Daniel found himself wondering whether that decision had not been overly hasty.

From the look of things, the perpetrator of those notes — and, possibly, of the silent phone calls as well — had eased off, if not abandoned the project entirely. Daniel's earlier fears were slowly calming themselves, to the point where he felt almost ready to reverse his decision. Sukkos with his parents would be wonderful. The children always enjoyed their Bubby and Zaydie, and he himself looked forward to spending time with his father, whose health was worrisomely less than robust, and with his mother, who rarely failed to lift his spirits.

Somewhere between the last bite of steak and cleaning the grill, Daniel's mind was made up. With the water running in the kitchen sink as Yael and Tzippy did the washing up and Mordy tapped away at the computer in the study, Daniel went upstairs to his bedroom to use the phone there.

"Mom? Hi, it's me. How was your day?"

"Very nice." Was it his imagination, or was there still a touch of frost in her voice? "How are the children?"

"*Baruch Hashem,* they're doing well. Mordy aced a Gemara test this week, and Yael just started piano lessons with a new teacher. So she's happy."

"Very nice," Hilda Newman said again. Her tone seemed to imply that she was waiting for him to state his business. She must be even more annoyed with him than he suspected. Well, he was about to put an end to that.

"Mom, I have good news."

"Oh? You found someone to marry, maybe?"

He laughed. "Not that good. You remember your kind invitation to have the kids and me join you in Miami for Sukkos? On reconsideration, I've decided that we can make it after all!"

"But what about the children? Won't they miss their *friends*?" Hilda was as close to sarcastic as she could come.

"Sure they will. But it'll be worth it, just to spend the time with you and Dad."

There was a pause, like the hush before a speech. Then Hilda said, "It's too bad you didn't change your mind a little sooner, Daniel."

"What do you mean? There's still plenty of time until Sukkos."

"When you said you couldn't come, we decided to rent a vacation apartment upstairs from us in Miami, and bring Chaim and the family down instead."

"Really? "Daniel was taken aback. This would be the first time his brother had agreed to such an arrangement for *Yom Tov*. Usually, something — his desire to be home for the holiday, or his pride, financially speaking or both — had precluded his accepting his parents' generosity for this sort of thing. Daniel had grown accustomed to spending the holidays with his parents since Ella's death, but he, of course, had always paid his own way.

"How nice!" he went on, genuinely pleased for his brother. "Well, we can all be together then. I'll make reservations in a hotel close enough so that we can walk over to join each other for meals and things."

Again, the pause. Hilda's voice, after she had marshaled her thoughts, had lost its cool edge. She sounded distressed now. "Daniel, I don't know how to say this —"

He stiffened in apprehension. "I've always found that the best way is just to state it flat out, Mom. What?"

"Well, they accepted our invitation a few days ago, and last night

Gila called me to ask about a few things. She kept saying how nice it would be for their kids to have Bubby and Zaydie all to themselves this Sukkos. It's usually you and Yael and Mordy with us, you know."

"I know. And Gila is absolutely right, Mom," Daniel said quickly. "The kids *do* deserve a *Yom Tov* with you that's exclusively their own. We can hop down to see you later on — say, Chanukah time."

His answer was reasonable, and Daniel sounded perfectly composed as he gave it. But inside, his heart had dropped with a dismal thud. He had not realized how much he was looking forward to spending *Yom Tov* with his parents. As long as he had thought the choice was his, he had been able to be stoic about it. Now he felt as bereft as an abandoned child.

"Are you sure it's all right, Daniel? We did ask you first, you know."

He was no child, after all. He was a full-grown man, with a responsible job and two wonderful children — and no wife to lend focus and meaning to it all. Pulling himself together, he put a determined smile into his voice. "I know you did. And of course I don't blame you. You're going to have a wonderful time, and my kids'll get to stay right here at home with their friends. It'll be great."

He ended the conversation soon after that, knowing that his mother was upset at the way things had turned out but fairly confident that she had no idea how upset *he* was feeling.

Yael knocked on the door just as he was hanging up the phone. "Yes?"

"Daddy, Tzippy's parents are running late. They won't be back in Cedar Hills till at least 11 tonight. Can Tzippy sleep over?"

"Of course. Does she have her things?"

"That's just it. We need you to drive us over to her house for pajamas and her schoolbag and things."

"Fine." Daniel walked to the door, the same fixed smile on his face. The smile remained in place as he summoned Mordy to come along for the ride, and did not vanish when they returned home and he sat down to learn with his son. He might be reeling beneath the weight of his loneliness, but neither his kids nor his parents would ever know. Once again, the judge had spread his protective wings over the people he loved.

When the learning was finished and Mordy opened the study door, girlish laughter floated down to Daniel from somewhere upstairs. The children were happy — that was the important thing. That was the only thing that mattered.

He sat in the study, alone, long after Mordy had gone. In semidarkness, with only a single small lamp switched on, Daniel nursed his unseen wounds in the aftermath of as perfect a day as they had had in a long time.

36

Two things happened on Monday.

In a Baltimore courtroom, the prosecution concluded its case against Henry Downing for the murder of Al Simmonds.

And in the Cedar Hills office of Miriam Schumacher, MSW, Sara Muller experienced her first genuine breakthrough in her quest to rise above the rage and insecurity that had, for five long years, made an emotional quagmire of her life.

Martin Bedeker's long, aristocratic face was impassive as he called his last witness, but a tiny pulse throbbed rhythmically in his temple to betray an inner excitement. He was overdue for a dramatic victory, and this case looked like the one that was going to hand it to him. He waited until the witness had settled himself in his chair, then gave him an encouraging smile. Theodore Winslow — Ted to his friends — was young, intense, and visibly nervous. He had dark, straight, and very fine hair that fell like a baby's over his forehead and into his eyes. From time to time, he lifted a thin wrist to flick it away. The greenish suit and tie were neat, but clearly on the cheap end of the scale.

"Mr. Winslow," Bedeker began, pitching his voice to a conversational key, as though he and the younger man were seated across the coffee table in his living room, "state your profession, if you please."

"I was an engineering student. I do a little tinkering on the side, too. I've patented three of my own inventions already." There was more than a hint of pride in the witness's voice, and a touch of something else that was more difficult to define.

"'Was'? Have you switched to a different career, then?"

"I've taken a sort of a sabbatical from engineering. I work for Mr. Simmonds now — or, rather, I was working for him until he — until the end. I'm still attached to the project."

"And that project would be — ?"

Winslow looked surprised. "The baby bottle, of course. I act as a consultant, overseeing production."

"How," asked Bedeker, beginning to stroll casually along the line of the jury box, "does a young engineering student come to work for a commercial entrepreneur such as Mr. Simmonds?"

Winslow was quiet a moment, plunged into the recollection of his first meeting with the wealthy, the unscrupulous, the sometimes notorious Alexander Simmonds.

"It was at a Labor Day barbecue that I met him," he said at last.

"Perhaps you'll be so good as to describe that meeting to the jury."

"Frances Kates — that's Mr. Simmonds' sister — throws a big Labor Day bash every year, and my mother — well, she does some sewing for Mrs. Kates, and I've done odd jobs there in the summers, so we were invited. There were a lot of people there, people we didn't know —" the young man paused, breathed deeply, and added defiantly, "*wealthy* people. Neither Mother nor I was very comfortable, so we stayed quietly at the edges of the party, planning to leave early. I was chatting with Mother when suddenly, a hand tapped me on the shoulder from behind. Turning around, I saw that it was Mr. Simmonds himself. He joined our conversation, which surprised me. Even more surprising — he ended by inviting me to an informal supper at his home that night."

"Just like that?" Bedeker's brows rose theatrically to the edge of his hairline.

"Just like that. Later, he explained that he was always on the lookout for promising young men to work for him. He said that guys like me, self-educated people from poor backgrounds, were the bread-and-butter of America. He'd eavesdropped on my talk with Mother, and was interested in hiring me."

The prosecutor gave the jury time to absorb this information. Winslow's story painted Simmonds in a rosy, sentimental light, very different from the portrait of the shrewd businessman that had emerged till now. He was shown as a compassionate figure, a sort of fairy godfather, as it were, with a hand outstretched to help those less fortunate than himself actualize their potential. This, presumably, was why Bedeker had saved Winslow for last.

"Did you accept the invitation?"

"Yes, sir."

"So you had supper with him. Did he offer you the job that evening?"

"No. We met again the following day, at my workroom. Actually, our converted garage. Mr. Simmonds was interested in seeing my inventions."

"Was he impressed?"

There was no mistaking the pride in young Winslow's dark eyes as he answered, "I think so. In any case, he offered me a job right then and there."

"He thought that your talents were particularly suited to helping with his own invention, the new baby bottle?"

Winslow nodded, then glanced up at the judge, cleared his throat, and said, "Yes. He made me an offer I couldn't refuse. I didn't refuse it."

"You began work immediately?"

"As soon as the bottle was legally patented. Production started almost at once."

Bedeker stopped his strolling and turned to face the witness. "Mr. Winslow, what were your impressions of your employer?"

"Mr. Simmonds?" A reverent note crept into the young engineer's voice. The dark eyes looked away, over the heads of the spectators, as though they glimpsed his benefactor floating benevolently there. "He was brilliant," Winslow almost chanted. "And he gave me the chance to better myself, a chance to make some real money without waiting years to finish my education."

Bedeker opened his mouth to ask another question, but Ted Winslow had not finished answering the previous one. With a look on his face that could only be described as worshipful, the young man burst out emotionally, "I think Mr. Simmonds was the most wonderful man I ever met. It's a crying shame that he's dead. Whoever did that to him deserves to be put away for life!"

The prosecutor nodded once, ponderously, and glanced at the jury. Several of the jurors were nodding their heads in silent empathy. Winslow lifted a hand to brush away some hair that had fallen into his eyes, and when the hand came away there was a clear glitter of tears. Bedeker decided to leave well enough alone.

"I'd have to agree with you there, Mr. Winslow," he said quietly. Turning to Judge Newman, he said, "I'm finished, Your Honor."

Palladin's cross-examination shed no new light. In a broken voice the young engineering student repeated his glowing praise of the murdered man, and one or two members of the jury were seen to nod their heads in sympathy. Elsa Downing put a hand to her mouth to stifle a sob.

Palladin beat a hast retreat. "No futher questions, Your Honor."

All eyes turned to the prosecutor's desk. Martin Bedeker rose, suave and complacent.

"The State rests its case."

Later that day, after school, Sara walked into Miriam Schumacher's office with an attitude that can only be described as impatient. She was not in an introspective mood today.

The holidays were approaching, holding out the promise of a much-needed break from her teaching routine and an equally longed-for visit to her beloved family in Brooklyn. The weather was perfect for traveling: blue skies, cool breeze, vivid autumn colors intensifying daily. With her sights set so eagerly on the immediate future, the past seemed particularly unappealing, like a meal warmed over too many times and then left to congeal. That morning, she had almost but not quite found the courage to cancel the appointment. Sara admitted as much a few minutes into the session, when Mrs. Schumacher commented on her unusual restlessness.

"I can understand why you thought about canceling," the therapist said quietly. "But why did not you follow up on that impulse?"

Sara thought. "I guess I didn't want you to be disappointed with me," she confessed, cheeks coloring a delicate pink.

"*Me*, disappointed? Whose life is on the table here, Sara?"

"Uh — mine, of course." Sara was startled.

"Yes. Your life, not mine. Then why would your failure to keep the appointment disappoint *me*?" Mrs. Schumacher paused. "Did you think I'd be upset about losing the fee for the session?"

On the verge of replying in the affirmative, Sara suddenly reconsidered. "You know, I *thought* that was the reason. But now — I don't know."

"What other reason might I have for feeling disappointed in you?"

"You might think that I should be more energetic about solving my problems. Going around canceling sessions is not exactly the best way to do that."

The therapist smiled. "Let's not exaggerate, Sara. A no-show for one session is not the same thing as 'going around canceling sessions.' Why do you persist in seeing yourself in the worst possible light?"

"Do I do that?" Again, Sara was taken aback. "I didn't realize."

"Yes, you do. Pretty consistently, as a matter of fact. But let's get back to the more intriguing topic of my possible disappointment in you. What does that remind you of?" When Sara did not answer right away, she added, "The feelings you experienced when picturing my 'disappointment' — the discomfort, the fear, the shame — when have you felt those things before in your life?"

Suddenly, and poignantly, Sara was awash in those feelings again. She was 5 years old, watching her parents delight in her baby sister and feeling an uncomfortable heaviness in the region of her chest — a burden of unshed tears — because they did not find *her* as delightful. She was 9 years old, bringing home a new friend for the first time, and scared of losing that friendship if the fun she offered fell somehow short of the other girl's expectations. She was 14 and acutely self-conscious, terrified to open her mouth when the popular girls were around, lest her attempts at sparkling conversation fall flat and shame her.

She was 26, ecstatically engaged to be married but knowing, on a level so deep that she could get by without acknowledging its presence, that her expectations were not returned. Every word must be measured, every action must be just so, for fear of angering him, of disgusting him — of losing him.

"When?" Sara repeated, beginning to cry. "Always. Always."

Mrs. Shumacher handed her a box of tissues. "It's always the other person who sets your value, isn't it? Always the other guy who decides what you, Sara Muller, are really worth."

Dumbly, blowing her nose, Sara nodded.

"Well, when are you going to finally put a stop to that kind of thinking? No one can assess your self-worth but yourself! Or, as Eleanor Roosevelt put it, 'No one can be made to feel inferior without his consent.'"

"It's not only that. I was so afraid —"

"Afraid of what?"

Crying harder, so that she was almost incapable of coherent speech, Sara clenched her fists and whispered, "Afraid of losing their love — if I wasn't everything they wanted me to be."

She was deeply and thoroughly miserable. The tears poured from her in a continuous hiccuping stream, bubbling up from a profound well of sadness, drenching Sara, drowning her. But behind the pain was a blinding light. The light dazzled. It made her scrunch up her inner eye. But she felt that she had only now — this moment — truly begun to *see*.

The rest of the session was essentially a deepening and a restructuring of that first, basic flash of understanding. When it was over, Sara was herself again, pale but calm and aghast to think that she had nearly canceled this pivotal meeting.

Her work was by no means over. She was probing for buried treasure without a map, and there was no guarantee that she would strike gold. But at least she now had an inkling of where to dig.

Every interaction in life was an exchange, a barter: I will give you this, in exchange for that. You will provide me with an education, and I will sit quietly in class and listen. You will be a considerate and supportive friend to me, and I will do the same for you. You will give me your name and the security of marriage, and I will be a devoted helpmate.

Sara had a wealth of perfectly fine qualities to offer, yet she had fallen into the unhealthy habit of seeing herself as a pauper, and every exchange as an offer of charity. If someone cared for her as a friend, she was doing Sara a big favor. If a man offered his hand in marriage, she must be abysmally grateful — even if his heart did not come along with it.

As she thanked the therapist and prepared to return to the life outside the office doors, Sara pictured herself as a package on an auction block, with a price tag written in her own, and nobody else's, hand.

The sky shone just as brilliantly when she stepped outside, and the wind held a tang that would add spice to a long road trip. She had regretted not having a companion for the drive up from Cedar Hills on *erev Yom Tov*. Now she was grateful for it. She would have some very interesting thoughts to keep her company.

37

The phone rang in Vinny Fouza's cluttered bedroom. Without removing his eyes from the computer screen to which they were riveted, he groped around with his left hand. He pushed aside two Internet manuals and several pairs of dirty socks before the phone shrilled again, right under his hand. He picked up the receiver. "'Yo, Vinny here."

"Hey, Vinny. It's me."

"Joey?"

"Yeah. You sound nervous, Vin. Any problem?"

"No problem. It's just that I haven't seen you around in a couple of days. I thought —"

"Thought you got rid of me, huh? No such luck, buddy. Listen, I need a favor. A computer favor."

Judging by Vinny's expression, he had an idea what that favor was. Uneasily, he said, "Look, Joey, I'm starting to be sorry I ever introduced you to e-mail. Why don't you get your own computer and take care of your own mail? I'll set it all up for you and show you how to use it. It's easy."

"Maybe I will, when I lay my hands on a little cash. Meanwhile, I need you to send a message from me. Just a little one, Vin. No sweat."

"Why don't you come over and send it yourself?" The instant the words were out, Vinny regretted saying them. He wanted no part of Joe Mercutio, not these days, not when he was trying to get his own act together.

"I'm sort of laying low at the moment. A temporary problem, that's all."

"What?"

"No questions, okay?" There was an edge to Joey's voice. "Will you send the message for me?"

"Who's it to — that judge again?"

"That's none of your business!" Joey said sharply. "Just do what I tell you, and *don't ask questions.* Got that?"

Vinny could almost see the knife waving under his nose. The implicit threat in the other man's voice was impossible to ignore. "I don't want to get involved in nothing crooked," he muttered desperately. "I'm clean, and I want to stay that way, Joey."

"Crooked — me?" Joey laughed. "Just a little friendly correspondence, that's all. Now write this down. It won't take a minute."

Reluctantly, Vinny dug a pencil stub and a scrap of paper from the mess on his desk. "Okay, shoot." He winced. "I mean, I'm ready. Go ahead."

"This is in reply to that last message I got. Write, 'PLEASE DON'T TELL YOUR FATHER OR ANYONE ELSE. I DON'T REALLY WANT TO HURT ANYONE. I JUST NEED SOMEONE TO TALK TO.' Got that?"

"I think you're nuts."

"I said, *Got that?*"

"I got it, I got it."

"And remember, no questions. And no spilling the beans to anyone."

"Believe me," Vinny assured him fervently, "I don't plan to tell anyone about this crazy game of yours. I wish I never knew about it myself. I wish I never knew *you.*"

His mission accomplished, Joey relaxed. With a laugh, he said, "You won't feel that way when I'm rolling in the stuff and you want someone to treat you to a pizza. Or, hey, a champagne dinner! Old Joey Mercutio dishin' out the champagne — what do you think of that, buddy-boy?"

"Nuts," Vinny said again.

"We'll see who's nuts," Joey promised softly. "You send that message now, hear?"

"You gotta get off the phone first. I can't send it without a phone line."

"Well, the second I get off, then."

"I'll do it, I'll do it. Get off already."

"Good night, Vincent," Joey crooned, as full of himself as it is possible to get without bursting. "Sweet dreams —"

Vinny hung up.

Scowling at the screen, he weighed his options.

He could ignore the request — no, the demand. Joey had said that he was laying low, which probably meant he had the police out looking for him. But sooner or later he would be in circulation again, and Vinny was genuinely frightened by the memory of the strange glint in his old friend's eye of late — not to mention the knife. Joey had always been a wild kid, but this was something new. He just had not been the same since his brother Sal died in prison. Something in Joey had hardened. He was twisted and hard, like an old petrified root. Vinny didn't like it. He was afraid of it.

He could always *say* he had sent the message, but actually do nothing of the kind. Then again, Joey might have some way of knowing whether he had or had not, and if he learned the truth, Vinny did not want to find out what he could do with that wicked-looking knife of his.

The easiest thing — and the safest, as far as Joey was concerned — was to just send the stupid thing. After all, he had no proof that there was anything crooked involved in this e-mail business. This last message of Joey's did not sound violent or threatening. If anything, it was on the pathetic side, like the whine of a lonely kid looking for a friend.

With a shrug, Vinny clicked on his e-mail server and, in less than a minute, dispensed with the unsavory chore. That done, he moved quickly back to what he had been doing before the phone had rung.

In his absorption, he found it very easy to forget that he had ever heard from Joey that night.

Yael was waiting for her new piano teacher at the school's side entrance. Tzippy waited with her for a few minutes. Girls hurried by them in a ragged stream, heading for car pools and home. Like Yael and Tzippy, their shoulders were hunched inside light jackets which were proving less than effective against the sharp breeze. The weather had turned chilly again, Sunday's summery warmth only a sweet memory now.

They stood in a companionable silence, which Tzippy presently broke by saying, "I like your family."

Startled, Yael stared at her friend. "What do you like about us?" Then, with the beginnings of a slow smile, she added, "Not that I don't agree with you that there's lots to like. It just seems like a funny thing for you to say."

"Why? Don't you like my family?"

"Sure. But your family is —" Yael broke off.

"Is whole?" Tzippy shook her head. "You may have lost your mother when you were a kid, Yael, but your family doesn't *feel* broken. It just feels — like a little something is missing. I think your father's done a great job."

"So do I," Yael said softly. She peered past her friend's shoulder to where the various cars were pulling up to collect their quota of kids. As usual at this time of day, the parking lot was a sluggish sea of cars and the lanes leading to and from it were congested, the traffic slow and uneven under the direction of two or three harried teachers. When their own car pool arrived, Tzippy would be climbing aboard — but not Yael. She was going home with Miss Muller for her piano lesson.

"Yael?" Tzippy hesitated.

"What?"

"Do you think your father ever plans to get married again?"

Yael stiffened. "I don't know. He doesn't talk about it."

"Don't you think he'd want to?"

"Why do you keep harping on it? If he wants to, he will! It's none of my business."

Tzippy pressed, "But of course it is. You're his daughter, and Mordy's his son. Whose business *is* it, if not yours?"

Yael turned slowly. Facing her friend, she said, "Look. This is painful for me, okay? I don't want anyone to take my mother's place, ever. If I can't have her — I don't want anyone. Wouldn't you feel the same way if you were me?"

"I don't know," Tzippy said honestly. The sandy freckles on her forehead creased with the effort of thought. "It might be kind of nice to have someone older around. Someone to ask questions, to do girl-stuff with, and to cook and all that."

"I can cook. And Mrs. Marks is great," Yael retorted quickly.

Tzippy saw her ride car edging into the parking lot. "Whoops, there she is. Gotta run. Look, Yael, I'm not trying to put anyone down. It's just that your family is great, and would be even better if your father had a partner and you had someone around to be a sort of new mother. I didn't mean to hurt your feelings —" Her eyes darted anxiously from Yael to the waiting car, then back to Yael.

"I'm not hurt." Yael relented, touching her friend briefly on the arm to prove it. "I just can't imagine anyone taking my mother's place, that's all. And I'm not sure I'd want anyone to."

"Well, think it over," Tzippy advised. "Gotta run. Talk to you later. 'Bye!" And she was off at a scamper, ponytail flying.

Yael knew that she *would* think it over. The topic was not a totally new one to her, of course. In the secret places of her mind, in the darkness of her nighttime room, she had often mulled over the possibility of her father taking another wife. For five years, that possibility had seemed remote. Occasionally, he had make a rueful joke about *shadchanim* and blind dates, and she knew that he actually had taken the plunge once or twice. But that was all. She had believed she wanted it to stay that way.

Lately, though, she had begun to look wistfully upon her friends and their mothers. It was not that she wanted another *mother*, exactly. More like a much older sister, or a beloved aunt — Someone to talk to who would understand, the way a father or a brother or even a female housekeeper could not.

But there was no time to pursue the subject now. Miss Muller was hurrying along the side of the building, waving as she went. Pink cheeked from the brisk wind, the teacher looked breathless and excited and happy to see her. Why was *she* not married? Miss Muller was pretty, and nice, and she played the piano like nobody else. Rumor had it that she was pretty old, but right now she looked almost young enough to be in high school herself!

Yael waved back, stooped to pick up her schoolbag, and flew to meet her halfway. She, the piano, and Miss Muller were a magic threesome that came together only once a week and Yael was anxious to savor that time.

38

S ara paused with her key in the car door. "Yael, I'm afraid there's a small problem," she said.

"Problem? Oh, please, don't tell me you can't make our lesson today!"

The door swung open. Sara motioned for Yael to climb aboard, then rounded the car to the other side and let herself in. Buckling up, she said, "That's up to you. You see, I'm driving up to New York tomorrow to spend *Yom Tov* with my family. Last night, an old friend of my mother's called me. She lives in Baltimore, and wants me to take a package up to New York for her. The problem," she continued, anticipating the question that blazed from Yael's eyes, "is that I have to pick it up right now."

"Couldn't you get it after our lesson?"

Sara was apologetic. "That would be too late for that person. But there is a solution. If you don't mind having our lesson *after* I pick up the package —"

"Sure! Great! I have no problem at all with that. I could even come along to Baltimore with you now, if you want. That'll save time."

"What about your family? Will the change in plans cut into your dinner hour?"

"No problem. I can eat later." Yael added candidly, "I'd much rather play the piano than eat, anyway!"

Sara laughed, but her answer, when it came, was direct and to the point. "I think you'd better ask your father first."

"Oh, Daddy's not even home from work yet. I could say something to Mrs. Marks. But I'm sure it'll be fine."

Sara started the motor and drove slowly, against the current of the other cars, back to the school entrance. "Why don't you go inside, then, and call her?" Gentle as a suggestion, it nevertheless carried the ring of command.

Obediently, Yael got out of the car and went into the building. She was out again a moment later to borrow change for the call, and then she was talking to Mrs. Marks, explaining the situation. As she had hoped, the housekeeper had no objection to holding dinner for her. "Your father's bringing home that new clerk of his — that Jake fellow," she remarked. "I'm making pot roast and noodles."

"Yum. But he's not exactly a clerk, at least not yet. Daddy told me."

"Whatever he is, he's a bag of skin and bones and could use a good, home-cooked dinner. What these law students live on is beyond me!" Mrs. Marks suddenly went back to the matter at hand. "Go ahead with your teacher, Yael. I'll explain to your father when he comes in."

"Thanks a million, Mrs. Marks! See you later!" Yael hung up and ran back to the waiting car. Her shining eyes told Sara what she wanted to know. She turned the key in the ignition once more, and made a careful U-turn before heading away from the school, out towards the open highway.

The drive from Cedar Hills to Baltimore was a very familiar one to Yael. She kept up a running commentary on the landmarks they passed.

"See that sign? That's the exit you'd take if you want to get to the Reisterstown shopping district. The next one, Park Heights Avenue, takes you right to the heart of the *frum* community, and the one after that is the Greenspring exit."

"Thanks for the directions," Sara smiled. "I don't know Baltimore very well yet."

"If you stay in Cedar Hills, you'll get to know it pretty well. Most people go into Baltimore often, for the kosher restaurants. I can't wait till Cedar Hills gets kosher Chinese," Yael said wistfully.

"I know exactly how you feel — Let's see, I'm looking for West Strathmore. Which exit would be closest?"

"It depends," Yael said promptly. "Strathmore's a long street. You'd be best getting off at Greenspring and driving up in the direction of Park Heights until you find the number you want."

With that taken care of, the talk turned to other channels. Sara asked Yael how she was enjoying the tenth grade, and Yael asked Sara how she liked Cedar Hills, and especially the Bais Yaakov. Sara was enthusiastic in her response to the first question, more guarded about the second.

"A new teacher is always on probation," she said with a wry smile. "Talk to me again in a few months from now."

"Miss Muller —" Yael broke off, blushing.

"Yes?"

The words tumbled out all in a rush. "There are some mean girls in your class. I hear they're trying to make life miserable for you. Don't let them!"

Eyes on the road, Sara said calmly, "I don't intend to let them. There are some very nice girls in the class, too. If I can just persuade them to stop playing follow-the-leader, we can have a good year."

"You'll persuade them," Yael said with complete conviction. There was admiration in her eyes, and it filtered into her voice. "I know you will."

"I hope so." Sara said it lightly, but her hands clenched a little more tightly around the steering wheel. In a different tone, she said, "Look, there's a sign for the Greenspring exit. Get ready to direct me, Yael —"

Some five minutes later, the car was crawling its way up West Strathmore, with Yael's head halfway out the window as she peered at the house numbers. They found the one they wanted just a short distance from the junction with Park Heights Avenue. Sara hopped out, walked up to the front door, and rang the bell. The door was opened by a middle-aged woman in a neat, short wig, a housedress and slippers.

Yael observed the interplay from her window. It was like watching a pantomime: the welcoming hug, the invitation for Sara to come in for a few minutes, the polite refusal, the turning away to fetch the package, the thank-you, the good-bye hug. Sara was back behind the wheel in less time than Yael would have believed possible.

"Boy, that was fast," she marveled, as the teacher started up the car. "I thought for sure I'd be waiting ten minutes, at *least*."

"The trick is to be polite, but firm," Sara said, pulling out.

"I know how to be polite. But firm?" Yael grimaced, making Sara laugh.

"You need firmness lessons," she said. Holding the wheel with her left hand, she gestured grandly with her right. Her voice dropped a dramatic octave. "For one half-hour after each piano lesson, I shall undertake to instruct you in the fine art of saying 'no.' "

"I'd need at least three hours of instruction, and definitely more than once a week," Yael giggled.

"Ah, but you don't know my methods! I guarantee, young lady, that within an incredibly short amount of time, you'll be saying 'no' with an ease you've never dreamt possible!"

"I still don't think it's possible. I'm just not a firm kind of person."

"You're not?" Sara feigned enormous surprise.

"No."

"There, you see? You just said it!"

Teacher and student laughed together. A gentle warmth flooded Sara. She liked this girl very much; more, she liked what the girl did for her. Confronted with coldness and hostility from her own students, Sara relished Yael's friendliness and reveled in her frank admiration. Faygie Mandelbaum and Yael Newman: the only two people, to date, in all of Cedar Hills that she could call 'friend'.

As she approached the light at the top of Strathmore, where it intersected Park Heights, Sara began to see vaguely familiar territory. She had not been here for five years, but she recognized this area. Not far away was a place she did not like to think about. A block that was a focal point for shattered dreams. A block that had long represented everything she dreaded and wished to shun.

But now, at this moment, filled with good feeling in this jaunt with Yael, and with the determination to grow that had arisen in yesterday's emotional therapy session, Sara decided that it was time to start exorcising those old demons. At the corner, the light turned green. She turned left.

"Miss Muller, where are you going? The Beltway is that way!" Yael pointed urgently to the right.

"This'll only take a minute. I'm going to make a tiny detour. I want to see a house I once knew."

"Did you have a friend there?" Yael asked curiously.

"You could say that." Sara would say nothing more. She concentrated on driving. A short way up the road from Strathmore, she found the street she was looking for: Menlo Drive. It was filled with Jewish homes and families now, as it had been then. Slowly, she turned into the block and made her slow, relentless way up the street and into the most painful region of her history.

"We used to live on this block," Yael remarked suddenly.

"What?" Sara's head abruptly swiveled, like a puppet's.

"Before my mother died. We lived right over there." She pointed to a modest house on the left, sitting primly on its neat patch of lawn, trim bushes fronting the brick facade. Then she turned her head away. "I don't like seeing it this way, with other people living there."

"I'm sorry. We'll get right off the block, then."

"Did you see the house you wanted, Miss Muller?"

"Yes. As a matter of fact, it's just two doors down from the one you lived in."

"It is?" Now it was Yael's turn to stare.

"Yes."

"What a coincidence!"

"Yes," Sara said again, gazing at the house in which her former *chasan* had lived, and where his parents still, presumably, resided. "Yes, it is."

With a feeling of vague discomfort, she glanced over her shoulder again at the house Yael had pointed out. The memory was crusted over with time and with anguish, and it had been formed in the first place in a cauldron of darkness and fog. But she was certain nevertheless; there was no question about it. The former Newman place was the one from whose driveway the overalled stranger had come running out, in the dead of that mist-filled night on which Sara's engagement, and her heart, had broken in two.

39

Had Yael been her contemporary, Sara might have used the return journey to tell the story of her ill-fated engagement. She would have received the other woman's sympathy, and they might have continued, perhaps, in a far-reaching discussion of men and marriage. Somewhere along the line, the description of the man in the overalls might very possibly have surfaced. The grown-up Yael might have mentioned to her father the stranger's odd presence at their former home. How far that might have taken Daniel on the road to understanding the exact nature of his wife's "accident" can only remain a matter of conjecture.

But Yael was not Sara's contemporary; she was a high-school sophomore, and Sara was not about to confide in her about so sensitive a topic. So the two rode home in high spirits, each determined to banish the momentary cloud that Menlo Drive — for other people, a perfectly pleasant block — had cast upon them. As they drove out of the city the talk turned to music, and that topic held them enthralled the rest of the way home.

Daniel and Jake had not yet arrived by the time Yael entered the house with Sara. After the briefest of greetings to Mrs. Marks, Sara settled her pupil at the piano. She wanted to get the lesson out of the way as quickly as possible. She had inconvenienced the Newmans enough today.

Daniel walked in ten minutes later. The strains of piano music had enveloped him and Jake almost before they were out of the car. He smiled, picturing Yael at the keys, then listened further and frowned as he realized that his daughter could not be the one playing the instrument. The music was too expert, surely beyond Yael's abilities. Pushing open the door, he nodded at the sight that confirmed what he had expected to see: the new piano teacher on the bench beside Yael.

"She's good," Jake whispered to Daniel, as they shed their coats. Neither Sara nor Yael, caught up in the intricacies of the piece, heard the door open or turned around. The melody soared from the piano like birds freed from captivity, then sank to a quieter pitch, a deepfelt throb of peace and rejoicing. When the last note had pierced the air, lingered there a moment and faded, both men enthusiastically applauded. Sara leaped off the bench like a pheasant startled out of the undergrowth.

"I didn't know anyone was listening," she gasped, a hand to her heart.

"We didn't want to disturb you," Daniel apologized. "You were playing so beautifully. Is Yael supposed to master that piece? It sounds very difficult."

"I think she can do it." Sara was regaining her composure. "Sorry — I'm Sara Muller."

"Daniel Newman. We spoke on the phone, remember?" As Sara nodded, he motioned to the younger man. "Jake Meisler, my — um, associate." Jake smiled broadly. Yael, jiggling with impatience, said pointedly, "Mrs. Marks is holding dinner until the lesson's over."

"In that case, we won't be disturbing the two of you any longer," Daniel said smoothly. "And hello to you, too, my darling daughter."

Contritely, Yael smiled and said, "Hi there, Daddy. Sorry."

Smiling, he motioned for them to continue. Sara reseated herself at the bench, where she waited self-consciously until the men had left the room before resuming the lesson. Yael's father was much younger than she had expected. Somehow, one imagines a judge as silver haired and stately. Not that she would know much about it, never having laid eyes on one in her life.

Until now, she thought, with an inward chuckle.

She called her wayward mind to attention. "This *is* a difficult piece, Yael. It's going to stretch your abilities a little. But then, that's what we're here for, isn't it?"

"You bet," Yael said happily, and plunged down hard on the keys to form the first glorious chord.

Mordy had come in just minutes before his sister. He made a beeline for the computer in his father's study. His practiced eye ran down the column of new e-mail, checking the senders' names. There it was! *"Vincent Fouza."* Who *was* this Fouza character, and what foul threats was he going to spout this time?

To Mordy's astonishment, the new message was completely out of character with the others he had received — so much so, that he checked the name again before rereading it. There was no doubt about it; it was the same person.

PLEASE DON'T TELL YOUR FATHER OR ANYONE ELSE. I DON'T REALLY WANT TO HURT ANYONE. I JUST NEED SOMEONE TO TALK TO.

What was *that* about?

Interestingly, it was this message that made Mordy, for the first time, seriously consider confiding in his father. An angry, blustering threat he could (he thought) deal with. It was this sudden about-face that threw him off balance. Was it a ploy to win his confidence? Or did the writer have a real change of heart? I DON'T REALLY WANT TO HURT ANYONE. Had the threats been a sham all along? Was he dealing with a madman, or a coward, or something else entirely?

He did not know. But, being Mordy, he meant to find out. He would not throw the whole puzzling business into his father's lap. He would try to ferret out the solution to this mystery all by himself. I JUST NEED SOMEONE TO TALK TO. *Well, here I come,* Mordy thought, pressing the REPLY button.

He thought a moment, composing his answer. Dimly, he heard his father's voice in the living room, and some other man's, and then the piano music again. Daddy was liable to bring his guest into the study any time now. Rapidly, he typed, YOU CAN TALK TO ME. AND YOU CAN START BY ANSWERING THIS: IF YOU DON'T WANT TO HURT ANYONE, WHY DID YOU SEND ALL THOSE THREATENING LETTERS? WAS IT SOME SORT OF SICK JOKE, OR WHAT?

Hastily, he pressed SEND and waited the three interminable seconds that it took to send his message winging toward its electronic destination. And not a moment too soon. Footsteps sounded on the hardwood floor on the other side of the study door; it opened, framing his father and Jake Meisler in the doorway.

"Hi, Mordy. How was yeshivah today?" Daniel greeted him.

"Fine, Daddy. Not much homework today. We had a substitute for math and science." Mordy managed a real smile.

"That's good. It'll give us some extra time for our learning tonight."

Mordy nodded. "I was just about to print out your e-mail messages, Daddy."

"Can it wait? I'd like to enjoy a little chat with my guest before dinner. You remember Jake."

"Sure." Carefully, he clicked out of the e-mail program. All record of his correspondence with the threatener was out of sight, where his father would never dream of looking for it. "I'm allergic to computers," Daniel frequently joked. Mordy, for one, was fervently glad — especially now — that this was so.

Jake had strolled over to stand behind him. "Like computer games?" he asked, making conversation.

"Uh, sure," Mordy said uneasily. He wondered how much Jake had seen. Not much, he decided. Even if the e-mail program had still been on screen, the name Vincent Fouza would mean nothing to the law student. Jake's manner was casual, suspicion free. Mordy breathed easily again.

Before he left the room, he had time to note the way his father sat in his armchair, facing his guest. He had one ankle hooked over the other knee, his manner relaxed and contented. How different from the Daniel who had faced Detective Garrity in this same room, and not so long ago, either! Mordy had not been able to see his father then, of course — but the strain in his voice had been plain to hear, even filtering up through the ventilation system to the bathroom where Mordy had crouched in fascinated dread, listening.

The change had come about because he, Mordy, had taken it upon himself to protect his father from the knowledge that the stalker had not vanished into silence, as Daniel thought, but had merely transferred to a different medium.

He hated keeping secrets from his father. It made him feel vaguely guilty all the time. But if that was what it took to keep Daddy looking calm and happy, the way he looked right now — well, a guilty conscience was a small price to pay.

Mordy left the study, intending to spend the remaining time until dinner in his room. The smell of pot roast and gravy wafting out from the kitchen was going to drive him crazy with hunger if he remained down here. But the doorbell's ring stopped him halfway to the stairs.

"Mordy, is that you? Can you get that, please?" Mrs. Marks called from the kitchen.

"Sure!" Mordy executed an about-face and trotted to the door. The ring sounded again just as he reached it. Sara threw one curious glance over her shoulder, but Yael never stopped playing. Mordy peeked through the peephole. Reassured by what he saw, he threw open the door. "Yes?"

A moment later, he was trotting back to the study. At his knock, his father called out, "What is it?"

"It's me, Dad. There's someone at the door to see you. She says its important."

"Come in, son." As Mordy stepped inside, Daniel said, "*She,* you said?"

"Yes. It's a woman, middle aged, I guess you'd call her. She says she needs to talk to you, and it's urgent."

Daniel exchanged a quizzical glance with Jake, then asked his son, "Did she give you a name?"

"Uh-huh. She said to tell you it's Elsa Downing."

40

There was a poignant silence after Mordy pronounced the name of his father's visitor. Daniel looked at Jake, who stared back, shaking his head. Mordy, mindful of his duty as host — he had, after all, been the one to open the door to Mrs. Downing — asked, "Dad, what should I tell her?"

Daniel roused himself. In seconds, he was on his feet and heading for the door. "I'll take care of it, Mordy. Thanks." Over his shoulder, he called to Jake, "Want to join us?"

"Wouldn't miss it for the world," Jake assured him, hurrying to catch up. Mordy followed at their heels, a curious third.

They found Elsa Downing waiting patiently on the doorstep. Despite the petite frame that looked as if it could be carried away by a strong breeze, there was a rocklike quality to the way she stood, as though she had been planted there at the beginning of time and had not moved since. She looked much the same as she did, day after day, in court, except that she wore outdoor clothing. The coat was of recent vintage and good quality, but she wore it with a careless air that lent it a drabness it did not deserve. Her hair, and face, too, appeared neglected. Sleep, it was obvious, was a rarity these days.

Gently, Daniel greeted her, "Good evening, Mrs. Downing. Won't you come in?" Nowhere in his manner did he betray a sign of the astonishment he had to be feeling. Conscious of this consideration, his visitor bobbed her head and followed the direction of his outstretched arm into the living room.

Sara and Yael were still seated at the piano, but the music had stilled with Daniel's entrance. "Go on," he urged. To Elsa Downing, he said, "Please, this way." He led the way back to the study.

"Now," he said, when she was seated comfortably in one of the two red-leather armchairs opposite the desk — Jake took the other — "Can I get you a drink, Mrs. Downing?"

"No, nothing. Thank you." The accent was broadly Baltimore. Her hands were folded neatly in her lap, but their placidity was belied by a tiny muscle that jumped with every pulse. "I apologize for intruding, Judge Newman. I know it's unheard of, and maybe even a misdemeanor, though I hope to heaven it's no crime! But I had to see you." The strained eyes, sunk in two charcoal hollows and wrapped in a network of fine lines, pleaded with him to be generous. Daniel's heart wrung with pity. He himself had lost his wife, and now this woman's husband was fighting a losing legal battle for his own. Yes, he admitted to himself — a losing battle. Slowly, methodically, ruthlessly, the state had built a circumstantial case against Henry Downing that no evidence, so far, had come to light to refute.

"What can I do for you?" he asked simply. Aware of Jake's piercing gaze, he added quickly, "Though legally, you understand, there isn't much I *can* do. You are aware of that, are you not, Mrs. Downing?"

She nodded. "I know. I didn't come here to try to bribe you or anything. I'd never do a thing like that!"

"Of course not. But you do have legal counsel, Mrs. Downing. Your lawyer is the one you should be consulting, not me. I'm helpless here — my hands are tied."

Elsa Downing looked down at her own hands for a long moment. They were thin and veined, dotted with age spots that she took no trouble to conceal. When she raised her head, her eyes were swimming in tears. "Mr. Palladin's a good lawyer, I know that. And I believe he's doing everything he can. But he's young, so young. How can he understand?"

Daniel felt the weight of his years pressing on him, because he *did* understand. He understood the impossibility, for this devoted wife, of contemplating a life without her Henry. If asked, a little more than five years earlier, he, too, would have declared, "Life minus Ella? Impossible!" But the impossible grievously, tragically, happened. He had been forced years ago to come to terms with that chilling fact. The woman before him was clearly shaken by the gargantuan task of facing it now.

"They're going to convict him, Judge!" she cried suddenly, in a passion of despair she made no further effort to control. "They're going to take my Henry away from me!"

"You don't know that, Mrs. Downing. There could —"

"He's trying to make Henry out to be a greedy monster," she continued, as if he had not spoken. "That prosecutor — the Roman-looking one, lean and hungry — he's doing everything in his power to make it look like my Henry would do anything for money. But anyone who knew him would tell you just the opposite! Henry never cared a bit about money — never! When we won the jackpot, the first thing he did was give thousands away to our relatives and to charities. We live very simply, even now. There's enough to last us to the end of our days, if we're careful. And that's even without the money he invested with that — with Simmonds." She clenched her fists in her lap. "Henry would *never* go after a man with a knife like that — and certainly not because of *money*!" She had run out of breath. Mutely, she filled her lungs and begged the judge to understand.

He did understand. Even more, he believed her. And that frightened him. The strength of his personal bias in the Downings' favor was growing daily. Though it would not be he who passed down the verdict, he had already, in his heart, passed judgment.

"Mrs. Downing," he said, choosing a tone that tried to convey his sympathy without subtracting anything from the firmness that had to be there, "You will be given every opportunity to say all this as a witness in your husband's defense. But for now — well, I'm afraid you were correct in what you said earlier. This conversation is improper. We shouldn't be having it. I am the judge in a case in which your husband is the defendant." He shook his head, appalled at himself for having allowed matters to proceed even this far. It had been the shock of hearing her name on his son's lips, and the pity that had wrenched through him at the sight of her, so frail and so patient, on his doorstep. She tried to speak, but he held up a hand. "If I listen to another word, I may be forced to declare a mistrial, and your husband will have to go through the whole thing again."

Elsa Downing looked stricken. She whispered, "I didn't realize —"

"*I* can't listen to any more," Daniel continued. "But my friend here,

Jacob Meisler, will be happy to hear anything you have to say. He is not connected to my court in any official capacity. There is no law against his having a conversation with you, though I'll admit that having it here in my home might be considered highly irregular." He sighed. "We are bound by the rules that govern our lives, Mrs. Downing — not by our humanity or our compassion. I'm sorry."

"But you *are* compassionate!" the older woman cried. "Ninety-nine out of a hundred judges would probably have thrown me out the minute they laid eyes on me. I knew I shouldn't have come. And I wouldn't have, except that I was feeling so desperate —"

Smiling, Daniel held up his hand again. "Remember, not another word." He stood up. "I'll leave you two to confer in here. Jake will see you out when you're done, Mrs. Downing. It's been a pleasure to meet you in person." He hesitated. "I sincerely wish you the best of luck." He turned to go.

"But —" Mrs. Downing stopped herself, biting her lip.

Daniel turned around.

"Yes?" he asked in a surprised tone.

Looking at Jake, she said, "I don't mean to sound rude, young man," she said, addressing him directly for the first time. "But if you're not connected to the court, what earthly use can you be to me — or to Henry?"

"That," Jake said, almost gaily, "remains to be seen. If the good judge will deprive us of his company, I'd like to hear more of what you were saying earlier. Your words greatly interest me."

Daniel smiled gratefully at his young friend, inclined his head at Mrs. Downing, and left. The study door closed behind him, leaving the improbable pair facing each other in their matching armchairs.

Jake plunged in. "I'm sure you've spent hours and hours going over in your mind what happened at your house that night. You must have some thoughts that could help shed light on this whole business. You're positive that your husband could not have murdered Al Simmonds in your garden that night."

"That's right."

"Then who," he asked, deadly serious now, "do you think *did* do it?"

When he had finished talking with Elsa Downing, Jake escorted her to the door and saw her out. He wore a thoughtful expression. Sara and Yael were winding up their lesson. Daniel, unwilling to exchange so much as another word with his surprise visitor, was in the kitchen, trying to be helpful and succeeding mainly in getting in Mrs. Marks' way. When he heard the front door close, he stepped out into the living room again.

Yael and Sara did not stop their low-voiced dialogue, which, from snippets that floated Daniel's way, seemed to be heavily musical in nature. Jake, on the other hand, hurried over to the judge, face alight.

"Judge Newman, don't even say it. I'm not going to repeat a word of my conversation with Elsa Downing to you. But I'll tell you this much, sir: *I believe her*. And I can think of one or two places where her lawyer can dig a little deeper than he has, or maybe hasn't even thought of digging at all." The keen gray eyes met Daniel's squarely. "Permission to contact him, sir?"

Daniel hesitated, then nodded. "I did tell her to turn to you. Do whatever you think best, Jake. But remember: I mustn't be involved in any way. Don't tell me what you're up to." He grinned. "Good thing I didn't take you on as my clerk, hmm?"

"As the man said, *Gam zu l'tovah*," Jake agreed. He sniffed the air. "Something smells awfully good," he said plaintively. "Will dinner be ready soon?"

Laughing, Daniel returned to the kitchen to find out.

41

Mrs. Marks was just putting the finishing touches on her pot roast. When Daniel next appeared in the living room, carrying a bowl of salad in both hands and a bottle of dressing tucked under one arm, Yael and her piano teacher were at the door saying their good-byes.

"Have a wonderful Rosh Hashanah, Yael," Sara said warmly. "And, of course, a *kesivah vachasimah tovah.*"

"You, too, Miss Muller. When do you start out for New York?"

"At the crack of dawn. It's a four-hour drive, you know, and I want to get there in plenty of time to visit with my twin nieces, and the baby, and to help my mother with some of the cooking. Though, knowing her," Sara smiled, "she'll have it all done before I get there."

Yael caught sight of her father. She was bursting with the day's news. "Daddy! Miss Muller took me into Baltimore before, and we drove right down our old block. She has friends there."

"Not really," Sara said quickly, blushing slightly. "Former friends, I guess you could call them."

Before Daniel could ask their name, Yael, oblivious to Sara's discomfort, chattered on, "The new people at our old house put little lights all along the path up to the door. They must be pretty at night, all lit up. Can we get them, too?"

"We'll see." Daniel smiled as he set down the salad bowl. Looking up, he noticed that Sara was smiling at his daughter, too, and with the same indulgent fondness he himself was feeling. Yael had made no secret of the fact that she adored her new music teacher, and from the looks of things, this Miss Muller returned his daughter's sentiments. It lifted Daniel's heart to see the quick hug the two exchanged, and to hear Yael's, "Have a safe trip, Miss Muller. Our next lesson is next Wednesday, right?"

Sara laughed. *"Im Yirtzah Hashem,* yes. Right after school."

Only then did Yael open the door for her, as though she had been unwilling to let her go before extracting the promise. Daniel walked to the door, too, and nodded courteously. "Have a good *Yom Tov,* Miss Muller. And thank you."

Sara did not ask what the thanks were for. Seeing the way the father's eyes rested on his daughter, she did not have to.

The rest of them assembled at the table for dinner. The meal was comfortable and homey, the food outstanding. Mrs. Marks had, as usual, outdone herself. After sampling the fare, Jake announced with enthusiasm, "This meat just melts in the mouth." The housekeeper, wreathed in smiles, turned to her boss. "I like this one," she told Mr. Newman in a stage whisper. "He's invited here all the time."

"That, ma'am, would be my pleasure," Jake said with old Southern courtesy. Yael giggled. Then a contented silence descended on the group.

It was Jake who broke the silence presently, to tell one of his funny stories, which soon had Mordy laughing so hard that he succumbed to an attack of the hiccups. Yael brought him a glass of water, which he got down with difficulty. Playing to his audience, Mordy made the most of the situation, coughing and sputtering and interrupting himself at intervals with enormous hiccups, so that a generous amount of the water in his glass ended up spraying the table and some of those seated around it. Daniel remarked, "Sure you can handle dessert, Mordy? Maybe you'd better lie down in your room for a while." Miraculously, first the sputtering and then the hiccups vanished without a trace.

Dessert over, Yael and Mordy were off to their rooms to attack their homework. Daniel and Jake retired to the study, both carrying steaming mugs of apple-cinnamon tea.

"I can't stay long, sir. I meet my *chavrusah* at 9 o'clock," Jake said.

"Oh? What are the two of you learning?"

Torah topics held the two absorbed for some time. Soon, however, Jake's eyes took on an inward quality.

"What's on your mind?" Daniel asked. "You're suddenly very quiet."

Jake replied. "Oh, sorry. I was thinking of Elsa Downing, actually."

Daniel made no answer. Jake went on, "I wasn't even thinking specifically about the case just now. It's more the way she *seemed* than what she said, sir. She's awfully tied to her husband, isn't she?"

"That's exactly the impression I had. In fact, Judge Lionel remarked on the same thing; he presided over the indictment. As if an invisible bond stretched between them through the courtroom, he said." Daniel shook his head. "I've seen it myself. *Felt* it, almost — like a rope you could touch with your hand. He never leaves the courtroom without turning around to smile at her. As though she's the one who needs comforting more than he does."

"Sad," Jake said. With a wistful grin, he added, "I wouldn't mind having a wife someday who was that wrapped up in *me*!"

"Wouldn't we all," Daniel sighed. He took a tentative sip of his tea. "Seems to be cool enough to drink by now."

Jake grew still. In the short time they had known each other, the judge had never touched upon the tragedy that had so permanently disrupted his life. Daniel knew that he could let his comment go at that, with no further elaboration. Jake did not expect any more. But he liked Jake, he respected him, and he found that he wanted to confide in him. Gently, he set down his mug.

"My wife and I had a wonderful marriage, Jake. These last years, I simply couldn't imagine sharing my life with anyone else. Now, though —"

Jake leaned forward to prompt softly, "Now, sir?"

With another sigh, and a half-smile, Daniel roused himself to continue. "I never believed it could happen — but, lately, I've been feeling differently. It's as if time has created a bridge between the *me* that was then, and the me that's around today. *That* Daniel Newman was firmly wedded to Ella Newman, and to even contemplate anything else was unthinkable. But the man I am today is a five-year widower, and a single father with two growing children who need a mother as much — as much as I know I need a wife."

He paused, as though to let himself absorb the import of the confession he had uttered aloud for the first time. Jake watched him, not moving a muscle.

"A wonderful marriage," Daniel repeated softly. "If I knew I could have the same thing again, I guess I'd be less reluctant to take the chance."

Deeply flattered by the confidences, Jake tried for the right blend of deference and empathy as he said, "I'm sure, with the right person, it could be just as good. Different, maybe, but good."

"You're probably right. But I'll never know until I take the plunge. And I'm afraid I'm still a little too much of a coward for that." Daniel smiled suddenly, and sent a keen glance at his guest. "So, what about you, Jake? You're certainly of marriageable age. Anything cooking in the *shidduch* department?"

"Now and then," Jake replied. "But I have to admit, I haven't been the best candidate for the matchmakers. Having started my learning so late, I wanted to catch up a little before searching seriously for a wife. I want to have something to offer, when I do find her."

"Something more than a law degree?"

"A lot more," Jake answered seriously. "But lately, I've been thinking that — well, enough is enough. I've prepared myself for a long time now. Maybe it's time, as you say, to take the plunge. If I wait until I'm perfect, I'll be waiting forever. Getting married doesn't mean you stop growing. You just do it together with someone else, that's all."

"Sounds like a wise move."

The two men sipped their tea and thought their thoughts. It was Daniel who broke the silence.

"Tell me, Jake, what do you think of my kids? Five years without a mother is a long time. I'm always wondering if there's something I'm missing, something I'm not getting right."

"You've done a great job with them," Jake said quickly. "They're a real credit to you."

"Thank you. But still I'm not a mother."

"Can't argue with you there, sir!" Both men chuckled. Then Jake said, "I see both Yael and Mordy as healthy, normal kids. They're also mature and respectful — and very likable! You have nothing to worry about, sir." He cleared his throat. "That is, in my humble opinion."

"Thank you. And you have my wholehearted permission to leave out the 'sirs.' "

"Yes, sir," Jake grinned. Chuckling, Daniel let his gaze wander to the window, its shades still open to the night. The gift of Indian summer seemed to be passing; a keen wind had sprung up and was making the tree branches sway and bend.

They sat silently awhile longer, each lost in a dream of the future. Finally, Jake glanced at his wristwatch and struggled reluctantly to his feet. "It's that time."

"Want a lift home?"

"No, thanks, it's not far. I'd like to walk. It's a nice night, and walking's the best way I know for putting my thoughts in order."

"I know what you mean." Daniel stood up to walk him to the door. The house was quiet. Mrs. Marks had tidied the kitchen and departed for her own home. The children were upstairs, presumably busy with their assignments, though a murmur from Yael's room told him that his daughter was once again doing her studying courtesy of Ma Bell.

At the door, Jake turned impulsively and said to the judge, "I have a feeling about this. About all of it — the Downings, and myself, and you, too, sir. I think it's going to turn out all right. I think our hearts' desire is there for the taking. We're just going to have to be clever enough to recognize it, that's all."

"Let's pray for wisdom, then." Daniel's words were spoken lightly, but the gravity in his eyes said otherwise. Jake held the other's gaze, and nodded. Without exchanging another word, he slipped out into the night.

Despite his appointment with his *chavrusah*, Jake did not hurry away at once. He lingered for a few minutes at the end of the path that led from the Newman's front door down to the sidewalk, lost in thought. The streetlight above his head cast a bright yellow glow. An identical lamp, across the street, shed another shaft of light that bounced sharply off something in the open basement window of the house there. The glint caught Jake's eye, but he was too absorbed in his musings to do more than subconsciously register it.

Vaguely, he had a feeling that something was wrong, that the reflection he had glimpsed had no business being where it was. His perfunctory gaze swept the peeling paint and sagging shutters of the house across the street, and the unkempt lawn with its straggling weeds and the FOR SALE sign sitting in discouraging fashion in the middle.

Whatever he had seen was gone now. It had not been important enough to make him do more than pause a moment in his own thoughts. Besides, he was late.

With his long, rapid stride, Jake was halfway down the block before the man in the basement picked up his binoculars again.

42

The Jewish New Year dawned clear and unseasonably cool. Mothers who had gambled on wool or velvet holiday outfits for their little ones beamed with pleasure, and prayed that their more important decisions in the coming year be just as much on the mark. Those who had chosen garb more suited to the vanished summer shrugged philosophically: *Zohl zein ah kapporah!* May such trivial disappointments represent the sum total of our discomfort this year!

Sara, ensconced in her childhood bedroom in Flatbush, shivered as she stood by the window she had just thrown open. After filling her lungs a token few times, Sara hastily pulled down the sash. It was time to get ready for shul.

The drive up from Cedar Hills had been blessedly uneventful. Recalling other trips that had been otherwise — a smoking engine in the middle of the Delaware Memorial Bridge came vividly to mind — she could only be grateful. In fact, she had determined that gratitude, and not self-pity, would be the motif of her personal Rosh Hashanah this year. If she thought she had plenty to be frustrated with in her life, she had just as much to be thankful for. Though she was unmarried, she was also healthy and strong. Though she had a difficult class this year, at least she had a job!

What kind of person dismissed the good and focused exclusively on only those things that were missing from the scheme of her happiness? Not a person of very much character, she had decided. And if there was one thing Sara needed to cling to, to develop, to treasure as her greatest asset, it was her character. Age would steal whatever beauty Hashem had endowed her with, but it could also season her with grace, insight, and wisdom. Character.

Feeling more at peace than she had for many Rosh Hashanahs past, she prepared to speak to her Creator formally, in a shul filled with other worshipers. She would still beseech Him for what she lacked. But this time, it would be different. This time, she would begin by acknowledging everything that He had already given her, and by expressing her faith — a faith she arduously worked on, every day — that the lot He had seen fit to apportion to Sara Muller was, by definition, the right one for her.

She put on a suit her mother had not seen yet, something she had picked up on sale in Baltimore. It was a pale, mint green — a color that complemented the gray-green of her eyes and brought out the rose in her cheeks. It was a fine suit, a suit that would make Ma smile, and then sigh. Was everybody blind, that they could not see the pearl that was her daughter?

That would be the beginning. Then would come the meal, with Debby and her family there, and Sara would have her twin nieces climbing all over her, begging her to play — and making Ma sigh again at all the wasted years. This, in turn, would inevitably remind her mother of Moish, the once favored son-in-law-to-be. The memories would stir up all of Ma's pain and resentment and anger, like an ugly sediment that should have been left to lie undisturbed at the bottom of some lifeless and forsaken pond.

Sara could only hope that the sanctity of the day would prompt Ma to omit at least some of the scathing observations she usually made on the topic. She had known her mother to ride that particular, bitter hobbyhorse for a full half-hour at a time.

If Sara's own heart had been broken when her engagement ended, her mother's had been cruelly lacerated. Sara doubted if anything short of a new, happier, and more permanent attachment would ever really heal it. For that matter, she could say the same about herself.

For Chaim Newman, this Rosh Hashanah had a sweeter flavor than usual.

With his daughter's room nearing completion, Tova was ecstatic. In her joy, she was especially helpful around the house, lending her mother a willing hand with everything from the cooking to the entertaining of her younger siblings. This, in turn, made Gila happy. And a happy Gila meant a more contented Chaim. If he was still nowhere near the man he longed to be, there was no denying that there were fewer feelings of anxiety and inadequacy gnawing at his innards these days. He could approach the holiday knowing that he had provided his wife and daughter with the home improvement they wanted, *and* was about to whisk them all away to sunny Florida for Sukkos. That was enough to make any man feel pretty good about himself —

Except that the new bedroom was being financed by a *gemach*, and the Sukkos trip by his parents. As a provider, Chaim was exactly where he had been last year, and for far too many years before that.

Tying his tie, as he gazed at his reflection in the mirror, he felt a resolution forming out of the mishmash of yearnings that made up so much of his inner life. As surely as the tie was taking shape beneath his practiced fingers, he would take his courage in hand and ask for a raise this year. He did not know when, exactly — but next Rosh Hashanah, he planned, with G-d's help, to be able to hand his wife a larger paycheck than he had been handing her until now.

He smoothed the tie, adjusted the knot, and tightened it to the perfect degree of tension. Crisp and elegant, it hung down to the precisely perfect point on his shirt. Gila always said that no one had Chaim's way with a necktie.

It was a talent, he thought with dry humor, that just might stand him in good stead. Asking for the raise he wanted was not without its risks. The powers that be could very well justify his darkest, most secret fear — and decide that he was worth only as much as they were already paying him, and no more. To save face, Chaim might have to reluctantly resign his position.

Well, if that happened — Heaven forbid! — he could always find work as a rich man's valet.

Hilda Newman felt less than sanguine this Rosh Hashanah. Leaving the shul just before the end of *davening* to prepare their lunch, she walked heavily, aware of a new hollowness as she peered into the face of the upcoming year. She saw an empty space, tinged with fear.

A woman who spent nearly all of her time serving either her family or her shul and community, she brought a fairly clear conscience to the High Holy Days. Of course, there were always faults to be acknowledged, amends to be made, and sins atoned for; she was only human, after all. But she had always felt herself to be a woman blessed by Heaven with special favor. Her life read like a menu of delights: a delicious childhood, followed by a well-done marriage and scrumptious years of childrearing. Finally, with both boys married and raising fine families of their own, her cup had been full.

Then came Ella's accident. The shock had lingered a long time, and the pain at seeing her son so bereft never really left her. Still, her own life ticked along much as before, filled with meaningful and enjoyable activities. Between sisterhood functions, fund-raising teas and luncheons for other charitable causes, and hostessing her extended family on summers and holidays, she had hardly had a moment to herself — and that was the way she had wanted it.

It was all different now. From here on, time would hang heavily on her hands. There would be the stir and bustle of settling Jon and herself in Florida, but that would soon subside. Then, the new routine would set in. She winced at the prospect of the life she might anticipate there: long, sedate days and nights, punctuated by nothing more strenuous than a stroll along the boardwalk or more exciting than a sale at Saks.

There would be visits, of course. Chaim, Gila, and the family for Sukkos, and then Daniel, she hoped, for Chanukah. Daniel had promised to drive into Baltimore with the kids sometime before they left for Miami. She had not seen much of them lately.

She set the table slowly, relishing the touch and the look of the fine china and crystal that had lain hidden in cupboards, biding their time, while the boys were growing up. The wide bay window beyond the table invited in the sunlight while denying entrance to the chill wind. Light danced off the crystal goblets, sending an arrow of pleasure through Hilda.

Maybe this was the way it was going to have to be from now on, she thought. Small pleasures instead of large ones; significance in tiny, everyday acts. Like a warm, voluminous blanket, she would drape her active, giving, take-charge nature over her husband. He would become her sole focus, his continued good health her aim. Please G-d, the two of them would enjoy the gentle companionship that would be their reward for all the hectic years that came before.

It would have to be enough.

"So what's new in that school of yours?" Faygie Mandelbaum's father asked over the brisket and tzimmes.

Faygie shrugged. "Nothing much. Same old place." She had been teaching there for three years, ever since her move from her parents' home in Silver Spring into the Cedar Hills apartment she shared with two friends. "They hired a new teacher this year. She and I are becoming good friends."

"What's her name?" her mother asked, the serving spoon poised in the act of ladling some more mashed potatoes onto Faygie's plate. Faygie had learned years ago not to bother protesting. To Mrs. Mandelbaum, her youngest would always be the one who needed the extra portion, the added dollop of attention, the little indulgences that, in a younger child, might be called "spoiling." The fact that Faygie was a mature 25-year-old seemed to have escaped her notice.

"Sara Muller," Faygie replied. "Originally from New York. If you know of anyone for her, she could really use a *shidduch*. She's over 30 already."

Her mother made a tsk-tsk sound with her tongue. "A pretty girl? Smart?"

"She has to be smart if she teaches for Rebbetzin Goodman. And she's pretty, too. She was engaged once, years ago. It left her burned, I think."

Again, the sympathetic click. "I'll have to think. Why don't you invite her over for a meal?"

"Yeah, let her join the crowd," chortled Tzvi, Faygie's oldest brother-in-law. At every festive meal, he made a great show of complaining about the crowded conditions at his in-laws' table, which was always loaded with as many children and grandchildren as it could hold.

"Really, Faygie," her sister, Tzvi's wife, urged. "Invite her to come tomorrow. We can meet her, and maybe think of someone for her."

"Sara's gone back to New York to be with her family for *Yom Tov*."

"At least she has family." With that comforting remark, Mrs. Mandelbaum lifted her spoon and turned to her husband. "More potatoes, Heshy?"

Fagyie regarded her mother fondly. She had been in her mid-40's when she had Faygie, so she was 70 now — and feeling her age. Faygie did not like the new slowness that had come into the older woman's step. "Brittle bones, the doctor tells me I have," Mrs. Mandelbaum had explained when questioned. "I have to be careful not to fall." She had made a face, laughing at herself, at impending old age, at life. "I'm like a baby again, taking baby steps!"

For her part, Faygie found nothing to laugh about. Her thoughts ran, as they frequently did these days, to Yoni, the man she was seeing. He would be returning to Israel after the *Yamim Tovim* — and taking Faygie's decision with him. Though she had determined not to think about it over Rosh Hashanah, she found herself irresistibly drawn to the opposing tugs of the arguments, *for* and *against.*

She wanted to get married. That was indisputable. She wanted to marry, to raise a family, to give her parents *nachas* — not to mention the joy and security she longed for herself. She gazed at her mother's face, and then her father's, seeing there the lines that the years had drawn, and knowing that time, implacable, would not wait for her forever. If she wanted to give her parents that *nachas,* it would have to be soon.

But that same reasoning was also pulling her away from the commitment that Yoni wanted. Marrying him would mean moving across the world, far from her aging parents. It would mean not being near when they needed her. It would also mean, as she had told Sara, missing her precious nieces' and nephews' growing-up years. The thought of meeting them as near-strangers on formal, once-a-year visits made her shudder. It was not the life she had envisioned for herself — or the life she was ready to embrace.

Well, she did not have to decide now. She had nearly three more weeks, until the end of Sukkos. Much could happen between then and now. When she saw Yoni again after Rosh Hashanah, she would be carefully noncommittal. What they might have together would have to be pretty special to tear her away from what she already had.

She would wait and see.

Ari Rabinowitz's Rosh Hashanah, on the West Coast, began three hours after that of his relatives back East. His *Yom Tov* meals were a little different, too, as his mother — the former Judy Stavinsky — liked to use local produce in her recipes. Her chickens tended to be baked with such improbable partners as oranges and artichokes, or even grapefruits. Ari did not mind the avocado salad, which his mom insisted on calling guacamole, though, personally, he preferred the old-fashioned meat and potatoes that his Bubby would have prepared. But it was no use telling his mother so. She always had a tendency to be different. Moving thousands of miles away from her native city had not been enough; she had turned Californian, heart and soul.

Yom Tov passed quietly, and then Shabbos. Ari's father recited the *Havdalah*. Ari was nearing his bar mitzvah, so he would fast the next day, *Tzom Gedalyah*. He and his parents discussed the advisability of waking up before daybreak to eat an early breakfast before the fast began.

"If you decide to set your alarm clock, then please wake me, too," he said. "I'm not going to set my own."

He liked these little games of chance, liked not knowing exactly how things would turn out. Maybe there was a little bit of his mother in him, too — He wandered up to his room and switched on his computer.

There was a new e-mail message from his cousin Mordy in Cedar Hills.

GOT ANOTHER MESSAGE FROM EL CREEPO JUST BEFORE YOM TOV. HE SAYS HE'S LONELY AND NEEDS A FRIEND. WANNA APPLY FOR THE JOB? HA, HA.

P.S. REMEMBER, THIS IS STILL A SECRET!!

Ari stared at the screen, then shook his head. That Mordy — what a whacky imagination! He belonged out here in Lala Land, not back in staid old Maryland.

The first message he had sent, the one where he had talked about the death threats, had sent shivers up Ari's spine. This one, though, only confirmed what Ari had suspected from the first: that the whole thing was a giant joke, a representative specimen of his cousin's strange sense of humor.

Grinning, Ari wrote back: NO, THANKS. YOU'RE PROBABLY MORE HIS TYPE. SEND MY BEST REGARDS, THOUGH!

Still wearing a grin, Ari pressed the SEND button.

After that first chilling message, he had seriously considered breaking his cousin's confidence and telling his parents what Mordy had written. Now he was glad he had held his tongue. What a fool he would have looked like!

43

Henry Downing's trial resumed on Monday, after a four-day recess over the Jewish New Year and the weekend that followed. It was the defense's turn to present its case.

Counsel for the defense, Neil Palladin, stood up, slightly rumpled as usual, his demeanor solemn but guardedly optimistic. Over the attorney's shoulder, in the row just behind the defendant's table, Daniel spotted Elsa Downing in her usual place. He could not see the pale, age-stained hands, but could easily imagine them clasped in her lap, the way they had been in his house — fingers grasping each other tightly as if to draw from a depleted wellspring of courage. After a single glance at the strained white face, Daniel studiously avoided looking at her. If any semblance of objectivity were to be maintained in this trial, it was vital that he treat the defendant's wife exactly as he would any other spectator at this trial.

But even as the resolution formed and hardened, Daniel found himself wondering whether Jake had spoken to Palladin, and what — if any — new insights he had offered.

The defense opened with a series of character witnesses. Each in turn, Downing's former employer, two old friends, and the woman who cleaned his house, sat in the witness box to heap praise on the man standing trial for murder.

His former boss described Downing as hard working, steady, and scrupulously honest. The old friends spoke of Henry's loyalty, integrity, and his willingness to lend a hand to a pal who was down. The cleaning woman swept a thatch of grizzled gray hair off her brow with one calloused hand and stated flatly, "I not work for no one as good to me as the Downings — Mister *and* Missis. Always treat me like I am a visitor, instead of come to scrub their house. They pay me on time, too — and a big bonus two times a year."

"Do you still work for the Downings, Ms. Willis?" Palladin asked.

"Miz Downing, she give me a leave of absence when her husband got took away. Say she rather keep busy herself, cleaning the house, or she go stark, starin' crazy. Pays me right along, even though I don't come in no more."

Palladin nodded. "Thank you, Ms. Willis. That's all." Turning, he announced, "I would like to call Mrs. Elsa Downing to the stand."

Like a woman in a dream, Elsa rose slowly from her bench and made her way to the witness box. The walk seemed to take an eternity. Every eye followed the slight, erect figure, and more than one heart beat in sympathy with her plight.

Whatever her husband might or might not have done, this suffering woman was innocent of wrongdoing. She had shared a decent existence with the man she had married, stood by him through the vicissitudes of life, and risen with him on the wings of good fortune when they had come into their unexpected pot of gold. Now, that same man stood accused of the vilest of crimes: the taking of another's life. The silence as she seated herself in the witness's chair was total.

"Mrs. Downing." Palladin's voice was deeply respectful. "I'm sorry to have to call on you at this difficult time. Truly sorry."

"Whatever I can do to help Henry, I'm prepared to do." She spoke quietly, but with resolution.

"Tell us," Palladin said, "what kind of man you married — how many years ago?"

"Forty-two. For forty-two years I've been married to Henry Downing — and every one of them has been a blessing and a joy! No woman could have a kinder, more faithful, or more generous husband." So profound was her emotion, and so acute her stress, that the words emerged almost stonelike, dropping like hard little pebbles into the pool of silence in the courtroom. At the defendant's table, Henry Downing watched and listened with grave absorption.

"What about your husband's financial integrity, Mrs. Downing?"

"Henry is as honest as the day. I've never known him to cheat anybody, or to demand what wasn't rightly his." Suddenly, Elsa came startlingly alive. Leaning forward to grasp the rail of the box, she said in ringing tones, "Money, for its own sake, meant nothing to him! You have to understand this, to understand who Henry was . . . who he *is*. He gave away thousands of dollars from the lottery money without blinking an eye. We bought a nice house and live quietly there, not extravagantly at all. Anyone who could believe that my husband would *kill* someone — for money —" The words trailed off in a burst of incredulous laughter. The laughter had an almost hysterical edge to it.

Palladin waited until she had regained a measure of calm before asking, "If money means as little to your husband as you say, why did he make such a fuss about the money Mr. Simmonds owed him?"

"Henry is no fool, "Elsa said, flinging up her head. "Right is right. Business is business. He made an investment in good faith and expected to be treated the same way. No one wants to see himself cheated. Why should he?"

Palladin waited a beat, then asked, very gently, "Was that the only reason, Mrs. Downing?"

As abruptly as it had come, the animation left her. With bowed shoulders and drooping gray head, Elsa Downing said, "No. We — Henry had been to the doctor. His heart isn't very strong. They've already done one bypass operation and don't think it advisable to do another. Henry — Henry wanted to make sure I'd be provided for —"

There was a stir in the courtroom at this. Angrily, Bedeker jumped to his feet. "Objection! Irrelevant, Your Honor!"

Daniel gazed at the prosecutor thoughtfully. "I'm afraid I'll have to disagree there, Mr. Bedeker. This case is essentially about money. Anything that pertains to the defendant's financial situation is relevant. Overruled."

A few minutes later, with Palladin retired, Bedeker approached the witness box.

"Mrs. Downing, you say your husband wanted desperately for you to be well provided for in the case of his — er, untimely demise. Is that correct?"

"Yes."

"That desperation might, in fact, have led him to view Mr. Simmonds' reluctance to share the profits of their joint enterprise in rather

a panic-stricken light, might it not? It might, in fact, have led him to —
shall we say, desperate measures?"

"*Objection!* "Palladin was furious. "Counsel is leading the witness."

Bedeker bowed his head, urbane as ever. "I withdraw the question.
Mrs. Downing, did your husband discuss his business affairs with
you?"

"Some of them," Elsa answered cautiously.

"Did he discuss, specifically, his difficulties with Mr. Simmonds?"

"Yes, he did. He was upset. Mr. Simmonds had promised —"

"Thank you, Mrs. Downing. Did you ever hear your husband
threaten Mr. Simmonds with physical violence?" His voice took on a
casual, almost chanting tone. "You know how it goes. The two of you
are discussing the whole frustrating situation, and he'll make a
comment such as, 'Wait till I get my hands on that old so-and-so . . .' "
Bedeker paused. "Well?"

Elsa hesitated.

"The truth, Mrs. Downing. You are under oath."

"Oh, you know how men talk when they're aggravated. He might
have said something like that now and then, but it didn't mean any—"

Once again, the prosecutor cut her off. "Thank you. So, by your
testimony, your husband, who now stands accused of murdering Al
Simmonds, actually threatened, in your hearing, to do him violence. Is
that correct?"

"You're twisting my words! You know as well as I do that Henry
never actually meant —"

"*You are under oath, Mrs. Downing.* Now, is that correct?"

Palladin jumped up again. "Objection. Counsel is bullying the
witness. She has already answered the question once. Permission
requested to let Mrs. Downing step down, Your Honor."

Daniel looked with compassion upon the woman in the witness box.
To Bedeker, he said, "I believe the witness *has* answered the question.
Let's hear the transcript, please."

In a wooden voice, the court stenographer read aloud, "Did-you-
ever-hear-your-husband-threaten-Mr.-Simmonds-with-physical-vio-
lence? You-know-how-it-goes-the-two-of-you-are-discussing-the-
whole-frustrating-situation-and-he'll-make-a-comment-such-as-'Wait-
till-I-get-my-hands-on-that-old-so-and-so . . . '-Well?-The-truth-Mrs.-
Downing-you-are-under-oath. Oh-you-know-how-men-talk-when-

they're-aggravated-he-might-have-said-something-like-that-now-
and-then-but-it-didn't-mean-any—"

The stenographer broke off, regarding the judge questioningly.

"Thank you. That's all." Addressing Bedeker, Daniel said, "As
you've just heard, Mrs. Downing did answer the question the first
time you asked it. I am going to sustain Mr. Palladin's objection." To
Elsa, he said gently, "Do you feel capable of continuing, Mrs.
Downing?"

"That will be unnecessary," Bedeker said crisply. He was already
halfway to his table. "As you've just pointed out, Your Honor, the
witness has already answered my question — quite adequately."

With a triumphant smile at the jury, the prosecutor took his seat.

"He's good," Jake said.

Paul Hencken, the judge's clerk, nodded as he sipped his coffee.
Setting down his cup, he said, "Oh, Bedeker's one of the best. I've seen
him turn a case right around on its head, taking a sympathetic jury
and getting them to bring in a guilty verdict." Sagely, he nodded his
head, and repeated, "One of the best."

Hencken's air of vast experience did not sit well with Jake, but he
concealed his irritation. With Daniel refusing to discuss the case with
him any longer, since his unexpected visit from Elsa Downing, Jake
felt a burning need to hash it over with someone. Hencken was on the
spot, and he was knowledgeable.

"What do you think of Downing's chances?" Jake asked. His own
cup of black coffee lay cold and ignored at his elbow. Courthouse
coffee was nothing to write home about; he had only ordered it to
keep Hencken company. "Will Palladin get him off?"

"Are you kidding? Unless he has something pretty dramatic up his
sleeve, I'd say Downing's goose is definitely cooked."

"The medical testimony from his wife might sway the jury. A few of
them are middle-aged men, probably with some heart problems of
their own."

"That has nothing at all to do with the question of Al Simmonds'
murder, and Bedeker is going to make very sure that the jury
remembers that."

"Well, what about all those character witnesses? Downing came up smelling like a rose there, for sure."

"Character witnesses," the clerk told him, "are worth zilch when it comes to a murder trial. Oh, they can help if the case is extremely shaky — which this one is not. Downing had motive, opportunity, and means. Who's going to believe that he *didn't* step into his own garden and stick that knife into Simmonds?"

"Anyone could have sneaked into that garden after dark! Security wasn't all that tight at the Downings' place, you know that," Jake argued. "And, from the sound of things, Simmonds was the type to have more than one enemy. He was slimy, he was ruthless, he was —"

"He was killed in Henry Downing's back yard," Hencken said implacably. He took a final sip, then set down his cup and stood up. "Thanks for the coffee. I've got to be going. The recess is nearly over."

Jake rose to accompany him. "You never know. Palladin just may *have* something up his sleeve." He refrained, with difficulty, from adding, *I've been speaking to him about one or two little ideas of my own . . .*

Paul Hencken hurried on, saying nothing. His silence spoke volumes.

Neil Palladin did have something up his sleeve. Scarcely had the courtroom settled down when he stood up and addressed the judge.

"The defense requests a week's recess," Palladin announced.

The jurors, newly seated, jerked around in surprise. Daniel frowned. "Our intention was to wind up this trial as speedily as possible. A lengthy ordeal is of no benefit to anyone."

"I'm aware of that, Your Honor. But a new line of inquiry has just presented itself to me. I feel that it would be grossly irresponsible of the defense not to look into it."

Daniel motioned for both counselors to approach the bench. Leaning forward, he asked quietly, "What's this all about, Neil?"

"A possible new suspect, Your Honor. As defense counsel, I feel it would be negligent to ignore this avenue of inquiry." Palladin spoke formally, but his face looked young and anxious.

"Does this suspect fall into the realm of genuine possibility?" Daniel asked, his tone gentle. "Or wishful speculation?"

Palladin hesitated. "I think it's worth pursuing, sir. If I could only have a week to check into it —"

"You can have three days," Daniel decided. "I dislike calling a recess in the middle of a trial, and we've just come out of a four-day break. However, I will respect your effort to aid your client to justice."

"Your Honor!" Bedeker sputtered. "This is highly irregular. I must protest!"

"You can do that, if you wish," Daniel said agreeably. "In my judgment, the cause of true justice will best be served by giving the defense the time it needs, in light of this new avenue." He cocked an eyebrow at Palladin. "Another suspect, you say? Want to give us a hint?"

Palladin hesitated. "With respect, sir, I'd rather not at this time."

"I expect an updated witness list," Bedeker told him coldly.

"You'll have it."

"Three days," Daniel said, nodding to dismiss the counselors. He waited until they had reached their own tables and sat down, before picking up his gavel. With a single sharp rap, he called, "This court is adjourned until 10 a.m. Thursday morning. Mr. Palladin, I trust you will help us come to a speedy conclusion at that time?" Daniel did not plan to work on Friday, which was *erev Yom Kippur*. Though he had acquiesced to the defense's request, he was not pleased. The trial appeared to be dragging on, and his calendar bulged with upcoming cases.

"Yes, sir," Palladin said, looking more nervous than grateful.

With a few final instructions to the jury about refraining from reading about, hearing about, or discussing the case over the course of the next few days, Daniel adjourned the court.

The last thing he saw, before retiring to his chambers, was Elsa Downing rushing over to the defense counsel, an urgent question stamped all over her wan, tired, but still hopeful face.

44

Before he left, Daniel met with the court clerk to rearrange his schedule. During the next three days, while the Simmonds trial was on hold, he would preside over some of the arraignments and minor hearings that lay at the head of the pipeline.

Business taken care of, Daniel slung on his coat and, with an air of unaccustomed repose, walked out of the courthouse. Jake, as usual, was right beside him.

The sense of freedom arising from the unexpected recess in the Simmonds' trial was sharply heightened by the sight of his car in the parking lot, blissfully bare of threatening notes, anonymous or otherwise. It had been weeks since he had received the messages, and he was inclined to believe the whole matter dead and buried. Someone had played a cruel and malicious prank on him once, twice — three times, if you included the series of silent phone calls — and then lost interest. It was as simple as that.

Remembering his reaction to the first note, discovered on this very spot, Daniel felt his blood begin to surge. But there was no point in letting himself get angry all over again. The nightmare was over. He could breathe easy now. Lucky he had never officially called in the police, as Garrity had urged. The kids need never know about their brush with terror. A new year had been ushered in, and with it a sense of having been reprieved. It was a jaunty and smiling Daniel who unlocked the passenger door for his young friend.

"Thanks," Jake said, slipping inside. Daniel rounded the front of the car and took his place behind the wheel. To his own surprise, he found himself saying — almost casually — "Did I ever tell you" (though he knew quite well that he had not) "that I once found a death threat on my windshield at the end of the day's work?"

"No! Who was it from?"

"Anonymous." Daniel started the engine.

"Did you inform the police?"

"In an unofficial capacity, yes. It happened not so long ago, actually. There were two notes, and then the whole thing died down. *Baruch Hashem*," he added, not quite so casually.

"What did the notes say?"

Daniel was beginning to regret having opened the topic. Maneuvering carefully out of the lot and blending into traffic took all his concentration for a minute. Then he said, "Something about my wife's death being no accident . . . and that I would be next."

Jake ventured, "That must have shaken you up." Without waiting for an answer to the obvious, he asked in the tone of one thinking aloud, "Could it have happened that way? Is it possible that it *wasn't* an accident?"

Daniel was about to offer a firm denial, when honesty compelled him to rephrase his answer. "Strictly speaking, anything is possible. Some masked marauder might have tampered with the brakes. Some thug might have driven Ella, somehow, off the road in that storm. But the fact remains that there *was* a storm raging at the time, and the highway was slick, visibility poor. What happened to my wife might have happened to anyone." Unconsciously, his foot pressed harder on the gas pedal, making the car shoot forward. Somebody honked at him. Muttering to himself, Daniel slowed down.

"Are you saying there's no way of finding out the truth after all this time, sir?"

"I'm saying that nobody is about to do so on the strength of some anonymous note." The words emerged more sharply than Daniel had intended. "Sorry. It's not easy for me to talk about this. I don't know why I brought it up at all."

Obligingly, Jake changed the subject. Daniel was polite on the ride home, and bade Jake a warm farewell as he dropped him off at his apartment, but it was clear that his mind was a long way off.

Daniel was not, however, to be permitted to avoid the subject for long. That very evening, after dinner, Garrity phoned.

"It's been over a week since I reported in, but I wanted to let you know I haven't forgotten about you, Dan. We've had our hands full with that Beltway shooting and a couple of other things, or I would've gotten back to you sooner."

"We celebrated our New Year on Thursday and Friday, so I wouldn't have been available in any case."

"Good. Uh, Happy New Year — Anyway, Dan, I've set up a couple of reliable prison guards to keep a special eye on Mario Esplanada and Gerry Towson. Esplanada had his usual visitors last week. Nothing changed hands except a food package, and that was thoroughly checked out beforehand. He would fit the educational profile of the note-writer — that is, aggressive, mean, and poorly educated. There's no question that he has violent tendencies. He's also, according to his cellmate, been spouting off about the prosecutor who landed him there, and about some crooked pal who let him down — and you."

"Spouting off, how?"

"Just whining, possibly. He seems the whining kind. But this character definitely deserves having an eye kept on him. Like they say in the hospitals: We're keeping him under observation."

Daniel smiled. "You're mixing up two professions. In law, we call it 'innocent till proven guilty.' "

"We're talking about someone who's already been convicted, remember. Though not, of course, of sending death threats." Garrity paused. "Not yet, anyway."

"Why don't you just ask him?"

"I may just do that," the detective said thoughtfully. "Confront him head on, shake him up, see if he talks."

"And the other one? Towson?"

"Nothing suspicious on him so far. Doesn't get many visitors, and those that do come aren't regular. Freehy, on the other hand — the guy they've put on probation, theft and attempted arson, remember? — is an interesting prospect. One of my men followed him into a stationery store yesterday, saw him pick up a white ruled tablet and a package of pens. *Black* pens."

"My notes were written in indelible marker. And the paper wasn't ruled."

"I know. Still, he bears watching."

"Why? Because he bought himself a pad to write his shopping lists on? Mark, aren't you grabbing at straws here?"

There was a brief, exasperated silence. Then the detective burst out, "Dan, we're doing what we can. Do you or do you not want the perpetrator caught?"

"Of course I do," Daniel said slowly. "But it's been weeks since the last threat. The whole thing seems to have blown over. Maybe we should just let it die."

Garrity's voice sharpened. "Sick minds can be very, very patient, Dan. What's a few weeks to a guy who's been nursing a grievance for years, maybe?"

"So when do we declare the case officially closed?" Daniel asked testily. "How long do we have to wait?"

"Listen, buddy, it's no skin off my nose if you want the investigation dropped. I'm only trying to protect *you*, see?"

"Yes," Daniel sighed heavily. "I see. And I'm sorry I rode you so hard, Mark. It's just that this whole exercise is beginning to seem pointless. You have more important cases to solve than an anonymous note-writer who seems to have vanished into oblivion."

Garrity relented. "Okay, you're forgiven. And I'm not letting it die yet. I'll keep you posted, Dan."

"Thanks, Mark. I mean that."

"I know you do." The connection was abruptly severed.

Daniel replaced the receiver, staring straight ahead of him at nothing. There was a tap at the study door.

He roused himself. "Yes?"

Mordy's head popped into view. "Okay if I use the computer now, Dad?"

"Fine. I was just leaving, anyway."

"Where to?" Mordy asked, seating himself in front of the monitor.

"Just the kitchen. Going to see if there's any more of that pie Mrs. Marks served for dessert tonight. Suddenly, I'm starving —"

When he had the room to himself, Mordy quickly activated the e-mail program. Nothing from Vincent Fouza tonight.

Half-pleased, half-disappointed, he switched to a game of solitaire and busied himself with its mindless competition for a few minutes.

Less than fifty yards away, "Vincent Fouza" was sitting in the darkness of his basement, the notepad in his lap illuminated only by the beam of a palm-sized flashlight on his knee. He was composing another message to his pen pal across the street.

This one he was determined to send himself — police or no police. Nine days had passed since his abortive attack on the liquor store. If he went out after dark and was very careful, he would make it to Vinny's house without a problem. It was time he took back control of this all-important aspect of his plan. It was not that he distrusted Vinny. This was just too important to leave to others, that's all.

The pot of intrigue was rapidly coming to a boil. A gleam of malicious anticipation shown in the dark eyes of Joey Mercutio.

45

Driving back down from New York on Sunday, Sara was filled with a pleasant sense of well-being. The wind that blew great, cotton-puff clouds around the sky was exhilarating; her car purred along like a tiger, swallowing the highway in one smooth, continuous motion; a new year was starting. If the *school* year had not exactly begun on exactly the right foot, there was plenty of time to change that. In time, her class would come to respect and even like her. The radical leap to Cedar Hills would justify itself. She would even (might as well dream big!) meet her *bashert* and live happily ever after. All was right in the world.

It was easy to feel this way as she drove along, her family's affection still clinging to her like smoke after a campfire. It was a simple matter to nurture optimistic dreams, while munching on Ma's delicious brisket sandwiches and the cupcakes the twins had made as a bon voyage gift: slightly lopsided, but liberally sugared with love. She carried all the warmth of her visit along with her, to shelter her from the chilly solitude of her own life.

The warmth, and the well-being, lasted exactly until bedtime.

Crawling into bed in her very quiet room, in her very quiet apartment, Sara felt her illusions pop like so many overfilled balloons. She pulled the covers up to her chin and listened to the silence. It was no friendly thing, that silence. It held out no promise of being broken at any time by a loved one's voice. To Sara, it sounded like silence eternal. And it closed in on her like a great muffling blanket, to stifle the flickering flame of hope in her heart.

She thought of the dreams she had nurtured in the car on the way down. Might as well dream big, she had decided then, with a laugh. And why not? Dreams, after all, were all she really had.

Turning over with a despairing thump, she closed her eyes and tried to sink into the memories of the *Yom Tov* just past, and the love that had enveloped her then. Her parents and sister could not have been warmer, and Debbie's children were a delight; but she wanted more. She was way overdue for a family of her own, for the husband and children that should belong to *her*.

For the moment, though, this was all she had. So she squeezed her eyes shut against tomorrow's harsh reality, and spent her last few waking moments remembering what it felt like to be cherished.

And then, at last, came sleep, to drop a curtain of blessed oblivion over both yesterday and tomorrow.

It was a good thing, Sara realized as she entered her classroom the next day, that she had descended from the pinnacle of her rosy dreams the night before. The reception accorded her by the class was no friendlier than it had been before the holiday. Sara plowed through the lesson she had so carefully prepared, fighting the bitterness that threatened to rise up in her throat and choke her. She did not deserve this!

She threw out a question. A tentative hand flickered upward.

"Yes, Nina?"

Nina, petite, blond, and timid, volunteered her answer in a soft voice.

"That's correct!" Sara beamed. Nina gave her a shy smile in return. Encouraged, Sara turned to her nemesis, Simi Davidowitz. "Simi? Can you tell us what conclusion Nina's answer must lead us to?"

Simi's face went blank. "Nina's — an — swer?" she drawled, playing for time. "Sorry. I didn't even hear the question!"

This elicited a storm of giggles from the army of supporters who flanked her on every side. Sara was not amused.

"Shall I ask the question again," she offered patiently, "and repeat Nina's answer? Maybe that will jog your memory."

"I wouldn't bother," Simi said, with a sideways, laughing glance at the friend seated beside her. "I probably wouldn't get it anyway."

The girl's voice — and even more, her attitude — definitely, to Sara's mind, crossed the border of disrespect. Had she felt herself on more solid ground, she would have sent Simi to the principal without a second thought. Instead, she bit her tongue to hold back all the things she wanted to say, and turned to another girl who, hung only at the fringes of the anti-Miss-Muller contingent.

"Rochel? Can you help us?"

As she listened to the girl start and stop and stammer her way to the correct answer, Sara was conscious of one bleak thought: "Things can't go on this way much longer. Something has got to change."

The question was, what? And — even more germane to the issue — how?

Wednesday afternoon found Yael in hot debate with several of her classmates. It was a blustery day, with heavy clouds trudging intermittently across the face of the sun. All the girls wore jackets zipped up to their chins.

"Come *on*, Yael!" Tzippy urged. "Cancel your stupid lesson for once, and come home with us. We can all study for the test together. We'll have a blast! Maybe our mothers — er, our parents — will even let us have a sleepover."

The invitation was a tempting one. Had it meant putting off anything but her piano lesson, Yael would have accepted it instantly. As it was, she shook her head.

"Sorry, people. I can't skip it. Maybe," she offered, "I can join you later on, after supper."

Malya, Debby, and Tzippy looked disappointed. Tzippy was most upset of all. It was she who had come up with the beautiful plan to have their carpool drop the girls off at her house, where they would have dinner together, with the possibility of a sleepover to cap it all off — and maybe even get in a little studying for the following day's big math test. Yael was her best friend, and it hurt to have her turn her nose up at the plan. Malya began to launch a counter argument, but Tzippy interrupted with a glum, "Oh, don't bother. With Yael, the piano will always come first." She paused. "Not to mention Miss Muller." Disappointment had made her turn nasty.

"That's not true!" Yael cried. "Of course my piano is important to me, but since when do I put it before my friends?"

"Since right now," Tzippy flung back.

"What's this about Miss Muller?" Hinda Shechter asked curiously. "You do mean the new teacher, don't you?"

"*And* Yael's new piano teacher," Tzippy said. "The two of them are really tight these days. Miss Muller even drives her home on Wednesdays."

"That's when I have my lesson," Yael explained quickly.

"Better watch out," Hinda giggled. "People are going to look at you funny if you're the teacher's pet *outside* of school."

Flushing, Yael was about to declare that she did care *how* people looked at her, when a ninth-grader came trotting up to them. She burst unceremoniously into the knot of girls, asking breathlessly, "Yael Newman?"

Yael stepped forward. "That's me. What is it?"

"Got a note for you." She thrust a folded piece of paper at Yael, then turned to hurry away.

"Who from?" Yael yelled after her.

Over her shoulder, the ninth-grader called back, "Miss Muller!"

Tzippy, Hinda, and the others exchanged meaningful glances. Hinda said, "Oh, now they're writing letters to each other! What's it all about, Yael?"

"How do I know?" Yael asked irritably, a splotch of red high up on each cheekbone. "I haven't even read it yet." With elaborate casualness, she flipped open the note, scanned it quickly, then refolded and shoved it into her pocket. "She just wants to make sure we're on for tonight."

Tzippy snorted. "As if you'd let *anything* stand in the way of your precious piano lessons!"

Anxious to mollify her friend, Yael said, "I'll see if my father can drive me over to join the rest of you at your house after supper, Tzippy. Okay?"

"Whatever." Tzippy turned away.

When Sara pulled up in front of the side entrance to pick up Yael a little later, she was struck by the troubled look on the girl's face. Was it something in the air? Faygie Mandelbaum, too, had been preoccupied all day, and unusually uncommunicative. In fact, Faygie had been walking around inside her own little bubble since their return from the Rosh Hashanah break. Thinking about her Yoni, Sara supposed. Sara missed talking to her colleague about her classroom troubles, and she especially missed Faygie's brand of good-natured humor, which had a way of making even the bleakest situation seem more bearable.

And now, Yael.

They started the drive in near-silence. At the first red light, Sara smiled at Yael, willing her out of her inward mood. "Nobody seems to be talking much today. Is anything the matter?"

A maroon Dodge Caravan had pulled up at the light directly in front of them. Yael knew the car. At the moment, it was filled with her friends, en route to Tzippy's house. She scrunched down in her seat as though trying to make herself invisible.

"Nothing," she said, with a sigh she could not keep from escaping. "Nothing at all."

46

That week was a week of preparation.

On the general front, of course, all Jews were preparing for Yom Kippur, the awe-filled Day of Atonement that would see them packing into their shuls, clad in white and trembling with fear, that very Shabbos. These preceding days were a special time for introspection, for repentance, for repairing relationships. Children went around reciting, "Please forgive me if I've done anything to hurt you," while their parents went about the more serious business of scrutinizing their souls. Prayers were said with a special intensity that week, in anticipation of the hour of judgment that would be upon them all too soon.

For Daniel, spiritual ready-making advanced side by side with emotional preparation. Like a pair of cars moving parallel to one another along two highway lanes, his heart was trying to keep pace with his soul. Even as he pondered the ways in which he might improve his character, he was increasingly aware of his need for a partner in life, to act as mirror and guide to that character. It is hard enough for a man to grow and change under the best of circumstances; doing it in a solitary state was beginning to seem to him as bordering on impossible.

He made some new-year resolutions. Right after Yom Kippur, he would phone a few of the matchmakers who had shown such interest in him over these past years. But even before that, he intended to pay a visit that he hoped would clarify his direction and cement his purpose.

"Rabbi Mintzer?" he said into the phone, using the reverent tone he reserved for this special man. The rabbi, aging now, had been his long-ago teacher and still served as Daniel's mentor and most compelling friend, in the best sense of the word.

"Yes, Daniel? How have you been?"

"*Baruch Hashem*, I'm feeling fine. I'd like to wish Rabbi Minzer a *gemar chasimah tovah* — and to ask whether I can come to see him sometime after Yom Kippur."

"Of course, of course." Advancing years and declining health had not robbed the rabbi of his warm voice or hearty manner. "Can I help you with anything, Daniel?"

"I'm hoping that you can, Rabbi. When can I come?"

"No point wasting any time. After Yom Kippur, you said? How about *right* after Yom Kippur? Make *Havdalah*, break your fast, and come on over."

Daniel's heart lifted. "I'll be there, *im yirtzeh Hashem*," he promised.

The talk meandered a little further before ending in mutual good wishes for the new year. As Daniel hung up the phone, he felt readier to face the future than he had in a long time.

On a more mundane level, there were other preparations moving forward that week. Gila Newman hurried the contractors unmercifully, and emerged the triumphant owner of a brand-new room for her eldest daughter. The room was tiny, and many finishing touches remained to be added, but Tova would be able to sleep there for a night or two before the family left for Miami.

The family had much to do in advance of their upcoming Sukkos trip. They were due to leave, together with the grandparents, on Sunday, the day after Yom Kippur. None of the children had ever been on a plane before, and the prospect was almost more exciting than the actual stay in Florida.

"My friend flew to Israel last year," Gila overheard Tova telling her younger brothers. "She says they serve you meals on trays that come right out of the seat, and some planes give out snacks and as many sodas as you want!"

Her brothers exhaled in awe. Gila hesitated, then decided to gently deflate their bubble now, before life itself had the chance to do it. "This is a very short trip, kids. I doubt there'll be a movie, *or* a meal." As her children's faces fell, she added, "We can bring along some snacks, if you want."

Their disappointment was acute. The boys looked as though they were still deciding whether or not to believe her, while Tova simply looked sad. Gila almost regretted saying anything. Turning away from the reproachful young faces, she clapped her hands smartly together. "It's never too early to start packing. Who wants to help me bring up the suitcases?"

This had the effect of dispelling the boys' gloom, and even Tova brightened. While her mother and brothers went down to the basement for the luggage, she picked up the phone and dialed her cousin's number.

"Hello, Yael? It's me, Tova."

"Hi, Tova! Long time no hear! What's new?"

"Wow, we haven't spoken in a while. Let's see — Well, my new room is just about ready —"

Yael interrupted at this point to ask what new room.

"Boy, it *has* been a while!" Tova exclaimed. In the next few minutes, Yael was treated to a description of the delights in store for her cousin in the unused balcony that had been converted into her own perfect little domain. When Yael had warmly congratulated her on this step up in life, Tova went on excitedly, "And, of course, we're all busy getting ready for the trip. I can still hardly believe we're actually going! My mother and the boys just went down for the suitcases."

"What trip?" Yael was puzzled.

Tova's breath caught in her throat. "You mean you haven't heard?"

"Heard what? Spit it out already, Tova! The curiosity is killing me!"

"We're all going down to Bubby and Zaydie in Miami for Sukkos!"

At the other end of the line, Yael's heart did a funny, slipping dance step. "All?" she repeated cautiously. "Us, too?" Had Daddy been keeping this a secret?

"Well — I don't think so. I asked my mother why you guys aren't coming along, but she didn't really give me an answer." Tova frowned. "I wish you *were* coming, though. It would be much more fun."

"My father hasn't said a word," Yael said. They had always spent *Yamim Tovim* with her Bubby and Zaydie — ever since her mother had died, at any rate. It would be strange spending Sukkos alone this year. And *why* couldn't they join their cousins in Miami?

When she asked her father later, he had a plausible answer. "Zaydie's not feeling so well these days, honey. It would be better for him if he's not surrounded by a huge crowd. Besides, you don't really mind being home, do you? We'll have fun, right here."

Yael accepted that answer — for the moment. Thinking it over afterwards, however, she had to wonder why her cousins' large, noisy family was considered better for Zaydie's health than herself and Mordy.

But, as often happened when dealing with the adult world, there were no satisfactory answers. She had to go to bed with the question dangling on her mind, and the prospect of a familyless Sukkos this year.

No, not exactly familyless. Wherever Daddy and Mordy were, she had family. Besides, Cedar Hills was where she had her friends — and at 14, that was almost more important than anything.

Comforted, Yael turned over and promptly fell asleep.

Jake Meisler was busy that week, too. He had pledged his word to Elsa Downing to do what he could to help in her husband's defense, and he had kept it by arranging a meeting with Neil Palladin, defense counsel, the very next day. That meeting had resulted in Palladin's request for a recess. They had three days.

"I stuck my neck out on a limb for this," Palladin said gloomily, running both hands through hair that already looked as though a windstorm had passed through it. "I hope this idea of yours pans out, Meisler."

"So do I," Jake answered, deadly serious, the engaging grin nowhere in sight. The two were seated in Palladin's office, surrounded by open law texts and scraps of paper on which various notes, unintelligible except to someone versed in the law, had been scribbled. "It just seems to me that a man like Simmonds was bound to have more than one enemy, and not all of them as decent as Henry Downing."

"Makes sense," Palladin agreed. "But who?"

"That's what we've got to find out," Jake sighed.

"Three days." As though his chair had suddenly turned red-hot, the defense lawyer leaped up out of it and began pacing the room with short, nervous strides. "Three days to make a miracle happen!" He ran his hands through his hair again, and groaned.

"The One Who makes miracles happen," Jake said softly, "can do it in a lot less than three days, or even three hours. Cheer up, Neil. We do have some possibilities to work on. We hired a private detective, and I'm going to do everything that I can to help."

"A lot of good *possibilities* will do, when Thursday comes and the judge finds out I've stretched this trial out with nothing more substantial in my hand than 'wishful thinking,'" Suddenly, he stopped pacing and turned to face Jake. "You told me that it was Elsa Downing who asked for your help, Meisler. How well do you know the Downings?"

Jake looked embarrassed. "Actually, I don't know them at all."

"Then what's the connection?"

"Judge Newman. I've admired him and his work for a long time now. I've been following the case because he's presiding over it. You probably haven't noticed, but I've been in the courtroom most days."

"I thought your face looked familiar." Palladin sank back into his chair. "You're a third-year law student, you said?"

"That's right."

"Where on earth," Palladin demanded, "do you find the time, what with classes — and studying for exams?"

"Oh, here and there," Jake said vaguely.

"You're either a genius, or not very interested in becoming a lawyer. Which is it?"

Jake's grin was wry. "Who says the two have to be mutually exclusive?"

Palladin merely shook his head.

Jake suggested, "Well, time's a-wastin'. Let's get started, shall we?"

Rousing himself, the defense attorney grunted, "I've had a look at the names on your short list. There are no obvious grudges against Simmonds, no overt threats, nothing to take hold of. This is going to take some digging, Meisler."

Jake stood up.

"Lead me to the shovels," he said.

47

The forces of evil, as represented by Joey Mercutio, were busy preparing, too.

He had never claimed to have the brains in the family (if, that is, any of the Mercutios could lay such a claim), but he had spent long, long hours in the seclusion of his borrowed basement, weaving his plots.

It occurred to him that he owed the police department a debt of gratitude: Without their intervention in his attempted holdup, and the subsequent urgent need to go into hiding, he might have wasted even more time. Here, he had no distractions. No noisy neighbors annoying him through paper-thin walls, to drive him out of his apartment in search of a reason to live. If there was no excitement in this dismal basement, there was at least plenty of leisure for doing some serious thinking.

It was dangerous to make the trip back to the old neighborhood to send his e-mails. For all he knew, the police were having his mother's house watched. He always made the trip after dark, and always in some innocuous disguise, but each visit left him jumpy and irritable. A man does not want to be forever looking over his shoulder when planning his finest moment.

Unexpected help came through a chance remark of Vinny's. Joey showed up at the Fouza residence late Tuesday night after a long, circuitous journey, and sat down to type his next e-mail to the Newman kid.

He was going to lay his story on thicker this time. He just had to make sure the kid's heart was touched. Grimacing, he wrote:

"MY FATHER NEVER LOVED ME. HE WAS A LOW-LIFE, USUALLY DRUNK AND ALMOST ALWAYS OUT OF A JOB. YOU'RE LUCKY YOU HAVE A RESPECTABLE DAD WHO CARES ABOUT YOU. I'M SORRY I THREATENED HIM — I JUST COULDN'T STAND SEEING YOUR DAD SO LUCKY WHILE I'M DOWN HERE IN THE DIRT. BUT IT'S NO USE. NOTHING WILL EVER CHANGE. I'LL NEVER HAVE ANY LUCK . . .

I'LL WRITE MORE IN A DAY OR TWO. THANKS FOR LISTENING. IT MEANS A LOT TO ME.

The revolting *weakling* words made the bile rise up in his throat. It was almost a physical pain to press the button that would send them wheeling their way through cyberspace toward their destination. No self-respecting guy would be caught dead spouting such garbage. He sneaked a quick look at Vinny, lounging on the bed behind him, his nose six inches deep in some computer manual. Vinny had not seen.

He punched the SEND button viciously, as self-disgust changed suddenly to rage.

He was angry at the Newman kid, who would soak up this sissy stuff and maybe even laugh at Joey while he read it.

He fumed at Vinny, who was getting his life together in such a conventional, but undeniably successful, way.

He was furious with every circumstance, large and small, that had contributed to his present down-at-the-heels situation. What he had written was no less than the truth! The judge *was* lucky, while he, Joey Mercutio, had never known a day's genuine good fortune — until now.

His fantasy soared again, over the borders of today and into the very near future, when everything would change. All it would take was the guts to see it through. And then *vengeance would be his.*

Vengeance — plus a lot of good, solid greenbacks. He sure could use it. In his mind's eye, he had already spent his winnings and basked in the newfound respect of all his acquaintances who looked down on him now. Impatience burned in him. He knew it would not be smart to rush things — but it was getting harder and harder to wait.

Vinny interrupted his musings with a remark that Joey did not catch. With something like a snarl, he twisted around and asked, "What's that you say?"

"Hey, don't bite my head off, Joey. I was just telling you that you don't have to send e-mails right away, you know. You can always use the "Send Later" option." Struck by the venom in his friend's face, Vinny shrank back, adding in confusion, "Er, only if you have a reason for doing that, of course."

"Send later?" Joey considered this, then nodded slowly. "I might find that very useful. What if I write an e-mail now, and get you to send it later? Like tomorrow."

"I could do that, I guess," Vinny admitted reluctantly. Under cover of his manual, his fists remained clenched. In his compulsive desire to show off his computer smarts, he had dug himself in deeper into Joey's mess, just when he had been longing to extricate himself!

"Can you do it without reading what it says?" Joey demanded.

"Sure. Just move it to the "Outbox," where messages stay until they're ready to be delivered. Then, whenever you give me the word, I press a button to send it off. I don't have to look at what you wrote at all."

"Good." Joey prepared to type in the next e-mail. He was taking a chance, he knew. There was no telling how the kid would respond to tonight's message. His own response to *that* response would be a stab in the dark. Still, it was worth a try, especially if it saved him a trip down here.

Steeling himself, he wrote:

IT'S HARD TO BE GOOD, OR EVEN THINK ABOUT BEING GOOD, WHEN LIFE'S SO HARD. NO ONE IN THE WHOLE WORLD EVER LOVED ME. I WISH I HAD A LIFE LIKE YOURS. CAN YOU GIVE ME SOME ADVICE? LIKE, HOW TO PULL MYSELF OUT OF THIS SLUMP AND MAKE SOMETHING OF MYSELF?

No one, Joey believed, could resist giving advice. He hoped the Newman kid was like all the others, eager to dispense the words of wisdom that they were sure would solve all his problems. Like his Mama, who was convinced that he would "straighten himself out" if only he went back to school and got his high school equivalency.

"Then you could get yourself a good job," she had whined countless times. As if he, Joey Mercutio, was looking to spend his days driving a truck, or even — the acme of Mama's ambitions for him — supervising a warehouse somewhere.

"No, thanks," he thought, dark eyes aglitter as he reread the message. Turning to Vinny, he snapped, "How do I put this thing in that Outbox you were talking about?"

With a reluctance he worked hard to hide, Vinny talked him through the simple procedure. As his unwanted visitor got up to leave, Vinny said, "Your Mama's mad at you, Joey. She says you don't come see her anymore."

Joey was not about to confide that he was on the lam from the police. "Next time you see her, say hi from me," he said laconically. "I'll be around one of these days." He pointed a finger at Vinny's chest. "Can I prepare some more messages right now, for sending out on different days?"

"That would be complicated. I'm not sure how."

"Then I'll be back Friday. You send this one out Thursday — and don't make it too late. Early evening is good."

"Okay." Vinny hesitated. "H-how long is this gonna go on, Joey?" he asked plaintively.

"Not much longer," Joey bared his teeth in a smile. "If all goes well, the note I write on Friday — and that *you'll* send out for me on Saturday night — should be the last one."

Vinny brightened. "Well, that's not too far off. I guess I can handle that."

Joey's smile was swallowed instantly in a dark frown. "You'll handle it just as long as I say you have to handle it. Got that, Vinny?"

It was on the tip of Vinny's tongue to shoot back, "Sez who?" A guy had his self-respect, after all.

Then he remembered the gleaming knife in Joey's pocket, and the even wilder gleam in his eye.

Prudently, he folded his self-respect into his own back pocket, and merely nodded.

Without another word, Joey slipped out of the room. The night was his best friend now. It would conceal and protect him as he made his way back to his hideout, and his intoxicating plans.

48

From Daniel's vantage point on the judge's bench, Jake looked awful.

There were deep charcoal hollows in the space beneath the law student's eyes, which glowed greenly now with exhaustion. His shoulders sloped downward, as if it were only by stubborn effort that he managed to keep them erect. Even the auburn hair had lost its spring and lay subdued beneath the yarmulke. He looked like a man who had not slept in days.

It had, in actual fact, been thirty-six hours.

During the first day-and-a-half of their "digging," he and Palladin had labored urgently, but with a sense of still having time ahead of them. It was only when the halfway mark was crested, and their goal still unreached, that a certain frantic quality had entered their labor. The hourglass was dropping its grains of sand at its own implacable rate, and when it emptied, a man's fate would be decided. Neither Jake nor Palladin had closed his eyes in sleep since the night before last.

Apart from running back to school to take one exam and to show his face at one or two crucial lectures, Jake had been at the defense's disposal for the entire past three days. He seemed to have embraced Downing's cause as his own. If there is a knight-errant hiding inside every man, Jake Meisler's had been summoned forth by the strain in Elsa Downing's worried eyes.

A more cynical observer might have come up with various ambitions to act as fuel for such devotion: a desire to gain valuable legal experience for his resume; a wish to shine in his hero, Judge Newman's, eyes; even boredom, and the yen to escape the confines of the classroom for a time. But Jake was spurred by none of these. It was an aging woman's pain that goaded him on — and on. And if, in helping Elsa Downing, he also injected a little more meaning into his own life, that was a bonus to be cherished.

Palladin's initial approach, in preparing Downing's defense, had been to dispute the circumstantial evidence that had led to his client's indictment. But this tactic, in the crucible of the real-life courtroom, had been fast melting into an unconvincing blob. Circumstantial or not, the jury seemed to be embracing, with increasing certainty, the state's case against Henry Downing. It was a simple matter to believe that, with the motivation, the means, and the opportunity to do away with his hated partner, Downing had done just that. The only defense now was to find another viable suspect, to sow reasonable doubt in the jurors' minds.

Without Judge Newman's three-day reprieve, Neil Palladin was fairly sure that Downing would be facing his punishment this very moment — convicted for murder. Even with it, he was not at all sure what they had accomplished.

The defense had launched its quest from the "short list" of likely and unlikely suspects — possible enemies of Al Simmonds — that Jake had devised. Each potential suspect had to be as thoroughly researched as time would allow. Alibis must be checked and proved or disproved, grudges assessed, motives analyzed. Friends, relatives, and neighbors were questioned, and they reacted with wildly differing degrees of willingness to cooperate. Palladin, with his greater experience, took on the toughest cases; his assistants tackled the next level of informants; and Jake dealt with the rest. His youth and his boyish grin stood him in good stead here, but the work was discouraging.

Jake stared at the back of Henry Downing's head with eyes that burned with sleeplessness. Neil Palladin, with the faintly rumpled look that never seemed to leave him, stood up at the defense table. All but swaying on legs gone rubbery with fatigue, he prepared to mount his client's last defense.

Daniel motioned for Palladin to step up to the bench. Quietly, he asked, "Is the defense ready to continue?"

"Yes, sir. I would like to thank Your Honor, personally, for the three-day recess you granted us. Justice has been well served," Palladin said simply.

"I hope it was worth it. Such delaying tactics are very hard on the jury and they always raise the chances of a mistrial. Let's move along now."

Counsel for the defense nodded, then walked slowly back to his table. In a clear, ringing voice, he called, "For my next witness, I would like to call to the stand — Allen Thatcher."

Amid a stir of curiosity, a thickset young man with a massive head of sand-colored hair ambled up to the witness box, where he was quickly sworn in. Allen Thatcher took his seat, flexing his fingers and shrugging his broad shoulders in an apparent effort to loosen the knots. Palladin waited for him to settle down, then asked, "What is your full name, sir?"

Visibly startled at being addressed as "sir," it was a full five seconds before the witness answered. "Allen F. Thatcher," he blurted finally. "The 'F's for 'Frederick.' "

"Where do you work, Mr. Thatcher?"

"I'm the bartender down at the Misty Green. That's a pub — a bar and restaurant — downtown."

"I see." Palladin strolled along the box. "From your place behind the counter, do you ever hear the conversations of people seated at the bar?"

"Sure. Lots of them. Drink will loosen the tightest tongue; you don't have to be in my line of business to know that."

"Does the Misty Green provide any background entertainment? A piano, or a band?"

Before Thatcher could answer, Martin Bedeker was on his feet. "Your Honor, I must object. Who is this witness, and why should we care about the quality of the entertainment at the, er, Misty Green?"

Daniel lifted a questioning brow at defense counsel. Palladin said quickly, "My point is not the quality of the entertainment, Your Honor, but its presence in the pub. I wish to establish that the place is generally quiet enough for the bartender, Mr. Thatcher here, to clearly overhear conversations taking place at the bar. This fact is vital to my case, sir."

Daniel thought a moment, then nodded. "Objection overruled. You may proceed, Mr. Palladin. But please let the jury see where you're headed fairly soon."

"Yes, sir!" Palladin wheeled back around to face the witness. "Mr. Thatcher? Can you answer my question?"

"We have a piano-player for about three hours a night. He plays tinkly music, not my taste."

"Loud?"

Thatcher shook his sandy head. "No, not at all. Real quiet, he plays. Just background."

"So you are positioned to hear people talking near you, at the bar, without too much noise to drown out their voices?"

As Thatcher began to nod, the prosecutor called out wearily, "Prosecution will concede the point. The witness could hear what his customers said. Must we waste any *more* time, Your Honor?"

"I'll move on," Palladin said hastily. "Now, Mr. Thatcher, one night last year, did one of your customers come into the pub in a euphoric frame of mind?"

The bartender looked blank. Palladin clarified, "On top of the world? Thrilled to pieces?"

"Yes. He came in with a friend, talking in a kind of excited babble, nonstop, even while they ordered their drinks."

"They sat at the bar?"

"Yes. He always did."

"He was a regular customer?"

"Well — I wouldn't exactly call him 'regular.' But he did come in now and again. About three or four times a month, I'd say."

"And the other customer?"

Thatcher shook his head. "He was new to me. A pal of the other one's."

"I see. Now, what was the subject of conversation between the two men?"

"Well, they were talking about some sort of breakthrough the first guy, the more-or-less regular customer, had made. An invention of some kind."

"Did you involve yourself in their conversation? Did you ask what the invention was?"

"Yes, sir. I was curious."

"And what was the inventor's answer?"

"He didn't say what it was, not in so many words. He just grinned like a cat who's found the cream — sort of ear-to-ear, you know?— and said that the children of the world were going to thank him."

"Children?" Palladin repeated.

"That's just what *I* asked. 'Children?' I said. 'What would the kids thank you for?' "

"And he answered —?"

"He said, 'Not exactly kids. Babies. The babies of the world will thank me — or they would, if they knew what I've just produced for them!' "

"Did he say anything further? Anything to give you a hint as to what, exactly, he'd done for — uh, for the babies of the world?"

"No, sir. I had to tend to other customers. The two of them left not long afterwards. Going to get something to eat, the second guy said — something more serious than the sandwiches we serve at the Misty Green. 'My friend here doesn't remember to eat when he's hard at work,' he told me. 'Look at him, skin and bones!'

" 'Well, go fatten him up some,' I said. They laughed, and then they walked out."

Neil Palladin stopped strolling and came to a halt directly in front of the witness box. Placing both hands on the rail, he peered intently into the bartender's face.

"Mr. Thatcher, do you know the name of the customer your recognized? The first one, the inventor, the one you say comes into the pub more or less regularly?"

"Sure. He's been in once or twice since this trial started. We talk about it sometimes."

"And why do you do that?" Palladin held his breath.

"Why? Because he was a witness in this trial, just like I am now! He worked with the guy who was knifed — Al Simmonds."

"His name, Mr. Thatcher?"

The bartender's eyes roved the spectator's benches, and came to rest on the face he wanted. He pointed. "He's right here in the audience. Don't know his last name. Down at the Misty Green, we just call him Ted."

"Thank you, Mr. Thatcher." Palladin glanced at Bedeker. "Your witness."

The State's Attorney walked up to the witness box in a forthright manner, planted his hands on the railing to squarely face the bartender, and asked, "How many drinks do you enjoy on the job, Mr. Thatcher?"

"Er — Excuse me?"

Bedeker spoke very slowly and clearly, as to a young child or half-wit. "How-many-drinks-do-you-have-while-on-the-job?"

"Well, that depends. On an easy day, maybe one or two."

"And on a hard day?"

"Er, well, a little more."

"How many more?"

"Maybe three or four."

"Three or four drinks? Or three or four *more* drinks?" Thatcher threw an uneasy glance at the defense counsel. "More," he answered sullenly.

Bedeker turned away, his face a mask of contempt. "No further questions."

As an attempt to discredit the witness, it was a masterly performance. Daniel wondered how effective it had been. The jury's expressions revealed nothing, but they were following the proceedings very closely indeed.

As the beefy bartender stepped down, Palladin turned, pale but composed, to face the man to whom Thatcher had pointed.

"Your Honor, the defense wishes to call Theodore — Ted — Winslow to the stand!"

For a moment, nothing moved. Then the young engineering student rose from his place, staring sightlessly over the heads of the murmuring rows of spectators. Slowly, he began the walk to the box in which he had been sworn in as a witness for the prosecution, ten days earlier.

49

"Please be advised that you are still under oath, Mr. Winslow."

Vaguely, as if in a dream, Ted Winslow nodded. The movement dislodged a shower of fine, dark hair, which fell over his forehead and into his eyes. A quick flick of one thin wrist pushed the hair back into place.

"Mr. Winslow, earlier in this trial you testified that you worked for Mr. Simmonds on his baby-bottle project, and that you still, in fact, serve there in a supervisory capacity. Is that correct?"

Winslow nodded.

"Speak up, please," Daniel called down from the judge's bench.

Winslow cleared his throat painfully, then found his voice. "Yes. That's right."

Counsel for the defense tapped a thoughtful finger against the knuckle of his other hand in an unconscious gesture, as he mapped his strategy for the next crucial questions. Ted Winslow stared straight ahead as though, on some level, he had removed himself from the proceedings. The courtroom was quiet, save for the scratching of the artist's pencil.

"The last time you sat in this box, Mr. Winslow," Palladin began, his tone friendly and conversational, "I asked you why an engineering student with several patents to his name would be working in a baby-bottle factory."

"I don't work in the factory." Winslow's tone was not nearly as friendly as Palladin's had been. "I am production supervisor. I sit at a desk."

"I see. Now, if memory serves, you accepted this, er, *desk* job because, in your own words, Mr. Simmonds 'made you an offer you couldn't refuse.' Am I right in my recollection?"

"Yes."

"May I ask about the nature of that offer, Mr. Winslow?"

The witness hesitated a beat, before saying, "Frankly, he offered more money than I could say 'no' to. My mother is a seamstress. And a darned good one, too. But a seamstress, no matter how talented, has a limited earning capacity. Here was a chance to see that my mother was comfortable and secure, and to continue my own private work without money worries. I grabbed it with both hands."

"And your private 'work'? How far have you come along on that, since you took up employment in Mr. Simmonds' empire."

Winslow flushed. "I haven't accomplished as much as I'd have liked, I'll admit that much. There's been too little time —"

"You'll admit 'that much'?" Palladin asked, moving up very close to the witness box. "What else might you be prepared to admit, I wonder, Mr. Winslow?"

"OBJECTION!" Bedeker roared. "Counsel is badgering the witness!"

"I withdraw the question," Palladin said, his eyes never leaving Winslow's face. He walked a few steps away, then turned so that he faced the jury box. Projecting his voice over the jury members' heads, he said, "Now, Mr. Winslow, I'm going to ask you to throw your mind back to the Labor Day picnic where, according to your testimony, you had your first encounter with Alexander Simmonds." He paused. "You do remember that meeting?"

Sullenly, Winslow nodded, then muttered, "Yes."

"A pivotal meeting, was it not? An important encounter, a red-letter event. This was the first time you and your mother had been invited to attend one of Mr. Simmonds' sister's big Labor Day barbecues. And then you met, and conversed with, Mr. Simmonds himself."

Winslow glared at him. "It *was* pivotal — but, no, I did not consider the barbecue a 'red-letter event.' My mother and I have no need to mix socially with that set. We have our own circle of friends."

"Why did you attend, then?"

"My mother is a polite woman. She went along out of respect for

Mrs. Kates, who had thrown a good deal of business Mother's way. And I went along to keep Mother company."

"Your father — ?"

"Is dead. He left nothing behind. My mother and I are forced to be self-sufficient."

"I see," Palladin said, nodding his head as if he did see — something that was not being said. "So your mother and yourself, still a student, were largely dependent on the goodwill of Al Simmonds' sister for your bread and butter. Is that true?"

Winslow hesitated, an ugly, mottled red spreading over his forehead and down his cheeks. When he did not reply at once, Palladin said softly, but insistently, "Please answer the question, Mr. Winslow."

"Okay, so we needed her! What's so bad about that?"

"Nothing at all." With a disarming smile, Palladin threw up his hands. Bedeker rose ponderously from the prosecutor's table to raise an objection. "Your Honor, I fail to see where this line of questioning is leading. I believe we all share a wish to end this trial in timely fashion?"

"We do, indeed. Mr. Palladin? Is there a point in all of this?"

"I'm getting to it, Your Honor," the defense attorney said, his manner for the first time betraying a suppressed excitement. "Please bear with me. Just a few more minutes will do it, I think."

The judge granted him those minutes. In the spectators' benches, there was a curious silence: suspense made almost tangible. Elsa Downing's eyes looked large as saucers as she kept them rigidly fixed on the witness stand. Palladin allowed the tension to stretch for ten interminable seconds before shooting an abrupt question at Winslow.

"What were you and your mother discussing when Mr. Simmonds overheard you?"

Winslow stared at him, startled. "What?"

"In your previous testimony, you mentioned that you'd been talking with your mother — at the edges of the crowd, I believe you said — when Mr. Simmonds suddenly tapped you on the shoulder and joined in the conversation. There is no knowing how long he stood there, listening. What were you speaking of, Mr. Winslow?"

"I — I don't remember."

"Try hard," Palladin urged.

"OBJECTION!" Bedeker was beside himself. "Irrelevant!"

"Not at all, Your Honor!" Palladin shouted. "As you will see in a minute." At the judge's brisk, "Overruled," he faced the witness again, a flush mounting in his wan cheeks and a new fire in the sunken eyes that had known no sleep in preparation for these next few moments.

"Mr. Winslow, I suggest to you that you were discussing a new invention that you had just completed. I suggest that you had devised a whole new concept in baby bottles. I suggest —"

"Objection! Counsel is declaiming!"

"Sustained," Daniel said. "Mr. Palladin, let's have a question, please."

"All right. A question. Mr. Winslow, did you hear the testimony of the witness who sat here just previous to you this morning?"

"Yes, I heard." Winslow was breathing hard, as though he had just completed a race. Strands of hair had fallen back over his forehead, but he seemed oblivious.

"Then tell me this: Is it true that you were the 'Ted' whom the bartender described to us — the young man who had just invented something *that would make 'all the babies of the world thank him'?*"

A swell of voices rose from the spectators. Daniel banged his gavel, hard. "Silence! We will not continue unless there is silence in the court!"

Gradually, the babble subsided into a tense, expectant hush. Palladin approached the witness again, gazing directly into his eyes. "Mr. Winslow," he said in a voice that was sincerely sympathetic, "I can understand your plight. There you were, a poor student with a mother to help support, and a wonderful talent for invention that you hoped would help you take your rightful place in the world — Then along comes a man who has everything — a man with a whole menagerie, who set his sights on your one little lamb — a man who had no scruples about stealing your idea and then had the cool nerve to force you to help him produce it! What did he threaten you with, Mr. Winslow? Did he —"

Bedeker was on his feet. His usual pallor had given way to twin crimson badges of outrage on either cheek. But before he could say a word, Ted Winslow cried out, in a voice that pierced the air with its anguish and fury: "*He was the scum of the earth!*

It was a full five minutes before order was restored in the court. Daniel had to bang repeatedly with his gavel, and the bailiff's voice rang out again and again until he was hoarse — "Order in the court. *Order in the court!*" — before the swelling tide of speculation began to subside.

Bedeker had sunk back into his seat, gazing at the witness in open befuddlement. The judge waited to see if he would go on to voice the objection he had apparently intended to make. When nothing came, he nodded to Palladin. "Go on," he said quietly.

Counsel for the defense had never left the witness's side. In a voice that just carried to the jury box, he asked again, "What did he threaten you with, Mr. Winslow?"

The young engineer seemed, at last, to welcome the chance to unburden himself. "He threatened to make sure Mother would never work again. And he said that if I didn't cooperate, he'd see that I was expelled from engineering school!"

"Could he have done that?"

"How do I know? He had money, lots of money. And in this world, money can unlock and lock any door —" He sounded bitter as death.

"He wanted to patent your invention as his own?"

"Yes." Winslow trembled with a rage that was too large, still too powerful, to suppress even now. "The fruit of *my* mind — of thousands of hours of work, alone at night when the rest of the world slept! He made me pass it off as his — and then oversee the production of *my* baby bottle! Do you know what that was like? Day in and day out, hearing the world rave about Simmonds' genius, watching the name 'Simmonds' stamped on bottle after bottle after bottle —"

"It must have been torture," Palladin murmured, watching Winslow closely.

"Torture! You have no idea. *My* work — with *his* name on it. I tried to take it back once — told him I'd spill the beans. He just laughed. Said it would be his word against mine. Everyone thought he was my benefactor! Even Mother was so grateful, so slavishly grateful — While all along —!"

"You must have hated him."

"Hate! That's too weak a word. He was the scum of the earth, I tell you!"

"He stole Henry Downing's profits," Palladin said softly. "But he did worse to you. He stole the fruit of your brain. You must have pictured your revenge — pictured the villain dead — pictured yourself with a hunting knife in your hand —"

"It was Mother's carving knife," Ted Winslow said, almost casually.

Then he covered his face with his hands and burst into wracking sobs, the thin shoulders heaving like the waves of a tormented sea.

50

"Thank G-d," Elsa Downing breathed.

Two enormous, pear-shaped tears were traveling slowly down the cliffs of her cheeks. She seemed unaware of them. With blind urgency, she pushed her way up through the throng surrounding her husband and his attorney. Palladin's assistants and Jake Meisler, and a small knot of perfect strangers who had been faithfully manning the spectator's benches all through the trial — all of them blocked her way. Elsa elbowed them aside with astonishing ruthlessness — and then, smiling and crying at the same time, she was at her husband's side.

It was Daniel's usual practice, at the conclusion of a trial, to vanish into the privacy of his own chambers; this time, he permitted himself to linger a few extra minutes. The jury's returned verdict of acquittal had led to a kind of mad explosion from the observers' rows, with dozens of figures leaping up, chattering, exclaiming, and converging on the defense table like a human tidal wave. Amid the uproar, Ted Winslow was led out of the courtroom through the same door by which Henry Downing had been led in.

Daniel's eyes were very bright as he watched the Downings' reunion. Ignoring the seething, yammering mass around him, Henry bent his gray head close to his wife's and whispered something that made her smile grow even broader. Their hands — roughened and reddened from years of blue-collar work, and not much changed since they had stepped into the world of the privileged — met and clasped. Daniel brought his own hand quickly to his eyes, whose vision, he found, was fast blurring.

He watched a little longer. His intense personal interest in this case, from the moment he had learned he was going to preside over it, made Daniel feel as though he ought to be one of those pumping Neil Palladin's hand. That being out of the question, he caught Jake's eye and motioned for him to step up close to the bench.

"I don't know what your role was in all of this," he said, low voiced and smiling, "but thank you."

A flicker of surprised gratification came and went in Jake's face. Grinning broadly, he said, "Actually, I had the time of my life. If I ever pass the bar, I think I'll become a defense attorney. Palladin says he'll give me a job in a minute."

"What?" Daniel feigned extreme hurt. "I thought you were banking on clerking for me!"

"Sir?" There was a deferential cough as his present clerk, Paul Hencken, materialized at Daniel's elbow. "I've got some hot coffee waiting for you in your chambers. I thought you might need it."

Daniel turned to rest smiling eyes on the younger man. "Bless you, Paul. I can almost smell it from here — I'll be right there."

He rose. The judicial robes fell in graceful folds around his ankles as he stood still, taking in the scene below for one last moment.

The tide had turned, and the crowd was beginning a slow but steady drift toward the courtroom doors. On the other side, Daniel knew, the press would be flocking like a horde of vultures, greedy for comment to fill their news columns and their on-the-air news slots. Palladin's dramatic and unexpected victory would make his reputation glow like a new-risen star in the sky. The attorney pushed eagerly for the doors, a protective arm raised to shield the Downings from the coming onslaught.

They were at the threshold, and Palladin was beginning to push the doors open to face the clamoring media circus, when one of their numbers abruptly defected. Elsa Downing broke free of her husband's grasp, darted around a bevy of Palladin's assistants behind, and ran up the aisle of the nearly deserted courtroom, back to the judge's bench.

Daniel looked down at the aging face that had become, in a short space of time, so familiar to him. All its lines were curving upward now, as Elsa Downing smiled radiantly at him.

"Thank you, Judge," she said, breathless from her short sprint. "Thank G-d, and thank you."

"It's Jake, here, that you should thank," Daniel told her, enjoying the blushes that suffused his young friend's face at the words. "Ask Mr. Palladin to tell you the whole story sometime."

"Oh, I will, you can be sure of that! And I do thank you, young man, for whatever help you might have given my husband. But it's you," she turned back to Daniel, "I'm really grateful to. I — I know how a judge can be. I've heard about some who can slant a whole case against a defendant if he's taken a dislike to him. You behaved fairly and objectively all the way through, but — but somehow, I couldn't help feeling that you were sympathetic, in your heart, to my Henry." She lowered her voice discreetly. "That's why I came to see you the other day."

"Shall I tell you a secret?" Daniel twinkled. "I *was* sympathetic. But only in my heart," he added hastily. "I hope my judicial behavior was completely unbiased and impartial, all the way through."

"You were lucky," Jake Meisler told Elsa. "You're right about there being different kinds of judges. It's the luck of the draw; and you drew the best."

"Come now, Jake," Daniel protested, sensing the pink beginning to creep into his own cheeks. "Enough of that."

"No," said Elsa Downing, gazing up at the judge with eyes that held the simple wisdom she had garnered in long, hard years of living on this earth. "No, he's right, Your Honor." Like a fervent litany, she repeated, "Thank G-d — and thank *you*, Judge."

"I appreciate the thought, Mrs. Downing. But G-d is the One who dispenses justice. The rest of us" — Daniel waved a hand to encompass prosecutors, defenders, witnesses, courthouse, and the entire judicial process — "are no more than His messengers."

The older woman regarded him silently for a moment, then smiled her understanding. Without another word, she spun on her heel and made her way, more sedately now, back up the aisle to where her Henry was waiting.

The car seemed to steer itself home. It purred along like a tame tiger, responsive to Daniel's lightest touch. Traffic was unusually sparse, even for the time of day — midafternoon — and what there was seemed to defer respectfully to Daniel's every wish. The other cars practically bowed out of his way as he sped along. If he had not known better, he would have sworn that his vehicle was floating above the road. But it was not the car that was flying; it was Daniel's own spirit, which felt lighter than at any time in recent memory.

All was for the best in G-d's good world. He felt filled to the brim with a shining new optimism. With his anonymous threatener silent so long, it was safe, he thought, to assume that the attacks were at an end. Daniel would have liked to learn his tormentor's identity — but he could easily live without knowing, if indeed the torment was over. It would be just one of the many, many things he did not, and would probably never, know.

Even the mighty Judge Newman was humble enough to understand that there were questions he would never learn the answers to. Questions about life and death — especially his Ella's death. And did he have, even, the right to ask?

With every fiber of his being he believed what he had told Mrs. Downing back in the courtroom: that G-d is the one true Judge. He, Daniel, was no more than a paid underling, scurrying about in his own small way, trying to see that procedure was followed and obvious outrages avoided. The only sensible way to live — even for a man who seems to be in control of his life — was by relinquishing that control to the One Who really wields it.

But controlling situations was one of the things that Daniel Newman did best. Even as his mind came to its inescapable conclusions, his heart was yet a little too full of its longtime conviction that he was still — in some degree, at least — master of his destiny.

The time was very rapidly approaching when his wayward heart would learn differently.

There was no point in going directly home. The kids would not be there for a couple of hours yet, and he would only get in Mrs. Marks' way. With abrupt decision, Daniel turned left at the intersection near his home, instead of right. A couple of hours of learning would be a bonus after this marvelous day: the icing on the cake. In these Days of Repentance, every extra bit counted.

Two hours later, he let himself into his house with a cheerful, "I'm home!" Mrs. Marks came hurrying out to welcome him. Yael called from her room, "I'm on the phone, Daddy, be down in a sec!" Of Mordy there was no sign.

"Where's the boy?" he asked the housekeeper jocularly.

"In the study, on the computer, where else?" She took his coat from him, and despite his protests, hung it up.

"Is there any of that good berry juice left?" he asked, starting for the kitchen. "I've got a sudden craving."

"Plenty," said Mrs. Marks. "If you'll just wait a minute, I'll pour you a glass." She hurried after him, puffing a little at the unaccustomed speed.

"Thanks, Mrs. Marks, but you're spoiling me. I've known how to pour myself a drink for ages!"

Chuckling, the housekeeper stood watching benevolently as the judge fetched the pitcher of juice from the fridge, then poured himself a glassful.

In the study, Mordy welcomed this brief delay. It afforded him the time he needed to finish the e-mail message he had been typing on the computer, and to press the SEND button. Vincent Fouza, whoever he was, had his answer.

With his mouse, Mordy clicked on the command that would close the program. Then, leaving behind him a screen that was reassuringly innocuous, he went out to greet his father.

51

Joey Mercutio had been correct in his assessment of human nature: people really *couldn't* resist the urge to give advice. And Mordy turned out to be as human as they come.

"FIRST OF ALL, YOU DON'T KNOW THAT YOUR FATHER DIDN'T LOVE YOU," he wrote, feeling rather foolish. He didn't know the first thing about Vincent Fouza, and he certainly didn't know Vincent's dad. But compassion bade him take the other's laments seriously, to do what he could to ease his pain — and guide him in a healthier direction.

By this time, Mordy had almost forgotten how his involvement with his unknown correspondent had started. Once the threats left off and the self-pity began, Vincent seemed far less alarming. Fear had been left behind, lost in a cloud of obscuring dust. Now he, Mordy, was in the superior role. He had plenty of good advice for this misguided young man (at least, he assumed he was young):

HE WAS PROBABLY JUST SAD BECAUSE HE COULDN'T GET A JOB. MAYBE THAT'S ALSO WHY HE DRANK SO MUCH . . . ANYWAY, ITS TIME TO FORGET ALL THAT AND MOVE ON. I THINK YOU SHOULD GO AWAY FROM HERE, FIND A NEW PLACE TO LIVE WHERE PEOPLE DON'T KNOW YOU AND START OVER, FRESH. YOU COULD FIND A JOB AND START A NEW LIFE.

Thinking that he had written enough, Mordy made a move to sign off. Then, on impulse, his fingers returned to the keyboard.

"YOU SAY THAT NO ONE'S EVER CARED ABOUT YOU. BUT THEY WILL, IF YOU GIVE THEM A CHANCE. REALLY."

That was *really* enough. Mordy pressed the SEND button, printed out a few innocent e-mails for his father, and exited the program.

He had expected to feel good after sending the message. Instead, inexplicably, his spirits plummeted. He was beginning to feel burdened by this strange correspondence. Besides that he was uncomfortable. The fear had left, but a strange depression had entered in its place. Mordy longed to see or rather, hear, the last of Vincent Fouza. He had never pictured himself as a kind of surrogate therapist to some stranger with (probably) criminal tendencies. What had begun in outraged self-defense had moved into a bizarre new place, and he felt unequal to the task of staying there much longer. He hoped with all his heart that the guy would take his advice and move away. Preferably, as far away from Cedar Hills as possible.

There was no question now of confiding in his father. What purpose could that have, apart from getting Mordy into a whole tankful of hot water? Any real threat from the whining stranger was obviously a thing of the past. Mordy felt a twinge of pride: *He had* been the one to ease this Vincent character away from the violent fantasies he had been acting out on paper. Not even Detective Garrity had helped Dad the way Mordy had.

His father might be proud, too, if he knew. But not even that prospect was worth the lecture he would doubtless be treated to, should the truth emerge. Daniel would tell his son with some justification, Mordy knew, that contacting the threatener had been a foolhardy move. The fact that it had all ended well did not detract from its foolishness.

In his heart, Mordy had to agree. He would continue to say nothing to his father.

He did, however, have one outlet for his pride. There was always Ari.

Ari Rabinowitz stood by the phone the next afternoon, *erev Yom Kippur,* watching as his mother dialed the Newmans' number in Cedar Hills. He could tell by the way she talked that it was Uncle Daniel himself who had picked up.

Judy Stavinsky Rabinowitz and Daniel Newman never spoke without the specter of Ella Stavinsky Newman, sister and wife, hovering between them. The tragedy bound the two irrevocably — and also placed a very real constraint upon them. It was with some relief that Judy handed the phone to her husband.

Reuven Rabinowitz enjoyed a brief, but heartfelt, dialogue with Daniel. As the talk wound down, he raised an interrogative eyebrow at his son. Ari nodded vigorously.

"Ari wants to talk to Mordy, if he's available," Reuven said. He listened a moment, then nodded at Ari. The boy listened to the final exchange of good wishes, then accepted the receiver from his father.

"Hello?" Mordy's voice came clearly down the line. Hard to believe his cousin was some three thousand miles away.

"Hi, Mordy! Two things. First of all, *gemar chasimah tovah* and have an easy fast."

"You, too, on both."

"And now what's the story with those crazy e-mails you've been sending me?" Ari chortled merrily into the phone.

"Ssssh! Are you nuts?" Mordy hissed. "I told you that's a *secret!* Are your parents still there?"

"Negative. But what's with the secret-agent routine, Mordy? The whole thing's just a big joke, right?"

Mordy's voice became suddenly louder, brisk and open. "Hi, Mrs. Marks! Going home already?"

Ari listened patiently as a short exchange passed between Mordy and the housekeeper, ending with Mrs. Marks' horrified, "Is that long-distance? And you're standing here talking to *me?*" Mrs. Marks was clearly of the generation who still found long-distance an exotic and extravagantly expensive luxury.

Mordy was back with his cousin. "She's gone," he whispered. "Ari, have you lost your mind? This is a dead secret, okay? I hope you haven't told your parents or anyone."

"Not a soul. But —"

"No buts. I thought I could trust you to keep a secret, and here you go and —"

"And nothing! I've *kept* your stupid secret, okay? But I don't see why you're making such a big —"

"My father's coming back," Mordy interrupted in an undertone. Aloud, he said, "Well, it's been nice talking to you, Ari. What are you doing for Sukkos?"

"What do you mean, what am I doing for Sukkos. I'll be sitting in a sukkah, that's what! Mordy —"

"Sounds great. So have an easy fast, Ari. Talk to you later." *Click.*

Bemused, Ari stared at the dead receiver in his hand for a long moment before, with an exasperated shake of his head, he replaced it in its cradle.

The sun sank into the horizon; candles were lit; sneakers were found to replace leather footwear. Many put on white clothing to greet the day that was suddenly, with breathtaking solemnity, upon them.

Yom Kippur passed as it always does, in prayer and fasting. Daniel and Mordy *davened* side by side, each lost in his own private world, each making his own private reckoning. On the woman's side of the partition, Yael kept her eyes glued to her *machzor*, determined to make her prayers as meaningful as possible this year. Sometime during the course of the long day, lightheaded with hunger, she found her thoughts turning to her father.

"Do you think your father ever plans to marry again?"

"It might be kind of nice having someone older around. Someone to ask questions, and to do girl-things with . . ."

On some subterranean level, she had been struggling to find the answer to the question Tzippy had posed. Now, as she waited for the *Minchah* service to begin, she sought an answer again; and came up with one that surprised her.

She actually wouldn't mind at all.

She, whoever it was, would never really take the place of Yael's mother. But she would make Daddy more complete, and also their home. And it *would* be kind of nice to let the burden of being the woman of the house slip off her own shoulders. A relief to just be a kid again. Nice to have someone older around.

As she launched into another round of prayer, she inserted a new request into her already loaded list. It was: "Please, Hashem, if it's Your Will that Daddy remarry, let it be to the right person, at the right time. And let me like her!"

She did not know it, but Daniel Newman, on the other side of the *mechitzah*, was *davening* for the very same thing.

Later, when the sun had made way for an array of stars in a sea of black, Daniel returned home with his children. As he recited the age-old words of the *Havdalah* that separated the Sabbath of Sabbaths from the rest of the year, he thought ahead to the visit he hoped to make that very evening, to discuss the subject that had been at the forefront of his mind all Yom Kippur. He wanted Rabbi Mintzer's blessing.

For some reason — call it fatherly paranoia — Daniel still did not like the idea of leaving his kids home alone at night. Even now, with his terror over the threatening letters subsided, he found he could not do it.

"Yael, Mordy, I've got to go over to Rabbi Mintzer's for a little while. After we break our fasts and have something light to eat, I'd like to drop you two at the Greenbergs' while I'm gone."

The proposal was met, as he had expected it to be, with a storm of protest. They were not little kids anymore; they could take perfectly good care of themselves; he was babying them, for goodness sake! But Daniel held firm.

"I'll be leaving in about five minutes," he said quietly. "Please get your jackets and whatever else you need — now."

He got away with nothing more than a couple of mildly rebellious looks from his offspring. Within five minutes, he had deposited them at the neighbors' house. And a quarter of an hour later he was ringing Rabbi Mintzer's bell.

In an entirely different part of town, Vinny Fouza entered his e-mail program and clicked the appropriate buttons to send off the message that Joey Mercutio had prepared the day before. Joey had promised that this would be the last one. Whatever crazy plan he was working on, it was apparently nearing completion.

Vinny, for one, could not wait.

The message flew through cyberspace to land in the Newman computer, where it nestled patiently, awaiting Mordy's return.

52

With the light at his back, Rabbi Mintzer was hardly more than a silhouette — a blank, black form without feature or detail. Then he stepped back, hands outstretched, and all at once there was a frock coat, and a beard, and a face dominated by a pair of the kindest, shrewdest brown eyes Daniel had ever known.

"Come in, Daniel. Come in." The rabbi grasped his visitor's hand with both of his own, and literally drew him inside.

The house was quiet, the way Daniel remembered it, filled with shelves and shelves of *sefarim* and the musty, leathery smell they exuded. Dimly, from the kitchen, he heard sounds that told him the rabbi's wife was busy there. She would undoubtedly make an appearance later, bearing a tray of tea and some of her homemade cakes. A sense of elation rose up in Daniel, filling his veins like liquid happiness and making his heart bubble with joy. This was a good place, a place that made him feel all the best things. Why didn't he visit this venerable man, this wonderful home, more often?

He knew why. As he moved toward the seat that the rabbi motioned for him to take, he had a brief but piercing glimpse of the thousand and one ways that time, and the world, and the evil inclination, drag a man away from that which is at his deepest center. While he might be seated in such a room, in consultation with a man such as Rabbi Mintzer, he spent it instead in boardrooms and courtrooms and the myriad marketplaces of the world, consorting with fools. It was a bitter realization.

But bitterness and despair had no place in this house. So Daniel shrugged off the sting of his thoughts and prepared to let the salve of the rabbi's wise and friendly concern soothe him. Rabbi Mintzer had finished with his preliminary questions about the children's welfare and was looking at him expectantly, waiting for Daniel to raise the real topic of his visit.

Daniel collected his thoughts and began to talk. He spoke about his life: as it had been, as it was, and as he hoped it would be. As the words flowed, his life's shape was sculpted in the air between them like a statue he was holding up for the rabbi's inspection.

The sculpture changed form with each sentence. Gradually, the past receded and the present flew away, and there was only the future that he was hoping — longing — to embrace.

For Faygie Mandelbaum, seated opposite Yoni Weiss of Jerusalem in the small Baltimore cafe, the future was about as tenuous as a butterfly's wing.

If she chose, that wing might grow solid as a rug — a magic carpet to fly the pair of them into realms as yet untasted and unknown.

A different choice, and the butterfly would flit out of reach, tantalizing as a lost dream, and just as unattainable.

It was up to her.

From the earnest speech he had just made, it was very clear where Yoni stood. The dark eyes were riveted steadily on her own, as if to draw from them the answer he wanted. Yes, Yoni's position was clear. It was Faygie who felt as though she were blind and groping, in a fog. In place of tables and chairs and her fellow diners, she saw confusion and uncertainty, hovering about her head like a flock of lost birds.

"I'm sorry," she said, producing a smile with an effort. "I missed that last sentence. What did you say?"

Yoni held up a menu. "I just said, 'Perhaps it's time to order?' "

"Oh! Sorry." She buried her head in her own menu, her cheeks the same color as its scarlet cover. "I, um, well — What're *you* having?"

The selection of their light meal carried them safely if temporarily past the conversational snags Faygie wanted so desperately to avoid. She would not be able to sidestep them forever — not even for the whole of this evening. But right now, she wanted nothing more than to chatter about simple, inane matters, things that required no decision. Though she had no appetite, she was willing to plow her way through seven courses, if necessary, to avoid a resumption of the speech Yoni had just made.

He obliged, for the moment, by following her lead. They discussed the Yom Kippur that had just passed, and the upcoming Sukkos festival. Yoni spoke wistfully of Sukkos in Jerusalem.

"Over there, it's as if everyone is part of a single family, all hammering away days before the holiday, dragging *sechach* down the street from the piles that the city leaves for them, and then all singing at the tops of their voices outdoors in their sukkahs, competing with one another like a pack of happy kids." He smiled, remembering. Then he sighed. "It's very different here."

"From my parents' succah, we can sometimes hear the neighbors singing," Faygie said, a touch defensively.

"It's not the same. In America, the home is like a fortress. It takes a lot to drag Americans out of their comfortable houses and into the street. A block party once a year, maybe — and, of course, Sukkos. But where I live, there is not much indoors to hold you. A crowded little apartment, a living room the size of a postage stamp, and a balcony that gives you a view that pulls you outside like a magnet. So people go out, they mingle, they talk, they argue, they laugh together, and they build together —"

Where I live. This, Faygie realized with a leaden feeling, was the crux of the problem. Where Yoni lived was not where she lived. Or, as she was becoming increasingly certain, where she *wanted* to live, at least for now. The ties binding her to her family were too strong. Simply put, they were her life.

Some people just picked up and went, never looking back. Her new friend, Sara Muller, had left her parents' Flatbush home to start over in a strange city, and the experience did not seem to have left a mark on her.

Not me, Faygie thought bleakly. *Not me.*

These past weeks had been some of the most exciting in her life. She had been soaring on the wings of Yoni's attention, her pleasure in his company, and a dream of marriage and happiness. But real life is not a dream, and one's pleasure in even the finest company can quickly sour under the wrong conditions.

She drew a deep breath. The coffee lay untasted at her elbow, and the cherry blintzes were congealing under their sour-cream topping. She forced herself to meet his eyes.

"Yoni," she said slowly, "how would you like to spend Sukkos in Yerushalayim?"

A startled light sprang into his eyes — then an apprehensive one. "What do you mean?"

Gently, she said, "I mean, it's obvious that you're very homesick. And the only thing keeping you here over *Yom Tov* is —"

"You," he finished, regarding her intently.

She hesitated, then lowered her head and, very slowly, shook it from side to side. A tear slowly made its way down her cheek and fell into her coffee cup.

"That's the story, Rabbi," Daniel finished. He was leaning forward, almost at the edge of his seat, hands clasped between his knees. "Until now, I felt that the best thing I could do for the kids was to be mother and father to them. I thought it wisest not to get involved with anyone else. They'd been through enough horrifying change and needed a long, peaceful time to rest from all that. Time to just *be*. But now — "

"Now?" Rabbi Mintzer prompted, watching him closely.

"Now I feel that the kids might be better off — might actually benefit from — could really do well with —"

"A stepmother?"

"Well, yes." Daniel drew a breath, held it a moment, then exhaled. "Yes, Rabbi. That's what I mean. What does the Rabbi think?"

"A new stepmother for your children means a new wife for you."

Daniel was taken aback. "Why, of course. I know that."

"Do you? Do you really? Think carefully, Daniel: a new woman in your first wife's place. How will you feel when she walks through the rooms of your house — in Ella's place? How will you feel when your children begin to relate to her as a mother? Mordechai, especially, was very young when your wife died."

"He was 7," Daniel whispered.

"Already the memories must be fading, like an old photograph kept too long in a box. And what of Yael? She must want a mother very badly by now. How will you feel when she grows close to a new woman who is not Ella? Hmm, Daniel? I want you to think about this. It's important."

Daniel forced himself to think. Somewhat to his surprise, the process was not as painful as he might have expected. At some point in recent weeks, he had begun to accept the possibility of a new woman in his home, in his life, and in his children's hearts. As yet, she was still a phantom. But he thought he could handle the real thing, when he met her. Or, at least, he hoped he could.

"They're two separate things," he said, choosing his words carefully. "Ella was one thing — an incredible thing. That will never change. But — but a person has to live in the *now*, Rabbi. And *now* says that I'm just no good on my own anymore. It says that my kids need a woman around the house, and that I need one, too. I need a partner. Marrying someone new will not be a betrayal of Ella."

He reconsidered that thought, then nodded emphatically. "No, it will not betray her at all. Just as her dying didn't betray me. We each have to follow the road that Hashem lays at our feet. For nine beautiful years, he blessed me with Ella. And now, I find myself praying that He will bless me with someone else, someone different but just as right for me. Because He has commanded us to choose life. And this — living alone, and raising motherless children — is beginning to feel like no life at all."

Rabbi Mintzer sat back, beaming. "Very well put, Daniel! I am beginning to wonder if you did not choose the wrong profession. You would make a very wise and eloquent rabbi yourself, you know."

Blushing with pleasure, Daniel murmured, "It comes from being a lawyer — gives a person plenty of practice making speeches."

"But do you believe what you've just told me, Daniel? Do you truly believe it?"

Daniel straightened his shoulders, planted his hands on his knees, and met the rabbi's eyes squarely.

"Yes," he said. "Every word."

"Then our job now," Rabbi Mintzer said, suddenly brisk, "is to find you a *shidduch*. Perhaps my wife can help out here —"

As if on cue, Rebbetzin Mintzer emerged from the kitchen, carrying a tray laden with cups of tea and plates of cake. Steam wafted up from the teacups to mingle fragrantly with the aroma of old books. Daniel leaped up to take the tray from her.

"Daniel Newman is here, my dear," Rabbi Mintzer exclaimed, just as if she had not been preparing the repast just for him.

"Wonderful! I happen to have some cake I baked just yesterday. Maybe you'll have a little piece?" She held out the plate.

Smiling somewhat shyly into her creased, benevolent face, Daniel accepted the cake with thanks. As the Rebbetzin handed her husband a cup of scalding tea, he smiled across at her. "Why don't you sit down and join us? We have a little business to discuss."

"Business? What kind of business?"

"Your favorite kind," he said, twinkling.

"O-o-oh, *that* kind of business!" She took her place in an armchair, facing both men. "It's about time, too! Now tell me, Daniel — in detail, now — what are you looking for in a wife?"

Daniel had experienced this kind of conversation before, over the course of the past five years. But, before, it had always been an exercise in endurance. He had answered the questions mechanically, longing to be away, back home with his kids. The two dates that had resulted from those talks had been, not surprisingly, abortive. Now, Daniel spoke eagerly — outlining, explaining, imagining. Rebbetzin Mintzer listened with attention, inserting a question now and then to clarify a point. The rabbi sipped his tea, listening to the interplay with a benign joy.

When at last the visit had spun itself out and it was time to go home, Daniel all but floated to the door. Gratefully, he told the Mintzers, husband and wife, "I don't know how to thank the Rabbi and Rebbitzin."

"We haven't done anything yet," the Rebbetzin reminded him.

"Oh, yes. I feel confident now that this decision is okay — that I'm not shortchanging my kids by wanting to remarry. That's important to me."

Rebbetzin Mintzer glanced humorously at her husband. "Shortchanging them, by giving them a mother? Is the man a little crazy, or what?"

"Not crazy," Daniel said, suddenly very serious. "Just worried. I worry about them all the time, Rebbetzin."

"Of course you do. What parent doesn't worry?"

"But now I don't feel so worried anymore. I feel as if I've been given permission to start living again."

Stepping out of the house, he started down the path, leaving the couple standing framed in their lighted doorway. Halfway to his car, he turned back to wave. The light poured over and around the

Mintzers, turning them into a pair of featureless silhouettes. Shadow hands lifted to wave back at him.

"Thanks again," he called softly. "And good-bye."

He felt as though he were bidding farewell to a pair of guardian angels, and leaving behind a house that might have been situated in *Gan Eden* itself.

The car pulled up in front of the attractive, low-slung apartment building where Sara lived. Faygie sat at the wheel for a long moment, composing herself. Only when she was very sure that she had wrung herself completely dry of tears did she venture to open the door. A quick glance upward at a certain lighted window told her that her friend was home.

With short, deliberate steps, Faygie walked up the path to the front door and rang the bell beside the name Muller.

"Yes? Who is it?" Sara's voice sounded thin — and astonished through the intercom. Unexpected visitors were apparently not par for her course.

"It's me — Faygie. I'm sorry to disturb —"

"Faygie! Just a sec, I'll buzz you in."

The buzzer sounded in her ear, harsh and insistent as fate itself. She pushed open the door and climbed the single flight of stairs to Sara's door. It was already open, with Sara on the landing, waiting for her.

"Hi, Faygie!" Sara exclaimed. "What's going on? I thought you were going out with Yoni tonight."

"I did," Faygie answered, her voice even and calm, held under the tightest control.

"And —? Are you here to tell me some good news?" Sara held her breath.

"Can I come in?"

"Oh, of course! Why are we talking on the landing?" Laughing breathlessly, Sara motioned for her friend to enter the apartment, then followed her quickly inside. "Faygie, what's happening? Why are you here, instead of with Yoni, or with your family, drinking a *l'chayim*? What's going on?"

In response, Faygie simply turned to face her. She had been right: The tears were finished. For the moment, she had none left to weep. Her face was rigid and expressionless as a mask.

Then, right before Sara's eyes, the iron mask on her face began to slip. It slid slowly down and away, leaving the young woman underneath standing vulnerable and exposed. Sara winced at what she saw, there beneath the mask. It was sheer, raw pain.

"Oh, Faygie." She stepped closer and held out her arms. Wordlessly, her friend walked into them.

And then, to Faygie's amazement, she found that the well of tears had not been emptied to the last drop, after all.

The sobs, low and wracking, continued for so long that they left Sara's shoulder feeling sodden as a well-used towel.

"There," she said awkwardly, when the sobs had petered into a whimper. "Do you feel a little better now, Faygie?"

Her friend lifted a swollen, tear-stained face, and gave her a tiny smile. "Not a bit," she said. "But I do have a sudden, overwhelming craving for chocolate. Do you have any?"

"Loads," Sara said, pulling her into the kitchen and beginning to open cupboards. "Now, sit down, and have your chocolate, and tell me all about it. Every single thing."

With a deep, shuddering sigh, the kind that belongs to very small children after a good cry, Faygie sat at the kitchen table and obediently began to relate, from the beginning, the sad saga of the *shidduch* that didn't take.

Daniel drove home in a euphoric dream, stopping at the neighbor's to pick up Yael and Mordy. When they arrived home, Yael reached into their mailbox to scoop out a handful of envelopes and handed them to her father.

"Here, Daddy. You forgot to get these before."

"Thanks." Absently — his mind was still full of his meeting with the Mintzers — Daniel thrust the letters into his pocket and entered the house. In his absorption, he hung up his jacket without noticing that the letters were still inside it — or that one of them, in a plain white envelope, had been addressed to him in indelible black marker.

Yael went up to her room to call Tzippy. Mordy went into the study to turn on his computer. As he had feared, he found a message waiting for him from his buddy, Vincent.

He read it through, and then read it again, shaking his head with relief. The guy said he was beginning to feel like a real millstone around Mordy's neck and he was hoping to leave town on Monday. He was planning to catch a Greyhound to Las Vegas or some point further west, he said.

But first, he needed Mordy to do him a little favor.

53

Sunday was not a day that was destined to turn out well for Mordy.

First, he woke up with a crick in his neck. "Comes from sleeping in the wrong position," his father told him, gently massaging his son's neck. "Does that feel any better?"

"A little," Mordy said. "But it still feels like there's a knot in it. And it hurts a little."

"Do you think you can make it to shul?"

"Sure. But maybe we can drive today, instead of walking?"

"Of course." Daniel reached for his jacket. While putting it on, he discovered the stack of mail he had thrust into the pocket the night before. He put the letters on the hall table; he would get to them after *Shacharis.*

It had rained during the night. The morning was balmy and still damp, with the sun making valiant efforts to put in an appearance through the clouds. Cedar Hills was suburban enough to boast open, unpaved areas, and in these areas dirt had mingled with the rain to form some formidable mud puddles. As Mordy was climbing into the car after *davening* — holding his head stiffly erect because of the pain in his neck — he slipped in one of them and landed, with a mighty *squish!,* stomach-down in the mud.

He stared down at himself in dismay. "Omigosh, look at me!"

Daniel looked. An irrepressible smile touched the corners of his mouth at the sight. "You make — quite a picture, Mordy. We'd better get you home, and showered, a.s.a.p."

"But the car! I'll get mud all over the upholstery." For a minute, Daniel and Mordy stared at the car, nonplused. Each pictured its pristine tan interior splashed with the dark stuff with which Mordy was so liberally spattered.

"Guess I'd better walk home," Mordy sighed.

"That's a good idea. Will you be all right? How's the neck feeling?"

Cautiously, Mordy swiveled his head. "Hey, you know something? I think that fall actually helped." He grinned ruefully in the direction of the sky. "Thank You!"

"Well, they say that every cloud has a silver lining," Daniel remarked, ruffling his son's hair — the only part of him untouched by mud. "I guess that's true of mud puddles, too. See you at home, Mordy."

The boy set off, grumbling, "Hope I don't meet anyone I know." His father started the car and waved as he passed his son.

A surprise met Daniel as he walked through his front door a few minutes later. It was his daughter, fully dressed and waiting for him.

"Well, well, well — the new year is off to a good start!" he said heartily. "What's the occasion, Yael?"

"I've already *davened* and eaten," she said eagerly. "I need to go over to Tzippy's house first thing this morning. We have a huge project to do, and we've hardly even started yet! Do you think you can give me a lift to her house, Daddy?"

"So early?"

"I know you haven't had breakfast yet, but after you eat you'll have to take Mordy to school in Baltimore and I don't want to wait till you get back. Early this afternoon we're supposed to be going over to Bubby and Zaydie's to say good-bye, remember? So this is my only chance to get some work done."

"I could drop you off when I take Mordy," he suggested.

"But Tzippy lives in the opposite direction. Please, can't you just zip me over there now, real fast?" She looked up at her father appealingly. "Tzippy's waiting for me. I already called her."

"All right," he smiled. "Let's zip. I'll just let Mordy know we're going. Meet you at the car." He'd be gone for all of eight minutes — approximately four for each leg of the trip. No sense in dragging Mordy from the shower to accompany him. Besides, Daniel was feeling safe today.

"Mordy!" he called up the stairs.

"Yeah?"

"I'm running Yael over to Tzippy's. Are you in the shower yet?"

"Just about!"

"See you in a few minutes, then. Keep the doors locked and don't let anyone in, okay?"

"Sure, Daddy!"

Satisfied, Daniel went outside, making sure to lock the front door behind him. Yael was waiting by the car, sniffing appreciatively in the fresh morning air. "The world smells better this early," she confided, as he unlocked the car for her.

"Why don't you get up early every Sunday, then?" he teased.

"Um, maybe I will. We'll see —"

He laughed. "I'm sure we will."

He switched on the motor and started down the block, Yael prattling beside him as they went. The sense of well-being that had filled Daniel at the Mintzers' the night before, and that had stayed with him since, grew more pronounced. This was going to be a beautiful day. They would pick up Mordy at noon, when his Sunday classes ended, and go to visit Daniel's parents in Baltimore and wish them a good trip and an early *Gut Yomtov*. That done, it would be home for a quick lunch and then an afternoon of putting up the sukkah. It was perfect weather for it: neither too warm nor too cold, with a light breeze to make you want to sing aloud while you swung your hammer. There were plenty of Shabbos leftovers for dinner, including a surprisingly tasty cake that Yael had baked for dessert.

Exactly eight and one-half minutes later, he was walking through his own front door again. He paused in the hall to pick up yesterday's mail, shouting, "Mordy, I'm home!"

A still muddy Mordy poked his head shamefacedly over the banister railing.

"Oh, hi, Daddy —"

"You haven't taken your shower yet? We have to leave for school in a few minutes. What's going on, Mordy?"

"Sorry, Daddy. I guess I got distracted. I'm getting in right now."

"Hurry, or you'll be really late. You haven't eaten yet, either."

"I'll have a muffin or something in the car. I'm not that hungry, anyway —"

Daniel shooed him on his way, then went into the living room. Selecting his favorite armchair, he sank into it to look through the mail.

There were one or two invitations, an Israeli postcard from his friend Yehuda Arlen depicting the Kinneret at sunset, and a few bills.

He reached the final letter — and his eyes widened in horror. His heart began a mad dance as he recognized the heavy black lettering. After a frozen second, he slit open the envelope and, with trembling fingers, pulled out a single sheet of plain white paper.

HI, JUDGE, it read. I'M BACK.

He stared at the words for an eternity, mesmerized by their stark, terrible simplicity. *I'm back.*

The nightmare had returned.

Slowly, his brain began to function again. There were no explicit threats in this one — a major relief. The letter-writer was obviously engaged in a war of nerves, which, Daniel was forced to admit, he seemed well positioned to win. Garrity would have to be informed of this new development. Daniel was glad the detective had never fully signed off from the case. If the leads he had been pursuing this far turned up blank, they would have to go through Daniel's own case files again, searching for other possibilities.

He got up to phone the detective at once, before Mordy came down for his breakfast. But just as he reached for the phone, it shrilled under his hand.

Entertaining a wild notion that the caller was Garrity himself, Daniel grabbed the receiver and said quickly into it, "Hello?"

"Hi, there, Judge," a rough, muffled voice said hoarsely into his ear. *"Do you know where your daughter is?"*

"Who? — What? —"

The line went dead.

This time, there was no delay, no time out for shock. Reaching for the phone book that was never far away, Daniel fumbled through the pages until he found Tzippy's number. He literally shook with fear until a voice answered.

"Hello, this is Daniel Newman." It took supreme effort not to shout the words. "Is my daughter there?"

"Yael? Yes, she's here. Just a second, I'll get her."

His breath emerged in a single, powerful gust; he had not even been aware that he had been holding it. Yael's voice, puzzled and slightly scared, came on the line.

"Daddy? Daddy, is that you? What's the matter?"

He closed his eyes. "Nothing's the matter, sweetheart — *baruch Hashem*. Now, listen closely. I'm coming over to pick you up in a few minutes."

"Pick me up?" If Daniel had said he was on his way to Mars, Yael could not have been more dumbfounded. "But I just got here! We have tons of work to do. What's going on, Daddy?"

"I'll explain when I see you. Stay in the house until I get there, okay?"

"Where else would I go?" Now Yael sounded mystified *and* exasperated. "Can Tzippy come over to our house, then?"

"We'll see. I have to think. First, I want to get you safely home, then we'll see. Now, remember — *stay put, Yael*. I'm on my way."

He hung up to a fresh bout of trembling. His heart was slamming in his chest as though he had just run a marathon. Until he had his daughter safely beside him, he would not stop being afraid. The twin shocks of the anonymous letter and the follow-up phone call had shaken him, almost to the point of mindless obsession. He must get to Yael — bring her home — see that she was safe.

Do you know where your daughter is?

At the front door, through the beating of his terror, he remembered his son. He bellowed again up the stairs, "Mordy!"

There was no answer. He ran halfway up the steps, until he heard the sound of running water in the shower. Mordy would doubtless be occupied in there for some minutes, scrubbing away the morning's debris. Daniel would have Yael back even before Mordy knew he was gone.

Locking the door carefully behind him, he ran with frantic haste to the car and set off again for Tzippy's house.

54

The sight of his daughter brought a powerful rush of gladness to Daniel — a release that was almost terrifying in its strength. In his blind panic, he had run out of the house like a man demented, no other thought in his mind but whisking his precious Yael out of harm's way. He gazed upon her face as if on a destination he had traveled many hard miles, instead of a few short blocks, to find.

The face in question happened, at the moment, to be furious.

Yael got into the car, tight lipped and wrapped in a stony silence. She refused to give her father the satisfaction of her curiosity. If he had a good reason for dragging her away from her friend's house within half an hour of dropping her off there, he would tell her in her own good time. She pressed her lips even more tightly together, to keep in the questions that were aching to get out.

Daniel felt around in the glove compartment. Good: His cellular phone was there. Quickly, he punched in Mark Garrity's number.

"'Lo?" The detective's voice was groggy, almost unrecognizable.

"Mark, is that you?"

"Whoozzat — Dan'l? Dan Newman?"

"Yes, that's right. I'm sorry I woke you, Mark."

"Two all-nighters in a row," Garrity explained, becoming gradually more lucid. "That big jewelry heist up at Crawford Mansions — But what's up, Dan? You didn't call just to wish me a good morning."

"No. Mark, I got another letter this morning or, rather, last night."

Garrity was fully awake now. "Well, which was it?"

"The letter came in the mail yesterday, Saturday, but I didn't get around to actually reading it until this morning."

"I'll be down to your house a little later to take it from you. Just give me a chance to pull myself tog —"

"Wait, Mark, there's more." Succinctly, Daniel described the phone call. "I'm sure the guy was disguising his voice. It sounded definitely muffled, and deliberately hoarse."

"And he made specific reference to your daughter?"

" 'Do you know where your daughter is?' Those were his exact words."

At the memory, Daniel clutched the phone more tightly, his knuckles turning white with the added pressure.

"Danny-boy," the detective said, quietly but with great firmness, "I think even you'll agree that the time has come to institute some police protection here. No?"

"Yes," Daniel said at once. "Yes. Come on over, Mark, as soon as you can make it." He moved to hang up.

"Wait a second! Wait, Dan. I want you to do something else before you go home. Until we have your place secured, I think it would be best for your daughter to be somewhere else. Is there anyone you can leave her with? Someone you can trust? It would probably be only for a few hours or so, until we get our act together."

Daniel thought of his parents, due to fly out of Baltimore shortly, and of his brother and sister-in-law, slated to do the same. Yehuda Arlen, a man he trusted with his life, was far away in Israel. It would have to be someone else, someone not of his inner circle.

"I'll find someone," he said tersely. He glanced at Yael, sitting rigidly beside him, the ears practically standing out from her head at the things she was hearing. "I'll get her over there, wherever it is, and call you again when I get home."

"Make sure you're not followed."

"Will do. Thanks, Mark."

Garrity grunted, and hung up.

Daniel turned slowly to face his daughter. "I owe you an explanation," he said.

There was something in his expression that dried up Yael's anger faster than a puddle in the blazing sun. She bit her lip.

"What is it, Daddy? I have a feeling I'm not going to like it."

"I don't like it, either, but we're both going to have to deal with it as best we can. I'll tell you what's going on, and then we'll have to brainstorm a little.

"It all started back in the beginning of September. It was the last day of your summer vacation, I remember. I was coming out of the courthouse at the end of the day, when I saw something stuck into the windshield of my car. It was a letter ... "

Yael was absolutely silent during his recital. Several times, she opened her mouth to ask something, and then closed it again. There was nothing in the world but her father's voice, going on and on about things that sent a shiver straight up her spine to tickle eerily at the base of her neck.

He finished at last. Yael knew her father was waiting for her to say something. Her mind felt blank; all she could think of was an accusing, "All this has been going on since school started, and you never told me?"

"I wanted to protect you," Daniel said. "I didn't want you to be frightened. But there's no choice now. In order to protect you, Yael, we need your cooperation. Until this creep is caught, you're going to have to be on your guard."

"*Will* he be caught?"

"Of course! He's been delivering letters, hasn't he? With the police lurking in the shadows to observe anyone approaching our house, they're bound to nab him sooner or later. For all of our sakes, let's hope it's sooner — But I have the fullest confidence in Mark Garrity. He's already working on several possible leads."

Suddenly, Yael remembered what she'd meant to ask. "What did you mean when you said, 'I'll find someone'?"

"What's that?"

"You told Detective Garrity that. *Who* do you have to find — beside the letter-writer, I mean?"

He peered into her eyes. "Yael, Garrity thinks you'll be safer away from home today, until the police get the place secured and under surveillance. I guess he's afraid that someone might try to get to you, somehow, while we're still off balance —"

Yael paled. He knew he had frightened her badly, but he needed to do just that in order to put her on her guard against the danger that hung over her. At the same time, he did not want to paralyze her with fear. In his most calming manner, the kind he used to wear when one of the kids got hurt and was near-hysterical with pain and fear, he said, "*Hakadosh Baruch Hu* is going to be watching over you every minute, Yael. Just get through today, and then we'll be together. The guy will be caught, and we'll be able to go on with our lives." Dimly, as though from a distant era, he remembered his contentment of last night and this morning, his rosy plans, his dreams of future joy. All that would have to wait now. Danger, like sickness, had a way of putting normal life on hold.

"Now," he said, "the problem is to find you a secure place to stay."

"Why not Tzippy's?" she asked promptly, just as he had known she would.

"We could do that," he said slowly. "But that would mean letting Tzippy and her parents — and, probably, the rest of her family, too — in on what's happening. Pretty soon, it would be all over town. While this is no shameful secret, do you really want everyone at school talking about it? Do you want conversations to suddenly stop when you walk into a room? Or, worse — have strangers come up to you to ask all sorts of idiotic questions?" He paused. "You can go to Tzippy's, if you want. I leave the choice to you, Yael."

The scenario he had painted was not very attractive. Yael bit her lip, considering, and then shook her head. "I guess that rules out all of my friends from school. So who's left?"

"Bubby, Zaydie, Uncle Chaim, and Aunt Gila are practically on their way to Florida even as we speak. So they're out, too. We need an adult, someone mature and discreet, someone you can feel comfortable with and whose household won't be turned upside down by all of this —" His brows came together in a wrinkle of concentration.

But Yael was smiling. "I have it, Daddy," she said softly.

"You do? Who?"

"Miss Muller!"

"Miss — Oh, you mean the piano teacher?"

"She's also a teacher in my school. She lives alone, and is new in town so she won't blab the story all over the place. Not that she would, anyway. I'm sure Miss Muller is, um, what did you call it? Oh, yes — discreet."

"Do you think she'd agree to have you?"

"Why not? She likes me, I know that. And I don't mind spending the day with her. We won't be able to play the piano because she hasn't got one yet, but we can talk music, and — just talk."

Even in his relief to have found a reliable option, he was intrigued by something in Yael's manner as she spoke of her piano teacher. "You really like her, don't you?"

Yael blushed. "I do. Strange, isn't it? Maybe it would be different if she were my teacher at school — I know some of the kids in her class have a problem with her. But I think she's really nice. And the way she plays the piano —!"

For the first time since his double bombshell that morning, Daniel smiled.

He started the car and started moving slowly down the block. "Do you know where she lives?"

There was a blank silence. Then Yael remembered: "She once told me the name of the apartment complex where she's renting this year. I know it; there are only a few buildings there, and they're not large. It shouldn't take us long to find her name by one of the doorbells."

Daniel glanced down at his cell phone. "Do you happen to know her phone number?"

"Not by heart, Daddy. Sorry."

"Well, then, Detective Newman, looks like we're going to track down the lady all by ourselves." He pressed on the accelerator, picking up speed.

Yael gazed worriedly out the window. "I hope she's home."

"So do I, Yael," Daniel said, thinking of Garrity, who was expecting his call, and itching to get the ball rolling in search of the hoodlum who was turning all their lives upside down. "So do I."

55

Faygie had been in no state to go home to her empty apartment on Saturday night. That, at any rate, had been Sara's firm opinion; and it had not taken her long to convince her friend of its validity. When Sara offered her a bed or rather, a pull-out sofa for the night, Faygie meekly accepted. It was as if every last drop of her will had been drained in coming to her wrenching decision. For the moment, she was content to let herself be mothered. Mindless obedience was a balm.

Before they turned in for the night, there was a cup of tea for her guest and decaf coffee for Sara, at the little kitchen table that seemed so lonely when Sara ate her solitary meal there each night, but felt utterly cozy with a friend seated opposite her. And there was talk, too, a great deal of it: woman-talk, friend-talk, wistful, bittersweet, keeping-back-the-darkness talk. Many words were spent on Yoni, at first, and on the relationship that would never be. Gradually, in deference to Faygie's still-raw wound, they abandoned that topic and wandered into others. Apart from her piano lessons with Yael Newman, they were the most content few hours Sara had spent since moving to Cedar Hills.

Faygie passed a restless night; Sara could hear her tossing and twisting in her blankets whenever she herself awoke. Her own night was no better. She was genuinely grieving for her friend. So many near-misses, the *almosts* that left the heart ragged and breathless, zigzagging from hope to hopelessness — When would it finally be right for Faygie — and for Sara herself, for that matter? When would

Hashem see fit to grant them what they each so profoundly craved: a loving husband, children, a home? For so many other women, these were things to be taken for granted. For those other, luckier women, these things made up the very fabric of which their lives were woven. Sara and Faygie were still bobbing at the edges of their own potential lives, filling useful functions but bringing joy to no one, and finding little enough of it for themselves.

The old self-pity threatened to consume Sara entirely, until she forced the useless thoughts from her mind and drifted finally into a light sleep. She woke early, despite her unrestful night, and got up to prepare breakfast for her guest.

Faygie slept on for a full hour after Sara arose. Sara used the time to make her bed and set the table and recite her morning prayers. When Faygie did wake, it was with bleary-eyed indifference to pain's hangover. She tried to be polite, but Sara saw through the pretense.

"What you need," she said, "is something hot to eat and drink, and then a nice, long, leisurely Sunday spent doing absolutely nothing. Read, relax, listen to music — Let the day heal you, Faygie."

"Sounds good," Faygie said, groping morosely for her slippers. "I need coffee, lots of it, black. And then I think I'll take your advice. I thought at first that I'd spend the day with you, but I can see I'm just not good company today. Besides," she sighed, inserting her feet into the slippers at last, "I've got to call my mother and break the news about Yoni."

"Good luck. I'd suggest you get that over with first thing, and then stay away from the phone."

Faygie brightened. "That's just what I'll do! Somehow, I can't picture myself spending a relaxing, *healing* Sunday with my entire family calling me to commiserate."

Breakfast was quiet but companionable. Faygie had hers while dressed in a borrowed robe of Sara's. Then after downing a large serving of scrambled eggs and three cups of coffee, she seemed to cheer up a little. A hot shower did the rest. By the time she had dressed and *davened,* she looked almost ready to face the world again.

"Here I go, bruised but undaunted," she announced, a hand on the doorknob. "Thanks for everything, Sara. I don't know how I'd have survived last night without you. I owe you one."

Sara thought of her own difficult first weeks on the job, and of the way Faygie had persisted in battering down her walls, bringing friendship and hope and cheer back into her life. "You owe me nothing," she said firmly. "Let's just say that we're almost even now."

Laughing, Faygie opened the door. "Oh, I never got around to asking — what are *your* plans for the day?"

"I haven't made any yet. Maybe I'll go out, do a little shopping. With winter coming, I can use a new pair of boots."

"Well, enjoy. 'Bye."

"'Bye, Faygie. Take care." Sara watched her friend down the steps, then closed the door.

Faygie descended the last step and reached the glass doors that fronted the building. She was about to push them open when two people, a man and a girl, walked up to the building from outside. The girl looked familiar. Someone from school, maybe.

They had stopped to peruse the names over the doorbells.

"Do you see hers anywhere?" the man asked. "This is the last building in the complex."

The girl squinted at the smudged name-tapes. "Yes! There it is — Sara Muller. Oh, I hope she's home." She reached for the bell.

"She's home," Faygie said, smiling.

The man turned quickly. Faygie added, "I've just come from there. Sara's home. First apartment, at the top of the stairs. Why don't you just go on up and knock on her door?" She held the glass doors open for them.

"Thank you." Inclining his head courteously, Daniel and Yael passed through the doors and started up the stairs.

Because of Faygie's helpful gesture, they did not ring the bell, and Sara did not buzz them in. She had no grace period, no warning at all that an undreamed-of upheaval was about to be ushered into her tidy, solitary life. The simple knock brought her to the door.

"Miss Muller? We're terribly sorry to disturb you at home, especially so early on a Sunday."

"Please. It's no trouble." Flustered and pink, Sara let her wondering eyes travel from one to the other. "Won't you come in?"

Daniel and Yael stepped inside. Through the open kitchen door Daniel saw the remains of a breakfast set for two. The open sofa, with its tangle of blankets, told the rest of the story.

"That was Miss Mandelbaum, wasn't it?" Yael asked shyly. "We met her downstairs."

"Yes. She spent last night here." Sara stopped talking and turned questioning eyes on Daniel.

He cleared his throat, suddenly tongue-tied. "You must be wondering what brings us here. It's important, or we wouldn't have come. I hope you understand that."

In the face of his obvious discomfort, Sara seemed to regain her own composure. She walked briskly over to the sofa and began gathering up great armfuls of linen, which she set on the floor to one side. As her visitors watched, she snapped the sofa back into its usual shape, then reached for the cushions, heaped against one wall. Daniel and Sara sprang into action to help. In a twinkling, the bed had become sofa again.

"Please," Sara said, gesturing at it. "Have a seat. Then tell me all about it."

She waited until father and daughter were seated side by side before asking, "Can I get you anything? Coffee? Juice?"

Daniel remembered that nothing had passed his lips yet that morning. "Coffee would be great," he said gratefully. "Medium-light, one sugar, please."

"Fine. Yael?"

"Nothing for me, thanks." Yael's gaze was raking the living room with open curiosity. It was not often that she got to visit a teacher's house. She pointed at a blank stretch along one wall, where until recently the sofa cushions had rested. "A piano would go well there, don't you think?"

Sara laughed. "From your mouth to G-d's ears. Maybe someday, when I've saved up enough, there'll be one." She made for the kitchen.

Daniel sat on the sofa, looking out at a view of autumn foliage through the window but not really seeing it. A stripe of sunlight snaked down one curtain fold. What strange twist of fate had brought him here, to the home of a woman he hardly knew, but to whom he was about to consign his beloved only daughter for protection? He felt the reins of control slipping, very slowly but just as inexorably, from his fingers. One event was piled relentlessly on top of the one that came before, until a structure had been erected that had nothing to do with his will at all.

And so he sat, hands clasped together between his knees like a supplicant, wondering how to begin explaining the situation to Sara Muller, nerving himself to ask for her help and hoping like an anxious schoolboy that she would say yes.

She returned, with a tray bearing a saucer, a mug, and a small plate of cookies. "They're from a box," she apologized. "I don't have much time, or inclination, to bake these days."

"Are you enjoying your new job at the school?" Daniel asked politely, reaching for the coffee.

She hesitated. "Most of the time, I do. There's one class that's giving me a little trouble — it's my official class, too. But I'm determined to get them to work with me. It might take some time, that's all."

"You strike me as a person who usually accomplishes what she sets out to do." He sampled the contents of his mug. "This is terrific coffee, by the way. Thank you."

"You're welcome. Well, what I'd like to accomplish right now is to hear your story. Whenever you're ready, of course."

He remembered something. Abruptly, he set down the mug. "May I use your phone first? This will only take a minute."

"Of course. It's in there."

He went into the kitchen and dialed his home. Mordy answered on the fourth ring, out of breath. "Hi, Daddy! Where are you calling from? I didn't even know you'd gone out until I came down from my shower and found an empty house."

"It's a long story. I'll be home soon. Just wanted to make sure you're okay."

"I'm about to have some breakfast. Do you mind if I finish off the Cheerios?"

Daniel laughed, buoyed by his son's sheer, high-spirited normalcy. Thank G-d, *someone* was out of this nightmare loop. "Take all you want, we've got more in the basement. Hold down the fort till I get there, all right?"

"Will do, Dad. Over and out."

Still smiling, Daniel hung up and returned to the living room, where Sara and Yael had begun a highly fascinating — for them — comparison of the merits of the various piano brands on the market. Sara interrupted herself when he came in, saying, "Okay, Mr. Newman. I'm all ears."

He sipped some more coffee while he collected his thoughts, then said, "To make a long story short, I've been getting threatening letters from an anonymous source. Today, it escalated into a phone call — one that made direct reference to Yael. The police are on the case and are preparing to set up surveillance at my home, but they've suggested that I find another place for my daughter to stay until it's all set up. Yael thought of you."

"Of course I'll be glad to help. You must be on pins and needles! I hope they catch whoever's been bothering you — and soon, too!" Sara was pink again, with indignation this time. Daniel hid a smile at her understatement: "bothering" him, indeed! When he thought of his pounding heart, his shaking hands, the visions that left him sweating and trembling — *Bothering* him —!

"That's very good of you. Yael assures me that, though you haven't got a piano yet, the two of you can spend endless hours of pleasure just *talking* music. I hope she's right, and that you had no important plans for today."

"She's right, and I didn't. I was thinking about shopping, but that can wait. Or maybe I'll take Yael with me — if the police think that would be okay?"

Daniel considered. "I think it would probably be best if you sit tight here until I call to give you the word. A friend of mine, a police detective, will be advising me soon."

"Fine." Absently, Sara took a cookie. "Will Yael be sleeping over, do you think? Because, if so, her car pool should be notified."

"No, no! At least, I'm pretty sure it won't come to that. Garrity, my police friend, said a few hours, that's all. I hope to bring Yael home in time for dinner, if not sooner."

"Then there's no problem at all." Sara stood up with decision. "You can leave her here, Mr. Newman. She's in safe hands. And please —" She faltered.

"Yes?"

"Try not to worry. It'll be all right, you'll see."

Her words, banal as they were, comforted him. Or perhaps it was the knowledge that he had an ally, someone who was clearly devoted to Yael, that provided the comfort. He stood, too, and brushed off his pants. "Thanks for the coffee, and everything else. You're very kind —"

"It's my pleasure. Now go home and catch that *rasha* already!"

Chuckling, Daniel moved toward the door. Yael followed him, with Sara Muller a close third. After kissing his daughter and offering a last smile to her protector, Daniel said, "Okay, I'll go now. Yael, stay cool. I'll call in a little later."

With that, he was out the door.

There was almost a bounce to his step as he ran down the stairs to the glass doors. He found his car in the parking lot and drove home quickly, eager to start the manhunt in earnest. He should have let the police in much sooner, he reflected as he negotiated the traffic lights. If he had, all this would not have dragged on so long. He had thought, after such a long silence, that he was home free, but the stalker had apparently been biding his time. Anger rose up in Daniel, swift and sharp — anger at being somebody's victim. The judge was supposed to be up on his bench, a figure of authority — not the hapless defendant standing manacled on the floor —

By the time he pulled into his driveway, the anger had given way to a steely resolution. He and Garrity were going to lay their hands on the fellow, he vowed silently, and see that he got the full measure of punishment allowed by law. He checked his watch: It was much later than he thought. Time had passed very quickly in Sara Muller's apartment, and his talk with Yael before that had run on, too. It was, in fact, a ridiculously late hour for Mordy to be starting his trip to school.

The boy would just have to stay home today; there were only three hours of classes on Sundays, a simple matter to make up. Once Daniel had explained everything — and he had made up his mind to fill Mordy in, just as he had done with his sister — Mordy would be anxious to be part of the action.

He fumbled for his key, making plans. He would phone Garrity immediately, get the ball rolling. Then he would talk to Mordy. And after that, if there was time, he might even grab something to eat. His stomach had been sending up urgent "empty" messages, which the single cup of coffee at Sara Muller's place had done little to assuage.

He opened the door, calling out at the same time, "I'm home!" Three steps took him to the phone. He waited impatiently for Garrity to answer; when he did, Daniel said again, "I'm home, and waiting."

"Stay put," Garrity said. "I'll be over in a little while. Your daughter okay?"

"She's in a safe place. But the thought of that creep knowing that she was out of the house at all makes my skin crawl."

"Relax. This was probably just a shot in the dark. For all he knew, Yael could have been curled up in bed when he called. Chances were, on a Sunday morning, that she would have been. He was lucky, that's all."

Some of Daniel's tenseness dissipated. "You're probably right."

"Of course I'm right. Ninety-nine out of a hundred anonymous threateners are spineless wimps — and not usually very intelligent, either. We'll get him, Dan."

"We'd better," Daniel said grimly.

He hung up the phone and went into the kitchen. The remains of Mordy's breakfast were visible, though the boy had made some attempt to clean up after himself. Daniel went to the foot of the stairs. "Mordy!" he shouted. "Can you come down? I want to talk to you!"

There was no answer.

"Mordy? *Mordy!* Where *is* that kid?" Grumbling, Daniel climbed the stairs to his son's room. He found it empty.

The bathroom was empty, too. And so, when Daniel ran back downstairs to check, was the study. The computer had been turned on; a star-studded cosmic screen-saver swirled gently over the face of the monitor.

Daniel stood quite still in the center of the small room, oblivious to the books on the walls, to the whirling cosmos on the monitor — to everything in the world except the deathly hush of the house, and his own blood, turning slowly to ice in his veins.

56

I n laying his plans, Joey Mercutio had counted on three things. None of them was the smile of Lady Luck, whose usual habit was to give him the cold shoulder — Though all that was changing now.

No, his three assumptions had nothing to do with luck. He had thought them out over the course of many long, lonely nights in his basement hideaway. They were solid.

The first assumption was one of ignorance: Judge Newman's. The judge could have no idea that he — the anonymous letter-writer — had for some time been in e-mail contact with Newman's own son. The proof of that was simple enough: Had he had any inkling of their correspondence, it would have been cut off immediately.

His second assumption was that the police had not been called in. He had been watching the house for weeks now, and there had been no sign of police activity, even undercover activity, across the street at the Newmans'.

The third thing Joey Mercutio was relying on had nothing to do with facts, but everything to do with human psychology. While he lay no claim to being a deep thinker, even he knew this much: For a man of courage, a threat to his own safety will make him mad — but a threat to his children will make him afraid. If Joey was right, then Judge Newman ought to be shaking like a leaf right about now. And a man in the grip of fear is not a man whose thinking is at its razor-sharp best.

Joey watched the house a moment longer, then lowered his

binoculars. The police would undoubtedly be pulling up in front of the Newman house soon, and he did not want any keen-eyed young officer noticing the flash of the sun off the lenses. He turned, placing the window at his back. Time enough for another peek in a little while, before the curtain rose on the last, glorious act. Anyway, he had something of greater interest right here in the basement.

A wheelbarrow stood propped up against one wall. It was full of something large and inert, covered with burlap. Joey walked over to the wheelbarrow, lifted the burlap, and peered greedily inside. He could almost imagine he saw stacks and stacks of greenbacks lying there.

It was hard to be patient, but he had to do this thing right. Everything — his whole future — hinged on that. The greenbacks would come soon enough now.

And of course (he'd almost forgotten), there was also the small matter of revenge.

As his father had predicted, it had taken Mordy quite some time to scrub the mud off. After that, he had to find another set of clean clothes — no easy feat on a Sunday, with Monday being Mrs. Marks' wash day. He had managed to scrape together a clean, light-gray sweatshirt, navy pants that he had only worn once before that week, and a pair of gray sweat socks to wear with his sneakers. He had cleaned his glasses, which were mud speckled too, and brushed his hair. Planting his yarmulke on top, he'd felt clean and vigorous, ready for anything.

But mostly, he was ready for his breakfast.

He had run downstairs and had just walked into the kitchen, stomach rumbling, when he remembered last night's e-mail. That Vincent character was planning to leave town, or so he said. But before he did, he had penned a handwritten letter and delivered it to a location not far from Mordy's house. "I GOT YOUR ADDRESS FROM THE WHITE PAGES," he'd explained. "HOPE YOU DON'T MIND ... I WANTED TO WRITE YOU A LONG LETTER, WITH ALL KINDS OF STUFF FROM MY PAST, SO YOU'D UNDERSTAND ME BETTER. PLEASE READ IT, AND WRITE ME AN ANSWER. THEN I'LL LEAVE HERE HAPPY. I WANT TO TAKE YOUR LETTER AWAY WITH ME

WHEN I GO, SO MAKE IT FULL OF GOOD STUFF — YOU KNOW, ABOUT HOW PEOPLE WILL LIKE ME ONCE THEY GET TO KNOW ME, THINGS LIKE THAT. I'LL READ IT WHENEVER I'M FEELING LOW, AND I'M SURE IT WILL HELP ME STAY ON THE STRAIGHT AND NARROW. YOU SURE HAVE HELPED ME ALREADY . . . "

The message had gone on to describe exactly where he left the letter for Mordy. "I SCOUTED OUT YOUR BLOCK THE OTHER DAY, HOPE YOU DON'T MIND."

Frankly, Mordy *did* mind. He did not want characters like this Vincent prowling around his block. Moreover, he was heartily sick of playing therapist or wet nurse to an unbalanced stranger. But a sense of responsibility kept him from ignoring the other's plea. While it was true that Vincent had started this whole business — by sending sick, threatening letters to Mordy's dad — it was Mordy who had taken up the ball and run with it afterwards. One look at the guy's letter, and another few minutes to scribble back a heartening note of his own, and he would be free, in good conscience, to wash his hands of the whole sordid business.

Mordy couldn't wait.

In fact, he *wouldn't* wait. He went into the study, switched on the computer, and quickly pecked out an all-purpose missive of encouragement. He used such lines as "Under all the dirt, there's often gold; you just have to dig it out," and "With hard work, you can turn your life right around and make something of yourself that you'll be proud of." The details of Vincent Fouza's own letter did not really matter. This note was vague enough, and peppy enough, to cover all bases. And typing it now would save him a lot of time. He had already spent enough of it on the guy.

He would grab some breakfast — he was really hungry now — and then run over to leave the letter in the place Vincent had described. He would take away the letter that was supposed to be waiting for him, and Vincent would never have to know that he had written the second one before he had read the first.

Satisfied with his plan, Mordy finished his note and printed it out. The phone rang just as he was signing it. Though there was an extension in the study, he decided to pick it up in the kitchen, where he was headed in any case. Pen and letter in hand, he sprinted for that room, and rather breathlessly grabbed the receiver off the hook. It was his father.

"Hi, Daddy! Where are you calling from? I didn't even know you'd gone out until I came down from my shower and found an empty house."

"It's a long story. I'll be home soon. Just wanted to make sure you're okay."

"I'm about to have some breakfast. Do you mind if I finish off the Cheerios?"

With a laugh: "Take all you want, we've got more in the basement. Hold down the fort till I get there, all right?"

"Will do, Dad. Over and out."

Placing the letter to one side, Mordy poured himself a heaping bowl of Cheerios, slathered on the milk, and dug in. It took him no more than five minutes to devour the contents of the bowl. He briefly considered another, but the Cheerios were gone and he did not care for any of the other available cereals. Shrugging off whatever empty pangs still remained, he picked up the letter and let himself out the back door.

A few seconds brought Mordy around to the front of the house. Through narrowed eyes he surveyed the street. The block was quiet in the sun, and empty as a graveyard. Not a figure to be seen except a lone man clad in a jogging suit, walking his dog. As Mordy watched, man and dog rounded the far corner and were gone from sight.

No car moved through the street on this still fairly early Sunday morning. By rights, Mordy should have been on his way to school well before this, but — for reasons he did not entirely understand — the morning was not working out according to its normal schedule. He had no idea where his father had run off to, or where he had called from. His guilty knowledge of the letter he had just finished typing — and that he had been holding it in his hand, in fact, as he spoke to Daddy on the phone — had made him forget the questions he had been meaning to ask. He hoped his father would come home soon and clear up the mystery.

But not *too* soon. He would pick up and deliver the letters first, and be rid of Vincent Fouza forever. Looking up and down the street to make sure no one saw him, Mordy crossed over to the other side.

The FOR SALE sign hung crazily at an angle; one nail, apparently, had worked itself loose in a recent wind. "I LEFT THE LETTER UNDER A LOOSE STONE ON THE LEFT SIDE OF THE PATIO, OUT BACK," the e-mail had informed him. Feeling unaccountably nervous about trespassing on the neglected property, Mordy hurried around back. He wanted to be finished with this business as quickly as possible.

The patio was made all of stone, in the cracks of which sad-looking weeds sprouted in dreary profusion. A couple of large, earthenware urns kept vigil on either side of the kitchen door; each looked as though it weighed at least a ton. In one corner, looking derelict, was a stained wheelbarrow. A quick inspection told Mordy that more than one patio stone was loose, but only one of them was located at the furthest edge to the left. Gingerly, he lifted it. A beetle scuttled out, annoyed at having its privacy disturbed.

And there, as promised, was the letter.

For a long moment, Mordy just stared at it. Like his father a little earlier, he was overcome by a powerful sense of life's weird convolutions. What in the world had led him to this bizarre situation, crouched on the patio of an empty house not his own, exchanging letters with a pen pal he didn't want?

Well, it was almost over. Vincent was leaving tomorrow; it heartened Mordy greatly to remember that. He reached in and picked up the plain white envelope.

The flap was tucked into the back, unsealed. He flipped it open with one finger, pulled out a sheet of paper, and unfolded it.

The page was blank.

A sound behind him — just the faintest scrape of a foot against a loose stone — made him turn quickly.

A man stood there, in his 20's perhaps, dark haired and unshaven. He wore dirty jeans, and a T-shirt that hung almost down to his knees. On his hands were thick work gloves, the kind gardeners use. A faded Yankees cap sat on his head at a disconcertingly jaunty angle.

"You're trespassing," the stranger said.

Mordy's heart took on a nervous, fluttering action. He was beginning to suspect that he had walked into trouble. Desperately, he decided to brazen it out.

"So are you," he retorted. "What are you doing here?"

"Looking for you," the man said softly, and stepped forward, a folded handkerchief in his palm. A sickly-sweet smell wafted to Mordy's nose.

What he had suspected before turned now to certainty. But there was no time to react before the handkerchief was pressed ruthlessly against his nose and mouth. With one iron hand clamped around his forearm, the boy's struggles were futile.

The frantic kicks grew more feeble as the chloroform took hold. At last, Mordy's eyes closed and he went limp.

Joey's face, as he loaded the boy into the waiting wheelbarrow and covered it with a length of burlap, was impassive. But his legs felt like dancing as he bumped the wheelbarrow down the steps to the basement of the deserted house.

57

"**T**wenty minutes," Daniel said dully, for the fourth or fifth time since Detective Mark Garrity had walked into his house. "Twenty minutes. That's how long it took for me to get home after speaking to Mordy on the phone. Maybe a quarter of an hour to wind up at Sara Muller's place, and another five to drive home." He shook his head, a man in the grip of a reality too overwhelming, still, to fully take in. "Twenty minutes —"

"Take it easy, Dan," Garrity said. "You'd better have something to drink, something strong. You're in shock, and I can understand that. But we've got work to do. I need you alert, and thinking. For the kid's sake."

When Daniel did not answer or make a move, Garrity swung around to the breakfront that stood against one wall. A quick opening and closing of its various doors brought to light a half-full bottle of whiskey. The detective poured a generous splash from one of them into a paper cup and handed it to Daniel. "Drink up," he ordered.

In a dream, Daniel did as he was told. The fiery liquid made him gag as it went down his throat, but immediately a warming sensation began to spread through his chest. Daniel took another sip, and felt the cobwebs start to uncoil from around his brain. A third sip cleared his mind enough to let the full horror of Mordy's predicament strike. He staggered to an armchair and sank heavily down.

"My son — Mordy — That guy *must* have him. First the letter, to soften me up — to scare me, set my nerves on edge. Then the phone call, to make me jump out of my skin with worry over Yael. I didn't think — I was sure Mordy was safe. It was Yael he was after . . . " He was babbling like a child, or a fool. But he could not stop himself. The words themselves were only a tissue-thin veneer, papering over an inner cry that resounded through Daniel like the howl of an abandoned infant. "*Hakadosh Baruch Hu,* help! My Mordy's in danger! Why, Hashem? Why my son? Why this? Please, oh, please — *help!*"

"Is there anyone I can call for you, Dan? A relative, maybe, or a close friend? You shouldn't be alone at a time like this."

"No — no. I can't think of anyone. My family's on their way to Florida, or will be shortly. My best friend's gone on sabbatical —" With an effort, Daniel pulled himself together. "I'm okay, Mark. Really. I'm glad you're here." He took a deep breath, then said through clenched teeth, "Let's catch this piece of slime."

"I've radioed for backup." Garrity came to sit on the couch facing him. "But while we wait, I want to make absolutely certain that we can rule out an innocent reason for Mordy's disappearance. Could he have gone to visit a friend?"

"His friends are all in school this morning."

"To a store, maybe, to buy something? Some kids'll go anywhere for a chocolate bar."

"Not my Mordy. He's not that kind. Anyway, the nearest supermarket is a seven-minute drive from here, which would make it a *very* long walk for a kid to take, especially on a whim." Daniel shook his head with emphasis. "Forget it."

"Someone offered him a lift, maybe? And there's always the bus."

"I tell you, Mordy wouldn't do such a thing! As far as he knew, I was about to come home and drive him to school. Besides, if for any reason he did have to go out for more than a minute or two, he'd have left me a note. He was — *is* — responsible that way."

Outside, a car pulled up. It was an unmarked police car, with no blazing lights or sirens to alert the neighbors that something catastrophic had just taken place on their block. Until they knew that Mordy was safe, the police would keep the news as quiet as possible.

With a slamming of doors, two plainclothes police detectives emerged from the car. They sauntered up to the house, appearing to the curious as nothing more than another couple of casual visitors for the judge. With their backs to the street, they never noticed the man behind them, directly across the street. He wore work clothes and gardening gloves, a cap pulled down low over his eyes against the sun. He was lumbering a wheelbarrow down the block.

The detectives entered the Newman house and began to confer with Garrity, while Daniel took another sip of his restorative and tried to keep the panic from spreading, faster than the liquor, through his veins. His mind was like one of those toys that jump when you touch them. Over and over, it touched on Mordy — who was Heaven-only-knew-where at this moment — and then jumped away again, as though burned. If only he had not panicked that morning, and dashed out after Yael without thinking. If only he had thought to take Mordy with him. If only . . . And meanwhile, his darling boy, his Mordechai, light of his life, was languishing somewhere in the hands of some stranger, surely scared, possibly hurt, maybe even . . .

Jump. There was only so much pain his mind could bear.

The wheelbarrow moved ever farther down the block. It reached the near corner and rounded it. A dusty black jeep was parked at the curb. The man tipped his load into the back of it, threw the wheelbarrow in after, and was driving away down the quiet street even before Mark Garrity had finished filling his colleagues in on the situation.

Many kids run away from home each year, only to return, tails between their legs, within a day of leaving. Bearing this in mind, the police generally do not file missing-persons reports until 24 hours have elapsed from the time of disappearance. But this case was different. It had a history. Based on the threatening notes and phone calls, the police decided to treat Mordy's disappearance from the first as a possible kidnapping.

With Garrity in charge, they set up headquarters in the Newman living room. Another pair of police detectives, a man and a woman this time, arrived to round out the team. Garrity introduced them all: Jim Stewart and Luis Mendez, Lucy Fenwick and Pete Rheims. Garrity's own partner, Richie Burns, was out of town until Tuesday.

"Most kidnappings are solved within the first 24 hours," Garrity told Daniel. "This one appears to have been perpetrated by a local. The notes you received from him in the mail had local postmarks. Must be in some little hiding place in town, possibly quite near here. If we can just get a handle on who he is, we'll be able to track him down using our sources on the street."

"He may have left town," Daniel objected.

"Maybe, but at this point it seems unlikely."

"How do we find out —" Daniel's question was cut short by the ringing of the telephone.

There was an instant's electrified silence.

"That could be him. There may a ransom request," Garrity said quietly. "Answer it, Dan. They're already alerted down at the station house to trace any calls coming in to this number. If it's him — the kidnapper — try to keep him on the line as long as possible." He walked quickly into the kitchen to pick up the extension there. The other officers took up positions close to Daniel.

With legs that felt as though they had turned into rods of lead or petrified tree stumps, Daniel walked to the shrilling phone and picked it up. His first effort at speaking drew a blank: His throat didn't work. He cleared it painfully and tried again. "H-hello?"

"Hello, Mr. Newman?" asked a bright young voice. "Is Yael there?"

It was Tzippy. Daniel closed his eyes as unused adrenalin rushed through him in a dizzying torrent. Pooling his fast-dwindling resources, he managed a convincingly normal, "No, I'm afraid she's not here at the moment. She had to go out for a while."

"Oh. Well, can you ask her to call me back when she gets in? We still have this project to do, and I'm getting kind of nervous. It's due Wednesday. *This* Wednesday."

"I'll tell her," Daniel promised mechanically. He closed his eyes. "Good-bye, Tzippy. Have a nice day." He hardly knew what he was saying. Vaguely, he heard a puzzled "'Bye," and hung up.

The tension eased. The detectives began moving again, setting up their headquarters. In an amazingly short space of time, the living/dining room took on a whole new identity. It was no longer part of a private dwelling, but a hub of police activity. The police shifted the dining room table to one side and opened a folding card table under the window to accommodate the overflow. Already, the large table where the Newmans ate their meals was unrecognizable, strewn with one officer's styrofoam coffee cup, another's cellular phone, a third's hat, notebooks and car keys.

From outside, the noises of suburbia began to filter in. The season of the droning lawn mower was past, replaced by the roar of the leaf-blower. Every Sunday, huge trash bags filled with leaves were left at the curb for pickup. Mordy would probably have done a stint with the rake this afternoon, if there had been time after putting together the Sukkah . . . Daniel winced, willing the thought away. To be of any help at all to his son, he had to retain a sharp edge. He must be dispassionate, unemotional. It was the lawyer's brain that Mordy needed now, and not the father's heart.

But the father's heart refused to be stilled. Out of sight of the milling detectives, out of sight even of his own surface consciousness, it keened mournfully, longing for its beloved child —

The officers stood in a tight knot, speaking to each other in low, purposeful voices. Daniel had told Garrity that the front door had been locked when he entered, and the detective detached himself presently from the group to dust the back door for fingerprints.

Jim Stewart and Lucy Fenwick approached Daniel, notebooks in hand. Pete Rheims joined them a moment later. He was the shortest of the lot, sturdy and reliable looking, with a steady blue gaze and a penchant for colorful analogy. Last of all was a slim, olive-skinned Hispanic who wore a mustache and a nonstop smile that never quite touched his eyes: Luis Mendez. Mendez carried a cup of coffee.

"Mark's already given us the broad outlines," Stewart said. He was a tall man, even taller than Garrity, with a thatch of black hair, a slightly pockmarked face, and eyes that were half-hooded, as though he were either tired or secretive. A closer look showed Daniel that the eyes were also very kind. "Mind going over it with us again? From the beginning."

"I don't mind." This would be the third time today. Was it only yesterday that he had stood in shul reciting the Yom Kippur liturgy, confident that the danger was past? And only last night that he sat with Rabbi Mintzer and his wife, sipping tea and feeling like a man with a future?

"I found the first letter on the windshield of my car in early September," he began wearily. The detectives listened attentively, jotting notes and inserting an occasional question. Daniel told of the other letters, which Garrity had already produced for their scrutiny.

"Anything else? Any other phone calls before today?" Rheims asked.

"No — Or rather, maybe." He described the series of silent calls that had spooked him one evening. "But that must have happened all of two weeks ago. There's been absolutely no sign of the stalker since then — until last night."

Garrity walked back into the living room from the kitchen, fingerprinting kit in hand. "No sign of forced entry," he announced.

Bewildered, Daniel asked, "Then how did he get to Mordy?"

Lucy Fenwick snorted. She was a thickset woman with pale blond hair pulled straight back from a squarish face devoid of any trace of makeup. For some reason, she seemed extremely irritable, almost hostile. Maybe, Daniel thought charitably, she just was not a morning person.

"Obviously," she said, "your son must have gone out to *him*."

"But why would Mordy?"

"The guy wouldn't have come knocking at the door, saying, 'Hi, I'm a kidnapper, can I come in?' now, would he?" Lucy said testily. "He would obviously be wearing some sort of disguise. Postman, milkman, meterman —"

"On Sunday?" Rheims said skeptically.

"Well, something then. But Mordy opened the door to him —"

"And the guy took him out," Stewart finished.

"Without much of a struggle, apparently," Garrity said. "No sign of one in the kitchen, at any rate."

"Nary a sign," Rheims agreed.

Mendez spoke up for the first time. "Could the guy have lured Mordy out willingly? Said he had something to show him outside, maybe?" He turned to Daniel. "What's out there?"

Daniel said, "The back yard. Patio, swing set, grill. The usual."

Garrity turned to Daniel. "You told me that you went into the kitchen right after you came home, and found Mordy's breakfast things lying around. Think, Dan. Did you notice anything — *anything* — out of the ordinary?"

Daniel thought hard, then reluctantly shook his head. "Nothing. It looked just the way you see it now, Mark. Placemat, the one bowl and spoon in the sink, the empty Cheerios box. Nothing that shouldn't have been there."

"What about the pen?"

"Pen?" Daniel repeated blankly.

"Yes, this." Garrity held up a black, medium-point Parker.

"That's my pen, from my study." Daniel stared at the writing implement as though it could spill secrets they were agog to hear. "How did it get to the kitchen?"

"It wasn't there before you left this morning?"

"I don't think so." Daniel frowned. "At least, not that I noticed."

"Maybe the boy *did* leave a note!" Pete Rheims suggested, snapping his fingers. "I say we take a good look around before we rule out that possibility."

Garrity nodded. "A good idea. Lucy, Luis and I will take the upstairs; you and Jim search down here. We'll —"

The phone rang again.

This time, Daniel hurried over to it without coaching. The detectives clustered around, watching his face intently, as Garrity scurried back into the kitchen to listen in on the extension. On the fourth ring, Daniel ventured a "Hello."

His face grew blank with astonishment.

"Ari?" he said. "Ari Rabinowitz, in California? My *nephew* Ari?"

"Yes, Uncle Daniel. I know this is a little unusual, but I need to speak to Mordy. Is he there?"

"But you just spoke to him on Friday. *Erev Yom Kippur.*" His faculties were overloaded this morning, his nerves stretched almost to the snapping point. Daniel was finding it difficult to adjust to the unexpected caller. In all the years since Ella had died, he did not recall Ari ever calling, on his own initiative, to speak to Mordy. Usually, he grabbed the opportunity presented by his parents phoning before a holiday to snatch a few words with his cousin. And, of course, they e-mailed one another.

"I know." Ari sounded nervous. "But there's something I want to ask him. It'll only take a minute. Is he there?" There was a sudden pause, then the boy exclaimed, "*oy,* I forgot all about the time difference! He's at yeshivah, right?"

Daniel drew a long breath. "Mordy's not here at the moment. I'll make sure he knows you called — when I see him."

"Um — Uncle Daniel?" Ari broke off.

"Yes?" When his nephew still hesitated, Daniel said firmly, "Ari, things are a little busy here right now. I'll tell Mordy you called, okay?"

"Uh, sure, Uncle Daniel. Well, 'bye."

"Good-bye."

Daniel hung up and turned away from the phone. The little group around him dissolved. He had an odd sense of dissociation, almost schizophrenic in nature, as he watched the police officers move about his living room, speaking into their radios and cell phones about *his* son — his Mordy. The couch where he curled up with his children to read countless bedtime stories sagged now under the heavy bodies of two police detectives. Garrity was emerging from the kitchen where, in happier times, Mrs. Marks had dished up so many suppers for them. Lucy Fenwick was gloomily slouching around the place.

His eye snagged the decorative clock that sat on one of the small tables flanking the couch.

Eleven o'clock. It was only 11 o'clock. Mordy had been gone less than two hours.

It was going to be a long day.

58

The next two hours passed excruciatingly slowly, though they were not without their share of activity. First, the detectives divided up to search the house. They made a thorough job of it, inside and out.

"No sign of a note," Garrity sighed when they had finished.

"It was a long shot," Stewart said. "It would most likely have been in plain sight on the kitchen table, if he'd written one."

"Then what about the pen?" Rheims asked.

"Could be nothing," Garrity said. "A coincidence." But he was frowning.

"The kidnapper — and my son — might be far away by now," Daniel said. "Is anyone checking the roads, rest stops, gas stations, that kind of thing?"

"The bulletin is out," Garrity nodded. "The station house is routing the calls through to here."

"What about the public? Shouldn't they be alerted? I can give you a picture of Mordy. Maybe someone will recog —"

"Not a good idea — at least, not yet. First of all, until we hear from either Mordy or the kidnapper we have no actual proof that he was snatched. And second," Garrity said, as Daniel made a move to object, "the powers-that-be have decided that, for now, this stays under wraps. Believe me, the police are keeping their eyes peeled." He patted the cell phone in his belt. "We won't bother you with the false alarms."

"Have there been any yet?"

"Sure. One officer noticed a nervous-looking guy at the pump next to his at a gas station. He had a boy with him. They filled up, then went into a nearby diner for some breakfast."

"And?" Daniel found himself suddenly short of breath.

"Turns out the kid is 8. The man is definitely his father — they look alike as two peas in a pod." Garrity grinned laconically, saving the best for last. "And, just another little detail: They're both Chinese! Guess the officer didn't get his facts straight."

The other detectives chuckled, except for Lucy Fenwick, who volunteered only a sour smile. Daniel did not feel much like laughing, either. He listened to the others: brief, technical spurts of talk, interspersed with the kind of humor that belongs to people who know each other well and are comfortable in each other's company. Enveloped in his own exotic, anguished atmosphere, Daniel might have been sitting on a different planet instead of two feet away.

The phone rang.

Garrity lifted a brow and gave the judge a quizzical grin. "You're a popular guy today, Dan."

But Daniel could not respond in the same casual fashion, not with his heart slamming against his ribs at the prospect of picking up the receiver to what just might, *this* time, be his son's kidnapper. The routine was seamless: Garrity disappeared into the kitchen, Daniel picked up the living-room extension, and the rest of the crew gathered around him, all at once deadly serious again.

"Hello?"

"Is this Daniel Newman? Judge Newman?"

It was a man's voice this time. An unfamiliar voice. Not the harsh, muffled voice he had heard on the phone that morning, but a stranger's voice just the same. In a blind panic, Daniel gripped the receiver hard.

"This is he."

"Glad I caught you, Judge. Henry Downing here."

If a horse had just thrown Daniel in a wild, bucking arc to land hard and disoriented on the ground, he could not have been more startled.

"D-Downing?" he stammered.

"Yes." A puzzled pause. "This *is* Judge Newman, isn't it?"

"Yes. Yes, it is. How can I help you, Mr. Downing?"

"You've already helped me plenty, sir," Henry Downing said warmly. His voice was rough, the accent very middle class: a working man's man. Daniel could picture him at the other end of the line, relaxed and smiling now, wearing his own well-tailored Sunday clothes instead of the drab suit he had worn in court. Elsa would doubtless be hovering at his shoulder.

"I'd like to thank you in person, sir. Maybe you could join us for dinner some night? It would be our pleasure — our honor!" When Daniel did not answer immediately, he added heartily, "Just a token of our appreciation, Judge. I know my wife's already thanked you, but I wanted to add my own two cents in person."

"That's very kind." Daniel swallowed, closing his eyes. He opened them again and gave a tiny headshake at the police officers. They nodded, and drifted away. "But I'm afraid I can't commit myself to anything just now. Something's — something's come up. A family emergency."

"Oh! Sorry to hear that, Judge. Maybe some other time, then?"

"Maybe." Tardily, as if reading a lesson from a meaningless book, Daniel remembered his manners. "It's very kind of you. Thank you."

There was a muffled dialogue at the other end, then Henry was back on again. "The wife says to tell you that everything's going to turn out all right. You're too good a man for it not to, she says." He paused. "And also that we're going to pray for you."

"Thank you." Absurdly, the words made Daniel want to cry, as he had not yet cried since his precious only son had disappeared.

It was almost 1 o'clock when Jim Stewart said something about lunch. He and Rheims volunteered to go out and bring back some fast-food for them all. Garrity, who knew that Daniel kept a kosher home, vetoed the idea.

"We'll go out for lunch, in shifts. You two and Lucy go first. Luis and I will take the second shift."

Stewart asked Daniel, "Want us to bring you back anything? Got to keep your strength up, you know."

"No, thanks." Daniel smiled faintly. He had not eaten yet that day, and all he had had to drink was a cup of coffee at Sara Muller's house and the liquor that Garrity had all but forced down his throat. It was like a second Yom Kippur — with his son's life hanging in the balance. He had not the faintest desire in the world to eat, though he thought, in a vague, dull way, that he ought to. Maybe some cheese and crackers in the kitchen later.

The call from Henry Downing would not leave his mind. Whenever Daniel closed his eyes, a vision of the courtroom sprang to the fore. Up on the bench sat Judge Newman, resplendent and awe-inspiring in his black robes — supreme authority within those four walls. He wielded his gavel the way a king might wave his golden scepter: ultimate symbol of his power.

And down at the defendant's table, haunted and silent, sat the accused. Henry Downing listened intently to every word the judge uttered, knowing how deeply it could affect his fate. Judge and judged had sat locked together for a few tension-packed days — days whose outcome would reverberate down the years of Downing's life like footsteps echoing down a hollow corridor.

And now?

Today, Downing was a free man, gazing into a future rich with the special joy that comes with a reprieve from disaster. And Daniel Newman, the all powerful, sat cowering in his own living room, abject as any prisoner and more terrified than the most cowardly defendant ever to face his bench.

The mighty judge could not even lift a finger to help his own precious son. His arms were handcuffed. His feet were shackled. The judge was utterly, and humiliatingly, helpless.

Restless, Daniel got up and began to pace the living room. Downing had been spared and he, Daniel, stricken. Was this Hashem's way of reminding him how tenuous are the roles we play in this world? "He uplifts the downtrodden and casts down the arrogant . . . " *Had* he been arrogant?

He had been secure in his role, certainly. He held the keys to other men's liberty in his own frail hands: a heady sensation. And yet, when all was said and done, the keys to his own life, liberty, and happiness were held in Hands other than his own. Had he forgotten that? Was that why he was being punished? Was Mordy suffering for the sins of his father?

He could not know. But there was one thing he did know, and that was the true source of his — and Mordy's — only possible succor. Daniel crossed to one of his bookshelves and did what he should have done a long time ago, and what he would have done if he had not been so shell-shocked and then so distracted by all the phone calls. He took down a small *Tehillim*.

"If you'll excuse me," he told Garrity quietly, "I'll pray a little now."

When the phone rang for the fourth time, Garrity was in the kitchen before Daniel had moved a muscle, so absorbed was he in his *Tehillim*. He got to his feet while murmuring the final words of the verse he had been reciting, then lifted the receiver. This time, because of the *Tehillim*, he was considerably calmer. "Hello?"

"Danny, is that you?" His mother's outraged voice came clearly over the line.

Angry. She was angry. Daniel tried to think why this should be so. He needed his mother now, as he had never needed her before — not even when Ella had died in that accident and his world had turned so completely on its head. Now it was Mordy who had vanished from his life with the same abrupt, violent lack of warning. *Mom, I need you.* Why was she so angry?

"For an hour and a half we've been waiting for you and the kids! You said you were going to pick up Mordy from school at noon and come right over. What happened? Did you stop for lunch somewhere? We have to leave to catch a plane in ten minutes!"

"Mom, I —"

"Do you have *any* idea how disappointed your father is? We haven't seen our grandchildren in the longest time — you've been *much* too busy for us lately! — and now you forget to come by like you promised. Danny, I'm absolutely furious."

"I can tell. And you have every right to be. But it's not my fault, Mom. Something came up. Unavoidable —"

"'Something'? Like what? What's more important than coming to see your parents off, like you promised?"

Daniel swallowed hard. "I can't tell you, Mom. I'm sorry."

There was a stunned silence down the line. Then, very frostily, Hilda Newman said, "All right, then. If you want to cut your mother and father out of your life, that's fine. We've stood by *you* through all the hard times, but now that your father's not well you can't find it in your heart to give us a few minutes of your precious time — *Your Honor!*"

"It's not that," he said desperately. "It's not that I didn't want to be there. I — I really can't talk about it right now. Maybe in a few days —"

"In a few days, we'll be in Florida and far away from our grandchildren. Maybe *they* care, even if you don't." Her tone grew elaborately formal. "Please kiss Yael and Mordy for us, Daniel. And have a good *Yom Tov.*"

"Wait! Don't hang up, Mom — please! Is Dad there?"

The answer was silence. Then, to Daniel's relief, his father came on the line. He sounded calm and content, as always. No anger here.

"Dad, I want to apologize for not coming to see you today. Believe me, I've got a good reason. I just can't tell you what it is, right now." He sighed. "Mom's furious."

"You have your own life to live," Jonathan Newman said tranquilly. "I know you well enough, Danny, to know that you'd have come if you possibly could. So all is forgiven."

"Mom, too?" he asked dryly.

Jonathan chuckled. "I'll work on her. But, Danny, remember one thing: We're here if you need us. Don't forget."

Gratefully, Daniel said, "I won't, Dad."

"Oops, there's Chaim honking. We're driving to the airport together. I'm sure we'll speak again before *Yom Tov,* Danny. Be well."

"Be well," Daniel repeated mechanically. There was a click in his ear.

They were gone. His parents, his brother, his sister-in-law and their children: gone to Miami for the next ten days or so. Well, that was the way he wanted it. He wanted all of them, but especially his father, well away from the nexus of danger that had become his home. Until the rogue who made off with Mordy was safe in police custody, Daniel was an unlucky charm. Much better for Mom to be angry at him than to be ridden with the same horrible, depleting anxiety. And it was certainly much, much better for his father to know nothing at all of this day's events — ever, if possible.

He might have confided in Chaim — not because he thought his brother more capable of solving the mystery of Mordy's disappearance than a team of seasoned detectives, but because, at the most basic level, Daniel longed to have family with him during this ordeal. Chaim had been a steadfast presence, solid as a rock, when Ella died.

It was inevitable that this crisis should bring back that other one. There were many points of similarity: the suddenness of the catastrophe, the police, the heartache. But there was a difference. When Ella died, hope had died, too. Once he had viewed his wife's body, twisted and broken behind the steering wheel of his car, there was nothing left to do but seek out a few desperate crumbs of comfort in his terrible grief.

He was suffering a different kind of agony today. The agony of hope.

The hope was pitted against the most heart-crushing anxiety he had ever known. There was an exquisite kind of torture in knowing that he might dare to dream he would have his Mordy back safe again — and that this longed-for outcome depended wholly on the whim of a crazed criminal.

No, not wholly! Fiercely, Daniel shook his head to push away the morbid dread that insisted on filling it. He would continue to storm Heaven's gates with his pleas. Good could yet triumph over evil. He opened his *Tehillim* again, and felt the warm solace of the age-old phrases flow over him.

Chaim's face floated over the page. How much easier it would be, were he praying shoulder-to-shoulder with his brother. There would not be a need for many words between them. Chaim was blood, as Mordy was blood.

But Chaim was not available, neither as confidant nor as a prop. He was off to Miami along with the rest.

Daniel had never felt more alone.

59

More time passed. For Daniel, the hours had the consistency of smoke: fluid, opaque, somehow not really there. He was sitting in a timeless zone. There was a single image fixed in his mind's eye: Mordy, as he looked when he raised himself ruefully from that morning's mud puddle. And he, Daniel, father of this golden boy, had chuckled at the sight and let him walk home alone, instead of grabbing him with both his own strong arms and never, ever letting go.

As a judge, he was all powerful in his courtroom. As a father, he dominated his household. But all his authority meant nothing now. He was as weak as the frailest child, his hands bound as surely as any prisoner's in the dock. A higher Authority than Daniel's had issued His judgment. Daniel could only bow his head under its weight, and pray.

So — he prayed. Chapter after chapter, he plowed his way through the Book of Psalms. The rest of the world came and went in flashes, like glimpses of daylight as a train speeds in and out of tunnels along its track. Elsewhere, people were raking their leaves, sitting down to meals, building sukkahs. Here, time and space had constricted into a single black-on-white square: the page of his *Tehillim*.

Dimly, as he *davened*, he monitored the progress of the investigation. After a short lunch break, Pete Rheims and Luis Mendez made a slow, discreet circuit of the neighbors, asking if any of them had noticed anything out of the ordinary that morning — a stranger on the block, or a strange car; any unusual activity. The results were ungratifying.

No one had seen a thing. Most had been asleep at the time in question. To explain their presence, the officers left the neighbors with a vague impression of attempted robbery. Not a word was said about Mordy.

In making their rounds, they did not neglect the empty house directly across the street from the judge's, the one with the FOR SALE sign hanging drunkenly on the lawn. Rheims and Mendez bypassed the sign, to peer through the windows at rooms that gaped back at them. They made a cursory check of the basement, too; Mendez crouched at the window to see if there were any signs of recent habitation. The window he chose happened to overlook the laundry room, where a decrepit washing machine and even more ancient dryer stood abandoned among the dustballs.

"Nothing here," he reported.

"Ah, this is a waste of time," Rheims said disgustedly. "The guy's probably over the state line by now."

"Mark thinks he's holing up somewhere close by, in town," Mendez said, rising and brushing off his pants.

Rheims shrugged. "Well, wherever he is, he's not here. Let's get back and see if anything interesting came in while we were gone."

They found the situation at the Newmans unchanged. The Newman place slumbered in the sun, as peaceful to the observing eye as any of its neighbors on that quiet suburban street. Inside, the story was far different. Garrity had clamped a complete news blackout on the potentially explosive story of the judge's kidnapped son. Tension charged every room, but especially the combination living/dining room where the police had set up their headquarters and Daniel pored over his *Tehillim*.

Rheims and Mendez tendered a succinct summary of their findings: in Rheims' words, "Basically, zilch."

"We even took a peek at that house for sale across the street," he finished. "Zip. Empty as a lady's handbag after a shopping spree."

Garrity glanced at the house in question. Pointing with his pen, he asked Daniel, "Any folks come by to look at the place lately?"

Daniel had put aside the *Tehillim* to hear the officers' report. He fingered it now as he said, "I don't remember seeing anyone recently. Of course, I'm not home much during the day. You'd have to ask my housekeeper, Mrs. Marks."

"Why don't you do that now, Dan?" Garrity said. "We can

interview her formally later, but I'd like to save time — and she'll talk more openly to you. Tell her about Mordy, and that it's to be kept quiet for now. We want this guy to feel confident — overconfident. We don't want a lot of publicity driving him even farther underground, or leading him to panic and maybe hurt the boy." As Daniel winced, he urged, "Go ahead, call. Ask her if Mordy mentioned anything unusual to her over the last few days. Tell her to phone us if she thinks of anything. All night, if necessary."

"Where will she be able to reach you?" Daniel asked, starting for the phone.

"Right here, of course." Garrity's brows rose into his hairline. "You didn't think we were going to walk off the case to get our eight hours, did you?"

"*I* wouldn't mind getting a little beauty sleep," Stewart said with a grin.

"Heaven knows, Lucy could use some," Rheims deadpanned. Lucy Fenwick frowned ferociously and buried her face in another mug of steaming coffee.

For Daniel, the prospect of having the police there through the night ahead carried immense relief. "I don't know what to think anymore," he murmured wryly, dialing Mrs. Marks' number.

It was, to put it mildly, a difficult call. Though he tried to shield the older woman from its harsher aspects, she caught on at once to the gravity of the situation. Someone had Mordy — *her* Mordy — and no one knew who, or where. By the time Daniel hung up, he was perspiring freely.

"Whew, that wasn't easy," he said, dabbing at his forehead with his handkerchief. "The poor woman was nearly hysterical. Mordy is the apple of her eye."

"The house?" Garrity prompted.

"As far as she knows, no one's been to see it in a long time. It's not very attractive; been neglected too long. As for Mordy, she can't think of anything out of the ordinary." His impression, after delivering his devastating news, what that poor Mrs. Marks hardly found herself capable of any thought at all. "But she'll call back if anything occurs to her." He started back for the couch, and his *Tehillim*.

"Dan," Garrity said, "I know you said that Mordy wouldn't have left the house voluntarily without letting you know. But it would be irresponsible of us to leave any stone unturned. I want you to call three or four of his closest friends and try to find out, without asking directly, whether they know anything about any plans Mordy might have made for today."

Daniel started to protest, then broke off. Argument was futile; these were the professionals. He went for the family phone book and did as Garrity had asked. Feigning ignorance as to Mordy's exact whereabouts, he sounded out his son's friends, now home from school. They all commented on Mordy's absence from yeshivah that morning.

The general line of the dialogue went as follows:

"Hi, Mr. Newman! Mordy was absent today. Is he sick?"

"Not exactly. In fact, he was well enough to go out, but I'm a little confused about where he is and I need to reach him. Do you have any idea?"

"Sorry, no, Mr. Newman. Mordy didn't say anything to me."

One boy did mention that on Thursday he had invited Mordy to come over to his house this Sunday afternoon. "But when I saw he was absent today, I figured that he was sick. Is he, Mr. Newman?"

Twenty minutes after he began his research, Daniel was finished. He said heavily to Garrity, "Nothing. No one knows anything."

Garrity shrugged. "We had to try."

Somehow, even making an effort that he had known ahead of time to be futile had raised hopes, however faint. These hopes were now dashed to the ground, leaving Daniel, if anything, more depressed than before. He started again for his *Tehillim*, his sole weapon against the steady hammerblows of disappointment and terror.

Before he had taken two steps, the phone rang again.

The silence between the first ring and the second was electrifying. "It's *him*," Mendez whispered, breaking the spell. With the smoothness of clockwork, the detectives took up their positions.

Daniel hurried to the phone, actually eager to hear the kidnapper's voice — to find out what he had done with Mordy, to learn his terms — to hear anything but the horrible silence that surrounded his son. "Yes?" he barked into the phone.

"Hi there, sir! It's me — Jake!"

It was like a voice from another world. Affection for his young friend flooded Daniel, but the feeling was immediately washed away by the much stronger tide of anxiety. The worry made him impatient.

"I'm sorry, Jake, but I can't talk now. I'll call you back when I get a chance." In his own ears, he sounded beyond curt: he was stiff as cardboard.

Jake held his peace for so long that Daniel began to hope he had gotten away with it. Then Jake said, "Judge Newman? Is something wrong?"

"Wrong? What should be wrong?"

"With all due respect, sir, your voice sounds funny. And I don't mean humorous."

"You're imagining things, Jake."

"Again with respect, I don't think I am." A pause. "I'm coming over, sir."

"You'll do no such thing. I'm fine, Jake. I appreciate your concern, but —"

"I'm coming over." Jake hung up.

Slowly, Daniel replaced the receiver. He turned, to find Garrity at his elbow.

"What is it?" Garrity demanded.

"A — a new friend of mine. Young law student, third year. He says he's coming over. He sensed something wrong —"

"Will he be a help or a hindrance?" the detective asked.

"A help, I think. He's certainly bright enough. In fact, he just helped bring a criminal to justice in a case I was trying."

"Then let him come. You need someone besides policemen to talk to, and if he's as bright as you say, maybe he'll come up with an angle we haven't thought of."

Daniel regarded Garrity with somber eyes. "There hasn't been much progress, Mark, has there?"

"It's frustrating!" Garrity spat out, almost angrily. "Until we hear something from the kidnapper, we haven't a clue. Your boy seems to have vanished into thin air."

Half an hour and seven chapters of *Tehillim* later, Daniel found Jake on his doorstep. He was carrying a small overnight bag slung over one shoulder.

"I brought my *tefillin,*" he said simply, then walked past Daniel into the police-strewn living room. His eyes widened a little, but he showed no other reaction. Seating himself in an armchair, he said quietly, "I suppose that, sooner or later, someone will tell me what's going on," and composed himself to wait.

Jim Stewart came over and began talking to him in an undertone. Daniel watched with a sharp upwelling of gratitude. Now that Jake was here, Daniel wondered why he had tried so adamantly to dissuade him. Heaven knew he needed a friend.

The phone rang.

"Positions," Garrity said softly, before vanishing through the kitchen door. It *had* to be the kidnapper this time, Daniel thought desperately. There had to be some word of Mordy soon. It had been — hastily, he checked his watch — nearly six hours since his son had vanished. More than six hours of his son's life unaccounted for.

He forced his mind to focus. "Hello?"

"Danny, is that you? Finally! I've been trying to reach you all day — since midmorning, your time. The line's been busy, busy, busy. Is Yael running a phone marathon, or what?"

"Yehuda?" Daniel gasped in disbelief to his best friend, in Jerusalem. "Yehuda Arlen, is it really you?"

"Who else? I couldn't get through on *erev Yom Kippur,* the circuits were busy just about all day long. So I thought I'd try my luck today. I wanted to wish you and the kids a great new year, Danny."

"Th-the same to you, old friend," Daniel choked.

Instantly, Yehuda was on the alert. "What is it? Danny, is everything all right?"

Suddenly, the secret was too much to bear alone. It was hard just to draw breath, so great was the weight on his chest. "This has to be kept quiet, Yehuda," Daniel said. "For Mordy's sake —"

"What? *Tell me!*"

"He's gone, Yehuda. It happened this morning. The police think — It looks like a kidnapping."

The shocked silence spoke volumes. It stretched for ten interminable seconds. Then his friend said, "What can I do?"

"*Daven,*" Daniel whispered brokenly. "Go to the *Kosel* and *daven* — your heart out — for Mordy."

And that, after six hours of holding them manfully at bay, was when the tears finally came.

Through his own wracking sobs, he heard his best friend — weeping now, too — promise, "I'll d-do that. I'll get ten yeshivahs to do it, too. Mordechai ben Ella, right?"

"Right," sobbed Daniel. "Thanks, Yehuda."

"Oh, Danny — Oh, Danny —"

Somehow, the call ended. Somehow, Daniel found his stumbling way back to the couch. He felt rather than saw Jake come to sit beside him. Dimly, through his agony, he felt a faint, distant surprise that the austere Judge Newman should have let himself go in front of others like this. It was not like him.

But somehow, it did not seem to matter. It did not matter at all.

60

Hilda Newman was not a woman who was often angry, but this Sunday she found herself in the grip of a fury that would not release its hold on her.

The fury was directed at Daniel.

Beneath the anger was hurt, deep and cutting, over what she perceived as her son's ingratitude. "Sharper than a serpent's tooth" about summed it up, she thought, while staring out the window of the moving plane.

The sunlit fields of clouds were dazzling, but she did not see them. Jonathan's bulk beside her was familiar and comforting, but she did not sense him. Nor did she pay any real attention to her grandchildren, in the rows behind her — beside themselves with excitement over their very first plane trip. Hilda was caught up in her anger, as surely as a rabbit in a snare.

Daniel was an ungrateful son. When had his parents not been there when *he* needed *them*? As a student struggling to find his direction, he had Hilda and Jonathan to stand by him with their wisdom and experience. When he married Ella and needed money for a home, who else but his mother and father had come through with the down payment? They had doted unreservedly on Yael and Mordy, both as babies and as growing children — and still did. And when his Ella was lost in that terrible accident, hadn't it been Hilda and Jonathan who provided the support system Daniel so badly needed! Hadn't they been twice as loving to the kids; hadn't they made sure to spend every holiday with the bereft family; hadn't Hilda, personally, guided

Daniel through the maze of single parenthood?

And now — this. He had been unusually distant of late, but this was the final straw. It smacked of disrespect to one's parents and, worse, a real lack of a feeling of family. And that was not like Daniel at all.

Beneath the anger and the hurt, there lurked something even stronger, though more difficult to acknowledge: fear. Hilda Newman, formidable warrior in life's battles small and large, was frankly afraid. What was happening to her firstborn, the light of her life, her darling son?

With a tiny, muffled sob, she prayed that Daniel would never know the pain she was suffering at that moment: the pain of knowing one's beloved offspring distant and possibly in trouble, and being helpless to draw him back.

Two rows back, Chaim, her other son, sat in a brooding silence.

Nothing his wife said to him penetrated far beneath the surface of his manner, which was polite but remote. When, exasperated by his dullness, she asked, "What's the matter, Chaim? What are you thinking about?" he returned a reassuring, if not precisely truthful, "Nothing important, Gila. You were saying — ?"

In point of fact, he was brooding over the same thing as his mother. But where she had reduced the problem to a matter of raw emotion, Chaim was toying with a perplexing intellectual puzzle. What had come over Daniel?

Beside him, Gila was ebullient. In her freshly set wig and a three-piece knit outfit that particularly suited her, she looked ten years younger than the harried wife and mother that presided over his household. Chaim knew he ought to be listening more closely to her prattle, which revolved, as far as he could make out, around the upcoming delights in store for them this Sukkos. He tried. He said "Yes" and "Of course" at the right moments; but his mind was back in Cedar Hills — with Daniel.

It had been clear from the moment he had seen his mother's face, as he pulled up at the house to drive his parents to the airport, that something was wrong. Jonathan had been prevailed upon to take the passenger's seat in front, and so was able, at an opportune moment, to mutter a word of explanation.

"It's Daniel. He and the kids never showed up to say good-bye today. Mom's furious — and worried."

Chaim threw a quick glance at his father, then directed his eyes back at the road. Under cover of the children's noisy chatter in the back, he said in an undertone, "That's not like Danny."

"Not at all. And he wouldn't explain what happened, either. I had the sense that he's got something on his mind — but you know Danny. He'll walk over hot coals rather than let other people carry his burdens."

"I know."

The conversation had ended there, but not Chaim's brooding. He had been feeling guilty enough already about accepting this expensive trip as a gift from his parents, and about the fact that Daniel and his children would not be joining them. That decision had been made by the women of the family. Between them, Hilda and Gila had decided that the "other" Newman grandchildren had been shortchanged by Yael and Mordy's usurping the lion's share of their grandparents' time and attention. It would not hurt anyone, and could only benefit Chaim and Gila's kids, if this one holiday was configured a little differently.

If Daniel's initial refusal of his mother's invitation had set the stage for the decision, his subsequent change of heart had not altered it. Hilda, it was true, seemed regretful afterwards. Gila, on the other hand, still considered the notion of spending an exclusive Sukkos with Bubby and Zaydie a splendid one. And Chaim was weighted down with guilt-ridden worry.

It was not like Daniel to bear a grudge. Whatever his faults, his big brother did not have a resentful bone in his body. But if it was not resentment, then what *had* prevented Daniel from coming by to see his parents, as he had promised? Was one of the kids sick, G-d forbid? Had Daniel himself suffered some kind of reversal? Imagination was not Chaim's strong point, and he found himself stymied even for ideas.

I'll call him from Miami, he decided as the plane moved ever closer, through blindingly blue skies, to that city. He had planned to do so in any case, on *erev Yom Tov.* Now he would move up the timetable a bit. Tonight, after the kids were settled, he would make some excuse to Gila and slip out with his phone card to place the call. Just to reassure himself — and his mother — that all was well with Daniel.

In his seat two rows ahead, Jonathan Newman had just resolved to do the very same thing.

And, seated beside him, a fretful Hilda was wishing that she could put aside her anger long enough to do it, too. But, at the same time, an unconfessed part of her was afraid of letting go of the anger. If that went, what would be left but the fear that kept trying to encroach upon her heart?

Miss Muller was doing her best; Yael had to admit that. But even her best could not prevent the girl from feeling a little downhearted. Picturing her father at home with the police, looking for some crazy man who had written him threatening letters, she felt nervous, afraid — off balance. All this made her rather less than her usual loquacious self.

Sara pretended not to notice. With lightning movements, the teacher tidied the kitchen and washed up the breakfast things. Yael looked through the contents of Sara's bookcase while Sara made her bed and did a little quick dusting. Then, smiling brightly, she asked Yael how she would like to spend the day.

"Oh, I don't know. Whatever," was the girl's not very useful answer. It was clear to Sara that Yael would remain on edge until she heard from her father. In an effort to distract her, Sara showed her guest her enormous CD collection. During the years when other women were busily building families, Sara had been reduced to collecting music. But what a collection! It kept Yael interested and rapturous for a full hour.

Yael herself owned most of the contemporary Jewish stuff; it was the classical works that made her catch her breath. Here were the very songs that she was beginning to play on the piano. The melodies that fell from her own fingers only with the most diligent practice, sounded fluid and effortless here. They were incredible — majestic! Yael wanted to hear first one piece, and then another. A concerto by Haydn came hard on the heels of a Beethoven symphony. Mozart rippled through the room like a visitor from another dimension, followed by Bach, marching by in stately precision.

It was Tchaikovsky that finally brought Yael back to earth, with a painful thud. Listening to *The Nutcracker*, she remarked without thinking, "This is one of Daddy's favorites." Her own words brought her back to the reality that music had made her — temporarily — forget. Sara saw the frown settle over the girl's forehead. Her own heart sank.

"Listen, Yael," she said briskly. "I'll bet you're going crazy, waiting for some news about what the police are up to. I know your father said he'd call, but I don't see why you shouldn't give him a call instead. Just to set your mind at ease."

Yael brightened instantly. "You mean, right now?"

"Sure, why not?"

"I've only been here a couple of hours. My father is sure to call pretty soon anyway —"

"Yael," her teacher said. "Call."

Yael called.

Her father's voice sounded strange over the line, though he explained it away by saying that Detective Garrity was with him and that they had been discussing something when the phone rang. "You startled me, honey," he said. Then more sharply, he asked, "Is everything all right? Are you okay?"

"I'm fine. Did they found out who sent those letters yet?"

"Not yet. But we hope to make some real progress soon," he said with forced cheer. "Are you and your piano teacher having fun?"

"Well, we've been listening to music. Miss Muller has the most fantastic collection of classical CDs you've ever seen, Daddy! I just heard the Nutcracker."

"Mmm . . . One of my favorites."

"That's what I told her. Daddy, do you have any idea when I'll be coming home?"

"I'll be in touch just as soon as I know, honey. Be patient, okay? I need to know that you're safe." Without intending to, he laid the faintest emphasis on the "you're." But Yael did not pick up on it. She merely asked, "Is it okay for us to leave the apartment if we want?"

Alarm bells began clanging in Daniel's head. Though logic said that the kidnapper, with Mordy already under his wing, would not target Yael today, there was something deeper and stronger than logic that made him stumble over himself in his haste to say, "*No!* No, it's safer if you stay put. I know it's not easy, sweetie, but do it for me, okay?"

"Okay. I love you, Daddy."

"I love you, too. See you later."

Hanging up, Yael felt a little better. It had been good to hear her father's voice. She found Miss Muller busying herself tactfully in the kitchen.

"It's all right," Yael said, standing in the doorway. "They haven't found the guy yet, but Daddy says the police are hoping for progress soon."

"And meanwhile —?"

Suddenly, Yael found herself feeling much better. She had always relished Miss Muller's company, and here she was with hours ahead of her in which to bask in her music teacher's full attention.

"Meanwhile," she said, "it looks like you're stuck with me for a while — indoors. I guess the police think I'll be safer here than outside."

Sara was struck by an awesome sense of the responsibility she had undertaken in agreeing to harbor the girl. Determinedly, she swept it back. There was no time for such thoughts now. She must focus on Yael, help the hours pass as pleasantly as possible.

They started a game of Scrabble, but ended up with a half-finished board, too busy talking to play. At some point, Sara led the way to the kitchen to whip up a quick lunch. "I'm not much of a cook," she apologized. "Is pasta okay?"

Pasta was fine. Yael stirred the spaghetti while Sara made the sauce; then they both sat down to enjoy both the meal and the ongoing conversation. In the back of her mind, Yael was constantly aware of the phone that never rang, but she did not really mind. Daddy would call when he knew something; he had promised.

At 5 o'clock in the afternoon, the long-awaited call finally arrived.

"It's for you," Sara said, smiling as she held out the receiver.

Yael was smiling, too, as she took it. But the smile soon disappeared.

"I hate to do this to you, honey, but the police think it would be better if you stayed out of the house tonight." How could he bring his daughter into the police circus that had once been their home? And, even worse, how could he break the news about Mordy?

He could do neither; at least, not tonight. His only shred of comfort in this whole agonizing business was knowing that Yael was out of the way, and safe. If Mordy was not found by morning — Well, tomorrow would be soon enough to let Yael know what had happened. As his mother always said, bad news can wait.

Unwilling to leave the phone for even a short time in case the kidnapper tried to make contact, Daniel sent Jake Meisler over to the Muller apartment with Yael's schoolbag and a change of clothes. During his brief appearance there, Jake was friendly but noncommittal. Afraid of Yael's questions, he edged toward the door as quickly as he was decently able. He hesitated, debating the wisdom of saying something to Sara. But Yael was standing right beside her teacher; there was no chance of a private word without making the girl suspicious. With a solemn good-bye, and a reminder to double-lock the door, Jake made his exit.

Sara helped Yael unpack. Hanging the school uniform neatly in the guest room closet, she had a dizzying sense of loss — of the daughter she had never had, the years of happiness she had missed. It was not too late, of course it wasn't. It only felt that way. Melancholy clung to her with tenacious fingers, steely tendrils that seemed so fragile and yet refused to depart.

But they had to go. Sara had a job to do, and that was to usher Yael cheerfully and tenderly through this time of trouble for her family. Melancholy would have to wait.

The night before, she had shared hot chocolate and nighttime talk with a heartbroken friend. Tonight, she would offer the same thing — plus an extra dollop of warmth — to Yael, her young and surprisingly enjoyable companion.

Behind everything was the knowledge that the girl was in possible danger. Though her eyelids were gritty and she longed for sleep, Sara would stay awake, and alert, just as long as Yael needed her.

Across the United States, in California, Judy Rabinowitz stared at her son in a mounting bewilderment that was turning rapidly to horror.

"I want you to repeat that, Ari. Clearly, now. He told you *what?*"

Sighing, Ari told her again.

61

As dusk closed in with no word from the kidnapper, Daniel's spirits plummeted to their lowest ebb since he had discovered Mordy missing.

Night was when you drew the curtains and turned on the lamps and felt glad to be snug inside your own four walls. The thought of his son, far from home and facing the dark at the mercy of a ruthless criminal, was almost more than he could bear. To distract himself, he focused on the question of the kidnapper's demands, and why he had not yet heard what they were. He discussed the puzzling silence with any and every detective that moved into his orbit. When a police officer was not available, he discussed it with himself.

His conclusions were not comforting. Either the criminal was intent on fighting a war of nerves with Daniel — or the boy had not been taken for ransom at all. The motive in this snatching might be very different. Thinking of these conclusions, Daniel began to shake. Terrible as a kidnapping for money was, it at least held out the hope that Mordy was being kept alive and well in anticipation of future profits. The other alternative was a wide-open Pandora's box of fearful possibilities.

It was Jake who calmed him, and who reminded him over and over of his obligation to turn to his Creator for help. When Daniel's hands grew suddenly limp with terror and the *Tehillim* drooped in his fingers, it was Jake who gently picked it up and turned the page for him. And finally, at Jake's insistence, Daniel agreed to try his utmost not to indulge his fears even in his most private mind.

Ruthlessly, he clamped off his imagination the way a surgeon might tie off a spurting blood vessel. For Mordy's sake he must remain alert — ready for anything. He stayed close by the phone all through the afternoon, *davening Minchah* alone in his study and planning to do the same thing when *Ma'ariv* rolled around. At 6 o'clock, all the detectives except for Garrity went out to get some dinner. Jake rummaged through the refrigerator for some of Mrs. Marks' leftovers, then left for shul. Daniel dutifully constructed a sandwich and ate it, though he had no memory, afterwards, of taking a single bite.

He had just finished *bentching* when the phone rang again.

This time, it was the kidnapper.

The ringing of the phone produced, in Daniel, more weariness than excitement. All through the day the ringing had heralded other calls, so many calls, calls that had nothing to do with Mordy. Why should this one be any different?

He had eaten his sandwich in the kitchen; rising deliberately from his chair, he picked up the phone in that room. Garrity, in a synchronized motion, went for the living-room extension. Through the kitchen window, Daniel could see the streetlights turning on, one by one.

"Hello?" he said.

"Judge Newman?" asked a stranger's voice. Like the morning caller's, it was hoarse and muffled — both of which Garrity had described as classic methods of disguise. Daniel's heart set up such a painful slamming that he had to bite his lips to keep from crying out. As he began to hyperventilate, the room swam before his eyes so that, for one frightening moment, he felt himself in real danger of fainting.

Groping for the chair he had just abandoned, he called upon every source of strength he had ever possessed. He must not give way to weakness. Mordy's life depended on him doing and saying the right things now.

"Yes, this is he." Incredibly, he sounded calm.

"*I've got your son.* If you want to see him alive, you'll do exactly what I tell you. Got that, Judge?"

"I — have it."

"You'll get your instructions tomorrow about where to leave the money."

"How much?"

Hoarse laughter. "Forgot to tell you, did I? A million, Judgie. A cool million. A nice price for the kid."

"Is my son all right?" Daniel asked urgently. "Can I talk to him?"

"He's all right. But no talking."

Daniel calculated with lightning swiftness. Ignoring the still painful beating in his chest, he said coolly, "If I don't hear his voice now, how do I know he's alive? There's no point in exchanging money for nothing."

The kidnapper hesitated. "That's just a chance you'll have to take."

"Sorry," said Daniel. "Good-bye."

"Wait! Okay — You can talk to him."

There was a brief silence. Daniel used it to started breathing again. His bluff had worked. He strained his ear, determined to catch every last syllable.

"D-daddy?"

The voice was weak, probably with fear more than anything, but it was undoubtedly Mordy's.

"Mordy! Are you all right? Has he hurt you?"

"I'm all right, Dad. He —"

The hoarse voice broke in. "That's enough. You heard him, Judge. He's alive. Get the million ready." *Click.*

An instant later, Garrity came bounding into the kitchen. "Just under two minutes," he said in disgust. "Another few seconds, and we would have been able to trace the call."

"It doesn't matter," Daniel said. He looked haggard and drawn, but there was a glow in his eyes that had not been there two minutes earlier. "Mordy's alive."

The other detectives, returning to the Newman house with some stir-fry for Garrity, were chagrined at missing the call. Garrity had taped the exchange, and they wanted to hear every word.

"Hear that accent? It's faint, but definitely Italian, I'd say," Lucy Fenwick said. With the waning of the day, her mood had brightened considerably. The six cups of coffee she had consumed since morning, and the dinner she had just eaten, had joined forces to make her look far more alive, and almost cheerful.

"I agree," Rheims said.

"I thought he sounded more Hispanic than anything," Stewart objected.

"Not very educated," Luis Mendez volunteered.

"I'd agree there, too," said Rheims.

"So would I," Stewart said. "And he's young, I think." He pressed the play button and let them hear some of the dialogue again. "Listen to the way he talks."

"He was intimidated when Daniel seemed ready to hang up," Garrity said. "That speaks of inexperience. This is probably his first kidnapping."

"May it also be his last," Rheims said, putting his hands together piously. The others grinned.

"I should have told Mordy that help is on the way. I should have offered him some hope," Daniel fretted. The euphoria he had felt at speaking to his son had given way to self-recrimination. "He's so alone, and terrified — I could hear it in his voice. If only I'd said something to help him be strong."

"You said just the right things," Jim Stewart said firmly. "Besides, the guy didn't let you speak to Mordy for more than a couple of seconds."

"I like the way you called his bluff," Pete Rheims grinned. "Pretty cool customer, aren't you?"

"It didn't feel that way," Daniel grimaced. "I just wasn't about to give in without talking to Mordy at all."

Garrity stood in the middle of the living room, eating with a plastic fork right out of the container. "He's going to call again with instructions tomorrow, he said. This buys us a little more time. If we could only get a break tonight —" His voice trailed off. He dug again into the stir-fry.

Daniel stood up, too, and walked over to face Garrity. "Mark," he said, "tell me honestly. If we *don't* get a break tonight, what happens?"

Sighing, Garrity said, "Then we'll have to play the thing out. Raise the million bucks, bring it to wherever he says, secrete some police in the area, and hope that he doesn't spot us and hurt the kid — hurt Mordy."

"I don't want to take that chance," Daniel said quickly. "Leave the police out of it, Mark. I'd rather hand over the money and have Mordy back, safe and sound — even if it means the kidnapper gets away."

"And your daughter?" Garrity asked, his own powerlessness turning him suddenly harsh. "Will you be able to sleep at night, knowing that she's the next one at risk? Or why not Mordy again?"

Daniel had gone very pale. The detective's stark analysis shook him to the core. There was, he bleakly realized, no risk-free solution. If he agreed to let the police make a play for Mordy's captor, he was placing his son in even graver danger than he already faced. And if he did not, the long-term risk was exactly as Garrity had outlined.

If he got Mordy safely back, he could always take the kids and move away, trying with distance and cunning to keep one step ahead of the stalker. But what kind of life would that be for his children? And what, in the end, were the odds against the kidnapper's tracking them down and rekindling the nightmare all over again?

A wave of hopelessness washed over the distraught father. He hung his head and shook it from side to side, a man in the grip of utter despair. Garrity placed a comforting hand on Daniel's elbow. "Come on, sit down. Pray some more. That's about as useful as anything else right now."

"Yes — No. There's someone I want to call first." Walking as though in a dream, Daniel went to the phone and picked it up.

"Who're you calling?" Lucy Fenwick asked sharply. "This thing is supposed to be kept under wraps, remember? We've decided it's safer for Mordy that way."

"May I call my rabbi?"

Lucy glanced at Garrity, who said, "All right. If he can keep this quiet."

"Rabbi Mintzer knows how to keep a secret." Daniel dialed the number, preparing the words he would say. There had been many, many times in his life when he had refused to say them — to anyone. The phone rang once, twice, three times.

"Hello?" It was the rabbi himself.

Daniel closed his eyes and spoke softly into the phone. "This is Daniel Newman. Rabbi, I'm in trouble. I need you."

Rabbi Mintzer didn't hesitate a moment. "I'll be over just as soon as I can get a car service," he said. The old man had stopped driving several years before.

At that moment, the front door opened to reveal Jake, back from shul. His intelligent gaze took in the scene, sensing a change in the atmosphere. He moved forward, keen as a bloodhound on the scent of its prey.

"Don't bother, Rabbi," Daniel said into the phone, beginning to feel the life coursing through him again at the prospect of seeing his beloved teacher. "I'll send a friend for you in my car."

"Fine. Stay strong of heart, Daniel. Please G-d, I will be with you very soon."

A minute later, after the briefest of explanations, Daniel handed Jake his car keys. Without a word, Jake took them and left again the way he had just come.

Daniel sat on the couch, letting the police officers go about their business around him. His entire attention was focused on the front door. When it opened again, some ten minutes later, he jumped to his feet and greeted the newcomer effusively.

"Thank you so much for coming, Rabbi Mintzer. I wouldn't have bothered you like this, except that it's a real emergency."

The rabbi grasped Daniel's hand. Still holding it, he looked around, taking in the littered dining room table, the strange equipment, the hats and badges — and most of all, the officers themselves, looking distinctly ill at ease in his presence.

"I can see that," he said slowly. "Where can we talk, Daniel? I want to hear."

With a quiet, "Thanks, Jake," Daniel led the rabbi into his study and closed the door. He waited until the old man was seated comfortably before he ventured another word.

"Rabbi —"

"Yes, Daniel? What happened? Tell me!"

"My son has been kidnapped," Daniel said, his voice breaking. "My son is in the hands of a fiend — and it's all my fault!"

62

"**Y**our fault," Rabbi Mintzer echoed, taken aback. "How? Did you tell the kidnapper to take him?"

Daniel flushed darkly. He said, "Of course not. I'm talking about a judgment, Rabbi. A judgment on me."

"Suppose you explain, Daniel."

Leaning forward in his seat, Daniel burst into a torrent of unstoppable self-recrimination. It was as though he had been waiting only for the other man's presence to express what lay deepest in his tormented soul.

"Remember last night, Rabbi? Remember how I sat in your house and decided that I was ready to pursue my own happiness at the expense of my kids'? For five years, the kids have been the center of my world. I've been mother and father to them. I've been blessed beyond what any man can expect — two wonderful children, a son and a daughter any father could be proud of —"

His throat closed. It was only with tremendous effort that he was able to continue. His voice harsh with an anger directed at himself, he said, "I spoke to your wife about *shidduchim*, remember, Rabbi? And I went home last night filled with dreams of finding a new wife — of maybe, maybe being happy again at last. As if — As if what I already had didn't make me happy enough.

"Well, I've been punished. Like a child who reaches out for too much candy, I've had my wrist slapped. My wrist, and my heart." A spasm of anguish contorted the judge's face. "It hurts, Rabbi. It hurts so much."

For the second time that day, tears came. They literally poured from Daniel's eyes, down his face and onto his shirt. He made no effort to stem the tide. He openly wept, hardly aware of what he was doing. Not since he had been a small child had he cried this way. Ella's death had emptied his reservoir of tears, but the intensity of his present weeping surpassed even that terrible time. The child he had fathered and whom he had dedicated his life to protecting was in trouble, and there was not a thing Daniel could do about it. He shed tears of helplessness and frustration. He shed tears of rage. And he shed the tears that belong only to a parent, when his little one is lost or in pain.

Rabbi Mintzer allowed him his cry in silence. For long, unbroken minutes Daniel wept into his hands while the rabbi sat and watched, eyes soft with compassion. When at last the sobs were replaced by shuddering sighs, Daniel lowered his hands and wiped them unthinkingly on his pants. He felt curiously empty. Grief, fear, and pain had flowed away in the torrent, leaving him passive as a child. And, like a child, he waited for the rabbi to speak.

"This," Rabbi Mintzer said, "is arrogance."

"Wh-what?"

"Arrogance," the rabbi repeated firmly. "Why did Heaven decide that you merited this suffering? A humble man would answer, 'I don't know.' He would even say, 'I don't *have* to know. I will just plead with Heaven to help me, because I can't carry on alone.'

"But Daniel Newman — *he* knows. He has it all worked out. 'Heaven has punished me because of so-and-so. I am a bad person, a terrible person. I decided to remarry, after five years alone, and that means that I no longer love or appreciate my children. I don't deserve to have children. I am a monster!' "

Daniel stared at the rabbi. He seized on the one point he could sturdily refute. "But I *have* been pleading! All afternoon, I've been saying *Tehillim* — "

"That's fine. That's good. You should *daven*, Daniel — but you should not presume to understand Heaven's calculations." Rabbi Mintzer looked directly into Daniel's damp and swollen eyes. "Now, you are a smart man. A very smart man. I want you to tell me, honestly, using your brain and not your heart: Do you really believe that your marrying again would be to seek happiness at your children's expense? Didn't we agree, just last night, that they need a mother? That this would enhance not only your happiness, but also theirs?"

Daniel hesitated. In a low voice, he said, "I don't know what's come over me, Rabbi. It's as if I can't shake this terrible guilt — this feeling that it's somehow all my fault."

"That's the *yetzer hara*. A guilty man does not plead wholeheartedly with his Creator for the help he needs. He doesn't believe he deserves it." Shrewdly, the rabbi added, "I suspect that your *davening*, fervent as it's been till now, will be much better once you've purged yourself of this silly guilt. Who are you, little Daniel Newman, to try to second-guess *der Aibeshter*? Heaven's calculations are Heaven's calculations. You have a different job to do."

Daniel drew a long, ragged breath. The pain did not leave him, but the guilt began to drain away. Slowly, he felt a hollow place inside begin to fill with something that was warm and good. Haltingly, he said, "I needed to find something — to help me make sense of this impossible thing. Even if it meant that I myself was the cause of it all."

"Stop trying to make sense of evil. Evil has no sense, it has only its own dark imperatives. Your job is to storm Heaven's gates and throw yourself on Hashem's mercy."

Rabbi Mintzer reached out with one pale, veined hand and patted Daniel's damp one. "I will help you. In shul tomorrow, I will put Mordechai's name on the list, and many people will pray. In fact, *all* the shuls should be contacted. Why hasn't anyone thought of doing that? And what about Mordechai's yeshivah, do they know?"

"Nobody's supposed to know," Daniel said. "The police are afraid that it will reach the newspapers, and people will start trying to locate the kidnapper. And that could make him panic. It could also make him furious. Either way, in fear or rage, he might decide to hurt Mordy — I'll have to ask you to keep this very quiet, please, Rabbi."

Thoughtfully, the old man nodded. "I understand. It is a case of *pikuach nefesh* where silence is the best weapon. Our prayers, then, must be quiet ones. We will send them up in whispers. *Hakadosh Baruch Hu* has Ears to hear even that kind of prayer, you know, Daniel."

Daniel tried to find the words with which to thank the rabbi, who waved away his fumbling attempts. "Now," said Rabbi Mintzer, "tell me how the investigation is going."

"There's not much to tell. Everything has turned up blank so far. Mordy seems to have vanished into thin air." Eagerly, Daniel added, "But I spoke to him, Rebbi! I heard his voice! He said he was all right."

"With *der Aibeshter's* help, he will stay all right," Rabbi Mintzer said with certainty.

They were only words, but they struck Daniel like the beam of a powerful searchlight. He was dazzled with hope, down to his very soul. No — more than just hope. A bit of the rabbi's certainty seeped into the father's anxious heart. For the first time since Mordy had vanished, Daniel allowed himself a genuine smile.

"I believe you, Rabbi," he said simply. And, at that moment, he did.

"Do you want me to stay with you until he's found, Daniel?"

"Oh, no, no. I would never presume —"

"I would do it, happily."

"I know you would, Rabbi, and I'm eternally grateful. But there is really no need. I have a friend with me, and the police are very sympathetic, and I'd really feel much better knowing you were in your own home and shul instead of pacing the floors here with me."

The rabbi fixed him with a penetrating gaze. "You are sure? The only reason I hesitate is because the Rebbetzin hasn't been feeling so well today. I would like to be able to check on her during the night."

"Positive." Daniel stood up. "Rabbi Mintzer, I can't tell you how much better you've made me feel. I *know* now that Mordy will be all right — and I didn't know it before. Thank you. And a speedy recovery to the Rebbetzin. Please send her my best."

"Yes. I will not tell her about all this," the rabbi said, standing. "She will worry. But later, when it's all over —"

"Yes. There'll be time enough to tell her then."

Daniel decided to break his phoneside vigil long enough to personally drive the rabbi home. Garrity gave his reluctant approval, saying only, "Make it fast, Dan. There's no telling what may come through at any time."

Daniel made it fast. It was just under a quarter of an hour later when he walked back into his house, to the now-familiar sight of the police paraphernalia that had overtaken his living room. Mark Garrity met him just inside the front door.

"A woman just called — says she's your sister-in-law." He consulted his notebook. "A Mrs. Rabinowitz. Judy Rabinowitz, from

California. She says you should call her back, it's important."

Nothing that did not directly concern his son could feel important to Daniel. He was tempted to ignore the call; he had a very legitimate excuse for being less than perfectly considerate at this time. Judy would understand when she eventually learned the truth.

Then he remembered his nephew, Ari's, strange call that morning. It had puzzled Daniel at the time. He wondered whether Judy's call tonight had anything to do with that earlier one. In the end, it was curiosity, more than anything, that made him lift the receiver and punch in the Rabinowitz number.

"Oh, Daniel, thank goodness you're there! Who was that man who answered the phone before? He was so businesslike: 'Sorry, ma'am, he's not available right now. Would you like to leave a number, ma'am?' What have you done, Daniel, hired a butler?"

Though the remarks were lighthearted, there was an underlying strain in his sister-in-law's voice. If Daniel had not known better, he would have said she was nervous — very nervous. But what did she have to be so nervous about? He said, "He's just doing some work for me. I'm sorry, but things are a little hectic here at the moment. You called about something important, I hear. How can I help you?"

She drew an audible breath, as though to steel herself.

"How's Mordy?" she asked.

"*What?*" If he'd expected anything, it had not been this!

"Is Mordy feeling all right? My Ari said he sounded a little strange over the phone on *erev Yom Kippur.*"

Daniel steadied himself, then spoke very clearly into the phone. "Judy, if you know anything — *anything* — about Mordy, I need you to tell me now. This is crucial."

There was a dead silence over the line. Then Judy said, wonderingly, "He *is* in trouble, isn't he?"

"Judy, *what do you know?*"

His intensity threw her into confusion. "I — It's probably nothing, Daniel. I wouldn't have called at all, except that Ari was getting a little worried. He thought it was all a joke at first, but after talking to Mordy on Friday he began to wonder."

Daniel forced himself to stay very calm. His manner was extraordinarily gentle as he asked, "Do you mind starting from the beginning, Judy? I'm a little lost here."

"I guess you don't know then — about the e-mails."

"What e-mails?"

"A couple of weeks or so ago, Mordy sent Ari an e-mail message, saying that some guy had been sending you threatening letters. Mordy said that one of the letters came via e-mail, and that he sent an answer back —"

"*What?*" If Daniel's first shout had raised a few eyebrows among the detective squad, this one brought them running. He motioned desperately for them to wait. "What exactly did he write?"

"I don't think Ari knows. But Mordy boasted that he'd convinced the guy to stop bothering you, and that the guy was actually trying to make friends with him. Mordy swore Ari to secrecy. I didn't hear a word about all this until today. I don't like the idea of Mordy corresponding with such a person, Daniel."

"Neither do I," Daniel said grimly. "Now, listen, Judy, this is very important. Did Mordy mention the man's name?"

"No, I don't think so."

"Any details at all?"

She placed a hand over the receiver to consult with Ari, apparently standing at her elbow. Judy came back on the line and said, "Only that the guy said he was lonely and needed a friend. Mordy wrote as if it were all a big joke, Ari says. But when Ari brought up the topic on the phone the other day, Mordy became agitated and wouldn't talk about it until there was no one else in the room. That's what made Ari start worrying if there might not be something to it after all."

Daniel closed his eyes, aware of Jake's and the police officers' curious gazes on him. "Thank you, Judy. I'm glad you told me."

"Is everything all right? Mordy *is* okay, isn't he?"

Please G-d, he will be, Daniel thought. Aloud, he said, "Don't worry about him, Judy."

"And what's all this about death threats, Daniel? I don't like the sound of that."

"Oh, never mind. It's history now."

"And Mordy? You'll talk to him about what he was doing, won't you? He shouldn't be talking to strangers that way, even over the computer. It could be dangerous."

"Yes, it could," Daniel said. "I'll tell him, Judy. Thanks again. If anything else occurs to Ari, you'll call again?"

"Sure. But what —"

"My best to the family." He hung up.

Daniel turned, to find six pairs of eyes riveted on him, waiting.

"Our first lead," he exclaimed softly. "It seems that Mordy's been in e-mail contact with the kidnapper for a couple of weeks now." He paced the room, bitter. "While I was relaxing, thinking that the letters had stopped, they hadn't stopped at all. They'd moved into a different medium, that's all."

"Why Mordy?" Garrity asked.

"Oh, he's the computer genius in this family. He always checks my e-mail for me and prints out the ones I need to see. Somehow, he heard about the death threats — probably overheard us talking, Mark — and when he found another one of them on the computer, my big, brave son decided to do his Daddy a favor and tell the guy off —" Daniel teetered on the brink of hysterical laughter. "It's funny, isn't it? There I was, trying to protect him and Yael — and all along, Mordy was trying to protect *me!*"

"Get a grip, Danny," Garrity said sharply. "Do you have a name?"

Daniel shook his head, "No."

"Where's the computer?"

"In the study."

"Then come on," the detective said, the light of battle in his eye. "Our first break!"

There was a concerted rush to the study door. Pete Rheims, who was closest, beat Garrity by a head. For a full three seconds the two stood locked in the doorway, at a standstill.

Then Rheims, with a sweeping bow and his characteristic grin, stepped back and drawled, "After you, m'lord!" Behind them, someone chuckled.

"Not now," growled Garrity, and burst into the room.

63

The computer sat innocently on its table by the window. Garrity flung himself into the seat and, as the others gathered round, flipped the switch to set the monitor glowing. While they waited for the machine to boot up, Garrity said to Daniel, "What server do you use?"

"Uh, AOL, I think."

"You *think?*"

Daniel spread his hands. "I told you, I'm practically computer illiterate. The only reason I got the thing, originally, was to make my correspondence easier. It was the kids who urged me to get e-mail, and they're the ones who use it to write to their friends."

"You said that Mordy routinely downloads your e-mail messages," Garrity said, his eyes never leaving the screen. "If you don't use it, where are the messages coming from?"

"Oh, my name comes up on various lists. You know, legal societies and the like. They send things out, unsolicited, and Mordy prints out the ones that look interesting. I wouldn't even know how to, er, download them." Sheepishly, Daniel grimaced. "Not my cup of tea."

The screen was ready. Garrity studied it for a moment, located the server he wanted, and with a few deft clicks of the mouse entered the program.

"Here's the inbox," he said a moment later, eyes narrowed in concentration. "Your Mordy's an organized type, I see. He's got almost everything in folders."

"Where's the kidnapper's folder?" Jim Stewart asked eagerly, stooping to see over Garrity's shoulder.

Garrity glanced over his other shoulder, at Daniel. "We're going to need your help here, Dan. Mordy *may* have erased all the messages, but there's an even chance that he's kept them. In that case, they'd be in one of these folders. In order to find the folder with the kidnapper's name on it, we're going to have to eliminate all the others. Do you think you could recognize the names?"

Unhappily, Daniel said, "I'll try."

Some of the folders — there were nine in all — bore such obvious titles as ACLU and LAWREVIEW. One of them was titled "ARI." Opening it, Garrity found the e-mails that Judy Rabinowitz had talked about. He moved quickly on to the others. Four of the folders were marked with only a surname.

"Percy, Mandrake, McAllister, and Fouza," Garrity read aloud. "Any of these ring a bell?"

"Percy's a district court judge who occasionally passes on an interesting article or news item. Mandrake ... Let's see, I think Mandrake's the name of a state prosecutor, somewhere in the Midwest. He writes me from time to time with legal questions or queries about precedents."

"How about the other two?"

Daniel studied the list another moment before confessing, "I haven't the foggiest idea who either of them might be."

"Let's check, then," Garrity said. He opened the folder marked "McAllister." Close-printed lines appeared on the screen. On closer scrutiny, they proved to be recent courthouse calendars and various amendments to court procedure.

"That's right!" Daniel smacked his head. "McAllister is the court clerk. It makes sense that I would be on his mailing list."

Without a word, Garrity closed that folder and clicked on the one marked "Fouza." The messages there were untitled. He inspected the dates and clicked on the earliest one.

HEY THERE, JUDGE! YOUR DAYS ARE NUMBERED. YOUR KIDS, TOO. AND SO IS THIS LETTER NUMBER THREE, RIGHT? HA, HA.

STAND BY FOR INSTRUCTIONS ... UNLESS YOU WANT NUMBER FOUR TO BE YOUR LAST.

In the study, a hush of triumph filled every corner.

"This is just the first tiny crack in the case," Garrity cautioned, trying to suppress the excitement he was obviously feeling. "We've still got a long way to go."

Jim Stewart made no such attempt. "We've got 'im!" he whooped. Pete Rheims and Luis Mendez did a happy little two-step in the center of the rug, and even the sour Lucy permitted herself a broad smile.

Rheims stopped dancing long enough to fling his arms into the air. "We've got ourselves a perp!"

"Perp?" Daniel asked.

"Perpetrator. Criminal. Bad guy. You know, the kind we all love to lock away behind bars — The way we're going to be doing to this creep — and soon!"

Daniel stared at the computer monitor as though willing it to speak to him. "Vincent Fouza? Mark, I don't remember putting away anyone by that name. We didn't come across it in the files, either, did we?"

Garrity shrugged. "So we were wrong. The kidnapper doesn't have to be someone you put in the slammer; that was just a nice theory."

"Who else would do this to me?"

"We may not know the motive until we've caught the guy."

"Well, we're not going to catch him by gabbing all night," Mendez stated. "How about a look at those e-mails?"

The others peered over Garrity's shoulder as he examined the contents of the Fouza folder. Intently, they studied the kidnapper's words, marveling with a sort of disgusted admiration at the adroitness with which he had wormed his way into Mordy's confidence. What emerged was a chilling portrait of cold-blooded entrapment. Fouza had played Mordy like an instrument, using the boy's own goodwill and naivete to lure him ever deeper into his clutches.

Scanning one message after another, they saw Mordy's outrage turn gradually to pity. Daniel shook his head in bemusement when he read his son's pep talks to the man who would subsequently kidnap him. "I'M SURE PEOPLE WILL LIKE YOU IF THEY GET TO KNOW YOU." He wanted to fold Mordy tightly in his arms, and shake him like a rag doll, all at the same time. What courage his son had showed in these missives; what compassion — and what an utter lack of good sense!

But it was the very last message that electrified the small group. Garrity quickly read it, reread it, then said over his shoulder, "He left the boy a letter in back of the empty house across the street."

"That's why Mordy went out!" Daniel cried.

In a flash, talk turned to action. The six detectives stampeded out of the study, Daniel close on their heels. At the front door, Garrity collected himself.

"No, Dan, I'm afraid you'll have to stay here. In case the kidnapper calls again."

Nobly, Jake said, "I'll stay with you," though he looked longingly at the door as he said it.

"But —"

"No buts. You stay; we go check the place out. We'll be back with a report just as soon as we find something."

"If you find something." Daniel was still reeling from the notion that his son may have walked willingly out of his own secure home to play pen pals with a monster.

"We'd better," Garrity said grimly, and followed the others through the door.

Under cover of darkness, they abandoned all pretense of casualness. There were no neighbors to see them now. The police officers sprinted directly across the street to the empty house and dashed up the front walk. A shutter flapped somewhere in the wind. Weeds, knee high in places, drooped mournfully on either side of the neglected lawn. Garrity led the way around back, to the patio. Whipping out their flashlights, the detectives studied the stones to find the loose one under which Fouza had said he would leave his letter.

In short order, they found the stone. Carefully, Garrity removed it. There was nothing at all inside.

"Check out the yard," he instructed his men. Frustrated, he played his own flashlight over the rest of the patio and the adjoining back yard. It was then that he spotted something white, snagged on a spindly bush at the very edge of the patio. It was a piece of paper, its corners fluttering in the wind.

He stepped off the patio to retrieve the page. In the beam of his flashlight, he saw that it contained a brief letter. Garrity's eyes dropped to the signature at the bottom. While the rest of the document had been printed, the signature was handwritten. It said *"M. Newman."*

"What's that?" Stewart called softly, running over. The others quickly reassembled around them. Garrity showed them the letter. "Looks like the kid *was* here."

Scanning the letter, Rheims frowned. "It starts off, 'I read your letter. I want you to know I'm glad you decided to leave town and start a new life.' But the e-mail telling him about the letter on the patio only reached him on Saturday night — last night. When could the kid have found the time to read the guy's letter, let alone write back? Unless he picked it up early this morning and was snatched later, on his way back to deliver this one."

Garrity had been studying the page silently by the light of his flashlight. He said slowly, "If you read this letter closely, you can see that it's kind of vague. Mordy just may have typed this up *before* getting Fouza's letter. He may have wanted to save a little time, or to get the guy out of his hair. Or both."

"That sounds good," Lucy Fenwick nodded.

But Rheims was not so sure. "I still say he made two trips out here this morning."

"We'll have to check with Daniel to see whether Mordy had the opportunity to slip out earlier without his family noticing. Meanwhile," Garrity glanced around at the others, "anyone find anything else interesting?"

There was nothing. "Then let's go inside."

Stewart held back. "Don't we need a warrant?"

"This letter," Garrity said shortly, waving the paper in Stewart's face, "tells me that this is a crime scene. Come on."

Mendez, Stewart, and Fenwick started at the top of the house; Garrity and Rheims began at the bottom. When the upstairs produced no sign of recent habitation, the three joined the team in the basement. They found Garrity and Rheims poring over a small notepad, of the yellow legal variety.

Luis Mendez looked around at the cans, beer bottles, and empty take-out cartons that littered the basement shelves and floor. He whistled under his breath. "So the son of a gun was here all along," he said softly.

Jim Stewart said, "We'd better start dusting for fingerprints."

"A tidy little hideaway," said Lucy Fenwick. She seemed, in her grudging way, almost admiring. "How long do you suppose he's been hanging out here, spying on the Newmans?"

"Long enough," Garrity said curtly. He held out the pad. "The guy obviously used this to write things down; some of the pages are torn off."

Stewart shone the beam of his flashlight directly onto the top page, which, like the rest of the pad, was blank. "Look! There's an impression here. You can see it faintly if you look hard." He stared intently. "Seems to be numbers."

Standing almost on tiptoe to see over Stewart's broad shoulder, Mendez exclaimed, "It looks like a phone number!"

A smile began to curl Garrity's lips. He pulled a pencil out of his pocket and said softly, "Watch this, guys." Carefully, he drew the tip of the pencil back and forth across the faint indentation in the page, where the numbers had been written on the page above. He continued until the indentation was completely covered with a thin film of gray. And in the midst of the gray, standing out whitely where the pencil lead had not touched them, were seven digits.

"It *is* a phone number!" Stewart whooped with satisfaction, pounding one big fist into the palm of the other hand. "Who'd he call, I wonder?"

"I know how we can find out," Garrity said.

Sixty seconds later, the police officers were back at the Newmans. While Stewart briefed Daniel on their discoveries, Garrity pulled out his cellular phone. He punched in the double-digit number that connected him to the station house.

"Marge? We need a name and address, soon as you can get them." He rattled off the phone number. "That's right —"

"He was *there?*" Daniel asked, stupefied. "In the house across the street, *spying* on us?"

"For some time, from the look of things," Stewart nodded.

"So close — Why didn't I sense him? How could I *not* sense him?" As if evil gave off a distinct emanation that should have made itself felt all up and down the block — Daniel broke off, then said to Jake, standing at his shoulder, "I did see a light once! I was coming home from *Selichos* late at night, and there it was. I thought I was seeing things —"

"You couldn't have known," Jake said quickly.

Garrity hung up. "She'll get to work on it immediately," he reported.

"And now?" Daniel asked, as the detective put away the phone.

"Now," said Garrity, "we wait."

They whiled away the time discussing every possible scenario in Mordy's attempted exchange of letters with the kidnapper. Daniel was adamant in denying that Mordy had left the house without his knowledge earlier that morning. "We went to morning services at the synagogue together. As we were getting into the car he slipped and fell in a mud puddle, and went directly home to shower and change."

"He could have made a stop at the old house first," Rheims suggested.

"I suppose so," Daniel said reluctantly. "Though it isn't likely. I was driving, he was walking. I got home before Mordy did, but only just. He seemed to have hurried, which isn't surprising when you consider what he looked like. I don't think there was time for him to make any stops."

"And there's no mud on the letters," Lucy pointed out.

"I think Mark had the right idea," Stewart said. "Mordy prepared the letter *before* going out to get Fouza's. Decided to kill two birds with one stone, so to speak. He thought he'd save time that way, before his dad got home."

Garrity's phone shrilled. He snatched it up, saying, "Marge? Anything?" He listened for a moment, a slow smile spreading across his face. "Yes, that's the name we were looking for. Did you get me an address?" He scribbled quickly in his notebook. "Thanks, Marge. You're a lifesaver." He hung up.

Turning to the others, he announced, "The phone number is listed under the name Antonio Fouza. I've got an address."

"What relation to Vincent?" Mendez wondered aloud.

"I guess we're going to be paying this Tony Fouza character a little visit," Rheims said laconically.

"You bet we are," said Garrity. "Right now. You, me, and Jim. The rest of you stay here with the judge."

Lucy Fenwick and Luis Mendez were not happy at being left behind to babysit, but they had no choice but to defer to the team captain. Daniel watched the others run outside. With Jake at his side, he watched the police pile into their cars and hurtle away into the night — on the kidnapper's trail.

He mouthed a silent prayer, "Please don't let them be too late. Let them find Mordy and bring him back to me, safe."

The prayer sounded good to him, so he said it again.

Then he sat down in an armchair in the living room of his empty house, to do the hardest job of all: wait for news.

64

Very gradually, he became aware of himself. He was floating in darkness — a darkness that smelled of mildew and old mothballs. And there was another smell, too: a sickly sweet odor that seemed to be lodged permanently in his nostrils.

Presently, the floating sensation ended. He began to sense a solid surface beneath him. Solid, but in motion. A car. For a reason he could not begin to fathom, he was riding in the back seat of a jeep, with a scratchy, malodorous something — it seemed to be an old woolen blanket — covering him from head to toe. The blanket accounted for some of the smells that were making his head swim and his stomach turn, but there was more to it than that. The strongest odor was not really present at all, but a lingering memory. The memory of a cloth pressed to his nose, and of frantic terror before the blackness came —

With a jolt like a thousand amperes of electricity shooting through his veins, Mordy remembered.

He sat up with a jerk — or tried to. His efforts were hampered by the fact that both his wrists and his ankles were firmly bound. His squirming eventually caught the attention of the man behind the wheel, who glanced back at him and snarled, "Awake already? Lie still, kid, if you know what's good for you."

Mordy lay back, rigid as a statue. His heart, however, was far from still, being engaged in a kind of Indian war dance all over the inside of his chest. After a few moments, he felt a slackening in the car's speed, and sensed it swerving onto the shoulder of the road. There was a rustle from the front seat, and the rough blanket was pulled back from his face. Mordy stared into the eyes of his kidnapper.

"Had some sweet dreams back there?" The man's smile was not a pleasant sight, nor was the long white scar that ran down one side of his face. That scar was the last thing Mordy remembered seeing, before blackness had engulfed him on the wings of the sickly sweet smell that would not go away. He said nothing.

"The quiet type, I see. Well, that's good. Because that's what I want from you, kid. Quiet, and lots of it. 'Specially when we're in places where people can hear you." He paused, as though to let his instructions sink in. "Just in case you're curious, here's why you're going to do exactly as I tell you." He produced a nasty-looking pistol and held it inches from Mordy's nose. "A little pressure on the trigger, and *bam*. Right between the eyes. The judge is minus one kid. Get the picture?"

White faced, Mordy nodded. His eyes never left the gun.

"Good. Now, I'll just tuck you up again —" He lifted a corner of the blanket — "and we'll be on our way."

"Wh-where are we going?" Mordy ventured quickly. His throat was so dry that the words sounded like the rustling of last year's leaves.

"That's my business. Now remember what I said about quiet." He tossed the blanket over Mordy's face. The car started up again, and swung back onto the road.

Closing his eyes made no difference, but Mordy did so anyway. He was desperate to block out the horror of his situation, and right now all that seemed to stand between himself and Evil was the frail thickness of his own eyelids. He thought of his home, and his father and sister, and he fought back tears.

The jeep rolled on. The steady motion lulled the boy into a numbness that could almost pass for serenity. As the miles unwound, Mordy pushed his terror to one side and began to do the same things that his father was doing, back home in Cedar Hills — the only things he *could* do: pray, and worry, and wait to see what happened next.

"Mrs. Fouza?"

The woman clutched her faded bathrobe more closely around her.

She was thin and gray haired, and just now her face wore a matching grayish pallor — whether of exhaustion or fear, or a combination of the two, Garrity could not say. She stared up at the three police officers with dark, ring-rimmed eyes, and quavered, "Yes?"

"You *are* Mrs. Fouza?"

"Yes." The woman seemed to collect her courage. "Wh-why are you coming here at this hour of the night? My husband works hard, he gets up very early in the morning. We were already asleep."

"Is your husband Anthony or Vincent?"

"Anthony," she said, her voice sharpening in heightened anxiety. "What do you want with my Tony? He's a good man, a hardworking man. He's never done anything in his life to be ashamed of." The eyes opened wider, incomprehension battling fear.

Mark Garrity said quietly, "It's Vincent we want to talk to. We just need to ask him a few questions. Is he here, ma'am?"

"Vincent? What has *he* done? Nothing! He's a good boy, my Vinny. What do you want with him?" The woman's voice had risen almost to the pitch of hysteria. With a quick glance over her shoulder to the stairs, at the top of which her husband presumably slumbered, she lowered her voice and demanded again, "What has my son done?"

"We'd just like to ask him a few questions, ma'am," Garrity said patiently. "Do you know where he is?"

She hesitated, then said sullenly, "Upstairs. In his room. He sits at his computer till all hours of the night." Defiantly, she repeated, "He's a good boy, my Vinny. Not like some of the bums in this neighborhood. He takes computer classes at college at night. He's going to make something of himself!"

"I'm sure he is, ma'am. If we may —?" Politely but firmly, Garrity stepped into a vestibule inadequately lighted by a single dim bulb in an ancient fixture. Beyond, he could see the darkened shapes of a modest living-room suite; in the other direction lay a small dining room and, after that, a tiny kitchen. He made for the stairs.

Pete Rheims and Jim Stewart nodded politely at Mrs. Fouza as they passed, but their eyes were on the stairs and their minds on their quarry. At the top of the steps, Garrity said quietly to his colleagues, "He's probably armed." He pulled out his own gun.

"Wonder why he didn't bolt when he heard the doorbell?" Rheims murmured.

When Garrity pushed open the door, they saw why. Vincent was hunched before his computer monitor, a pair of headphones clamped to his ears, as he was listening to a CD, the cover of which was strewn among a number of other CDs on his littered desk. Garrity hesitated, then walked up to the young man and touched him on the shoulder.

Vinny spun around and whipped off the earphones in one startled motion.

"*Freeze!* Don't reach for a gun or you'll never reach for anything again." Garrity's own weapon was leveled at the center of Vinny's chest.

Blanching, Vinny lowered his hands very carefully to his lap. "I don't have a gun," he whispered. Then, a little louder, he added, "What is this? What's going on?"

Garrity kept his gun leveled on Vinny while Rheims searched him for concealed weapons. Stewart began slowly moving around the room, looking for evidence. "What are you looking for?" Vinny demanded. His face was still very pale, but he had not broken out in the cold sweat Garrity had seen on so many other guilty-minded men when questioned by the police. In a calm, conversational tone, he said, "I'd like to ask you a few questions, Vinny."

"Questions? About what? I'm clean, officer. I'll admit, I was a wild kid, but I've settled down. I don't even see the old gang anymore, hardly. I'm taking computer courses at college —"

"We've already heard all about that. Tell me, Vinny, about your e-mails to Mordy Newman."

Vinny went blank. "To who?"

"Mordy Newman. Judge Newman's son."

At the word "judge," the last remaining vestige of color drained completely away from Vinny's face. He swallowed convulsively, and licked his lips that had gone suddenly dry.

"I don't know anything about no — about any judge."

"You've been sending e-mails to his house on a regular basis," Garrity said, still pleasantly, but with a distinct edge that Vinny would have had to be deaf to miss.

"That wasn't me!" The words burst out of Vinny before he could stop them. He broke off, blinking nervously at the detectives. Now, Garrity noted, he *was* sweating.

He took a step closer to the desk, the gun held casually in his hand but still pointed at the center of Vinny's body. "It wasn't? Then suppose you tell me who did send those e-mails. They had your name and address on them. That means they were sent from this computer, doesn't it?"

Reluctantly, Vinny nodded.

"Well?" Garrity prompted, harshly now. "Tell me about those e-mails, Vinny!"

"I want a lawyer! You can't prove I did anything wrong!"

Another step brought Garrity within two feet of the younger man. He towered above Vinny, still seated in his swivel desk chair. The hand that held the gun was rock-steady. "You'll have your lawyer, Vinny. You'll also have your day in court. But right now, I want to talk about the kid you kidnapped. I want you to tell me where you've put him. And I want you to tell me now."

There was no mistaking the genuine shock in Vinny's face when he heard those words. "K-kidnapped?"

"Don't play the fool with me. We read your e-mail, instructing the kid to pick up your letter behind the empty house across the street. We also found your phone number in the basement of that house."

For the first time in the headlong rush of events, it occurred to Garrity to wonder why it was Fouza's number that had been found in the hideaway. If Fouza himself had been spying on the Newmans from that basement, wouldn't he have written someone else's number there rather than his own, which, presumably, he knew by heart? That fact alone pointed to the existence of an accomplice.

Added to that was the way they had found Vinny here tonight. Here he was, in his bedroom in his parents' home, whiling away the evening in an apparently normal manner. He certainly did not seem to possess the ruthlessness or hatred to effect a kidnapping, nor — if his present quivering manner was any indication — the cold-bloodedness to sit listening to music while the kid he had snatched lay languishing somewhere, or worse.

Acting on the intuition which had won him his greatest successes as a detective, Garrity asked softly, "Who is he, Vinny? Who sent those e-mails?"

"It wasn't me!"

"I know that. But I want you to tell me who it was. Because whoever it was did a very bad thing today, Vinny. He kidnapped the judge's son, Vinny. A nice 12-year-old kid who never did anything to hurt anyone. The kid doesn't deserve that, does he, Vinny?"

Vinny did not say whether he did or did not.

"Even if I decide to believe you when you say you didn't send those e-mails — and I'm not promising that I will — they came from your computer, right? That means that you'll certainly be up for accessory to kidnapping — if not accessory to murder. This is very, very serious, Vinny." Garrity paused. "Now, *who is he?*"

In front of Vinny's inner eye flashed the image of a knife, and a long wicked scar that belonged to a man who had lived intimately with violence before. He clenched his fists, deathly afraid. Danger stalked him from every direction. On one side was Joey, with his knife and his threats — threats that Vinny knew he would not hesitate to carry out. And, on the other, this police officer with his talk of being an accessory to all kinds of awful things. Just when Vinny had started getting his life together, too! He cursed the day he had found Joey on his doorstep and introduced him to the marvels of cyberspace. How stupid could a guy be? He, Vinny, had dug his own grave, and now either Joey or the cops were going to push him right into it.

Deathly afraid, he said nothing.

"All right," Garrity said, motioning to Stewart. "Jim, the handcuffs. We're bringing this guy in. Maybe he'll remember more down at the station house."

"No!" Vinny lunged to his feet — and found not one, but three guns pointed at him. Hastily, he raised his hands. "I'm not going to do any-thing. I just don't want you to arrest me. I want to help you, but —"

"But you're afraid, is that it? Afraid your friend's going to be a little annoyed when you tell us his name?"

Dumbly, Vinny nodded.

Sympathetically, Garrity said, "A tough choice, Vinny. But that's what life's all about, isn't it? Choices. So, choose. You protect your friend, and you fry alongside him. You sing to us, and we'll do our best to protect you. We aim to put your friend behind bars for a long, long time. You can go on with your life and play with your computers to your heart's content."

"You won't charge me if I help you?"

"That's for the state prosecutor to decide. But we'll certainly let him know how helpful you've been, Vinny. That goes a long way in this business."

Still Vinny said nothing. The muscles in his jaw worked nervously as he weighed his options. Garrity did not give him much time to think. They did not *have* much time. Insistently, he asked, "So who's your friend, Vinny?"

"He's not my friend. At least, not anymore. We hung around together when we were kids, together with the rest of the neighborhood gang. But I've straightened myself out, while Joey —" He broke off.

"Joey?"

The decision had been made. Deep down, Vinny had known all along which way he would go — which way he *had* to go. To protect Joey now, in the face of these men and the consequences they represented, would spell suicide to all of Vinny's dreams. This way, he at least had a chance.

"Joey Mercutio. His mother lives around the corner. I don't know where Joey hangs out these days."

Mercutio. The name triggered a piercing alarm in Garrity's brain. Hadn't that name been on the list he'd prepared with Danny? Hadn't he been the one who —

"Mercutio died in jail," he said sharply.

Vinny shook his head. "That was Sal. Joey's big brother."

Like tumblers clicking neatly into place, the whole picture became crystal clear to Garrity. Danny sending Sal Mercutio up for a long stretch — Sal's death in prison — a kid brother's revenge.

And Ella's death? Was that connected, too?

Pulse racing with excitement, Garrity had just begun to ask for Mrs. Mercutio's address when the phone rang. There was an extension in Vinny's room, half hidden beneath the pile of computer literature heaped there. Garrity motioned for Vinny to answer.

Vinny's hand snaked out toward the receiver. "Hello?"

Garrity saw Vinny's face go rigid with shock. The detective thrust his own face close to the young man's, asking silently, "What? Who is it?"

Blindly, as he listened to the voice in his ear, Vinny's fingers groped for a pen. They connected with one, then hovered over a piece of paper.

"*It's Joey,*" Vinny wrote in a shaky script.

65

I t was one of those strokes of luck that policemen can never bank on — but without which their work would often be all but impossible. Masking his excitement, Garrity motioned for Vinny to go on with his conversation. Inwardly, he railed against the fate that had decreed him helpless to listen in. All he could do was attend to a one-sided dialogue while carefully watching Fouza's face to determine whether he was trying to tip off Mercutio that the police were on his tail.

"But I don't *have* that kind of money," Vinny protested into the phone. He listened a minute, then said, in a resigned sort of way, "I guess so. But Joey —" A pause, during which Vinny blanched. "Okay, okay, you don't have to get nasty. I'll find the money for you. But you gotta promise to pay it back as soon as —" Again, he broke off. A moment later, he said, "Yeah, right. Wait a sec while I find a pencil . . . Okay, shoot." Wincing at his own choice of words, he began to write.

"Got it. If I mail it in the morning — What? Oh, all right, I'll send it by overnight mail. That'll mean a trip to the post office . . . Yeah, I'm looking forward to that. Thanks a whole lot, pal . . . See you around." He hung up.

Garrity and the others were at his side in a second.

"Tell me everything," Garrity ordered.

The lobby of the Miami condominium complex was quiet at this hour. With a resident body consisting largely of senior citizens, 10:30 usually found the building just about tucked in for the night. Feeling absurd — he was reminded of the secret-agent games he and Daniel had played as kids — Chaim gave the place the once-over. The easy-chair arrangements by the window were deserted and the elevator was at rest. Satisfied, Chaim nodded. He had the place to himself.

It took him a few minutes to track down a public phone, around a corner of the lobby behind the elevators and then down a hallway, and a few more to plow through a maze of access codes and PIN numbers until he heard the phone ring in his brother's Cedar Hills home. As he waited for Daniel to pick up, he had a guilty twinge, picturing Gila asleep in their apartment upstairs.

It was a well-deserved rest. She had been working tirelessly for weeks, first on the renovation of Tova's room, and then in preparation for this trip. Upon their arrival here, Gila had embarked on a personal tour of inspection of every corner of the rented condominium. Then she had recruited the kids in a frenzy of unpacking. After a quick, light supper, she bathed and herded them — all except Tova — off to bed. At last, Tova, too, had succumbed to the fatigue that comes with travel and strange surroundings. Only then did Gila stop puttering about the place and find her own bed.

Chaim, pleading restlessness, had said he would follow a little later. When he was sure that Gila was asleep, he had slipped noiselessly from the apartment and made his way downstairs, not even daring to use the elevator for fear its thump would somehow penetrate his wife's consciousness.

Now that he had arrived at the pinnacle of all his plots and subterfuges, he found that he was oddly nervous.

"Hello?" Daniel sounded wary. The single word also held a deep-seated undercurrent of emotional exhaustion. To Chaim, this registered only as an unusually low timbre in his brother's voice.

"Hi, Danny. It's me — Chaim."

"Oh! Chaim! How are you? How was the trip?" Was that relief in Daniel's voice — or disappointment? And why should it be either?

Chaim found himself babbling, as was his habit when unsure of himself. "The trip went amazingly well considering it was the kids' first plane ride. They were almost too excited to talk. Everyone is getting along so far, so Sukkos should be fine. Mom and Dad are doing well, too. Their place is two floors below the one they rented for us."

"And how's the condo? Roomy enough?"

"We wouldn't have cared if it were a matchbox, you know that. But Gila gave her stamp of approval to the apartment. It's the whole idea of the trip that gives us such a thrill. It's the first time we've ever been away for *Yom Tov*." Then, hearing the implicit accusation in what he had just said, Chaim hastily switched tracks. "And how are you, Danny?" he asked. "Is everything okay?"

It was the infinitesimal hesitation that gave Daniel away.

Deeply truthful by nature, lying was inherently stressful to him. It was this passion for truth that had made an outstanding prosecutor of Daniel, and then a formidable judge. He could dredge up a circumvention when necessary, or at least avoid telling the whole truth, as he had done with his mother earlier that afternoon. But Chaim had caught him at the end of one of the most difficult days he had ever lived through — and it was not over yet.

The police had disappeared on the trail of the man who had been sending e-mails to Mordy, the man who was most likely his kidnapper. Where Mordy was, and in what condition, only Heaven knew. Daniel had prayed till he was hoarse, and was no closer to finding the comfort he craved. Until his son was found, safe, he was a man in torment.

Daniel had, quite simply, reached the end of his reserves. There was no more strength in him to pretend, as he had been trying to pretend all day to those not in the picture, that everything was fine. Everything was as *un*-fine as it could possibly be, and something in Daniel was crying out for the release of telling someone so. His talk with Yehuda Arlen seemed ages ago. He needed to talk *now*, and to someone closer than 6,000 miles away. What better confidant than his own brother? And he had the added advantage of being out of the way, in Florida. It would be easier to keep the story quiet there.

Still, he hesitated.

Chaim said sharply, "What is it, Danny? What's the matter?"

Daniel sighed. "Believe me, you don't want to know."

"Yes, I do! I want to know what's going on — everything. And I want to help, if I can." There was a new note of command in Chaim's tone — a note that rose from a sense of his big brother's unusual vulnerability. "Tell me, Danny. Please."

Daniel hurled the news at him full force. It hit Chaim like a rock between the eyes. "Mordy's been kidnapped."

"*What?*"

"It's a long story. It happened this morning. The police have been here with me all day. We're keeping the story quiet for now; we don't know how the kidnapper will react to publicity."

Chaim clutched the receiver to his ear, as though the motion could bring his brother closer. Choking, almost incoherent, he stammered, "But but how did it happen? Do you have any idea where Mordy is? Oh, that poor child! Do the police have any clues? Is Mordy okay?" He ended almost in a shout. "Danny, *what's happening?*"

His brother's agitation had the curious effect of making Daniel calmer. "The police are out right now, following up some leads. We think we may know who did it, but we have no idea yet where he's holding Mordy. I did speak to him —"

"To the kidnapper?"

"Well, yes. To both of them, actually."

"You spoke to Mordy? Is he all right?"

"He sounded all right. Scared, of course." Once again, as he had at intervals throughout the day, Daniel entertained a dazed, dreamlike notion that none of this was happening. There was a surreal quality about the conversation. Was this *his* son they were discussing?

"*Baruch Hashem* for that, anyway." A pause. "How much does he want?"

"Who? Oh — the kidnapper. A million."

Chaim emitted a low whistle. "Can you raise it? If there's a problem, I know of several *gemachs* —"

"Thanks, Chaim, but we're not up to that yet. I haven't even been told when or where to leave the money." Daniel exhaled audibly. "I wish you were here, little brother. You have no idea how much."

"I'll come," Chaim said at once. "I'll explain to Gila, and we'll think of something to tell Mom and Dad and the kids. We'll —"

"Chaim, I appreciate the offer — more than I can say. Just hearing you make it is almost as good as having you right here in my living room. But the answer is no. Gila and the gang need you right where you are. Your flying off mysteriously is bound to raise questions, and

I don't want Dad to find out what's happened under any circumstances. Besides, there's nothing you can do here that's not already being done by the pros."

"I could just be with you."

"I know. And I wish. But — better not."

"Are you positive? I want the truth, Daniel."

"I wouldn't insult you with anything but the truth. I'm not completely alone, Chaim. I have a young friend here, Jake Meisler's his name; he's a real help. And Yael's out of the way at her teacher's, thank goodness, so I don't have to worry about her. You stay where you are, and just make sure to *daven* good and hard for our Mordy."

"That goes without saying."

The two conversed a little longer, short, meaningless sentences that were just a camouflage for the real things that were being said without words. A connection had sprung up between them in these last few minutes — a bond born of Daniel's confession and Chaim's impulsive offer. The bond had been there all along, perhaps, but family politics and sheer inertia had prevented it from coming to the fore until now. Sometimes it takes catastrophe to remind us of the things we cherish in life.

"Well, you have my number, Danny. Call me if there's *any news at all* — or if you just want to talk. If anyone's around, I'll find a public phone, like the one I'm calling from now."

"Will do. Thanks, little brother."

"I love you, Danny."

"Ditto. *Daven* good, Chaim, but don't despair." Daniel's voice cracked on the last word. Then, collecting himself, he said with forced brightness, "I have it on good authority that Mordy's going to be all right."

Chaim hung up, trembling. For a long moment he stood where he was, breathing deeply. Street noises filtered in from outside, and he could almost imagine hearing the swish of the sea as it made its endless round trip to the shore and back. But of course, that was impossible. Their condominium was situated a full two blocks from the beach. It was his own pulse he heard, thrumming in his ears like the surf.

It was some time before he felt capable of walking again. He made his way, cautious and shaken, down the hall. As he rounded the corner into the main area of the lobby, he came face to face with another, older man.

The two started in mutual astonishment, then smiled in guilty conspiracy.

"How is he?" Jonathan Newman asked.

"Basically fine, Dad," Chaim said. "He's — he's had some problems to deal with, but I'm sure they'll be cleared up in no time. He sends his love."

"No point in my calling then, is there?" Jonathan cast a look, half-amused, half-apprehensive, at the ceiling. "Your mother was only just dropping off to sleep when I slipped out. I don't want her to wake up and miss me."

"No, no point in calling. You go on back to Mom."

The two men rode up in the elevator to their respective floors without speaking. Bidding each other an affectionate good-night, they went to rejoin their wives.

Vinny took a deep, steadying breath, and sank into his chair. The three detectives formed a half-circle around him. He could not have asked for a more attentive audience.

"Joey needs money," he began, somewhat unnecessarily.

"How much, and why?" Rheims demanded.

"Five hundred. He says he's coming into some money soon — big money. He'll pay me back then." Suddenly, the significance of this information dawned on Vinny. He raised his eyes to the detectives, then banged his forehead, hard, with the heel of one hand. "Did he mean —? Oh, my G-d. What's that idiot done?"

"I told you," Garrity said calmly. "Joey Mercutio kidnapped Judge Newman's son this morning. He's holding the boy for ransom. Apparently, he's short on cash to cover his expenses until the ransom comes through."

Vinny groaned.

"What else?" Garrity asked.

"When — when I told him I didn't have that kind of money, Joey turned nasty. Said he'd got hold of a nice little pistol and was going to let me have a real close look at it — unless I helped him out."

"He didn't have a gun before?"

"Not that I know of. Usually, he liked to flick around a knife. Scared me to death." Indignantly, Vinny added, "Why else do you think I agreed to let him e-mail from here? Once I began to suspect he was up to no good, I mean."

"We'll get to that later," Garrity said. "So you said you'd get the money to him?"

"What else did you expect me to say — 'Come on over and kill me'? I have some money saved up in the bank. I've been working as a computer technician during the day while I go to night school. The salary's no great shakes, but I do have five-six hundred sitting in my account." Vinny produced a mirthless smile. "Joey promised he'd not only pay me back, but is planning to show me a 'real good time' with all the loot that's going to be rolling in — soon."

"When?" Stewart asked urgently. "Did he give any indication?"

Vinny shook his head. "He just said soon. Maybe he also said something about 'in a few days.' I'm not sure."

"You wrote down an address," Garrity said. He held out a hand for it. Vinny passed over the paper.

"P.O. Box 1321, Lincolntown, Pennsylvania," he read aloud. The sound of his escaping breath was clearly audible in the quiet room. Garrity glanced triumphantly at his fellow officers. "We've got ourselves a perp *and* an address."

"It's only a post office box," Vinny objected. "Joey didn't hide the kid in there!"

"No," Rheims said, smiling. "But it stands to reason that he's got the kid stashed away somewhere nearby, and will keep him there at least till the money comes in — Tuesday morning."

Garrity ordered Vinny, "Listen carefully. Go to your local post office first thing tomorrow morning. Write out a check for $500 and mail it to the address Joey gave you. Do as he says and send it by overnight mail."

"Yes, sir," Vinny said, eager now to be as helpful as possible. "And after that?"

"I'm going to post a couple of police officers here in the house until this is over. That's in case Joey contacts you again." *And*, Garrity added silently, *to make doubly sure that you don't chicken out, or give us away to your old pal. Right now you're anxious to please, but the threat of a bullet between the eyes can make a man do funny things.*

"I'm going to bring the officers in right away," he continued. "They'll accompany you to the post office tomorrow and stick close until we give the word."

"And how am I supposed to do my job?" Vinny demanded, both cowardice and helpfulness replaced — momentarily — by outrage.

"You won't be doing an awful lot of computer repair in a maximum-security prison," Rheims remarked pointedly. Vinny bit his lip. "You *are* going to cooperate, aren't you, Vinny?"

The brief spurt of aggressiveness crumbled like a tower of ash. "Yeah," Vinny mumbled. "I'll cooperate. Do I have a choice?"

Garrity called for backup. While they waited for the new policemen to relieve them, the three detectives retired to a corner of Vinny's bedroom, where they quietly reviewed the situation and laid out their plans. Vinny himself sat lost in a gloomy reverie. Life, he decided, was hard. You tried to keep your hands clean, then along came someone out of your past with mud on his clothes, and got you all dirty again.

When this was all over, he vowed silently, he would kiss the old neighborhood good-bye and start over fresh — someplace where there were no Joeys or Luigis or Marios from his earlier, reckless days, liable to pop up at any minute to haunt him.

The sound of an approaching vehicle made Garrity glance out the window. He nodded at Rheims, who trotted downstairs to open the door. A moment later, two police officers walked in. Garrity quickly apprised them of the situation, and gave them their instructions.

"We're going now," Garrity told Vinny. "These cops will keep you safe. Remember, if there's any contact with Joey — *anything* — they're going to want to hear about it. You tell the cops; they'll report to us."

"And what about you? What are you gonna do about the kid?" Vinny asked, his relief at seeing the last of his interrogators making him feel brave again.

It was Jim Stewart who answered.

"We're going to Lincolntown to get him, of course."

66

Not surprisingly Daniel spent the rest of that nearly sleepless Sunday night thinking of his son. What did come as a surprise was the fact that various other people — people who had no idea of Mordy's predicament — were thinking of him, too.

In the last, hazy minutes before sleep claimed her, Judy Rabinowitz, in California, found her nephew on her mind. Daniel had sounded strange on the phone this evening. When she had asked how Mordy was, he had not asked, "Why?" Instead, in a sharp, unaccustomed tone, he had demanded to be told what she knew. That meant, didn't it, that there *was* something to know?

Her thoughts flowed jerkily, on the edge of sleep. Shocking, the way the boy had become involved in writing to that lowlife. She wished Ari had told her about it sooner. Good thing she had called Daniel tonight. Fretfully, she wondered if there was anything more she could do. She would call in a day or two — not right away, that would seem like prying — and see if there was any more to be wormed out of Daniel. Or maybe she would ask to speak to Mordy himself. Though what could she possibly learn from him that his own father, on the spot, could not find out?

Judy Rabinowitz was not used to leaving questions unanswered in her life. This one, however, she was forced — for the moment, at least — to abandon. She would definitely make that call, she promised herself sleepily. In a day or two —

Her son, Ari, suffered a rare bout of insomnia that night.

The autumn moon flooded his room with a cool silver light, but it was not the light that kept Ari awake. Running through his head like a frightening litany were the things his cousin had written him about his unknown e-mail partner. Though Ari's mother had tried to convince him that Mordy was fine, he could tell that she, herself, was far from certain that this was the case. And he himself was certain that it was not.

Mordy was in trouble — and he, Ari, could have done something to prevent it. Just what that trouble was he did not begin to know, which was a blessing for whatever peace of mind he still retained.

Yael, in Sara Muller's comfortable guest bed, woke up suddenly in the small hours of the night and found herself wondering about Mordy.

If their father had insisted that *she* be out of the way, wouldn't he have done the same with Mordy? Or was her brother at home, having the time of his life "helping" the police with their detective work? She felt a pang of envy at the possibility.

Normally, Yael loved sleepovers. While these commonly took place at the homes of friends, spending the night at her adored piano teacher's would, under normal circumstances, have been a thrill. Tonight, she felt less thrilled than homesick.

She understood that Daddy had sent her away for her own protection; but if she had been the one to choose, she would have opted to stay with him even at the risk of her own safety. In any case, such risk — in her opinion — was more theoretical than real. She had a child's implicit faith in the ultimate goodness of life, and youth's confidence in her own immortality.

Staring up in the darkness at the unfamiliar ceiling, she thought about her own room. Then she pictured her father, doubtless asleep by now.

But when she tried to picture Mordy, she came up blank.

The police, after snatching a few hours' sleep in Daniel's house, departed at first light for Lincolntown, PA.

"Having crossed state lines with your son has now turned this into a federal offense," Garrity explained to Daniel over coffee and danishes, while the sun struggled to dispense a thin, pearly light through a thickening cloud cover. "We could call in the F.B.I. immediately, if we choose. But we've decided to go it alone, at least for now. For one thing, we've established a connection with Vinny — at present our only link to the kidnapper. And, for another, we're frankly reluctant to hand over the investigation unless and until we find ourselves stymied. We have a name and an address to work with. That's a lot more than most kidnapping investigations start with. I think we can do it."

Garrity looked exhausted, the haggard, unshaven cheeks lending him a raffish air that clashed oddly with the seriousness in his eyes. "I'm leaving Luis Mendez here with you, Dan. He'll be our liaison."

"What about Officer Fenwick?"

"She's coming along. We're going up to scout out the post offices and to see if we can't get a whiff of Mercutio before the money arrives tomorrow morning. Plainclothes, of course, no uniforms. A woman is invaluable for this kind of work. People tend to trust women more easily, open up to them more." He took a long swig from his mug.

"I see." Daniel took a sip from his own mug, cradling it between his palms for the warmth it offered. He had slept sporadically in the last few hours before dawn, then rose to *daven Shacharis* in tearful solitude before the others awoke. He felt worn down — ground, emotionally, to the very bone. His muscles ached as though with a fever. He longed for Mordy. He longed for Yael. He longed for an end to this long-drawn torture. *Ribbono shel Olam, end this agony and bring back my son to me!* The silent cry echoed all through him, but left only emptiness in its wake.

He looked up at Garrity and asked dryly, "Any chance I could come along with you, Mark? He is my son, you know."

"I know. And believe me, I sympathize. But you're needed here. The kidnapper has to be able to hear your voice when he calls again. Otherwise, he'll suspect we're on his trail and pull up stakes and vanish again — this time, more effectively." He paused earnestly. "You do see that, don't you, Dan?"

"Of course," Daniel sighed. "Just wishful thinking." Like an automaton moving without volition or hope, Daniel bent his head once again to his coffee.

The detectives, except for Luis, left at 7 o'clock. Garrity promised to phone from Lincolntown later in the day with his report of the situation there. Mendez busied himself with the morning news, making it clear that he neither expected nor particularly craved conversation with Daniel. For this, Daniel was grateful.

On his return from shul, Jake approached Daniel with an encouraging smile, and said, "Well, how are we going to spend the day?"

"Today's Monday. You're going to class."

"With all due respect, sir, I'm not. You need me here."

Daniel sighed. "I know I do. And I don't have the strength to argue with you, Jake. But I'm concerned. You've made it through more than two years of law school. Don't blow it all because of me. I couldn't bear the guilt." He spoke half-humorously, but Jake knew that he meant it.

"Not to worry, sir. At the risk of boasting, I'm a top student. *And* I brought along a couple of textbooks, which I plan to hit today. After we learn together, of course."

"Oh? Is that what we're going to do?" Daniel was finally smiling, too. He rubbed tiredly at his cheeks.

"What else?"

"There *is* nothing else," Daniel said softly. He pushed away his mug and got to his feet. "Excuse me, Jake. First, I have to make a phone call."

"Yael?" the young man guessed.

"No," Daniel said. "Her piano teacher."

Sara replaced the receiver with a hand that seemed to have gone unaccountably numb. She was seated at the edge of her bed, which she had been on the point of leaving, when the phone rang.

Who, she had wondered at the first muted ring, was calling her at such an hour? Wild, panicky speculation seized her mind in the two or three seconds before she answered. Her parents, her sister — Holding her breath, she finally picked up the receiver and offered a cautious greeting. The response came in a voice she had not even considered — though she ought to have. With Yael staying with her, it was only natural for her father to call.

"Good morning, Miss Muller. I hope I didn't wake you," Daniel said politely. Something in his manner struck Sara as odd, remote — as though his thoughts were not marching in time with his words.

"No, not at all. I've got to get ready for school. I'll be waking Yael in a few minutes."

"Before you do, there's something I think you should know. And after that, I have a request to make."

Her jaw tightened ominously. He sounded so terribly somber. "I'm listening."

Quickly, concisely, Daniel brought her abreast of the situation. With the same remote politeness, he listened to her exclamations of horror, answered her questions, and waited for the final, "What can I do, Mr. Newman?"

It never came. Instead, Sara said firmly, "Yael can stay right here until this is all over, if that's what you want, Mr. Newman."

"I do." He closed his eyes in relief. "I need to know that Yael is out of this. It's not even so much a question of her safety any longer — we know that the kidnapper has centered his activities up in Pennsylvania for now. He's not likely to make the long trip back, especially if he has no idea where Yael is staying."

"I agree. But, Mr. Newman —"

"Yes?"

"Forgive me, but I think you should tell her. Mordy's her brother, after all. I'm sure she'd rather know than be kept in the dark. She's not a baby any longer. At 14, she can handle it." *And be a support to you, too,* she added, but not aloud.

There was a pause while Daniel processed the suggestion. He dealt with it in a detached way, like a problem of logic. Then he said, "You may be right. Yael does have a right to know. But, sometimes, a person has to give up her rights so that another person can keep his sanity. I need Yael safe — and happy in her ignorance. I'm sure she'd understand."

Sara did not agree, but she made no further effort to persuade him. She had offered her advice, and it had been rejected. She shifted the conversation to practical matters.

"She'll need more clothes and things."

"I'll have Jake bring them over after school. And if at any time I decide that Yael needs to know, I'll be in touch with you."

"Be in touch anyway, Mr. Newman," she urged. "You were talking about sanity just now? I've got to know what's happening, if I'm to hold onto mine."

There was actually a hint of a smile in his voice as he answered, "Will do. Thank you, Miss Muller. And remember, this has got to be kept quiet. Not a word to anyone, please."

"I can keep a secret," she said quietly, and hung up.

Seated at the edge of her bed, Sara replayed every word of the phone call. She was grateful that she had picked it up in her bedroom where there was no chance of encountering Yael — which had no doubt been her father's intention in phoning so early. By the time she had dressed and left the room, she hoped, her features would be schooled to the required discipline. Yael would never suspect from *her* that there was anything amiss with her brother.

Fifteen minutes later, she was gently shaking her young guest's shoulder. "Wake up, Yael. Rise and shine. It's time to get ready for school."

Drowsily, Yael turned over so that she was facing Sara. One cheek was creased, and she wore a warm and sleepy smile. "I was dreaming about my mother. For a minute, when you said 'Wake up,' I thought you were her."

Sara's heart went out to the girl. "Did you? How nice! But it's really getting late. I couldn't bear to wake you up any earlier, you were sleeping so soundly." *And dreaming so sweetly,* she thought with a pang.

"I'll be up in a second," Yael promised. As Sara watched, the mists of sleep left her eyes and she grew suddenly, fully, alert. "Has Daddy called?"

"Yes. He thinks it would be best if you stay here a day or two longer, Yael. Until this mess is cleared up."

Yael moved to make some objection, then pressed her lips together. Without a word, she sat up and reached for her robe.

At the door, Sara turned. "There's Cheerios or Cornflakes for breakfast," she said cheerfully. "Or I can whip up something hot. I make a mean scrambled egg, you know." She laughed. "One of the few things I *can* make."

Immersed in her thoughts, Yael did not respond.

"Yael?" Sara prompted. "Breakfast?"

"What?" Yael looked up, startled. Belatedly, she heard the question, and saw the expectant look in her teacher's eyes. She smiled indifferently, then shrugged. "Whatever."

With a stifled sigh, Sara went to the kitchen to put together a semblance of a breakfast for her reluctant guest.

67

I t did not take long for Garrity and his team to learn that Lincolntown, PA (pop. 12,713) had three post office branches. Garrity dispatched Lucy and Pete Rheims to the first of them, Stewart to the second, and made his own way to the third. By flashing their police badges and insisting on speaking directly to the manager of each branch, they succeeded in securing the information they wanted just as the big town hall clock was striking the noon hour.

"A Joe Mercutio rented a box at the Moonview Road post office yesterday," Stewart reported. "He paid up front for a month — the minimum rental period. In cash."

Garrity consulted his map of Lincolntown, procured at a local gas station on their arrival. "Let's see. Looks like Moonview's a relatively small street. Let's go there now and check out the place — exits and entrances, parking lots, all of that. Then we'll start making the rounds of the campgrounds."

On the long drive up to the Poconos, the four had agreed that Mercutio must have had a reason for choosing little Lincolntown as the hiding place for his hostage, and that the reason might well have to do with the many campsites in the area. Each site was marked on the map with a tiny black triangle, with a definite cluster of them within a ten-mile radius of the town in which they stood. It was this cluster they had decided to investigate first.

"If we come up with nothing at the camp grounds," Garrity said, "we go ahead with the plan for tomorrow morning. What time does the post office open?"

"9 o'clock," supplied Stewart.

"9. So we get into position at 8. Someone to block each exit, some-one else loitering beside the bank of post-office boxes. We make a definite ID, we pull him in, we get him to tell us where the kid is."

"And if he doesn't talk?" Lucy asked.

"Oh, he'll talk," Garrity said. A vacant look swept his face clean as he plunged into a recent, favorite daydream: a dream of just what exactly he would do to Joe Mercutio once he had him in his clutches. "Just let him try to hold out on us. Oh, man, just let him try!"

The four piled into Garrity's unmarked sedan and drove slowly through the sedate streets toward the Moonview Road post office.

Sara had never considered herself a particularly adept actress, but this morning she had to give herself full marks for deception. Not by a single word or look did she betray Daniel's secret to his daughter.

Of course, she was helped along considerably by the fact that Yael was completely self-absorbed through breakfast and the drive to school. The girl made a few token attempts at conversation, then sank again into her thoughts. Under normal circumstances, Sara would have been upset by these signs of her young friend's distress. Today, she was grateful.

In the parking lot, she waved Yael ahead. "You go on with your friends. I'll follow in a few minutes."

"I don't mind being seen with a teacher," Yael assured her candidly.

Sara smiled. "That's good of you. But run along anyway. See you after school. We'll meet right here, okay? Remember where I'm parked."

Yael looked at the parking spot, and nodded slowly. She shrugged into her backpack and gave a small wave in farewell. After that, Sara saw only a slender back that looked as though it were weighted down not only with the bulging schoolbag, but with all the world's troubles. She sighed.

Her mind turned to the day ahead. With the Newman boy's plight looming so hugely in her mind, the last thing she felt like doing was teaching — especially to as unreceptive a class as she had ever had the

dubious pleasure of addressing. It would be a struggle just to concentrate.

But duty called. She hefted her briefcase and stepped out of the car.
Her own back, as she made her way along the parking lot to the side
entrance of the school building, was straight and squared as a soldier's
on his way to a battle he knows himself doomed to lose.

This fatalistic attitude stayed with her through the morning. But like
the proverbial camel, she needed but a single straw to demolish her
hard-won equanimity. Her last class before lunch — and her second
period of the day with *the* class — proved to be her breaking point.

She began the lesson with her usual animated concentration. But it
was like shouting into a fog. Part of the class stared back at her, stony
eyed, while the other part let their gazes wander to the windows.
Except for one or two of the better students who apparently could not
stop themselves from responding to *any* learning experience, no one
made the slightest attempt to meet her intellectual quest halfway — or
even partway. She might as well have been lecturing to a group of
trees.

Behind every word she uttered was her terrible worry over young
Mordy Newman. Her heart was with the boy, and with his father, and
with his sister, uninformed as Yael was. Still, Sara was prepared to
share that heart with her class, even at the cost of immense self-
discipline. Had the girls shown so much as a particle of interest in her
carefully prepared lesson, she would have forced aside all other
considerations and given them everything she had. As it was, she gave
them what she could.

Ten full minutes went into an explanation of an intricate Rashi.
When she was finished, she asked the class at large, "Is that clear? Any
questions?"

There were none.

"Devorah." She nodded at a girl in the second row — large, oval
face and frizzy blond hair. "Please explain to the class what is
bothering Rashi here."

Devorah gave her a blank stare. "Sorry, I don't understand it."

With an effort, Sara swallowed her impatience. "Why didn't you
speak up just now, when I asked if there were any questions?"

The girl shrugged.

Carefully, patiently, Sara explained the whole thing again. When she was done, she said, "Now, Devorah, can you tell it over in your own words?"

"Not really," Devorah said placidly. "I guess I'm dumb or something. I still don't get it." There was a muted chuckle from the back corner of the room where Simi Davidson and her friends held court.

Sara pointed to another girl, this one petite and dark. "Mindy? How about you?"

"I don't understand it either, Morah Muller."

The chuckle from the back of the room grew more pronounced. This was more than the usual nonreceptiveness, mean as that was. This was intentional harassment. Sara gripped the edge of her desk — the edge closest to her, which the girls could not see. It took every ounce of self-control to say pleasantly, "Well, it looks like either the Rashi is more difficult than I'd thought, or else I'm not making myself clear. Shall I explain it for the third time?"

This time, she laid out every word of the Rashi, one by one, like a row of stones beside a riverbank. They shone in the sun of her articulateness. The concepts they held sprouted wings of their own and became airborne. They should have flown, under Sara's coaxing, directly into every young mind in that room.

But those minds were closed hard against her, against anything she might try to teach them. Sara saw that clearly, even as she wound down her discussion. Helpless, she gazed into the empty eyes and concealed smirks of her students — and especially of Simi Davidson, her nemesis. And, as she did, something finally snapped.

Her anxiety about Mordy, her compassion for Yael, and her respect for herself converged in one heady rush of emotion. This was not what she had contracted for! She was a teacher, and a fine one. She was *not* Public Enemy Number One. She did not deserve what these foolish girls were dishing out — and, what's more, she had too much on her mind at the moment to swallow it a minute longer.

In a world where terrible things could happen to people — and *were* happening, that very moment, to people she was beginning to care about — she had no patience for the kind of behavior these girls were bent on doling out. It was a world where a beloved wife and mother could be bounced across a slippery highway like a fragment of paper and, like paper, plucked from her family on a sudden, cruel wind. A world where little boys and girls became, in an instant, bewildered orphans. A world where a happily engaged young woman could find disillusionment in the very place where she had looked for contentment and security. A world where young boys became prey to evil-minded criminals.

A reckless anger took hold of Sara. Frankly, at the moment, she did not care if she lost her job. She — just — did not — care! After all these weeks, she had enough of cringing and cowering, of trying to win the approval of a bunch of ill-mannered youngsters who were not about to give it to her, no matter how hard she tried.

She was going to tell them exactly what she thought of them.

Very gently, she laid her pen down on the desk. She moved around the front of it to stand directly before her class, the way she had stood when delivering her welcoming talk on the first day of school. Several front-row girls blinked nervously at this sudden proximity. Others — notably Simi and her pals at the back — challenged her with bold stares. Sara stared right back.

"There are some of you," she said flatly, "who are apparently determined not to learn a thing in my class this year. I don't know exactly what you hope to gain from this. Perhaps, if you bring home terrible grades, you think you can convince your parents, or the principal, that I am inept as a teacher. Maybe that's your goal. I don't know.

"But let me tell you this, girls: *It won't work.* Rebbetzin Goodman knows about my ten long years of experience. She knows about a certain difficult student I had last year, a student who just barely missed being asked to leave my old school because of her atrocious behavior. And she knows about the way certain members of this class are determined to capitalize on what they see as my vulnerability."

There was not a sound in the classroom. Not the shuffling of a single foot, nor the scrape of a single pencil, marred the absolute silence. Sara had faced silence in this classroom before — too much of it — but this silence had a different quality. The girls were finally listening.

"Let me set you straight," she said, looking directly into Simi Davidson's face. "It's not I who is on probation here. It's you. It's you who are called upon to learn, just as I am called upon to teach. Rebbetzin Goodman knows, and she will tell your parents, that I am a very capable teacher who has a great deal to offer this class. Unfortunately, this year she would be hard put to say the same about you as students. Not so far, at any rate.

"Now, here is my last word on this subject. You have a choice.

"You can choose to come along with me on the adventure of learning — to learn, to respond, to help me make the lessons interesting and challenging. To *succeed*. Or you can choose the opposite. Which course you choose makes no difference to me. But it will make a very, very great difference to each of you."

She swept the class with her steady gaze, holding some pairs of eyes a little longer than others. Most of the eyes dropped under her scrutiny. In seconds, the bell would ring to release them from the tension of their little drama. Sara continued, "Class is nearly over. I am willing to overlook what happened here today — in return for a completely different attitude from you. Starting tomorrow."

As the clamorous ringing filled the room, she rounded her desk again and took her seat. With lowered head, she began industriously sorting her papers as though it were a matter of supreme indifference to her whether or not anyone were watching. She heard the stamping of feet toward the door, and the low murmur of voices. Presently, a tentative throat-clearing made her raise her head.

She looked up. The classroom had largely emptied, but a small delegation stood by her desk — a bright girl by the name of Matti Rheinbacher at their head. Matti had straight brown hair that just touched her shoulders, and deeply set gray eyes under thick dark brows.

"Yes, Matti?" Sara said, trying to disguise the weariness she felt.

"Morah, we wanted to say that we liked the speech you gave just now. It was great! And — we're sorry."

A melting came to Sara, like the rush of liquefied snow that runs headlong down the mountains in spring. She smiled at the girl with a heartfelt gladness she took no trouble to conceal. "Does this mean that we'll see a change tomorrow?"

In ragged unison, the girls bobbed their heads. Matti said, "We can't promise for the others, but most of the class feels as bad as we do. I know they do; I heard them say so as they were leaving just now."

Sara smiled again. "I'm not surprised." Lowering her voice conspiratorially, she said, "Shall I tell you a secret?"

"What?" Matti edged closer, with the others pressing up behind her.

"Remember when I said that it makes no difference to me what you choose? Well, I didn't really mean that. It matters a whole lot to me. I want you to succeed." She paused. "I want *us* to succeed — together."

Shyly, the girls smiled back. Someone from the back of the small group said indignantly, "It's that old Simi and her friends. They run everything around here."

"Not anymore, they don't," Matti said with spirit.

Sara nodded firmly. "That's right. Not anymore."

She smiled a final time, in recognition of the delegation's gallantry and her own triumph. Then she dismissed them with a warm, "See you tomorrow, girls."

"See you, Morah."

"'Bye."

"See you."

Sara watched them go. When the door closed behind them, she lifted her eyes skyward and whispered, "Thank You." Then she heaved a long, protracted sigh, as though clearing the palate of her mind between courses.

Slowly, she pulled out her trusty *Tehillim*. She was going to *daven* with all her heart for Mordy's safe return home.

And after that, if she hurried, there would be just enough time to grab her lunch, hurry to the teachers' room, and fill in her friend Faygie on the morning's events.

It would be an edited version, of course — beginning just after the early-morning call she was not permitted to share with anyone yet.

Two hundred miles away, in Lincolntown, Pennsylvania, four detectives completed their surveillance of a modest post office and re-entered their car. No one had noticed their arrival, and no one noticed when they left town again, headed west for the nearest camping ground.

68

Once again, he was lying down.

This time, it was on a moldy bed whose springs jutted sharply into the small of his back. No matter how much he tried to adjust his position, he could not avoid the discomfort of that hard place. In a way, he was glad. The jutting spring kept him uncomfortable and did not let him fall asleep easily. It kept him alert. And that was the way he had to be, if he ever wanted to get himself out of this awful predicament.

It galled Mordy that, so far, his entire part in the proceedings had taken place in a supine position — first in the back seat of the jeep under a smelly blanket, and now in a lumpy bed in this small cabin in the woods. The kidnapper had tied a blindfold around his eyes for the five-minute walk from the spot where, after a very bumpy road along an unpaved track, he had parked the jeep.

Even after he could not see, he knew that they were in the woods. He recognized the woodsy scents and sounds from all the weeks he had spent at his Bubby Hilda's summer place through the years. There had been a forest there, too, and he had spent a lot of time playing at the outermost edges of it. There was something different about the air in a forest — more oxygen, he guessed. The rustlings and twitterings sounded very close all around him. But the clearest giveaway was the smell: that never-to-be-mistaken compound of moss and fern and bracken and rich, damp earth.

The kidnapper had not removed the blindfold until he had pulled the shades down on the windows of the cabin. Then he had ripped the cloth from Mordy's eyes and hurled a package at the bed, narrowly missing the boy's head. "Here's your dinner."

Mordy's legs were still tied, and his hands were securely fastened to the bedpost. Joey untied one hand so that he could eat, then stepped outside. Mordy could hear him prowling around the perimeter of the cabin like a lion marking his turf. He opened the bag and peered eagerly inside. He was ravenous. He had not tasted a bite since the single bowl of Cheerios (it felt like another lifetime!) in his own kitchen that morning. Hungry as he was, he steeled himself for disappointment: It was too much to hope that the kidnapper had taken the trouble to find him something kosher.

There was not much. Dumping out the contents of the brown paper bag, Mordy found several packets of chips, two chocolate bars, and a stale sandwich — the kind that can be found in vending machines in all fifty states — with some sort of paste filling. Ignoring the sandwich, he studied the packaging on the chips and chocolate, and found to his delight that two of the snack bags and one of the candy bars bore the OU symbol.

He was tempted to devour the simple repast, but forced himself to eat slowly. With an effort, he stopped himself halfway through the second snack bar, rewrapped it, and stuck it in his pocket against future emergencies. He recited the after-blessing. Then, his frugal meal over, he set himself to thinking about his situation.

He was lying on a lumpy bed in a cabin in the woods, though exactly which woods remained a mystery. By consulting his wristwatch, he calculated that the trip here — wherever "here" was — had taken them just under three-and-a-half hours. They might be in Virginia, or in Pennsylvania; he could not know for sure until he knew which direction the jeep had taken.

But did it really matter? What was important was not how he had arrived here, but how he was going to leave. He tested the strength of the ropes that bound him, and found them depressingly healthy. The knots, too, looked like a professional job. Did the guy do this for a living — go around snatching kids for ransom? Or *was* it ransom that he was after? Mordy was not sure. He had caught a glitter in the man's eyes once or twice that spoke of more than simple greed. There was something deeper and blacker there — something like hatred. It took Mordy's breath away, to be hated like that. And he did not even know what he had done to deserve it.

Joey came back to the bed, retied Mordy's free hand, and said, "I'm going out." He passed through the door again, closing and locking it behind him.

In the little cabin, utter silence reigned. The loneliness, and the terror, settled over Mordy's shoulders like a heavy woolen cloak. He tried to think, but the gears of his mind had turned to rust. He closed his eyes to blot out the room, and fell into an unexpected doze.

Two hours after he had left, the kidnapper returned. Mordy had been awake for the last thirty minutes of that time. Through the drawn shades, he noted the quiet fading of the day. One of the windows faced west, and he saw the shade turn rosy with the last rays of the setting sun. It was the after-dinner hour, the time for being at home with family, for hearing loved ones' voices bubbling in the background. In Mordy's case, it would have been the time to be close to his computer, but the principle was the same. Nightfall was the time to head for home. Mordy felt the rise and sting of unwilling tears. He blinked them away before his captor could see them, and mock him for the coward he was.

Mordy cleared his throat. "Excuse me, uh, sir," he said.

"What?" For an instant, the man looked as though he might burst into laughter. "Did you call me 'sir'?" As quickly as it had come, the impulse to laugh vanished and the scarred face darkened again. He snapped, "Call me Joey. Everyone else does. Well, what do you want?"

"I-I need to go."

"What?"

"I need to go. It's been hours —"

Comprehension dawned. Joey hesitated, then went over to the bed and undid the knots that kept Mordy tied to the bedpost, leaving his wrists loosely bound but maneuverable. He motioned for the boy to wriggle into a standing position by the bed — no easy feat with his legs still tied together. With his gun trained on the boy, he said, "Now bend down and untie your feet. Remember, no funny moves, or there'll be a bullet in here with your name on it."

"I won't," Mordy promised, bending painfully; every part of him ached after hours of lying stiff. After a few false starts, he managed to fumble the knots open and release his legs.

"Now walk," the man commanded. With the gun, he gestured at the door.

Mordy did as he was told. Outside, Mordy filled his lungs gratefully with the cool, pine-scented air — the atmosphere in the cabin, with the door and all the windows shut tight, had been very close — and walked obediently, at his captor's direction, around the side of the cabin to the rear. A tiny outhouse stood there.

Joe motioned Mordy back. With the gun still pointed at the boy, he walked over to the sagging structure and inspected it, inside and out. Mordy could have tried to make a break then, but he was not certain if his numbed legs were yet capable of running. Besides, he was afraid of the gun. The kidnapper's eyes flicked back and forth constantly, to the outhouse and Mordy and back again. At last, he stepped away from the door.

"You have five minutes," he growled, gesturing once more with his gun. "I wouldn't bother locking it if I were you. But it don't matter either way. If you don't come out when I call you, I'll blow this thing apart first — and then you."

On this cheery note, he moved aside and let Mordy into the outhouse.

Five minutes can be a long time. It was enough time for Mordy to do what he came in here for and to thoroughly check out the tiny place. It was not much more than a hole in the ground, but it did have four walls and someone had once tried to give it a window. The glass was long gone, the rectangular opening papered over.

The glass was gone — all except for a triangle-shaped sliver in one corner of the window frame. Moving in for a closer look, Mordy's breath caught in his throat. Excitement sent the blood rushing into his head and made his ears ring like a dozen alarm clocks going all at once. Carefully, very carefully, he lifted his loosely bound wrists and scraped one edge of the thick rope against the broken glass.

When he brought his wrists away, there was a faint but definite dent in the rope. Tiny, torn edges of individual strands stood out from its surface, undetectable except on close scrutiny. He had time for a few more sawing motions, frantic with haste, before he heard footsteps outside.

"Hey, kid! Time's up!"

Mordy came out. The rope was still intact, but perhaps an eighth of an inch of it had parted into frayed threads. His heart was pounding so loudly that he found it hard to believe that his captor could not hear it.

Joey followed him into the cabin and pointed the gun at the bed. Without being told, Mordy climbed on and submitted to being tied up again. His spine greeted the jutting spring almost as an old friend. Gradually, his heart resumed its normal beat.

Having disposed of Mordy, Joey settled in for the night. He ate a little and — after checking that the boy's knots were secure — slept a little. Mordy slept, too. But several times through that long, cold night, he awoke shivering. The shivers were due in part to the autumn frost high in the mountain woods, for which the single blanket he had been supplied was hardly any protection.

But the cold was only part of it. He shivered with fear, as he remembered the look in the man's eyes whenever they rested on him. And he shivered, too, with the sheer, heady thrill of knowing that another trip or two to the outhouse in back of the cabin would be enough to release him from the bonds that held him captive.

Sara heard the last bell of the day with genuine relief.

Hour by hour, the level of her internal stress had increased like the buildup inside a volcano, until she knew she would explode if she did not find out if there was any word about Mordy. For discretion's sake, she decided against phoning from school. She would get Yael over to the apartment, serve her a snack, get her started on her homework or listening to music, and then retreat to her bedroom to make the call.

Leaving the building, she restrained herself — barely — from running to the parking lot. A determinedly sedate walk brought her to the car. She unlocked it, slipped inside, turned up the heat against the crisp late-afternoon air, and waited.

And waited. Streams of girls poured out of the building, talking and laughing together before parting and climbing into the cars that pulled continually in and out of the parking lot. Two teachers stood at the lot's entrance and exit, guiding traffic. It was the usual after-school scene of carefully controlled mayhem. For Sara, there was only one disturbing note. Where was Yael?

Craning her neck to see past the milling figures, she caught a glimpse of Tzippy who, she knew, was a close friend of Yael's. She was on the verge of calling out when she thought better of it. No point in alerting others to the fact that Yael was coming home with her. Hopefully, the situation would stabilize itself very shortly, and Yael's life would return to normal. After that, it would be up to Yael herself to decide whether or not to confide in her friends. Sara's own lips were sealed.

Still no sign of Yael. As the lot emptied, Sara began to worry in earnest. She locked the car again and ran back to the school building. With the human equivalent of the screech of brakes, she pulled up in front of the office window and asked breathlessly, "Has anyone left a message for me?"

The secretary, a round-faced woman with small glasses and a perky short wig, looked up in mild surprise. "Nope," she said. "Are you expecting one?"

"I *thought* I was driving a student home, but there seems to be a mixup. Yael Newman?"

The secretary shook her head. "I don't know anything about it. Sorry, Sara."

"So am I," Sara muttered under her breath. She turned and made her way outside again.

There were now no more than two or three cars left on the school premises. Dusk had fallen; the cars' headlights cut long slashes of white through the settling night. As she moved toward her car, panic fluttered through her with the beating of powerful wings. She had been given a responsibility, an awesome one, and already — just one day into her guardianship — she had lost track of her charge. She hesitated, thinking of the phones back in the building, then decided not to retrace her steps. She broke into a run instead.

Quickly unlocking her car door, she got in and started it up. Sara pulled out of the parking lot to begin the short drive to the Newman house.

The door was opened by a muscular Hispanic man who eyed her in a way that definitely discouraged visitors. "Yeah?"

"Is Mr. — is Judge Newman home?"

"Who wants to know?"

Anger, fueled by anxiety, flared up. "Who are you to ask that — the new butler?"

An appreciative grin flashed across the olive face. He answered,

"Police, ma'am. What's your business with the Newmans, please?"

"I'm the daughter's piano teacher."

The man's eyes flickered to a spot just out of sight to his left, then returned to Sara. "I don't think there'll be any piano lessons today." He started to close the door.

She threw out a hand to stop it from shutting in her face. "Wait! Where is Mr. Newman? I need to talk to him. It's urgent!"

"Who is it, Luis?" a voice called from inside.

"Some lady, says she's the piano teacher."

Footsteps sounded across the parquet floor. Daniel came into view. With a shrug, the detective moved away. It was only then that Sara saw a smaller figure standing beside the judge. She gasped.

"Yael! Oh, Yael, I'm so glad to see you! When you didn't show up at the car, I thought —" Sara bit her lip. Involuntarily, she stepped forward, arms outstretched.

Yael lunged forward, right into Sara's arms. The woman hugged the girl tightly. "Why didn't you let me know you were going home?" she whispered, her anger dissipated completely in the immensity of her relief.

"I was afraid you'd say I couldn't come. But I *had* to come, Miss Muller. I needed to be with Daddy — and I thought that, maybe, he needed to be with me." Yael raised red-rimmed eyes to Sara. "And he does, Miss Muller! He does need me!"

Sara looked questioningly at Daniel, who nodded tiredly. "I just told her."

Before he could say another word, the phone shrilled insistently behind him. He held the door open wider, saying, "Come in, come in. I'll just get that. It may be the police. They promised to report."

With an uncertain smile at Mendez, still standing sentinel by the door, Sara walked into the house. She drew Yael down onto the couch beside her, an arm around the girl. Silently, they both watched Daniel pick up the phone.

As he listened, his face stilled, then hardened.

Mendez moved past Sara in a swift, graceful glide. "It's *him*," he said between his teeth. "Too late to pick up the other line . . ."

Then he fell silent, eyes riveted on Daniel and ears pitched so as not to miss a word.

69

The conversation was over almost before it had begun. The kidnapper was obviously afraid that the call would be traced if he spoke too long. Daniel hung up, ashen and trembling, and turned to Mendez.

"He wants the million by the end of the business day tomorrow. 5 o'clock, he said."

"Where?" Mendez asked.

"A town called Stanton, in Pennsylvania. He says it's about two hours north of Baltimore. He wants me to leave the money, in a briefcase, under a certain bench in a park. He'll call again at noon tomorrow with details." Daniel swallowed. "He warned me not to bring any cops along, or Mordy would suffer."

Yael moaned softly, clutching at Sara's hand. With her free hand, Sara smoothed the girl's hair. It was a meaningless gesture, but it seemed to comfort Yael a little.

"Stanton?" Mendez rushed to the dining-room table and bent over the large map of Pennsylvania that lay there. The team had used it to plan out their route to Lincolntown early that morning. He studied the map for a moment, then jabbed a triumphant finger on the spot. "Here it is! Just a bit south of Lincolntown. About an hour's drive, I'd say — maybe less."

"It's clear he doesn't want to bring Mr. Newman into Lincolntown itself," Jake spoke up.

Sara turned her head to look at him curiously. She had noticed Jake soon after her arrival, seated quietly in an armchair with a worn

Tehillim in hand, and had wondered what part he played in this crazy drama. They had first met when he had come to the house while she was giving Yael her piano lesson. The second meeting had been just yesterday, when Jake had dropped Yael's clothes off at Sara's apartment.

The law student continued, thinking aloud: "Wherever he's got Mordy, he figures it's safe to leave him alone for a couple of hours. One hour to drive into Stanton, a few minutes to make the pickup, an hour back."

"He's done it before," Mendez remarked. "He had to have left Mordy stashed somewhere when he made the arrangements at the post office. I doubt that he walked in with a gun in the kid's back."

Daniel fought to push aside the image the detective's words had conjured: Mordy trussed like a chicken in some dark, dank hide-away — Mordy scared and helpless, wondering why his Daddy was not there to help him — He clenched his fists. "I wish Mark would call! The last time I heard from him was at midday, when he said they were going to check out the local post office branches and then look into camping sites in the area. Not a word since."

"Means they've been busy," Mendez said dismissively. "He'll call. Meanwhile, let's talk about the ransom money. In the worst-case scenario — if tomorrow's plan flops and they don't get their man — do you think you can raise the cash by, say, 3 tomorrow after-noon?"

Grimly, Daniel said, "I hope so. I'd have to get on it right away, though." He glanced worriedly at the telephone. "It's already past banking hours. I hope I can arrange it all in the morning."

"Try persuading the kidnapper to give you one more day," Mendez advised. "He'll bluff and bluster, but remember: He wants that money. If you can convince him that the deal is in the works and you just need one more business day to wrap it up, my guess is he'll capitulate." He thought a moment, then added, "And ask your lawyer to make the arrangements for you. Less stressful for you that way."

"I will," Daniel said gratefully. "Good idea." He went to fetch his telephone book, and a moment later was in the kitchen, dialing his lawyer's number.

"I left a message," he said, returning to the group in the living room. "He's supposed to be calling me back soon. In the meantime —"

They never got to hear what he proposed that they do in the meantime. From the study down the hall there was a sudden beeping, then a whirring.

"The fax machine," Daniel said. He hesitated. "It's probably not connected to any of this, but I'll go check. Just in case —" Yael's eyes followed her father down the short hall to his study. She was still holding Sara's hand, having seemingly forgotten to take her own back. Sara found she did not mind at all.

When Daniel returned, he was walking very slowly, head bent to study the thin fax paper in his hand. One end kept persistently curling up, and he smoothed it down impatiently for a closer look. The other four watched with mounting curiosity until he had reached the entrance to the living room. Still Daniel did not say a word or lift his head. He merely took advantage of the increased light in the living room to examine the page more closely.

It was Yael, finally, who burst out, "What is it, Daddy? Does it have anything to do with Mordy?"

Daniel looked up. His eyes held a vacant look, as though they were seeing something other than what was before them — or trying to. He shook his head. "I don't remember —"

"What?"

Daniel seemed to suddenly become aware that he had an audience. He grinned sheepishly. "Sorry, I was trying to remember if I'd ever seen a face before." He held out the fax. "*This* face. It came in from the police station just now. Before he left, Mark asked them to look up Joe Mercutio, see if he has a record. This is what they came up with."

"What kind of record?" Mendez asked, walking over to take the fax from him. He skimmed the page, then answered his own question. "Petty larceny, joyriding, breaking and entering. Two indictments, one conviction, eight months in and out of prison." He studied the accompanying picture. "Nasty-looking scar," he commented.

"May I?" Jake held out his hand. Mendez handed the fax to him. Jake ran his eyes down the page, then politely passed it on to Sara and Yael. Yael took one look at the kidnapper's face and averted her eyes, shuddering. Sara read the fax thoroughly, top to bottom. Then she looked at the picture.

Her gasp filled the room, cutting sharply into Daniel's thoughts and into the low-voiced talk Jake and Mendez had been having.

Yael said in alarm, "Miss Muller? What's wrong?"

Sara looked at Daniel, white faced. "That man —"

"What about him?"

She took a deep breath to steady herself. Instead of directly addressing Daniel, she asked Yael, "Do you remember when we drove down a certain street in Baltimore, and you said you used to live on that block?"

Mutely, Yael nodded. Her eyes looked as large as saucers in the pinched, frightened face.

"And remember that I said I used to know people on that block?" Without waiting for the nod this time, Sara turned to Daniel and said in a rush, "Five years ago, I was engaged to a boy who lived on that block. On the night we — broke our engagement — I was out on the street very late. It was a foggy night, and I was looking for my car. I was running —"

She seemed to run out of steam. Daniel, clearly bewildered, said, "Yes? You were running —"

"I was crying, too. I didn't really watch where I was going. All I wanted to do was find my car and get away — Go home. And then, as I was passing under a streetlight, someone ran out of a driveway and nearly bumped into me. He was wearing overalls and a baseball cap, and he had a long ugly scar down one side of his face."

"Are you saying this is the same guy?" Mendez demanded. He looked skeptical.

Sara nodded. "Yes, that's the one. I'm sure of it. I was able to get a good look at him. And later, when I got home, I remember that I found an oily stain on my blouse. Black oil. I never did manage to get it out." For an instant, her face creased in pain, as though the weight of that night still had the ability to hurt her. Then it cleared, and she repeated to Daniel, "That's him."

The blood had drained completely from Daniel's face. On unsteady feet he walked over to the couch and sat shakily on Yael's other side. Leaning forward to see past his daughter, he asked, "The date, Miss Muller? Do you remember the date?"

Sara's look was half-amused, half-reproachful. Does a person forget the date she buried all her hopes of happiness? "It was October 7th, Mr. Newman. A Sunday night, about a week after Sukkos."

Daniel closed his eyes. His wife's accident had taken place on the morning of Monday, October 8th.

It took some time to bring Mendez and Jake up to date on the significance of Sara's revelation.

"My wife's death *was* no accident," Daniel said, in control of himself now, still pale but composed. "Just as the letter-writer — the kidnapper — said. And he ought to know. He's the one who was responsible for it!"

"Do you think he tampered with the brakes?" Jake asked.

"Maybe. My car was parked in the driveway that night, I remember that clearly. He did something to it, hoping to have his revenge against me for putting his brother in jail. But Ella borrowed my car the next morning. She was the one who tried to brake but found she couldn't. She was the one who skidded across the highway in the rain instead of me."

Yael snuggled closer to her father, her head on his shoulder and his arm around her. It was hard to tell who was comforting whom. Yael's memory of her mother was vague, and tempered by time. It was her father whose pain she felt so strongly now — the father who had struggled alone for five devoted years to raise Yael and her brother, and who had just seen his beloved only son snatched away from under his nose. Later, perhaps, she would weep again for her mother, and the evil that had so abruptly and tragically ended her young life. Later, she might even shed a few tears for herself. Right now, her concern was all for Daniel.

"It's not your fault, Daddy," she whispered.

He tried to smile. "I know. I've worked at trying to know it for the past five years. But that doesn't necessarily stop it from hurting."

"I understand." All at once, Yael sounded far older and wiser than her years. Sara's heart pinched painfully with sorrow and with affection for the girl, so valiant in her own loss, so filled with love for her father. She saw Daniel's arm tighten around his daughter's shoulder — and then suddenly lift away as he shot to his feet.

"Mark! He doesn't know what Mercutio looks like. We have to get this picture over to him right away, Mendez!"

The detective shook his head. "I don't have a fax number that will reach him over there in Lincolntown. If he calls in and gives me one, we can send it. Though how much a twice-faxed picture will help is anybody's guess."

"We can do better than that," Sara said suddenly.

Heads swiveled in surprise at the sound of her voice. Mendez said, "What do you mean?"

"I'm the only one here who's seen the man face to face. You say the police are hoping to spot him when he visits his post office box in the morning? Then I propose to go up to — Lincolntown, is it? — and point Mercutio out for them."

"You can't do that," Daniel said quickly. "It's too dangerous."

"Why? He'll never remember me or recognize me. To him, I was just a blur in the dark, five long years ago. I hardly think he saw me at all. But if it'll make you feel any better, I'll stay out of sight."

"It's not a bad idea," Mendez said. He eyed Sara thoughtfully, as though measuring her ability to keep her head in a crisis. What he saw must have reassured him, because he said, "I'm going to try to contact Mark and ask him what he thinks."

"It's a *very* bad idea!" Daniel exploded. "I won't have Miss Muller getting involved in this mess. There's no reason in the world for her to put herself in danger. I've seen the picture. *I'll* go up there!"

"You're staying right here," the detective told him flatly. "You're expecting another call from the kidnapper, remember? If he calls and you're not around, he'll be out of Lincolntown so fast your head'll spin. And we'll have blown our best chance of getting our hands on him — *and* the kid."

"Mordy," Yael whispered.

"I'm going," Sara said firmly.

Unexpectedly, Jake said, "I'll drive up with you, if you want."

Sara was surprised. She started to object, then realized that she had no desire in the world to drive alone, for hours, with the prospect of coming face to face with a hardened criminal at the end of it. So she simply inclined her head and said, "Thank you."

"I appreciate the offer, Jake," Daniel said, "but the same objection applies to you. There's no reason for you to walk into danger. I don't —"

"If — *when* — the police find Mordy, it would be nice if he saw a familiar face, wouldn't it?" Jake said. "Mordy doesn't know me well, but I have had dinner here once or twice. He seemed to like me."

"Of course he liked you!" Yael said eagerly. "It's a great idea. I wish I could come along, too." She seemed on the point of requesting permission to do so; a decided glare from her father made her quickly change her mind.

Daniel was still arguing about the matter as Mendez punched in Garrity's cell phone number. The detective held up a hand for silence, then said into the phone, "Mark? Luis here. Any developments?" He listened a moment, then shook his head. "No luck, huh? Too bad . . . I know. Well, listen to this. The station house just faxed over a picture of this Mercutio character, and guess what? It just so happens that we have a lady here who claims she's seen him before, face to face . . . . Yeah, it's a long story. The point is, she wants to go up to Lincolntown to help with the stakeout. She'll point the guy out for you, so there'll be no mistakes. What do you think?"

A few minutes later, he hung up. Daniel glared at him. "You didn't say a word about my objection to this ridiculous plan!"

"I'm sorry, Mr. Newman, but this is police business."

"It's *my* business. It's my son!"

"Sure. But *we* decide what's best for your son. And Mark Garrity thinks it best for the piano teacher to go up there. He had no problem with Jake here going along with her, but asked me to remind them both to stay strictly out of sight." He gave Sara a slip of paper, on which he had scribbled something during the course of the call. "This is the name and address of the post-office branch where the stakeout's taking place. You meet Mark and the others in the parking lot at 8:15. He'll give you your instructions then." Sara nodded.

Jake looked at Sara. "We have two choices. Leave this evening and stay in Lincolntown overnight — or set out at the crack of dawn. Your choice."

"Crack of dawn," Sara said promptly.

"This is ridiculous!" Daniel almost shouted. "Miss Muller, I very much appreciate your concern, but you have absolutely no reason to involve yourself in my problems. I forbid you to risk your life on my behalf!"

Sara looked him steadily in the eye. "With all due respect, Mr. Newman, I am not risking anything on your behalf. This is for Mordy."

Yael gulped loudly, then twisted around on the couch and threw herself at Sara. As the woman's arms encircled and enfolded his daughter, Daniel found his vision suddenly obscured. There was a mist in front of them — a mist of tears. They had nothing to do, this time, with his missing son. When the mist cleared, he had a moment of stunning clarity — a moment that few people ever experience, but never forget when we do. A moment when the future unfolds before us like a play on a stage. The glimpse made him catch his breath.

But Sara was waiting for his answer. He forced himself to speak evenly. He hardly knew what he was saying and could not have quoted a single word afterwards, but Sara took it as acquiescence. Over Yael's head, she said, "Thank you, Mr. Newman." Very low, she added, "If I can do anything, even the tiniest thing, to help bring Mordy back, that's all I want."

She left soon after that, with Mendez's slip of paper tucked securely into the zipper compartment of her purse. Her farewell to Yael was tender. She arranged with Jake to pick him up in her car at 4 a.m. The prospect of a severely curtailed night's sleep did not trouble her in the least: She doubted she would close her eyes much that night in any case.

70

The ride through the predawn darkness was pleasant — or would have been, had their goal been any less grim. At that hour, the roads were virtually empty. The sky, which had started out clear, gradually grew overcast, clogged with thick woolly clouds that obscured the moon and blocked out the stars.

Jake volunteered to take the wheel. He proved a competent driver and an easy conversationalist. Their mutual worry, and the high-risk adventure they were embarked on together, made confidences flow freely. Sara was a little surprised to learn that he was all of 26; in the Newman living room he had seemed much younger. With some adroit probing in the course of the three-and-a-half hour drive — and without making him suspect for a moment that he was undergoing an interview — Sara learned quite a bit about Jake's past, his present, and his aspirations for the future. Jake learned considerably less about Sara, but enough to engender the beginnings of a genuine sense of respect.

From time to time, the talk touched on Daniel. Sara could not help but notice the hero worship in the young man's tone whenever he spoke of the judge. By mutual consent, they steered clear of the reason for their drive. Both had poured their hearts out in prayer before they set out; now, as they moved inexorably toward their destination, it was easier to lock fear away in the trunk, out of sight. For the duration of the journey, Mordy was an untouchable topic.

Sara was, inexplicably, in a mood that might almost be called exhilarated. Though she did not quite see it, there was a sound reason for this. The best medicine for what ailed her was to step out of her world of isolation and self-pity, and what better way to do that than by extending a hand to help someone else? Judge Newman was the last person she would have thought she could ever help — but here she was, riding through the night on her errand of mercy. She might succeed in having some impact on Mordy's predicament and she might not — but she was trying. Her prayers that day were for someone other than herself. She had crossed a boundary into a territory in which self-absorption had no place. And so, in the midst of her very real anxiety, she was — exhilarated!

They reached the outskirts of Lincolntown at twenty minutes to 8.

It was an uninspiring town, although — in keeping with a recent face-lift in the Poconos in general — a cared-for one. Houses were neatly painted and the streets were clean. The sky had turned from charcoal to pale gray and stayed that way, windy and threatening. Jake expressed a hope that the rain would hold off. "It'll make it that much harder for us to see the guy clearly."

"I'll know him," Sara said, peering through her window. "Can you pull up there, please?" She pointed to a row of public telephones outside a bank. "I have to make a call. Then we can go directly to the post office."

"We're going to be a little early."

"No problem with that, is there?"

"Sure there is. The longer the wait, the more jangled the nerves. Or are yours made of steel?"

Sara made a face as she stepped out of the car. "No such luck." From her purse, she extracted her calling card.

The sidewalks were deserted. Her call went through with no trouble. "Sara?" a familiar voice said at the other end of the line. "Is that you?"

"Yes, Faygie, it's me. Listen, I can't go into the details right now, but I'm going to have to call in sick today. Or rather, you're going to have to do it for me. Please let them know in the office that I won't be in."

"What's the matter? Are you all right?"

"I'm fine. I'll tell you all about everything when I get ba — Uh, when I come in."

"And when will that be?" Faygie was agog with curiosity. "Is that a

438 / The Judge

bus I hear in the background? Where in the world are you calling from, Sara?"

"Never mind. I promise, I'll tell you all about it at the right time." She paused, eyes sparkling in the early-morning light. Talking to her friend was a note of normalcy in what was going to be as abnormal a day as she had had in a long time. This might be a ridiculous moment for it, but she gave in to an overwhelming urge to add, "And Faygie? When all this is over —" She broke off with a soft laugh.

"What?"

"— have I got a boy for you!"

There was a second trip to the outhouse on Monday morning, before Joey disappeared into town. Sometime during the endless afternoon that followed, Mordy realized that severing the ropes that tied his wrists carried its own dangers. He had to be prepared to run the moment the bonds were fully cut, or his captor would notice and take much better precautions to secure him next time.

So when he was led outside again that evening, he worked frantically to saw through all but the last few threads that held the rope together. He was fairly certain — though not completely so — that a few good yanks would separate those threads when the time came.

Monday night was as long as the previous night had been. The cold was, if anything, more intense — and Mordy's trepidation, now that escape seemed within tantalizing reach, climbed to new heights. With the moon clouded over, the darkness inside the unlighted cabin was total. In his mind's eye, he traced the outlines of its meager furnishings: the rickety wooden table in the center of the room; the "kitchen" along one wall, consisting of one small sink, three cabinets, and four feet of formica countertop; his own bed and the one on the opposite wall where Joey lay snoring. Eyes open in the dark, Mordy wondered again how he had arrived at this place.

To pass the time, he thought about his father and Yael. He even thought about his mother, something he had not done in a while. He was just 7 when she was killed, and the memories had become blurred and soft, like an out-of-focus photograph or the whiff of something sweet in a long-forgotten drawer. But he remembered the feeling he had when he was very small and woke in the night with a bad dream. He would whimper in his bed, not very loud — and she would come. She would always come.

Who would come to his rescue now?

Daybreak found him wide awake and shivering. As the second dawn of his captivity spread in a gray sky, Mordy murmured again the prayer he had been repeating, at intervals, since the nightmare had begun:

"Hashem, if I've done something awful to deserve all this, please forgive me. For my father's sake, and my sister's, please help me go home again soon."

Breakfast consisted of more chips and chocolate, washed down with a can of soda. Mordy ached for some real food, though with the way his stomach was churning he doubted he could have kept down anything more substantial. He waited tensely for a sign that his captor was getting ready to leave.

It came at 8:10.

"I'm going out," Joey said, as he held open the door. A blast of cold air, maliciously gleeful, swept through the unheated cabin. Under his thin blanket Mordy shivered uncontrollably.

Joey was different this morning. The kidnapper seemed caught in the grip of an inner excitement that made his eyes glitter even more intensely — and that impelled him to talk. "This is it, kid. I've waited a long time for this."

The black eyes rested on Mordy with the indefinable look the boy had come to dread — as if he were a bug to be crushed under a heel, or a wild animal ripe for the hunter's rifle. Certainly not as a human being deserving of the slightest shred of respect or compassion. Mordy clenched his fists, still tied together and then attached by a second rope to one of the iron bedposts. "What's going to happen?" he asked hoarsely.

Joey's laughter was harsh. "Believe me, kid — you don't want to know. But I will tell you this: I plan to have a nice chat with your Dad today. A very *profitable* chat."

The door slammed shut behind him.

Mordy stared at it, willing himself to relax. A "profitable" chat? That must mean that some ransom money was going to change hands.

That was good news for him, wasn't it? With the kidnapper's greed satisfied, Mordy might find himself freed as early as this very day!

But then he remembered the look in the man's eyes, and the harsh laughter that still rang in Mordy's ears. The boy knew that his freedom was not yet what Joey had in mind.

This is it, kid.

Mordy shivered again, and cautiously tested the bonds that still held him prisoner.

At 8:15, the parking lot was nearly empty. Garrity steered the unmarked car into a spot, and nodded with approval as he saw the white Mercury Tracer already there. He and his men stepped out and walked over to it.

"Miss Muller, is it?"

"Yes, I'm Sara Muller. And this is Jake Meisler."

Garrity nodded at Jake. "We've met." Then, to Sara, "I'd like to hear just how you happen to know the man we're after, Miss Muller. Think you can tell it to me in under sixty seconds? That's all the time I can spare at the moment."

Quickly, concisely, Sara told him. Garrity tightened his lips. "A chance meeting that just might serve us well. Now, here's what I want you to do . . . "

His first concern was to remove their cars from the lot, lest the suspect arrive early and become suspicious. They agreed to park far down the block and meet again.

The move made, the four detectives and two civilians huddled under the awning of a pizzeria to lay their plans. When everyone understood his or her role, they separated. Garrity checked his watch. Zero hour was 9 o'clock, when the post office would open its doors.

Already now, at 8:25, employee cars were beginning to drift into the lot. He took up his post near the exit. A quick look around showed Pete Rheims and Lucy Fenwick, positioned at strategic spots near the main post-office doors. Jim Stewart was guarding the back exit, on the off chance that a panicked Mercutio might ram his way through the branch's employees-only area in an escape attempt. Jake and Sara were seated in Sara's car, parked in front of the pizzeria. At the right moment, Sara would move into the post office itself, to try for a clear glimpse of the man they were hunting for.

Garrity checked the sky for signs of incipient rain, then looked again at his watch.

Zero-hour minus twenty-nine.

Never had half an hour crawled by so slowly. Sara and Jake tried talking, then gave up and listened to the local radio station without actually hearing it. Rain was predicted by midmorning but was supposed to give way to sunshine by late afternoon. At five minutes to 9, Sara took a deep breath, let it out, and said, "Okay, this is my cue. See you later, Jake."

None of Jake's confident good cheer was in evidence at the moment. "Good luck," he said soberly. "I'll be waiting here for you."

She nodded, then slipped out. The plan was for her to be among the first customers to enter the post office when it opened its doors. With both hands in the pockets of her lightweight navy jacket for warmth, she walked briskly up the block past the barber shop to the post-office parking lot. Was it her imagination, or had the air grown colder since their conference with the police three-quarters of an hour before?

Probably her imagination, she decided. Fear was a chilly thing.

At one minute to 9, there were three other people waiting in front of the glass doors. As a heavyset guard turned his key in the lock on the other side and swung the door open for them, she glanced casually at her fellow customers' faces. One was a middle-aged woman, the other two, respectively, a stolid businessman and a young, lawyerly type. Neither looked remotely like the person she was searching for. She did not know whether to be relieved or disappointed.

"Mercutio may not be here on the stroke of 9," Garrity had warned. "He could just as easily walk in at noon, or at 4 in the afternoon — or even tomorrow. But we know he's hard up for money and waiting for this check. We're keeping our fingers crossed that he's as eager to get his hands on it as we are to lay hands on *him*."

Sara walked over to a counter where some passport forms lay in readiness. Making a show of searching for a pen and reading the form took her to 9:05. Several more customers walked in: No Joey. She prepared herself for a wait.

Outside, Garrity and the others also waited. They were more patient than Sara in the post office, or Jake in the car down the block. These were experienced professionals, accustomed to a job which consists of more waiting than outsiders might imagine.

Jake found the wait particularly unbearable. After five minutes alone in Sara's car, he was itching for action. At the very least, he would have liked to get out of the car and stretch his legs. And why shouldn't he? He had promised Garrity not to enter the parking lot, but he could just as easily wait for Sara outside the car as in. He switched off the ignition, pocketed the key, and stepped outside. To passers-by, he presented the picture of a bored young man lounging by his car, waiting for a tardy someone — wife? co-worker? — to join him.

To Joey Mercutio, strolling up the block toward the post office, he looked — familiar.

Joey had parked a block away, electing for caution's sake to approach the post office on foot. He stopped now, just short of the pizzeria, wrinkling his brow in an effort to concentrate. He had seen that face somewhere — he *knew* he had. But where?

He started walking again, averting his head slightly as he passed the auburn-haired guy leaning on his car. The guy wore a baseball cap similar to his own, but it was not the cap that rang a bell, it was the face. He thought he had seen that car before, too, though not with the guy. Joey had a good memory for faces, and an even better one for cars. The puzzle teased him with every step. He walked more slowly, racking his brain.

It was not until he was within a few yards of the post office that he stopped short a second time, the hair on the back of his head pricking as though from an electric shock. He remembered.

He had seen both the face and the car in the same place, though at different times, and he had seen them through his own binoculars, outside the Newman house.

How, he wondered with racing heart, could anyone have followed him here? No one knew he was here. No one except — Vinny. But how in the world could Newman have connected him to Vinny? The questions knocked about his head, seeking answers that were not there. Joey took another step forward and then, without breaking stride, swerved around to cross the street.

The sudden movement caught Garrity's attention. Instinctively, he moved away from the parking-lot entrance for a glimpse of the man's face — or whatever he could see of it beneath the baseball cap pulled low over his forehead. As Joey, at the curb, glanced to the left to check for oncoming cars, Garrity got a clear look at his profile.

There it was: the jagged white scar running from eye to mouth down his left cheek.

Eyes on the man as he sauntered across the street, Garrity spoke, quietly and urgently, into his radio. "Suspect crossing the street. Meet me at the car, pronto!"

Seeing Garrity standing at the curb, Jake came running over. "What happened?" he asked breathlessly.

"Something may have tipped him off that we're here — or else he's just remembered something he forgot back home. He was about to enter the lot when he stopped and crossed the street instead."

"I know," Jake nodded. "He passed right by me."

Garrity looked at him in sudden suspicion. "Did he see you?"

Uncomfortable, Jake said, "Uh, I suppose so."

"Were you inside the car?"

"No, outside. Why?"

Garrity groaned. The suspect was still walking slowly, making his way down the block at a pace that would not excite undue curiosity. It stood to reason that he had a car parked somewhere nearby. Waiting for his colleagues to join him, Garrity snapped, "Has it ever occurred to you that the guy was spying on the judge for a long time before he made his move? You've visited the judge before, I gather?"

Dumbly, Jake nodded.

"So he recognized you. *That's* what tipped him off." For a moment, Garrity appeared ready to explode with frustration and anger. Then, with visible effort at control, he said, "It was a mistake to let you *or* the Muller woman up here. Get out of sight now, and *stay that way!*"

Fenwick, Stewart, and Rheims came running up. Without a word, all four sprinted to their car and opened the doors. Garrity motioned for Stewart to take the wheel. Stewart turned the ignition key, put the car in gear, and pulled away at a slow cruise. He reached the corner just as the suspect entered a dirty white jeep. Seconds later, the jeep swung into the street. Jim Stewart gunned his own motor discreetly, and followed.

Bemused, Jake stood looking after them for all of ten seconds. Then he ran up the steps to the post office and made for Sara, now on her third passport form.

"Hurry — he got away!" he hissed. He beckoned urgently, then ran back out the door, feeling his back impaled by the curious glances of men and women waiting in line. Sara dropped the forms and ran outside after him.

A short dash down the block and they were back in her car, Jake behind the wheel. He stuck the key into the ignition and turned it jerkily, peering into the distance where the two cars had disappeared.

"They went thataway," he gasped, and started off in pursuit.

Joey Mercutio reached the cabin at a breakneck run. He did not know how he had been betrayed, but the fact was that Lincolntown was over for him. Time to grab the kid and get out of there — fast! Breathing heavily, he pushed open the door and lunged over to the bed by the far wall.

It was empty.

And so, he saw with one wild, swift sweep of the room, was the cabin.

His captive had flown.

71

The first thing Mordy did upon achieving his freedom was dash out of the cabin and take a deep, swooping breath of fresh air.

The second thing he did was twist his ankle.

He had made the mistake of trying to run, forgetting that a forest floor is far different from kitchen linoleum. Trying to put distance between himself and the cabin as quickly as possible, he stumbled over a hidden root and went sprawling.

Dazed, he picked himself up, throwing an anxious glance over his shoulder. The cabin was still visible through the trees, though barely. Joey might return from town at any moment. Mordy would have to proceed more carefully, while trying to maintain his speed. By the time his kidnapper laid eyes on the cabin again, he wanted to be far, far away.

There was just one problem. It took a few seconds for the significance of what he was feeling to penetrate the fog of his anxiety. *Pain.* Throbbing, intensifying-by-the-minute pain, beginning at his ankle and shooting up his leg. Mordy bit his lip, blinking back tears of frustration. Why did this have to happen now, of all times, when he desperately needed both his legs in good working order?

He tried a step, then another. No good. For one thing, at this rate, he would not get anywhere. And, for another, each step only added to the pain. His ankle, he saw, was swelling fast. He would have to abandon the idea of running and find a secure hiding place instead.

And that might not be such a bad thing, he realized. The last place Joey would think of finding him would be within shouting distance of the cabin where he had been held prisoner for the past two days. While the criminal searched farther afield, Mordy would hunker down, waiting for his chance — To do what, exactly?

To wait. For his ankle to get better. For someone, some benevolent stranger, to pass by. For a miracle.

But first, to get to safety.

Wincing with every step — it felt as though knives were stabbing his foot each time he put it down — the boy made his determined way deeper into the woods. His pace was necessarily tortoiselike, and a full five minutes' effort did not get him very far. He raked the woods for a hollow tree, but the trunks he saw were smooth and unyielding. He would have to try branches. The thought of climbing a tree with the thousand knives in his foot almost made him cry again. Mustering all his resolution and his will to live, he hobbled over to a likely prospect and peered upward.

The tree was tall, and — more important — had not yet been stripped bare of its foliage. The blazing leaves formed an adequate curtain behind which a boy his size might hide — if he could get up there.

"Now, this is going to hurt," he told himself wryly, like a doctor about to inject a small patient. "But when it's over, you'll be safe. So just *do it!*"

He grasped the trunk with both hands, found a toehold with his good foot, and began to climb.

Using both arms and the one leg that was in working order, he inched his way up the trunk like some kind of crippled monkey. His hurt foot dangled as he went, a dead weight. With the single-minded intensity that often overtook him when working out a thorny math or computer problem, he focused on his upward progress. Nothing else in the world mattered at that moment but the need to keep moving, keep rising. When he reached the lowest limb, he pulled himself into a sitting position, parted the curtain of leaves, and looked out. From here he had a clear view of the forest floor below — too clear. He needed to be higher. Stifling a sigh, he steeled himself for another climb.

Ten minutes later, dripping with perspiration and aching abominably in every muscle, he was perched on a sturdy limb some twenty feet above the ground, amply camouflaged by the autumn foliage. His ankle was one screaming mass of agony, but he was pleased. From here, he would be able to see any figure that might approach the tree where he lay hidden. Unless that figure happened to look directly up at him through all the leaves, there was a good chance that Mordy would go unnoticed.

Of course, there was always the possibility that his erstwhile kidnapper, on the lookout for him, would do that very thing. Just what he intended to do if Joey spotted him was something Mordy was still too winded, and in too much pain, to consider. He just prayed that the leaves would keep him well enough concealed so that he could safely ignore that worry for now.

What he would do for food and water, and how he was going to find his way back to civilization with an ankle that refused to support his weight, were some other areas he refused to touch upon at the moment. The important thing was that he had escaped and was out of sight.

For now, that was more than enough.

Joey let out a bellow of rage. How could the kid have escaped? He, Joey, had personally tied those knots, and tied them good and tight. How had the kid got free of them?

But there was no time to unravel the mystery now. Flinging open the door through which he had just come, Joey ran out into the clearing that surrounded the cabin. The special attraction of this place was the privacy it afforded. Though loosely belonging to a common camp-ground, each cabin sat in lonely splendor in its own circle of woods. That had been Joey's prime consideration in choosing to bring his prey here. He had gone camping in this area once, long ago, with some friends from the old neighborhood. Though they had been more interested then in raising a ruckus in boring old Lincolntown than in the beauties of nature, the place had nevertheless stayed in Joey's memory. Miles away from anywhere, he had thought it the perfect cage in which to hold his captured bird.

But now the bird had flown, and he, Joey, was out of luck.

"NO!" He wasn't sure whether or not he had shouted the word aloud, but it reverberated inside him like the clanging of angry bells. He was not about to let this one slip through his fingers! Not after all the waiting, the planning, the tedious spying, and all those stupid, nauseatingly sweet e-mails he had written, letters that still had the power to make him cringe with shame. He was going to find the kid — and when he did, the little monster would wish he had never been born.

Whipping out his gun, he considered his options. The woods lay thick on every side, but from where he stood the walking seemed easiest directly ahead. Then again, the kid might have chosen the hard way, to throw him off the scent. Joey hesitated, then plunged ahead. If he were a kid who had just escaped his kidnapper, he would choose the fastest and easiest way out of there. He was gambling that Mordy had done the same.

He plunged through the woods, scanning the bracken underfoot for evidence that someone had recently passed that way. Not being a skilled woodsman, he was uncertain of the signs to look for. The fallen leaves seemed disturbed in some places, but he had no way of knowing whether that signified anything more interesting than the passage of some lively squirrels. He pushed on.

Twenty feet above his head, Mordy let out his breath in a long, long sigh of relief.

"Keep him in sight," Garrity ordered, "and don't lose him."

Jim Stewart knew the game. This was no high-speed cops-and-robbers chase — at least, not yet. Their first priority was to find Mordy. By following the white jeep circumspectly — and he was being so circumspect that they had nearly lost him twice, so far — they hoped that the suspect would lead them to the boy. Only then would apprehending the kidnapper move to the top of the list.

"He's moving into the camping area," Rheims said excitedly, from the back seat. "You were right, Mark. We must have just missed him yesterday."

"There are a lot of campsites," Garrity said. His tone was laconic, even bored, but his heart was beating fiercely with an urgent prayer that, this time, they would find the right site. As long as the jeep's driver remained unaware of the fact that he was being followed, they had a chance.

The country roads were narrow, choked with woods on either side. On a clearer day, the asphalt would have been sun dappled; this morning, a pessimistic gloom seemed to brood over everything. Garrity tried to shake off the feeling. They were, after all, hard on the heels of the man with the scar. He was going to lead them right to Mordy. This time, the campaign would be brought off successfully — not bungled, the way it had been back at the Lincolntown post office.

Remembering Jake Meisler, he ground his teeth in chagrin. Such a small detail, overlooked, had upset all their careful efforts. The suspect had apparently recognized Jake from his visits to the Newman home. Right now, he must still be uncertain whether this was mere coincidence, or something more sinister. But there had been no signs of police presence at the post office for Mercutio to see. And he was driving now at a reasonable pace, not like a man who knew he had a posse of cops on his tail.

A droning from the road ahead was the first indication that their smooth progress was about to be interrupted. Just as the white jeep passed a modest turnoff, out of it emerged a big, lumbering tractor. The jeep moved ahead, while the tractor took up the road behind it. Like an inescapable fate, it loomed between the detectives and their quarry.

"No room to pass!" Stewart growled, frustrated. He inched up as close to the tractor as he dared, but the farmhand driving it seemed oblivious. Short of forcing the larger vehicle off the road, there was nothing Stewart could do but crawl along behind it. Not daring to honk for fear of alerting Mercutio up ahead, he blinked his lights several times, and was rewarded by the sight of the tractor driver's grin and shrug. The driver pointed at the road ahead, presumably to indicate a spot further on where he could pull off for the car to pass. How far along that spot might be, the police officers had no idea.

Resigned, they followed the tractor down the road at a crawl, and wondered where the jeep was now.

A quarter-hour of fruitless searching through the woods left Joey in an even fouler temper than when he first discovered Mordy's absence. Physical misery had been added to his original fury. The humidity made his clothes feel unpleasantly damp against his skin. He was scratched and tired and, most of all, in need of a drink. He fought his way back to the cabin, with no clearer purpose than to gulp down a beer or two to slake his raging thirst.

He found the cabin still empty. He uttered a bark of derisive laughter, directed at himself: Had he really expected the kid to come sauntering back, all ready to be tied up again? He made straight for the ancient refrigerator in one corner of the "kitchen," popped the top off a can of cold beer, and downed it in three long, cool gulps. A second beer followed the first in quick succession. The third went down more slowly.

It was with the final drops of that third beer that he had his idea. The kid had flown — so what? His father did not know that he was gone. Joey would have to wait a little longer for the chance to eliminate the Newman family; right now, he was eager for the money he could make from them first. Vinny's check, for all the good it was doing him, was sitting in his post-office box back in Lincolntown. Maybe he would try again later today, or else tomorrow, to retrieve it. Seeing that red-haired guy hanging around near the post office had seriously shaken him.

But who cared about a measly five hundred, when he had a million waiting for him in ransom money? He had never intended to return the boy — not alive. The whole purpose of the kidnapping was to extract a cash fee. Why change his plans now?

He pulled out his cell phone and punched in the judge's number. He had made the previous calls from public phone booths in town, but a new recklessness, brought on by Mordy's disappearance and the three beers, made him too impulsive to find one now. Impatient, he listened to the flat, rhythmic sounds that meant the phone was ringing at the other end.

"Yes?"

"Judge, I'm the one who's got your son. Have you got the million I asked for?"

"I'm working on it. You can have it by tomorrow."

Joey's voice hardened. "I said by 5 o'clock today!"

"These things take time. Please, give me a few more hours. By noon tomorrow I should have it all for you. Any earlier is just impossible."

Joey forced himself to relax. What was one more night? He had a roof over his head and the prospect of becoming an overnight millionaire to sweeten his dreams.

"Okay, noon," he snapped. "But a minute later, and you'll never see your son again."

"Can I speak to him now?"

"No." About to hang up, Joey heard the judge say quickly, "Why should I get the money for you if I don't even have proof he's still alive?"

Joey thought fast. "He's asleep," he said, lowering his voice. "You wouldn't want me to wake the kid, would you?"

"Uh, no, I suppose not — No, don't do that. But I want you to call me back when he wakes up. Otherwise, there's no point in my getting the money together for you."

"No point? I'll tell you the point, mister," Joey said harshly. "Your son's life — *that's* the point! You get the money by noon tomorrow — or else." He slammed the disconnect button so hard that his thumb hurt.

By the time the tractor swung aside to let them pass, it was too late. The white jeep was nowhere in sight.

"This isn't going to do us any good," Mark Garrity said, as his colleagues gave verbal vent to their pent-up feelings. "We need to plan." He motioned for Stewart to make a U-turn, then twisted in his seat to face the two in back. "First of all, I want you, Pete, and you, Lucy, to go back to that post office. There's always the chance that the guy will head back there later to try again. We know he needs the money."

"What about us?" Stewart asked.

"We start going over campsites again. We saw the jeep enter this neck of the woods, so we can ignore the sites in other directions. I have already okayed our operating here with the local authorities but now its time to call them in — Lincolntown's sheriff and his men — to help us search. Pete, you and Lucy take care of that when we drop you back in town, okay?" Garrity waited for the affirming nod, then said unhappily, "And I've got to make a phone call."

"To Daniel Newman?" Rheims asked.

"To Daniel Newman."

Garrity picked up his cell phone and dialed.

"Hello?"

"Dan, this is Mark."

"Mark! What's happening? I just got another call from the kidnapper."

Garrity's pulse quickened. The man must be equipped with his own phone, then. "What did he say?"

"He talked about the ransom money. I got him to agree to push the transfer off until noon tomorrow, but he said not a second later or I'd never see Mordy again. I asked to speak to Mordy, but he was asleep."

"I see."

"Mark" — Daniel's breath caught in his throat — "Do you think the guy was telling me the truth? Is Mordy all right? Is — is he still alive, do you think?" Just asking the question made him want to rip his hair out at the roots. No one who had seen Judge Newman in his courtroom would have recognized the quivering mass of nerves he was reduced to now.

"I think he's still alive, Dan. We have to believe it, anyway. We have to act as if we know it for a fact. Chances are good that the kidnapper won't harm him, not with the prospect of losing a cool million." Garrity wished he could believe it.

Daniel struggled valiantly to control his emotion. "Well, what's the news at your end? I take it you didn't catch the guy at the post office."

"No, we didn't catch him. He turned tail and left at the last minute, just before entering. We think he might have recognized Jake."

"Oh —" The disappointment in Daniel's voice was keen.

"But we followed him into the woods, so we have a general idea of where he's hanging out. We're going to contact the local police to help us, Dan. You'll have your Mordy back yet."

After he hung up, Garrity pulled out his map and got down to business.

"Look, there are only three camping sites in this area. We'll drop you two off in town, then Jim and I will start on one of them" — he pointed — "Here. You get the sheriff's men to start in on the others. We'll stay in radio contact to keep abreast of developments."

They drove in silence back to Lincolntown. Stewart dropped Pete Rheims at the sheriff's office and Lucy Fenwick at the post office. Then he and Garrity turned back, to try their luck again where they had failed the day before.

As they entered the woods, it began to rain.

72

He was hungry, and thirsty, and wet. Most of all, he was terribly tired. For hour upon hour Mordy fought the urge to sleep, afraid that he would lose his hold on the limb and fall to the ground. His swelling ankle was a help here: Every time he nodded off, a fresh stab of agony prodded him painfully awake.

He had seen Joey rush off into the woods, searching. Then, nearly half an hour later, he had seen him stumble back. The slam of the cabin door told him that Joey had gone to roost there. Mordy had not heard a sound since.

Mordy had no way of knowing it, but inside the cabin Joey Mercutio was sprawled across his bed, sleeping off the effects of a six-pack of beer.

Within an hour of losing sight of the white jeep, a force of some two dozen local men was mobilized to comb the woods and campgrounds for the kidnapper and the boy.

Sheriff Will Brown had proved more than eager to assist in the search: It had been years since Lincolntown had known this much excitement. Under Garrity's overall command, the men swarmed over the area in and around the three camp sites closest to where the jeep had last been seen.

One reserve deputy was not on duty that day. Dave McAllister had gone out into the woods that morning to see if he could shoot himself a rabbit, but the threatening look of the sky had sent him hurrying back home with an empty bag. Unfortunately, in his haste he slipped and fell — not unlike Mordy's inglorious sprawl a bit earlier, in those same woods — and wrenched an arm. He was at home, nursing his injury, when the call came from the sheriff's office.

"Tell him I'm sorry, but I can't make it," he called to his wife, who picked up the call in the kitchen. "Explain what happened." Then, on second thought, he said, "Oh, never mind, I'll talk to him myself."

He found the sheriff's secretary on the line. McAllister asked, "Is Will there?"

"He's just on his way out — Oh, wait a minute, he's coming back. He says he'll take the call." McAllister and Brown were old friends.

"Will?" McAllister asked. "What's this about?"

Succinctly, the sheriff outlined the situation. McAllister frowned. "The woods south of the E-Z Camp Grounds, you say?"

"That's it. I've got men fanning out all over the place now. If they have no luck there, they'll move on to Hideaway Camping."

McAllister said slowly, "Will. This is going to sound funny — but I think I may have seen the guy."

"The kidnapper?" Brown asked disbelievingly. "Where?"

"In those same woods, about an hour ago. I was out with my rifle, on the lookout for a rabbit, when I fell and hurt my arm. While I was lying there, I saw a fellow walking past. Didn't see me — I guess I was hidden by some trees. Looked like he'd lost something — and he had a gun."

"A rifle?"

"No, a little-bitty pistol. He wasn't hunting game, Will. Looked mean, though. A scar as big as your hand, right down the side of his face."

Sheriff Brown did not waste a moment in radioing the information to the Baltimore detectives. Garrity's eyes met Jim Stewart's, speculation dancing wildly in both.

"Out searching the woods with his gun?" Stewart said. "What could he have been looking for, except —"

"Mordy," Garrity breathed. "Do you believe it? The kid's managed to escape!"

Stewart was forced to concede that the explanation was the only one that made sense, given the facts at their disposal. "So now we're looking for the kidnapper *and* the kid, in two different places."

"Yes!" Slowly, the sparkle in Garrity's eyes died. "Jim, we'd better find that kid before Mercutio does."

Stewart nodded in sober agreement.

Garrity picked up his cell phone to dial the Newman number again.

❧

Daniel stared dumbly into his daughter's eyes. "They think Mordy escaped. The kidnapper's out looking for him in the woods — and so are the police." He shook his head as though to assimilate this abrupt turnaround. "Mordy's somewhere in the woods — free."

Yael burst into tears of relief and strain. Moving as though in a dream, her father put an arm around her. But his mind had begun working again, and it hooked onto one salient point.

"I don't have to worry about getting that ransom money together now," he said into the air above Yael's head. "Mordy's gotten free of that monster. *Baruch Hashem!* Now all we can do is hope and pray that the police get to him before the kidnapper does —" Suddenly, he pulled away from his daughter. "No! Yael, do you realize what this means? I don't have to sit home with my hands tied anymore! I can start doing something, finally, to help my own son!"

"Daddy, where are you going?" Daniel had whipped away and run to the closet for his jacket.

"To Lincolntown. I want to be there, on the spot, when they find him — or, better yet, take a hand in the search myself."

"I'm going with you!"

Luis Mendez walked through from the kitchen, where he had been eating a snack. "Where do you think you're going?" he asked pleasantly, but with an edge.

"Garrity just called. It looks like Mordy escaped. He's somewhere in the woods near Lincolntown right now. I'm going up there to help find him."

Mendez hesitated. "I don't know if that's such a good idea. The kidnapper might still call here —"

"So what if he does? He has no leverage anymore. You can pretend to be me, if you like. Do whatever you want. I'm going."

"And so am I," Yael said grimly, clinging to the sleeve of her father's jacket as if no power on earth could shake her loose.

"Then so am I," Mendez said, grinning broadly at the prospect of action at last. "We'll take my car. Let's go!"

Daniel, Yael, and Mendez crossed into Lincolntown at midafternoon — just as the sun burst fully from behind the clouds for the first time all day. Mendez, who had up to that point maintained a prudent radio silence, contacted Garrity.

"Hi, Mark. Guess what? I'm here. In Lincolntown."

"Luis! What are you doing here?"

"Newman insisted on coming up to help search for his son. The daughter tagged along, too. I figured I'd better come along to keep an eye on them."

Garrity could think of nothing very damaging that might arise as a result of Mendez's zeal for independent action. In any case, he had no time to think. "You can join the others at the post office," he said shortly. "Bring Daniel and the girl to the sheriff. Let *them* figure out what to do with them!" On this rather incoherent note, he disconnected.

He and Stewart, together with the local men, had been on their feet for hours, through drenching rain for the most part, checking out cabins and calling themselves hoarse through the woods. His soles were blistered and he had the beginnings of a nasty head cold. Garrity was in no mood or had much voice left — for conversation.

When Mendez relayed Garrity's instructions, Daniel was none too happy. "I want to go look for Mordy," he insisted.

"With all due respect, Your Honor," Mendez said, "you don't know the first thing about these woods. Let the locals take care of that. At the sheriff's, you'll be on hand to hear developments as they come in."

With that, Daniel was forced to be satisfied. He had traveled more than three hours just to cool his heels in some office, when he had envisioned himself scouring the woods for his son. Still, he was much closer to the heart of things here than he would have been at home. And, best of all, he would be on hand to embrace Mordy if — when — he was finally found.

A few minutes later, the Lincolntown Sheriff's office was taken aback at the sight of a man in a skullcap and a girl in a long, modest skirt, seated side by side in the tiny waiting area and murmuring inaudibly out of identical small books. The secretary questioned a deputy with her eyebrows.

"Father and sister of the kidnapped kid," the deputy mouthed silently.

"Oh!" The secretary nodded in understanding. Family members in that kind of situation had free license to act as nutty as they liked. She wondered if she should go over and offer them coffee or soft drinks, then sank back in her seat. Better wait till they finished praying, or whatever it was they were doing with those little books.

Outside, the sun broke through the clouds for the first time that day.

Joey Mercutio awoke with a dry mouth and sweating palms. The gun was on the pillow beside his head, where he had had enough presence of mind to deposit it before he fell asleep. A steady dripping from the eaves told him that it had rained while he slept, but the sky had begun to clear and the sun was making a feeble attempt to penetrate the clouds. Checking his wristwatch, Joey saw that the time was midafternoon.

He considered trying the post office again, then decided that that would have to wait for tomorrow, on his way down to Stanton for the ransom money. Right now, though his head pounded and he was vaguely hungry, he decided to try one last search through the woods before calling it a day. He might be able to fool the judge into paying for nothing, but he would not rest until he had his hands around that infernal kid's neck.

He ripped open a package of pretzels, and stuffed some into his mouth as he left the cabin. As soon as the package was empty, he tossed it aside into the undergrowth and took the gun from his belt. He set off at a slightly different angle this time, grimacing as the damp seeped into his shoes from the soggy undergrowth.

From his perch, Mordy watched him go. It occurred to him that here was his chance to return to the cabin for some food before the night set in. A foolhardy thing to do, maybe, but in his opinion very necessary.

Frankly, he was starving. All he could think about was food and hunger was making him lightheaded. It seemed to him, with his empty stomach's impeccable logic, that food would definitely enhance his ability to keep himself safe. Joey was not likely to reappear in under twenty minutes, and it would take Mordy less than half of that, he reasoned, to run back to the cabin, grab a packet or two of chips and a chocolate bar from the stash on Joey's bed, and run back to his tree.

There was one snag: He could not run. But even at a slow walk, he could make it in time if he left right this minute.

Mordy slipped carefully down the trunk, literally biting his tongue to keep from crying aloud at the pain in his ankle. On solid ground, he stood for a moment with one hand on the trunk, fighting for his equilibrium. He was beginning to wonder whether, hungry as he was, a few mouthfuls of potato chips were worth this agony.

As he began a slow hobble toward the cabin, the sun broke for the first time through the clouds.

Garrity and Stewart had left the search of the woods to the local men, taking to themselves the task of investigating the three camping sites in the immediate area. One of these they had already checked the day before; they did it again now. The other two sites took them much longer, as they were the all-by-yourself-in-the-woods variety, with cabins set at enormous distances from one another to give the illusion of privacy in the wilderness. By late afternoon, they were down to a last handful of cabins. A local man who worked summers as a groundskeeper was their guide.

"There are two more cabins out here," he said, leading the way easily for the two exhausted policemen. "Not in great shape, either of them, but the folks who rent them don't usually complain. The price is right — and if it's solitude they're after, they get plenty of that here."

Garrity saw what he meant. The woods were thicker here, the path hardly defined against the encroaching undergrowth. Crimson leaves blazed from the trees that hid the next cabin from view.

"Around the next bend," their guide promised, just as the sun broke through the clouds.

73

The forest floor was damp and unpleasant after the rain. Disgusted, Joey turned back. This effort was wasted. He cursed the beer for putting him to sleep, and for fogging his mind now and sending him off on this wild-goose chase. Wherever the kid was, Joey was not likely to lay hands on him again in these woods. He was probably miles from here by this time, hitchhiking along some highway toward home. Joey would have to try again another day — but not before he scooped up his ransom money tomorrow. If his vengeance still awaited fate's pleasure, at least Joey could wait a rich man.

As he neared the cabin, the sun broke fully through the clouds for the first time that day.

Joey still had the gun in his hand, but it dangled limply as his alertness waned. He thought ahead to the cabin, and a quick bite of supper, and then some more sleep before setting out for Stanton in the morning. After that — who knows? With money in his pocket to burn, the world was his for the taking.

He stepped around a bend in the path — and came face to face with Mordy.

Mordy had been standing stock still, balancing on one foot and grimacing in pain. Now the grimace turned into a mask of terror. In an instant, the boy — pale enough before — turned absolutely white. He turned, cruelly hampered by his injury, and tried to run.

He never had a chance. Mercutio's steely arm was around his neck before he had taken two steps.

"So, thought you'd take a little walk, did you?" Joey's victorious laughter rang harshly in Mordy's ears. "Stupid of you to hang out so close to the cabin."

Mordy said nothing. But Joey was merciless in his triumph. He was also curious. Shaking the boy, he demanded, "Talk! Why'd you come back, kid?"

"I was hungry," Mordy said in a tiny voice. Again the laughter, harsh and overloud in the peaceful wood. Joey started shoving Mordy in the direction of the cabin, ignoring the boy's involuntary yelp of pain.

Suddenly, a voice rang out. "Hold it right there!" Joey twisted in a full circle, instinctively holding Mordy against him like a shield. His gun was pressed to the boy's temple. He saw three men facing him at a little distance down the path. Two of them were pointing guns at him.

"Drop those guns!" he yelled. "Drop them, or I'll shoot the boy, I swear it!"

Garrity felt the urge to batter every inch of Joey's body. Seeing that vermin with Mordy made his blood boil. But, slowly, he lowered his gun arm. He saw Stewart, at his side, do the same. Behind them, the guide stood stock still, watching in fearful fascination.

"Shoot him!" Mordy called in a voice that shook despite his best efforts. "Oh, please, shoot him! I don't care what happens to me!"

"Shut up," Joey snarled, yanking Mordy's head back in warning. Mordy winced, a hand clawing at his constricted throat. Garrity's heart lurched. He took in the boy's soaked and disheveled clothes, the swollen ankle grotesquely emerging from his sneaker — and the blend of despair and simple courage in his young eyes. He shook his head. "No can do!" he shouted back. "Your father would never forgive me."

Joey's laughter sounded again. "You're right about that. His father's going to hand a million bucks over to me tomorrow. We can't have him worrying himself sick over his little boy, now can we?" He tightened his grip around Mordy's neck. "You come with me, sonny. I'll take good care of you." In the slanting rays that filtered through the trees, the long scar on Joey's face looked livid.

"Leave the boy, and you'll still get the money," Garrity called.

"Yeah, sure," Joey shot back. "Stay where you are, cop. I'm taking this boy with me — and you and your men better stay far, far away, or the kid gets it." Ostentatiously, he lifted the gun a fraction higher and tightened the trigger finger. "Understand?"

The guide let out a strangled whimper. The detectives nodded.

Joey began slowly backing away down the path, not in the direction of the cabin but toward higher ground, where he had parked the jeep. He had progressed no more than a few feet when, from behind him, someone shouted, "Drop the gun!"

For the second time in minutes, Joey spun around, astonished. Garrity and Stewart were no less surprised. The newcomer advanced down the path, holding something concealed beneath his jacket. Its snout protruded beneath the cloth in a way that left little doubt as to the nature of the concealed object.

It was Jake.

The kidnapper hesitated. Then, without warning, he lunged off the path, making for the woods. Jake broke into a run, obviously intending to try to block him. It was difficult for Joey Mercutio to run with the boy stumbling along in front of him, impeding his progress. He veered leftward, in an attempt to throw Jake off and to shift Mordy's position so that he did not bump into the boy with every step. Mordy took advantage of the momentary lack of focus to twist out of his captor's grip. Sobbing raggedly under his breath, he ran — or rather, staggered favoring his one good leg — toward Jake.

Joey spun around and let off a shot. Mordy, hobbling and weaving like a drunkard on his bad ankle, was not touched. But Jake clapped a hand to his shoulder, where a spreading stain became quickly visible. The guide whimpered again.

"Stop right there, Mercutio!" Garrity shouted.

Joey whirled around to aim at the detective.

But the instant the kidnapper had used to shoot at Jake had been all the time Garrity needed to fix his own aim. Mordy was still on the criminal's far side, out of danger's way for the moment. Garrity ducked as Joey sent a bullet spinning fruitlessly in his direction, then saw him concentrate on getting the boy back. Mordy tried to run, but the man was much faster. Two steps brought him to the boy's side. A heavy hand landed on Mordy's neck. Garrity fired.

The detective had the satisfaction of seeing the cruel grip relax from around the boy's skinny neck. In slow motion, as if surprised at himself, Joey Mercutio sank into the bracken at Mordy's feet.

Mordy stared down at the man who had snatched him away from everything and everybody he knew and loved, and who had held him terrorized for two horrible days and nights. Garrity and Stewart came up, too, with Jake Meisler, very pale and with an unsteady hand to his hurt shoulder, coming last. Together, they watched the strength drain from the criminal's body. A small hole, the size of a nickel, was visible in his chest. It was rimmed with red. There was surprisingly little blood.

"He — killed — my brother," Joey croaked.

"Daniel Newman sent your brother to jail," Garrity said flatly. "He had nothing to do with your brother's death."

"Same — thing." A flickering smile flitted across the dying man's face. "I got — his wife, though."

"And tried to get his son, too."

"Yeah — that's right."

Garrity leaned closer. "But you didn't get Mordy, Mercutio. He's going back to his father, safe and sound. You have nothing now." Garrity was implacable, even in the face of death. The kidnapper had sown his own harvest.

"Revenge —" Joey whispered.

"A nice dream," Garrity said. "Enjoy it, Mercutio —"

Joey's eyes closed. There was a final, rasping breath — and then silence.

For a moment, no one said a word. The gunfire had silenced the forest creatures for a time, but now, from somewhere above their heads, an unseen bird twittered a scolding. Death, even of a man who had snuffed out at least one innocent life and had brazenly attempted to destroy others, seemed a sacrilege in those woods.

It was then that Mordy noticed Jake's upper arm.

"Jake, you're hurt!"

Jake grinned wanly. "It's nothing. Just a scratch, as they say in the cowboy books."

As the last of his fear drained away, the boy's natural curiosity reasserted himself. "Where'd you get the gun?"

Still grinning, Jake pulled away his jacket to reveal his weapon. It was a stubby stick of damp wood. "Best I could do at a moment's notice."

Garrity was smiling broadly as he stepped up to Jake. "I thought I told you to get out of the way, and stay that way," he said, pumping Jake's free hand.

"Sorry, sir. I was never very good at following orders."

"Where's Miss Muller?" Stewart asked suddenly.

"Back there." Jake gestured at the higher ground, out of sight around the bend, where Sara's car was parked beside (had she but known it!) the kidnapper's white jeep. "I made her wait in the car. Chivalry is not yet dead."

"You followed us?" Garrity asked, using his handkerchief to bind Jake's upper arm as best he could. That would have to do until they reached a hospital. The wound, mercifully, didn't look too deep.

"All day," Jake admitted.

Mordy turned to the police detective. "Mr. Garrity?" he said.

"Yes, Mordy?"

"Do you think you could drive me home now? It's a long drive, and my father must be very worried about me."

"I can do better than that," Garrity said, blinking away a sudden moisture in his eyes. "Come on."

Garrity radioed the news ahead. He arranged for some men to come get the body, leaving Stewart and the guide behind to guard it in the meantime. Then he led the boy to his car.

Mordy was quiet on the ride into Lincolntown. He remained that way as the detective led him into the sheriff's office. And he said not a word as his father and Yael sprang to their feet, staring at him as though struck dumb by the force of their own emotion. Behind him, Jake was grinning again. Sara watched, too, solemn but radiant.

It was Daniel who found his tongue first.

"Well, son," he said, the words coming thickly through his clogged throat, though he was smiling so hard he was afraid his jaws would break. "We'd better get going. We've got us a sukkah to build."

Only then, with a sob, did Mordy rush into his father's arms.

"Baruch Hashem," he said brokenly into Daniel's shirt front. "Oh, baruch Hashem!" He lifted his face, tear stained but glowing like the first morning of the world. "Daddy, I didn't know when I'd see you again. I was afraid I'd miss Sukkos altogether. I was afraid —"

"Never mind that," Daniel said, putting a finger to his beloved son's lips. "Never mind, Mordy. It's all right now. Everything — *everything* — is right now."

Mordy nodded. He leaned into his father like a very small and very tired child newly wakened from a bad dream, to find his pillow striped with sun and the danger nothing more than a puff of smoke, fading already into distant memory.

74

The plane cut through a layer of cumulus clouds, gray at first and then blindingly white, to emerge in a sea of blue. The flight would not be a long one, but what there was would take place high above the world, where light reigned perpetually. This seemed fitting, somehow. Daniel drank in the sight, which never, in all the times he had flown, failed to move him.

Below, they had left people huddled in their winter coats, glancing up at the ominous December sky and scurrying for cover. They did not know, or had forgotten, that the storm clouds held only temporary dominion. Up above was permanence — and light. Even obscured by the vagaries and falsehoods of this world, the Hand of Providence continues to shine, steady and strong. Daniel promised himself never to forget that again.

He had felt himself abandoned, in those dark, precarious days between Yom Kippur and Succos. He had believed his fate — and Mordy's — to be sealed. It had taken every ounce of his faith to open his lips in prayer and to believe that the prayer would be heard. Stripped of his own illusory power, he had been forced to summon up an old, childlike dependence on the One Who truly held the power. And his Father had not let him down.

"A drink, sir?" the flight attendant asked courteously, poised above her cart.

Daniel shook his head, smiling. "No, thanks. I'm fine."

And he *was* fine, with his children safely beside him and the nightmare behind them all. An immense gratitude had a way of swelling Daniel's heart at odd moments these days, catching him by surprise and rendering him speechless. He felt that way now. He had so much to be thankful for. More than he'd ever dared hope for.

As the plane droned through the sky, Daniel's eyes drifted shut and his thoughts grew less coherent. A tumble of associations came, disjointed in the way that thoughts are at the edge of sleep. Interestingly, the first image to come to mind was Henry Downing's solid, friendly face, stripped of the sadness that had marked it all through his trial. He and Elsa had paid Daniel a visit on *chol hamo'ed.* Together, over cups of tea in the Newman sukkah, they had tied up the loose ends of the trial — beginning and ending with young Ted Winslow's rage.

"Did you hear how he got into the grounds?" Elsa asked, still indignant at the thought. "He dressed as a BGE man and got the maid to let him in with some story about checking the gas lines. I was out of the house at the time."

"An old ploy," Daniel murmured. "But still surprisingly effective."

Henry took up the thread. "He hid in the garden until Simmonds came — four hours, at the very least. The man must have the patience of a rock!"

"An iron will," his wife said sadly, "but for what a purpose —"

"How did he know Simmonds was coming to dinner at your place that night?" Daniel asked curiously.

"They worked in the same plant, remember? He overheard Simmonds taking to me on the phone to set it up — and seized the moment, as they say." Downing sighed. "Poor kid. He must've gone over the edge."

Daniel was impressed with the sheer compassion of the man. Winslow's act of rage had cost Downing months of his freedom, and very nearly much more — yet he could still sigh with pity.

Very soon the talk moved away from the courtroom, as Daniel shared the story of the kidnapping.

"In a way, Henry, you had a hand in saving my son's life," Daniel had smiled. "You see, I met my young friend, Jake Meisler, through your trial. And it was Jake's timely appearance in those woods that helped turn around what looked like a no-win situation for Mordy." Daniel shook his head, recalling Garrity's description of the scene in the woods. "Jake took a hit that day. A hit meant for Mordy."

"Is he all right?" Elsa had asked, concerned.

"Thank G-d, he's just fine. He'll be finishing up law school this year, and after that, who knows? I predict a bright future for that boy."

"He certainly deserves one," Elsa said warmly.

Yes, Jake deserved everything that was good. He would be a part of the Newman family's life always, if Daniel had anything to say in the matter —

The scene shifted. Now he was talking to Mark Garrity again, thanking him in words that seemed all too inadequate for bringing his boy safely back to him. The detective had waved away the thanks. "All I ask for," he'd grinned, "is an ice-cold Coke."

"You shall have it!" Daniel cried, springing over to the refrigerator. "There'll be a Coke for you in here any time you want one, Mark." He watched the detective dispose of the drink with his characteristic dispatch.

"What's going to happen to Mercutio's friend?" Daniel had asked suddenly. "Vinny — was that his name?"

Garrity nodded. "With Mordy safe and Mercutio dead, I don't think it will be too hard to convince the state prosecutor to drop charges against Vinny Fouza — especially in light of the way he helped us get to Mercutio. It really does look like he was just a pawn in all this."

They were all pawns, Daniel reflected sleepily, only some were more obvious than others. The Master set up the chessboard, and then left it to them to make the choices that would take them around the board, falling sometimes on the black squares, and sometimes on the white —

He was nearly asleep now. Just before he finally floated away, his thoughts touched on Chaim, his brother, who had been prepared to fly to his side at a moment's notice. Good old Chaim. Ever timid, always marginally successful, never believing in his real worth. Well, he had surprised them all. He had finally, after all these years, asked his yeshivah for a raise — and had been turned down. Daniel would have expected his baby brother to dig a quiet hole and pull it over his head. But something seemed to have come over Chaim. Denied the pay he felt he deserved by the yeshivah he'd served faithfully for so long, what did Chaim do but go out and land himself a better, more responsible, and much better paid job at a different yeshivah! How happy Gila had been. How proud! Good old Chaim —

And his parents, too — But here the thoughts ended. Daniel was asleep.

Hilda had the door open before the peal of the doorbell had finished echoing down the condominium's corridor. She held out her arms. "Daniel."

He embraced his mother, feeling the wholeness of a family breach mended. They had spoken on the phone a number of times since the bitter parting before Sukkos, but it was not until he saw the warmth in his mother's eyes that Daniel knew that he was truly forgiven. Interestingly, he had never revealed either to her or to his father the reason for his failure to show up to say good-bye that Sunday. He had merely called them on *erev Sukkos* to wish them a good *Yom Tov*, silently asking for Hilda's understanding — and had been granted it, this time without question. Hilda could not remain angry at her son for long.

"Dad." Gently, Daniel detached himself from his mother's embrace, leaving her to turn her rapturous attention on the grandchildren. As Yael and Mordy hugged her, Daniel and his father took stock of one another. Jonathan looked good, better than he had the last time Daniel had seen him. He had a slight tan and seemed well rested. A prayer of thanksgiving rose up in the son's heart. This extended stay in Florida seemed to have been the answer. Daniel made a mental note to phone his father's doctor when he got back, and thank him.

"Come in, come in. Let's not stand on the doorstep all day!" Hilda urged, pink cheeked and laughing. She, too, looked fit — bubbling over with energy and, just now, with joy at having them there. As he followed his parents into the tasteful living room, Daniel sneaked a surreptitious look at his watch, which Hilda's eagle eye didn't miss.

"What, checking the time already? You just got here! And you're staying for five whole days," she said, glowing at the prospect. She sat beside Daniel on the couch. Mordy was on his other side. "What was it like up north when you left?"

"Cold," Daniel said, pantomiming an elaborate shiver. "We had some snow a few days ago, and the streets are all lovely slush now."

"Perfect Chanukah weather," Hilda smiled.

"We had a snow day off from school," Yael volunteered. "The first this winter!"

"The first of many, we hope," Mordy added ingenuously.

Joining in the general laughter, Daniel could hardly resist the urge to pull the boy to him. He had hugged Mordy so often since the kidnapping that Yael was beginning to complain of favoritism.

"I'm not playing favorites," Daniel had told her, earnestly. "It's not that at all. You do understand that, don't you, Yael?"

And Yael had melted. "Of course I do. And I'd hug him all day, too — if he'd let me!"

"Well, what'll it be?" Hilda asked, standing up again as though her happiness would not allow her to remain in one position for long. "Coffee, tea, soda, juice?"

"Maybe they want to unpack first," Jonathan said mildly.

"We'll unpack later, thanks," Daniel said. "And some juice will be fine. Right, kids?" Yael and Mordy nodded.

Jonathan settled back in his armchair, in his quiet, undemonstrative way relishing their presence as much as his wife. "So tell me all the news," he said. "You've seemed a little preoccupied lately, Daniel. Is everything all right?"

Daniel shot a fleeting look of warning at his children, who smiled angelically back. The kidnapping was off limits for their grandparents; they had been through all that with Daddy before they came. And other subjects would wait until he brought them up. Didn't he trust them?

Apparently, he did. Relaxing, Daniel said, "Actually, everything's just fine. More than fine. In fact —"

He was interrupted by the pealing of the doorbell. Daniel glanced again at his watch, then looked up with a secret smile to meet his children's eyes. Theirs were dancing with glee. He stood up.

Hilda was already emerging from the kitchen, wiping her hands on a dish towel. "Who could that be?" she wondered aloud, hurrying to the door. She reached it just ahead of Daniel, peered through the peephole, then flung the door open.

A young woman stood there, smiling shyly. She clutched a large, no-nonsense handbag as though it were a life preserver. Over his mother's shoulder, Daniel smiled back as he walked over to join them at the door.

"Actually," he said, before Hilda could frame the questions trembling on her lips, "I was about to tell you, Mom."

"Tell me what?" Hilda asked, bewildered.

"This" — he said softly, gesturing politely at the woman standing in the doorway — "is the reason for my — er — preoccupation lately. Since Sukkos, anyway."

From the corner of his eye, he saw Jonathan and the kids beginning to cross the room to join them. When they were all assembled at the door, Daniel said, "Mom, Dad, I'd like to introduce you to Sara Muller. Originally from New York."

"Muller?" Hilda said, instantly alert. "Do you happen to be related to the Nosson Mullers, in Queens?"

"No, we're Flatbush stock, through and through," Sara smiled. The smile looked a little nervous.

"In fact," Daniel said, "I'm guilty of practicing a small deception on you, Mom and Dad. We didn't fly here directly from Baltimore. We made a short stop first — in New York."

"In New York?" Hilda echoed, dazed. "What for?"

"To meet Sara's family, of course. Her parents, and her sister's family."

Suddenly, the significance of the unexpected visitor seemed to strike Hilda for the first time. She put a hand to her heart. "Oh, my goodness! Oh, my goodness! Daniel, why didn't you tell me you were bringing someone? And not just any 'someone'! I cannot *believe* that you just —"

"My dear," Jonathan said, smiling. "Why don't you invite Miss Muller in?"

"Oh, yes! Come in, come in. I don't know what I was thinking. Come in!" Again, the hand to the heart. "Oh, my goodness!"

"Have a seat, Miss Muller," Jonathan invited. At the moment, he was much more capable of coherent speech than his wife was.

Daniel escorted Sara into the living room and whispered, smiling, "Go on, sit down. They won't bite." Jonathan resumed his position in the armchair, but Hilda was too excited to sit. Sara's eyes lit on Yael and Mordy, as though seeing them for the first time.

"Hi, guys," she said.

"Hi! You're right on time! How's your hotel room? Did you have trouble finding a taxi?" Yael chattered busily.

Sara laughed, more at ease already. "The room's fine, and no, no trouble at all getting a taxi. The doorman flagged one down for me.

The hotel's just a short ride from here."

Jonathan, silver haired and patrician as ever, rested his gaze on the young stranger. "Well, let's get comfortable and become acquainted, Miss Muller."

"Please — call me Sara. And I'd love to get acquainted." A quick look at Daniel. "Daniel has told me so much about the two of you."

"Let me just get the drinks," Hilda said, "and then we'll sit here and talk all night long!"

But they did better than that.

They drank a *l'chayim.*

The moon was rising above the ocean as they stood on the balcony and raised their glasses.

"To our daughter-in-law-to-be," Jonathan said. There was a catch in his voice.

"To our darling Sara!" Hilda sniffled unabashedly. "Welcome to the family!"

Daniel looked at Sara. She stood framed in the window, backlit by the moon and flanked by his son and daughter, who were toasting her with glasses of sweet wine and hearty cries of "Mazel tov!" She looked elated and at peace — and a touch surprised, as though still astonished at her own good fortune.

There was so much hurt to make up for, in both directions; such a wealth of long overdue joy to be mined. So much building to do, together. He waited for silence, then raised his own glass in her direction.

"Here's one from me." Though he spoke quietly, it seemed to Sara that his voice carried clear across the ocean, to the ends of the earth.

"To my *kallah,*" he said. The glass rose a fraction higher. "Thank you."

She smiled. Then, as the others sipped their wine, Sara lifted her eyes to the velvet sky and whispered, "Thank *You!*"

And the moon spread a silver canopy over the heads of the happy couple and their rejoicing family, while the ocean rushed away from the shore to spread the glad tidings.

EPILOGUE

Daniel walked out of the courthouse into the cool of early evening in autumn. The day had started out promisingly enough, but now there was a brooding stillness that heralded a storm. With the clock already set back an hour, the parking lot was beginning to fill with shadows. He strode over to his car, dismissing the last of the day's cases from his mind and thinking ahead with pleasure to his home and family.

He had just reached the car when it began to rain.

The first fat drops made him, as always, think of the day Ella had died. The memory — and the pain it brought — was like an old war wound, quiescent except in bad weather. It had stormed the day she had taken his car and driven out onto the highway to meet her end. An end engineered by a ruthless individual, a man warped by his own thirst for vengeance. Though seven years had passed since that awful day, it still had the power to make him shudder, and to bow his head in sadness at the terrible waste of a precious life.

The strengthening rain had obscured something that he noticed only now, as he pulled open the door on the driver's side. There was something on his windshield. Something white.

An oblong envelope was tucked under one of the wipers, with his name in big block letters on the outside.

His heart froze. It was like time playing backwards.

When his heartbeat resumed, the sensation was painful, like a thawing after long exposure to the cold. He snaked a hand out into the rain to pull in the envelope. He waited a moment for the trembling to stop before he slit open the damp envelope. Another few minutes, and it would have disintegrated into a pulpy, illegible mass.

He saw the handwriting on the note. Slowly, he began to smile.

Hi, Daniel. I was shopping in the area and thought I'd leave you a little note — just to let you know I was thinking of you.

Hurry home, okay? Supper's your favorite tonight — chicken cutlets the way you like them. Isn't it a good thing Mrs. Marks gave me the recipe before she went away to live in Florida with her sister? I hope mine come out as good as hers always did.

Cutlets aside, we're having special guests for dinner. Faygie and Jake are coming — with their two-month-old princess! Yael and Mordy are going to have to toss a coin for who gets to hold her first — if, that is, Jake will let anyone get near his precious girl. Have you ever seen such a doting father? (Present company excluded, of course.)

Little Nafi is in the throes of cutting another tooth — his fifth — and has just informed me in no uncertain terms that he won't stand for my scribbling another minute. He also says "hi" to his Daddy — or would if he could talk. So I'll say good-bye for both of us now. Have yourself a great afternoon, my dear.

The last of his tension gurgled away like bathwater as Daniel slipped the page back into its envelope. The rain, though falling as hard as ever, seemed friendly now. The threat was gone.

Smiling, he tucked the note into his jacket pocket, next to his heart, and started for home.

The End

FROM THE AUTHOR

A novel is a friendly mixture of fact and fiction. To acquire the ring of truth, a story, though imaginary, must be rooted in a network of solid fact. When these do not happen to lie at the author's fingertips, she must seek help from the experts. For providing me with much valuable information about the Maryland court system, I am indebted to Mr. Gary Honick, Assistant Attorney General for Maryland. If I have erred in any of the legal niceties, it was due to my own ignorance or oversight.

My dear husband, Menachem, provided an endlessly patient sounding board for new ideas, as well as a number of exciting plot twists of his own. As a rebbi, his behind-the-scenes school stories were invaluable in helping me create a fictional heroine who is a teacher. Menachem, your loving encouragement was the prop that supported me during the long birth of this book, and means more to me than I can say. Thank you from the bottom of my heart.

A timely suggestion by my dear son, Naftali, literally changed the face of this story. *Yasher kochachah* — and keep those comments coming, Naftali!

Nothing is created in a vacuum. I want to take this opportunity to say "Thanks" to all my other children, for enriching my life (not to mention providing plenty of fruitful material to work with!). You're wonderful, each and every one of you.

Mrs. Judi Dick did a superb job editing this large work in record time and with an uncanny sensitivity to the nuances so dear to an author's heart. What better way to express my appreciation than to say I look forward to working together again in the future?

As always, my heartfelt thanks to my mother, who helped imbue me with the values that inform all of my work, and in loving memory of my beloved father, *z"l*, whose passion for the written word I inherited and who continues ever to inspire me from afar.

And of course, to the One Who guides me constantly in my every effort I offer my humble gratitude, and a prayer that the arrows will always stand out in bold relief to show me the way I must go.

Writing is a lonely business. During work hours, an author's best friends and only companions are the computer screen and the imaginary characters inside her own head. The knowledge that my words leave me to fly not into a void, but into readers' minds and hearts, is exhilarating. It gives me a thousand companions at each sitting.

When you curl up with something I've written, that's the next best thing to talking directly to each other. And when you take the time and trouble, as so many of you have done over the years, to let me know what you think, that makes me feel connected to you in a powerful way.

So it's to you, dear readers, that I dedicate *The Judge.* May it be Hashem's will that we continue as long-distance companions for many years to come!

Libby Lazewnik

May 2000
Baltimore, MD.